PRAISE FO
JEAN-CHRISTOPH
AND *AURORA*

"Combining Arctic adventure with Victorian fantasy, this page-turner is as sparkling and colorful as the northern lights."
—*The San Francisco Chronicle*

"A magnificent achievement, balancing serious intent with arch humour. It's also beautifully stylish, replete with inventive steampunk iconography and fantastical characters in a stunning polar setting." —Eric Brown, *The Guardian*

"Jean-Christophe Valtat's *Aurorarama* follows steampunk's basic conventions, but its influences and setting are of a different species. Narrated as a trans-Arctic alterna-history, *Aurorarama* harks back to Jules Verne, Raymond Roussel, and Marcel Allain and Pierre Souvestre... This surrealism is largely what distinguishes *Aurorarama* from standard-issue steampunk ... *Aurorarama* mesmerizes less for its intricate plot twists or descriptions of steam-powered gizmos than for its extraordinary dramatization of the birth and death of a civilization..."
—Erik Morse, *Bookforum*

"*Aurorarama* is perhaps what Jules Verne would write if woken from the dead and offered a dose of mushrooms. An enjoyable amalgam of thriller, fantasy, and polar adventure, topped off with a sprinkling of anarchist intrigue... Valtat's world is ingeniously imagined and peopled with an alluring cast."
—Jacob Silverman, *The National*

"*Aurorarama* entrances and delights. You could spend years picking apart the sly references and the particular myths, poems, novels and songs that inspired Valtat, or you can simply enjoy it for the experience. Valtat is making his American debut in a big way ... with his remarkable enthusiasm and bravery, it's completely possible he'll conquer the world." —Jessa Crispin, NPR

"Marvelous, perfect, and perfectly marvelous!... [*Aurorarama*] promises to attract discerning and sophisticated readers galore, those fans of the fantastical who are tired of second-hand visions and stale conceits.... Valtat's novel is *Little Nemo in Slumberland* as retold by a trio of Jeff Noon, Steve Aylett and William Burroughs. I can hardly wait for its sequels."
—Paul Di Filippo, *The Barnes and Noble Review*

"*Aurorarama* tells a tale of political intrigue (secret police! Eskimos! *Prisoner*-esque hovering airship!) with some truly lyrical prose." —io9

"As well-written as it is well-imagined... *Aurorarama* explicitly blends conventional narrative pleasures with the logic of dreaming." —*Strange Horizons*

"*Aurorarama* is an experience to be savored." —*Make Magazine*

"A terrific storyteller, Valtat mixes humor and poetry, romance and politics into a surprisingly thoughtful page-turner about social revolution." —Matthew Jakubowski, *Paste Magazine*

"[Valtat] has a magical sense of shape, and a gift for lyrical prose that are rare in modern writing." —*La Croix*

"Jean-Christophe Valtat is a writer of 'beautiful energy.'"
—*Le Monde*

"The most noteworthy contribution to steampunk in almost two decades.... *Aurorarama* rejuvenates an entire subgenre, adding creativity and accuracy (historical and, more importantly, tonal) to a field that risks being defined solely by corsets and airships. Beyond its importance in legitimizing steampunk, *Aurorarama* is a sparkling read—breathing, human characters wandering amok in one of the most captivating cities in fiction." —*Pornokitsch*

AURORARAMA

AURORARAMA

JEAN-CHRISTOPHE VALTAT

MELVILLE HOUSE
Brooklyn, New York

To Serge, who built this city with me.

AURORARAMA

Copyright © 2010 by Jean-Christophe Valtat

All rights reserved

First Melville House printing: March 2012

Melville House Publishing
145 Plymouth Street
Brooklyn, New York 11201
mhpbooks.com

Book design by Kelly Blair

ISBN: 978-1-61219-131-7

Printed in the United States of America
2 3 4 5 6 7 8 9 10

The Library of Congress has cataloged the hardcover edition as follows:

Valtat, Jean-Christophe, 1968-
Aurorarama : a novel / Jean-Christophe Valtat.
    p. cm.
 ISBN 978-1-935554-13-4 (alk. paper)
 1. Steampunk fiction. I. Title.
PQ2682.A438A97 2010
843'.914--dc22

                                        2010025659

CONTENTS

It was shewed us by Vision in Dreams, and out of Dreams, That that should be the Place we should begin upon; And though that Earth in view of Flesh, be very barren, yet we should trust the Spirit for a blessing.

A Blast on the Barren Land, or the Standard of True Community Advanc'd, Presented to the Sons of Adam by Henry Hotspur, Being a Platform to Plant the Waste Land Of the Northern Isles & Septentrional Parts, & to Restore the Regiment of Commonwealth, Printed in the Yeer 1649

Is not human fantasy,
Wild Aurora, likest thee,
Blossoming in nightly dreams,
Like thy shifting meteor-gleams?

Christopher Pearse Cranch,
To the Aurora Borealis, 1840

A Panorama of New Venice
by Samuel Elphinstone

A PROLOGUE

That Is Just That

•

"Here is the true City of the Sun."
William F. Warren, *Paradise Found, The Cradle of
the Human Race at the North Pole, 1885*

I n New Venice, every year around February 15, when the sun goes up for the first time after four months of polar night, it is customary for the inhabitants to gather on the bridges and embankments and take off their mittens and hats to salute the benevolent star. By this, as the Inuit do, they manifest their respect and also their hope that they will be alive at the same time next year. It is a well-known piece of local lore that, having mocked this ritual, the German explorer Mr. Wulff died from cold, hunger, and exhaustion a few months afterward.

As far as Gods go, the Sun may not have, it is true, the most impressive record. He has certainly none of the gift of the gab that runs in the Jehovah family and when it comes to throwing lightning bolts Jove-style, He is as inept as the aver-age mortal. But, down to earth as He is, when one needs a God who is punctual, reliable, and handy around the house, and that is *exactly* the kind of deity one needs above 80° North, good old Ray is likely to be the connoisseur's first pick. This is why, whatever confessions they claim to belong to, the New Vene-tians are at least once a year sun-worshipping heathens of the purest ilk. The sun, on this day, just stays around—more than up—for an hour or so, but when the night comes down again, the crowds throw a party in the streets that is noisy, spectacu-lar, and messy, full of dominoes, fireworks, confetti, screams, laughter, brawls, trysts, and vomitus.

There is, however, a corporation for which this could be said to be the worst time of the year: the shore-workers of the Septentrional Scavenging and Sewerage Service, whose ungrateful duty it is to clean the mess. It was during the long night of that short day that one of their "gangs" made a strange discovery.

The three men, clad in the traditional black overcoats, white bird masks and wide-brimmed hats of their plague doc-tors' outfits, operated in foggy Niflheim, the northernmost part of the city, right at the corner of the Pining and Pothorst canals. Their *chasse-gallerie*—as the shore men call their barges—was waiting just below the embankment, still in sled mode, for the ice on the canals had not been broken yet, as it would ritually be for the Spring Equinox.

Their sturdy silhouettes fading in and out of the thickening mist, the Scavengers were busy hooking an overbrimming large dust-bin to the crane in the barge when all of a sudden a faint jingling sound made them turn their long hooked beaks toward Byfröst Bridge. There, coming from where the canal dissolved into the night, passing the rare gas lamps that smeared the milky fog with blurs of livid light, emerged by and by, and much to their surprise, a sled whose pack of dogs had no driver at all.

The ghost sled approached, as steadily as allowed by the dreamlike strangeness of its apparition, and as it arrived next to the *chasse-gallerie*, stopped right there on its own. Wrapped in a cloud of breath and steamy fur that blended with the surrounding haze, the dogs stood still and, heads tilted, stared with intelligent eyes at the three Scavengers.

Such men, whether by trade or character, are not easily troubled, but this went, or came from, beyond the pale. They gazed at each other for a quizzical while. Chipp, who led the gang, eventually walked towards the edge of the embankment, snapped open the skates inserted in the soles of his hip boots, and lowered himself carefully onto the ice, while his gang mates reached for their lever-guns and watched over his progress. The dogs, however, showed no nervosity or fear as Chipp slid closer to them, his skates grating in the silent night.

The sled struck him as a curious hybrid of *Inuk* technique— its runners were obviously one of those complex mosaics of driftwood and animal bones—but its body was of a quite different nature: the platform was a copper cylinder, painted black, but with a pale green glass or crystal lid, over which Chipp leaned as far as his beak allowed, trying to see if there was something inside.

It was not something, but someone: a lady. Old enough. Dead, or so it seemed, as no blur of breath troubled the glass above her thin dark lips and her pale bony face. She wore a sober black dress of antique cut, and on her lap, her long fine hands were placed around an oval, silver-framed mirror that reflected a distant, dreamy image of Chipp's bird mask.

He thumped on the glass with his thick black glove, knowing that it was useless, that the heavily made up eyelids would not open at his signal. He wondered what he should do with this spectacular piece of *tosh*—as they referred to their findings.

Report it to the authorities? Certainly. But for Scavengers, the authorities were first and foremost their own tight community. They would decide together what to do.

What puzzled him most was that the sled seemed to have come straight from the North. And he knew that north of here there was nothing, and maybe not even that.

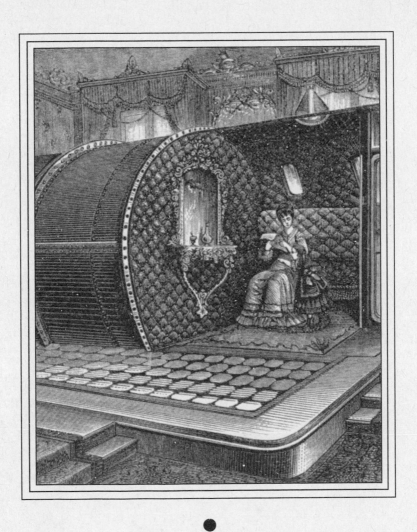

*He drew a curtain aside, and in the dim, glimmering light
of perfumed oil-lamps, found himself facing the incubator,
a huge brass cylinder with a small padded door.*

Book One

•

Qarrtsiluni

The form familiar to our stage of culture, which aims at weaving together and combining motifs into a whole, while gradually shaping itself toward a climax and tending to an explosive conclusion, viz. the dramatic construction, has no place in the intellectual life of the Eskimos.

C.W. Schultz-Lorentzen,
Intellectual Culture of the Greenlanders, 1928

CHAPTER I

A Mysterious Airship

●

"They have steam engines in the North Pole.
And the people there write books and raise bananas."
Polaris, To the editor of *The New-York Times*,
November 12, 1885

Strange as it seemed, Brentford Orsini had never been to Frobisher Fortress, and on the whole, especially now that he was freezing himself at the back of the speeding, shaking Dorset Dragoons' aerosled that had been sent, with a chauffeur, to fetch him, he felt he could have got through his life without ever going there.

The fortress was located some miles away from New Venice, as both Administration and Council had—untypically—agreed on the idea that the fewer soldiers you have hanging around in the city the less trouble you are going to have to deal with. The antics of the Navy Cadets (among whom Brentford had done his own service in some glittering, flickering past) surely enlivened many drab New Venice evenings, but the authorities did not deem it desirable to have more of the same. Brentford, on that grey, windy morning, almost regretted it, or, more exactly, he regretted that he had insisted on the meeting taking place so far away.

The silvery aerosled was noisily scraping west, following a track of snow-covered permafrost, which under the present cheerless light would have been dull unto death, except for the moving panorama it unfurled roaringly on each side of Brentford.

On his left, on the first slopes that led to the mainland mountains and glaciers, the "whirly woods" of the purring city wind vanes soothed him as he was propelled past their ever changing perspectives: they seemed to him like winged creatures of angelical nature waving semaphores of protection and peace.

But, if he turned his eyes to the right, toward the frozen ocean and the bristly white outlines of New Venice itself, he could still see the mysterious black airship that had been hanging over the city for a week or so like a dark cloud brooding and threatening to burst: it looked as if New Venice was in a bad mood, which, indeed, could well be said to be the case.

The fortress, he saw as he approached, barely deserved its name. There was a little fort at one end, but the place mostly consisted of rows of wooden barracks, each one decorated with the coat of arms of the units they housed. Brentford knew and recognized the insignia of the Northern Light Brigade (Dorset Dragoons, Lancaster Lancers, and Sirius Scout Squadron), the Sea and Land Battalion (the famous Sea Lions), the Ellesmere Engineers' Construction Corps, the Alert Armoured and Anti-Aircraft Artillery, the Boreal Weather Warfare Battery, and, in its own Tesla tower, the Tactical Transmission Team. From what he knew, the whole amounted to a force of a mere two thousand men, but it had been sufficient so far. The best defence of the city was its Arctic location, a challenge no invaders had so far chosen to take up.

Though the weather was rather chilly and wet, soldiers in fur-lined trapper hats, mittens, and kamiks were loitering in front of the barracks, playing curling or some rather clumsy soccer, with an air of relaxed resignation to the well-known drabness of the soldiering life. Brentford remembered with somewhat exaggerated nostalgia the time of his own military service, when life had seemed more romantic, full of fancy uniforms, dazzling waltzes, and half-serious duels fought with serious hangovers. Things were now less fanciful, and probably better adjusted to the time and place, however uncertain those notions could be in North Wasteland.

The aerosled swerved toward the fort, and Brentford could now perceive the hangars—where two immense Van der Graaff generators were being serviced—as well as the building site of his own brainchild, the new greenhouse, which would ensure the autonomy of the fortress in terms of food supply. On the whole, the Frobisher Fortress added to the sobriety of its military purpose the stripped-bare severity of an Arctic base, and Brentford really hoped that he would be back before nightfall in his safe, warm hothouse of a house.

The vehicle stopped at the entrance to the fort and a nauseated Brentford, the propeller still whirring in his head, was led by a sentinel to the Headquarters House. Captain-General Frank Mason, Brentford was informed, was waiting for him in his office.

The first time he had met with Mason over this greenhouse business, Brentford had felt something uncanny, as if the officer were a slightly older mirror image of himself—a possible Brentford Orsini who so far had not been allowed to happen, in spite of the prophecy, which he had heard in his youth from the mouth of an old fortune-teller, that he would spend or end his life among men in uniforms. ("I suppose she spoke of nuthouse wardens," as his friend Gabriel d'Allier always said, in a joke that had become rather tired.)

This apparent kinship went beyond their common tall frame, short-trimmed hair, and small, silver-sprinkled sideburns, even beyond a similar decency of demeanour that could sometimes border on a defiant stiffness. It was more the moral meaning of these hieroglyphs that Brentford could relate to: Mason was dutiful, determined, dependable, sound without being sententious, brave without being a daredevil, had a sense of honour without any vanity, and could even convincingly convey the impression that he found some civilians worthy interlocutors. He was, in many ways, the epitome of that bizarre, ill-understood breed of the human species usually known as "soldiers."

But if he was careful never to let the warrior out of the bag in public meetings, Mason also revealed some deep-seated traits that Brentford found a little harder to cope with. The officer had at times, in his sun-dried, cold-bitten, weather-beaten face, the stare of a man who had been once or twice splattered with the brains of a best friend, or who had himself plunged a few inches of solid steel in a total stranger's throat. If he was polite enough to make one believe that he thought his job was the "dirty" kind that "someone had to do," one could feel that that he was prepared to do it to the bitter end. Probably, his conscience would draw the line somewhere, but Brentford was not too curious to know where that would be. And he could presume that, were he to become the enemy, Mason's way of showing his respect would be to leave him no second chance.

So far, there had been no cause for alarm. Though officially taking orders from the Council of Seven, Mason had been clever enough not to meddle in the ongoing internal strife that pitted the Council against the Arctic Administration, to which

Brentford belonged. In a sense, the captain-general relished the isolation of Frobisher Fortress, and would rather be among his men than playing at "poletics."

Impeccably attired as usual in his grey and light blue battle-dress uniform, he welcomed Brentford in a courteous yet business-like way, thanking him for the wedding invitation and congratulating him on the happy event.

"I hope you will be able to make it to the banquet," said Brentford, sitting down.

"I hope so, believe me," answered Mason, with a noncommittal bow.

Brentford actually did not care that much if he came or not and had no intention, no more than Mason had, of discussing his oncoming wedding. He was, for one thing, unsure of how the bride came across socially and did not especially wish to dwell on the matter.

"The Inuit delegation has not yet arrived?" he asked instead, though he knew what the answer would be.

"I do not know if the notion of being on time has any meaning for them," said Mason, wincing, as if he had not sent an aerosled to pick them up from Flagler Fjord and bring them back to the fortress. Brentford pretended he had not heard this typical remark and quickly changed the subject again.

"I see the Greenhouse is well on its way."

"We'll be ready for the spring, don't worry," Mason assured him, almost dismissively. Brentford's plan settled the question of the food supply without involving any road to watch over and protect, but Mason had yet to develop an interest in discussing the positive effects of Pleasanton Blue glass on tomato plants. Looking out the window, his hands clenched behind his back, he clearly signalled that he had other food for thoughts. Since the big black airship had been looming there, all New Venetian attempts at communicating, or at simply gathering information, had proved unfruitful. Seen from any kind of field glasses or observation balloon, it remained opaque and mute, a suspended meteorite that always seemed about to fall.

"I suppose this airship worries you as much as it worries everybody," said Brentford.

Mason shrugged his shoulders.

"I have four anti-aircraft guns pointed at the thing. Whatever it is, it should worry as well."

He seemed to reflect for a while, then turned toward Brentford.

"What is your take on it, Mr. Orsini?"

"I hear a lot about 'aerial anarchists.' But I think anarchists would be either more discreet or more aggressive. So far, this airship has been more inoffensive than it appears." Brentford also thought that anarchist threats were a well-known trick used by the authorities to keep everyone in line, but he did not find it necessary to inform Mason of that opinion.

"In my trade, as you know, nothing is inoffensive," said Mason, walking back to his desk. "Either something is dangerous, or it could well be dangerous."

"Why not simply blow it up, then?" asked Brentford, faking naïveté.

"Some things or people can be more dangerous when they are destroyed. By the way, have you heard of this book, Mr. Orsini?" he said, with a smile that Brentford, busy trying to regain his balance and control his own reaction, did not have time to interpret.

The book that Mason was showing him was a thin black leather-bound quarto with silver lettering, that reproduced in font and style a seventeenth-century pamphlet. It was signed by a certain Henry Hotspur and was entitled *A Blast on the Barren Land, or The Standard of True Community Advanc'd*. In spite of its garb and guise, it was a transparent thrashing of the Council of Seven that bordered on a call to arms, and indeed it was not unknown to Brentford.

"By reputation," he answered, as coolly as possible. "I am surprised you have it in your hands."

"The Council wanted me to read it. Which I did. And what is *your* take on it?"

"It sounds like one of those hoaxes. People tend to get bored, you know."

"I have not been here for very long time," said Mason, "but I know that a hoax can be as effective here as any real thing."

"Certainly so," Brentford admitted. "Do you think it could be connected to the airship?" he asked, indicating the window with his chin.

"I also know," Mason persisted, "that everything has been, is, or will be connected at some point or other. This is a small place, after all."

"Once again, I could not agree more."

To Brentford's relief, Mason put down the book. But it was only to stare at him in a way that made him feel slightly uneasy. He welcomed the knock on the door and the announcement that the Inuit had arrived and were waiting for them in the maps room. They were, after all, not so late.

CHAPTER II

The Gentlemen of the Night

●

The romance of the police force is thus the whole
romance of man. It is based on the fact that morality
is the most dark and daring of conspiracies.
G. K. Chesterton, *The Defendant*

Since Gabriel d'Allier had discovered he could not allow himself to keep a full-time housekeeper anymore, he dined out more and more often. Not that he minded that much: he had always had a taste for market-stall and stadium food, and, as long as he could maintain a three-foot-radius bubble of empty space around him, he was perfectly happy to be among the busy crowds of his beloved city.

He was now having some shrimp from the smorgasbord at a Swedish specialties counter in the Pleasance Arcade, letting the spectacle of the food market alley paint itself on his retinas. As far as the eye could see, the mock castles and the nicely hand-crafted wooden shops extended under the iron-and-glass roof like mirrored reflections of one another, overbrimming with shiny cans, fish and seals beached on gleaming ice, muskox and reindeer carcasses hanging upside down, pyramids of shining fruits and thick groves of vegetables (Brentford seemed to be doing a great job running the Greenhouse), giving to the place a kind of Lubberland atmosphere that pleasantly lulled him. It was not the rush hour yet, and the crowd of passers-by and patrons was mostly composed of Inuit and Russian maids running errands for their employers, and of a few fur-coated, black-hatted flâneurs like himself, whose interest in the generous offerings of Nature was, it seemed, directed as much toward the kissable as toward the edible.

The bubble burst as two men arrived and sat on either side of Gabriel. As he could see from the mirror running behind the counter, one was a tall, broad-shouldered swell with a blond moustache, sporting a black overcoat of the finest cut, a white silk scarf and a top hat, as if he were just out of some theatre matinee; the other, of a lesser bulk, showed a rounder, black-moustached face, and his jowls were framed by a bowler hat and a fur-lined collar. From the corner of his eye, Gabriel could make out on the enormous signet ring worn by the fair buck an emblem showing a moonlit round temple guarded by an owl and a lion, and circled by the inscription *watch & ward*, thereby confirming his apprehension that this was one of the Gentlemen of the Night, whose path one does not cross without good reasons or bad feelings.

"Please, sir, excuse my indiscretion," said the tall dandy, turning toward him, "have I the honour of speaking with the Honourable Earl Gabriel Lancelot d'Allier de St-Antoine?"

Gabriel sighed ostentatiously.

"You have that honour, indeed."

"I am mightily pleased to meet you, Mr. d'Allier, a man who is preceded by such a reputation," answered the man, with an slight inflection that hovered just below the acceptable level of irony. "Let me introduce myself: I am Sealtiel Wynne and I have the honour to serve the Council of Seven."

Gabriel nodded, casting a wistful look at the smorgasbord, which seemed to dwindle in the distance, like some enchanted island disappearing in the fog as soon as apperceived.

"I am truly sorry to disturb you, but it happens that it is my unfortunate duty to ask a favour of you. Do you think, Mr. d'Allier, that you could follow us to a more comfortable place?"

"I suppose I *could*," said Gabriel, trying to face the blue eyes towering too many inches above his own dark brown, twin-barrel look. "But would I *want* to?"

"Let us say that it would be very *kind* of you, if you did."

"How much I regret it, that I am not *reputed* to perform random acts of kindness," answered Gabriel, as coldly as he could, which was not much, for a natural distaste for all kinds of authority quickly gave him the williwaws in such circumstances. "Now, please, would you be so kind yourself as to leave a peaceful citizen to have his lunch quietly?"

"A peaceful citizen. How I love this expression, Mr. d'Allier. It sounds almost as good as 'obedient citizen' or 'law-abiding citizen,' which, I must admit, are the sweetest music to my ears. But, as an intelligent man like you certainly must know, it is, alas, not the citizen himself who decides if he is peaceful or not. Let us imagine that, in a few seconds, a loaded gun should inadvertently fall from your coat pocket. Then, much to my dismay, it would be harder for me to simply take your word for it, and I would have to consider the unpleasant notion that you are a threat to your fellow citizens."

"Is that gun already about to fall?" asked Gabriel, turning suspicious eyes toward the reflection of the other man.

"Accidents happen quickly, by definition," Wynne answered, with a fatalistic shrug of his shoulders. "Listen, sir. We would certainly hate to embarrass you. What I propose to you is this: my friend and I are going to walk to that place I have been talking of, and which is, by chance, not very far from here. Why don't you follow us there from a *respectable* distance? We will not of course hinder you from finishing that appetizing lunch, so we can very well wait till you are done."

"I don't think I'm very hungry anymore. Why don't you leave now?"

The man rose from his stool and bowed in perfect synchrony with his silent companion.

"As you wish, Mr. d'Allier. And *au plaisir de vous voir.*"

The Hôtel de Police in Frislandia, a vast nexus of chiaroscuro corridors, muffled suites, and immense meeting rooms lined with gilt-framed mirrors and succulent plants, was like a five-star palace, except the shortest stay there was always deemed the best. The office in which they received Gabriel was, as promised, very comfortable. The floors were covered with thick woollen rugs, and the walls, of a subtle creamy tint, seemed to be padded with satin. A reproduction of Manet's *Bar des Folies-Bergères* was hung on the wall and its barmaid contemplated Gabriel with an air of weary concern as he sat in an upholstered club armchair, holding a glass of Courvoisier that had just been offered to him together with a cigar, which he had declined.

"Would you care for some music, Mr. d'Allier?" asked Wynne, coming back from the drinks cabinet and pointing at a phonograph standing against the wall. "We have just received the latest record by the Clicquot's Cub-Clubbers."

"Are we yet at the point where my screams have to be drowned?" asked Gabriel, with an archness not quite devoid of nervousness.

"Ah, wit! The next best thing after wisdom!" said Wynne, sitting next to his silent partner behind the mahogany desk that was, Gabriel reflected, as wide and black as the stone slab of a mortuary. "No, no," he continued, "we simply like our interlocutors to feel at ease. You see, Mr. d'Allier, our occupation, which should be counted among the noblest, as it deals with such valued and time-honoured notions as peace, order, and harmony, is too often marred by useless indelicacy, instead of the courtesy, protectiveness, and respect that would be only adequate. We see no reason why this should be so, and neither does the Council, in its generosity."

"Does this generosity extend to my having a lawyer with me?"

"It does, indeed. I am the lawyer," said the other fellow, standing up and offering his hand to Gabriel, who could not but take it. "Mr. Robert DeBrutus, to help and assist you in all legal matters pertaining to this interview and its consequences."

"This gentleman is controlling my activity on your behalf," said Wynne, as the other sat down. "I hope he has no reason to complain about the way things have been handled so far."

DeBrutus, nodding his head, radiated some shortwaves of approval.

"I must say I have none. Nor, I suppose, has my client."

Gabriel felt the arms of the Club chair tighten around him and the seat suck him down like some sort of tar pit. As far as he knew, he had not done anything *really* outside the law, but he was also aware, as Wynne himself had understated, that his own opinion was not of the greatest weight in the matter.

"And since we have your rights so much at heart," Wynne kept on, handing a leather folder to Gabriel, "I will let you know, as it is my duty and pleasure to do, that you are entitled to see the file that we have been carefully putting together about your honourable self."

Gabriel, casting a look dark enough to snuff out a candle, put down his glass, took the folder and browsed through it, his life passing in front of his eyes as if he were a drowning man. Everything, from his résumé and professional activities to his less official occupations, had been duly recorded and archived, including his (extremely rare) forays into "poletics" and his (more numerous) sexual proclivities and episodes of drug abuse.

"It is a truly engrossing read, isn't it?" said Wynne. "You have had a very active life in our community. You should write a book about it sometime."

"I can see it is already written," said Gabriel, handing back the folder to Wynne with a shudder that was a blend of fear, disgust, and aggressiveness.

"In a sense, yes. Though I admit it sadly lacks style, the content is certainly instructive. I hope you appreciate the lengths to which our Recording Angels have gone to get the facts down as accurately as possible, so that we, the Guardian Angels, can act at your service in the most useful and enlightened way. It helps us, gathering statistics on facts that you yourself are not necessarily aware of in the course of your everyday life, but that, from an objective and impartial point of view, draw interesting patterns. For instance," he kept on, pointing to some page in the file, "you may not have noticed it, but it seems that the age of your friends of the fair sex is getting increasingly younger. We certainly encourage the dialogue between generations, but we would not want your commitment as a professor to lead you into *uncharted* territories."

"Each profession has its own risks," said Gabriel, with what he hoped would come across as insolence.

"Certainly so, Mr. d'Allier, *les risques du métier*... We are also worried about your health. You seem to have taken, on a basis that can roughly be regarded as regular, products that have been subjects of stern warnings from the Surgeon-General. Mostly psylicates, from what we gathered. Are you not afraid that these habits might prove to be incompatible with your professional activities as well?"

"I think that they're not only compatible with my teaching, but necessary to it, though that would be long and probably boring to explain, should I ever want to justify myself on this."

"That will not be necessary, sir. We will fully trust you in that respect. As I suggested, we are just warning you for your own good. We have also been very surprised to learn that you have lectured to the Anarchist Circle in Blithedale. And this twice."

"I am sure you know that it is because I was invited to do so, on innocent topics such as literature and music," Gabriel answered, all the more impatiently as he thought that a good half of those anarchists were probably undercover policemen. "I do not see why these 'fellow-citizens' should not be 'enlightened' on these matters, as we can agree that, in the end, education brings more good than bad."

Wynne smiled a decent imitation of a real smile.

"Oh, we certainly agree. We would not want you to feel defensive, Mr. d'Allier. All these facts I have alluded to are not presently *seriously* held against you. We would just like to make you aware that, taken all together, they may, at some point that is not under your control, combine to endanger your position as a professor. Given the present economical difficulties some of our citizens go through, it really would be a shame if a man of your standing should happen to find himself in a delicate situation. Unpleasant as is the prospect, I am nevertheless relieved that we have had the occasion to discuss this before it is too late, as we have nothing but your interest at heart. But that is not exactly the main reason for your presence among us. I know you like books and I happen to have one I want to show you, and this one, believe me, should satisfy your sense of style."

Wynne unlocked his drawer, flourished a thin volume, bound in black leather, and handed it to Gabriel, who did his best to pretend that he was seeing *A Blast on the Barren Land* for the first time in his life.

"I suppose that a learned man such as you has already heard about or even read this book," said Wynne, before propping up his square jaw with his fists.

Not only had Gabriel done that, he had also proofread and rephrased some minute parts of it. But he decided that this piece of information was to be kept locked in the safe of his cranium, for that was what a skullbox, or sulkbox, as he liked to call his own, was meant for, after all.

"I am sorry to disappoint both you and myself on that point."

"I would not believe it, if I hadn't your word of honour for it," said Wynne.

"Consider you have it for all it is worth." ("Under the present circumstances, you bastard son of a sick circus seal and a bearded woman"), added Gabriel to himself. He had been raised at St. Ignatius High School, and about all he had inherited from the Jesuits, besides his hatred of all forms of self-righteous domination, was the point and practice of "mental reservation."

Wynne, though he still made his best effort to remain courteous, was now exuding impatience.

"We have it that you are very well acquainted with the Duke Brentford Orsini, the current Gardener-General of the Greenhouses & Glass Gardens."

"I am indeed. And proudly so."

"This honours you both, certainly. But the little problem that we have on our hands is that we strongly suspect that this libel, which could be easily be construed as defamatory, is the work of none other than the duke himself. Do you honestly think—as you, I presume, know very well both the style and ideas of your friend—that he could possibly be the author we are looking for?"

"Well. It is obvious that the book is written precisely to disguise any recognizable style, and does so rather efficiently. As to Mr. Orsini himself, privy to his thoughts as I am, I have always known him for an obedient, law-abiding citizen."

"May you be right, Mr. d'Allier, may you be right," said Wynne, in a tone that was now perceptibly threatening.

"There are many kinds of laws," interrupted DeBrutus, as if he sensed his colleague's subtle shortening of temper and sought to maintain a standard of decency throughout the proceedings. "Some are written, some are of a more implicit nature. One can be a 'law-abiding citizen' and still, consciously or not, be at odds with the most sacred principles that make common life possible. Mister Wynne's concern is that your friend does not make such a mistake, and for the time being, as your lawyer, my own concern is that Mr. Orsini does not make you his accomplice, when your own situation is not, if you'll permit me, exactly the safest as regards the law."

"Thank you, Mr. DeBrutus," said Wynne, who had regained some composure. "I could not have expressed it myself more accurately. Let us hope that, in order to avoid any misunderstanding, I am now able to make a clear summary of the current situation."

He leaned on the desk, staring straight into Gabriel's eyes.

"Mr. d'Allier, I will not hide from you that were you to gather, by hearsay or sudden recollection, some information about the authorship of that book and let us know about it, we would greatly appreciate your effort, both as a service to the general public and as a token of your own goodwill in the circumstances that surround you. On the other hand, we would not regard as very favourable to your own affairs any attempt to inform your friend about our inquiries, for were our suspicions unfortunately to be confirmed, that could be interpreted as a kind of obstruction, which, as Mr. DeBrutus could confirm, qualifies as a breach of the law. We would deeply regret it if things were to come to that point, for both you and Mr. Orsini, who are two highly valued members of our community, but you will easily understand that it is on the interest of that community that we must all set our sights. I hope you will forgive me if you feel that I have a been a little too straightforward with these explanations."

"Not at all," said Gabriel, trying to control the trembling in his voice. "They are quite fascinating actually, and certainly confirm the high regard in which the population holds you. Now, if you will excuse me, there is no company, good as it is, from which one must not eventually be parted."

"Let me see you to the door" said DeBrutus, and rose from his seat, while Wynne, standing up as well, bowed to Gabriel and bade him farewell.

It was a long walk before DeBrutus, who had vainly tried to strike up a conversation, followed a moody Gabriel through the marble reception hall and the gilded revolving door that opened on the Nicolo Zeno Embankment. Gabriel inhaled what remained of the daylight as if it were a bottle of Letheon.

"Shall I say *au revoir*, Mr. d'Allier?" asked the Angel of the Law with a smile that Gabriel saw himself punching to a pulp in some kinetoscope of his mind.

"I hope it's *adieu*," he answered, dashing down the stairs without, this time, taking the offered hand.

CHAPTER III

Unhappy Hunters

•

O dear native land! How well it is that you
are covered with ice and snow... Your unfruitfulness
makes us happy and saves us from molestation.
Paul Greenlander, a convert Eskimo, 1756

The first thing Brentford noticed about the delegation is that they had a watch hung around their necks: one wore the case and one the face while the others shared the works. Whether that was for ornamental purposes or meant as a comment, he could not tell.

The group consisted of four Inuit from the local Inughuit people. As far as Brentford could make out, their names were Uitayok (older than the others, and who seemed to be the riumasa, "the one who thinks"); Ajuakangilak (a clever-looking man with searching eyes, who, judging by his belt and amulets, may have been the angakoq, or shaman); Tuluk (tall for an Inuk, some sort of métis, no doubt, deemed useful when dealing with the Whites), and Tiblit (a long-haired fellow of rather uncouth appearance whose insistent smile could easily get on one's nerves). They lived at—or had been relocated to—Flagler Fjord, and were among those families who had not deemed it a good idea to live in New Venice, though they probably had some relatives among the Inuit workers and servants of the city. All now sat at a round table, watching each other with all sorts of forced smiles.

Brentford had come to New Venice at an early age and had almost always lived with Inuit around, had known a lot of them, befriended some (even, briefly, loved one), had some inklings of their culture, and had collected their art, for which he showed a connoisseur's appreciation. However, he had to admit that relationships with them were often a bit of a riddle and could be frustrating at times. When they were with the *qallunaat*, their word for Whites, unless some sort of personal friendship and trust had developed, Inuit often defended themselves with a blend of comic humility and unfathomable irony verging on contempt, which could make one uncomfortable. Brentford was used to it and had learned to live with it, but he could see that for Mason these meetings were still a source of uneasiness. The captain-general, not of an outgoing nature himself, seemed to subscribe to the classical military axiom about the "natives," according to which "they couldn't be trusted," and as a result, he had firmly settled on the curt side of courtesy. Today's palaver did not promise to inspire a more amenable attitude in him, as the situation quickly proved delicate.

Uitayok, who spoke a singular but almost intelligible missionary English, and who, when in trouble, was helped by the slightly more proficient Tuluk, put the matter with more succinctness than Brentford and Mason had feared. It was obvious these Inuit and their families were genuinely worried and in urgent need of a solution. Their problem was this: since self-sufficiency had become one of the goals of the Frobisher

Fortress, hunting parties had become the norm for patrols, and the use of noisy aerosleds and rifles had scared or depleted the game in a way that was starting to deprive the Inuit of their main source of food.

Brentford had already considered this possibility and foreseen it as a drawback to his plan. But he had not thought that the Subtle Army, for once unworthy of its self-bestowed nickname, would show so little understanding or restraint. Mason, on the other hand, assuming he could perfectly grasp what the problem was, had his own agenda: it did actually bring extra food to the fort, it was a welcome distraction for his bored men, and, not unimportantly, it was a show of strength that would remind the "Eskimos" of their real position in the food chain, in more senses than one.

There was, however, something else to be considered. These past few weeks the city "natives" had been rather "restless." Pro-Nunavut slogans, in both the Inuktitut and roman alphabets, had been painted on monuments at a more frequent rate than usual, and revolting *tupilaat*, made of various animal remains glued together in crude miniature human forms, had been found all over the city, probably intended less as spells than as warnings that trouble was brewing.

There was usually little connection between the urban Inuit independentists and their wilderness cousins, but a recent picture, mysteriously sent to the newspapers, of forty or so fur-clad Inuit defiantly posing with rifles in a barren polar landscape, had made the authorities wonder if this was not changing. In other words, though Uitayok was certainly not implying anything of the sort, it was maybe not the best idea to strengthen those ties by bothering the North Wasteland Inuit.

If their numbers were few and, in theory, not much of a match for the Subtle Army, they had a better knowledge of the theatre of operations, and one of Mason's missions was to avoid that kind of conflict at all cost. Then, too, he had to take into account the presence of the mysterious black airship that, as he had himself remarked, might sooner or later be connected, if it wasn't already, to his other concerns. If Eskimos were to be equipped, by some channel or other, with an allied air force, it might not do any harm to take into account what they had to say.

"I understand your worries," Mason said, articulating carefully as if he were talking to children. "I propose we come to an agreement to limit,"—raising his voice, for while he was talking, Tiblit murmured something into Tuluk's ear, so that Tuluk was lagging behind on the translation—"to limit the quantity of food we take. If our hunt exceeds this limit, the surplus will be returned to you."

Uitayok seemed to ponder this, but Brentford could guess what he would answer.

"This is very kind of you. But it happens that one likes to hunt for oneself, even if one is a bad hunter," he said, showing maybe more pride than he intended.

"Of course," said Mason. "So, I shall see that a decent limit is not exceeded."

Brentford doubted very much that Mason could control his men as well as he said, when they were patrolling in the wild. From hunters they would turn into poachers, and that was all.

"Why not collaborate?" he allowed himself to say. "It would be more convenient if our friends could set the limit themselves by offering their surplus or even by hunting for the Fortress. In exchange they could benefit from the surplus of the Greenhouse that is being built."

Brentford, who could not himself stomach even the sight of a plate of spinach, was well aware that Inuit would not be overexcited at the idea of eating their greens. But he hoped that they would know a fair deal when it came to them, waving a white flag. Mason was casting him a somewhat darkened look, but he could not admit that he wanted to allow his men to have some sport at the expense of the Inuit.

"But would there be surplus at the Greenhouse?" asked the captain-general, playing his last card.

"I do not know," conceded Brentford, "but I doubt very much that sweet peas and french beans run the risk of becoming extinct."

Uitayok and his cohorts followed the exchange with, Brentford could see, much curiosity and expectation but also, or so it seemed, some amusement. They had been witnesses to enough betrayals and murders between *qallunaat* to know that if white men could be bad to them, there was always a chance that they would be still more wicked to one another.

"But," said Mason, who had obviously found another card up the sleeve of his uniform, "if these *gentlemen* hunt for us," this with a note of contempt that made Brentford flinch inwardly, "we will not be as independent as *your* plan intended to make us. Why do not we define zones where we are allowed to hunt?"

Uitayok, after having listened to Tuluk's version, answered this better than Brentford could have done. He drew from a bag some pieces of driftwood that, to the *qallunaat's* amazement, he organized to make a map that corresponded precisely to the geography of North Wasteland, though there was little chance that he had ever seen the area otherwise than by paddling around. He pointed to various zones, miming the migrations of species.

"It happens that the animals move. The lines, they do not know. If *qallunaat* have them all what will the Inuit do? And the Inuit, they have to move with the animals."

Mason frowned, trying to grasp Uitayok's meaning, and eventually he turned toward Brentford.

"This *gentleman* knows the matter," said Brentford.

Mason returned him a frowning "whose-side-are-you-on" look, but he also knew a dead end when he saw one. However, he did not feel inclined to give in to Brentford in front of his guests.

"But you know I am not entirely qualified to decide on such important matters. I will have to refer to the Council of Seven concerning the possibility of this contract, as well as to the City Council for Customs and Commerce, and probably to the Nunavut Administration for Native Affairs to make sure everything is clear to all parties," he said, both to gain time and to embarrass Brentford a little, knowing of his strained relationship with the Council of Seven.

Tuluk translated as well as he could, but Uitayok had already understood and his face showed clearly that the word *administration* in an Inuk's ear sounded about as promising as the word *tupilaat* did to the *qallunaat*'s. Ajuakangilak said something to Uitayok who in turn repeated it to Tuluk.

"There is another matter," Tuluk announced.

"What is it?" said Mason, a little impatiently.

"Some of *qallunaat* soldiers. They are very scary."

"Some of my soldiers? What do you mean?"

"They are evil spirits. Dead and living. Very Hungry. Very Evil."

Mason turned toward Brentford with an inquisitive look. Brentford was not that surprised. He had heard the story before, when he was a child, actually. The Phantom Patrol was a popular legend when it came to scaring disobedient children: the living dead, mummified, mutilated corpses of British and American sailors or soldiers lost in polar explorations prowling the ice fields for blood, animal or human, on sleds of bones drawn at full speed by skeletal dogs. They were, beyond the lore, not an uncommon hallucination for today's strayed travellers or Inuit.

"They are hunting on your grounds?" asked Brentford, with a polite interest.

Ajuakangilak launched himself into a long explanation that Tuluk translated as an unequivocal yes. They had made their dogs *pillortoq*—crazy—and dug up graves and stolen one child.

"Can someone explain this to me?" asked Mason.

Brentford tried to smile. It was his experience that the less you heard or talked about some things, the less they were bound to bother you. Those who had never heard about the Phantom Patrol were not likely to see them. Or such had been the case so far.

"Oh, it's nothing that should concern you, really. Part of the folklore."

But he also knew, as the Inuit did, that here fictions were like animals: they could migrate, and they ignored the lines.

CHAPTER IV

A Teacher's Pet

●

And to adorne her with a greater grace,
And ad more beauty to her louely face,
Her richest Globe shee gloriously displayes
Michael Drayton, *Endimion & Phoebe,* 1595

For a prelapsarian sensibility such as Gabriel's, work was nothing but a curse, the sin committed against man. Seldom bored, which was not common at those latitudes, and always busy in his own mysterious ways, he had no spare time to lose in such a tasteless fashion: he would, normally, not have touched a "profession" with a barge pole and a pair of fur overmittens if he could have helped it.

But, years ago, as the Blue Wild catastrophe had left parts of the city in (beautiful) deep-blue ruins, he had been obliged, like all the other scions of the so-called Arcticocracy, all the more because he happened to be the son of a profligate father whose legacy consisted of nothing but debts, to become, in his own bittersweet words, the Earl of Real. He had been cunning or lucky enough to get into one of the rare trades he could tolerate, and the only one among those that could materialize a monthly paycheck. The task was mostly a bit of acting, which he handled competently enough, in a courteous yet slightly desultory way, always walking the thin line that separates discretion from uselessness. But it has to be said that since his interview with the Gentlemen of the Night, his already minimal commitment had dwindled to Lilliputian proportions. It had even come to the point where he sat in his Doges College office whitewashing his brain with cheap "snowcaine" freshly bought in Venustown from a certain Charley Sleighbells.

Today his excuse for doing this was not a class to teach but the "private conversation" he had just been invited to in the Dean's Office, by way of a none too polite letter, which we would gladly have shared with the reader if it were not at this very moment sulkily crumpled at the bottom of the wastepaper basket. Gabriel was fed up with people wanting to discuss things with him, and it was only when he deemed himself sufficiently sharpened that he could bear getting up and going down to the meeting.

The corridors looked their bleak mid-February selves, with a few stray students gliding about like ghosts and shadows against the dying daylight pouring from the arched windows at each extremity. There had always been, since his own student days at Doges, a light aura of unreality about this place, or maybe about himself, he reflected, sniffing and checking that his nose was not running too much.

Gibiser, who occupied the honourable and much-coveted position of Dean of Doges, was a white-haired but healthy man, with a sympathetic surface and tolerably murky depths, the kind who would pat you on the back to choose the best spot to stab you. But today, he was not even that cheerful when Gabriel sat before him in his large first-floor office with its view of the mock Parthenon and the—ridiculous—miniature Rialto bridge that marked the entrance to the Campus.

"I am glad to see you here," Gibiser said.

"I work here," answered Gabriel with typical snowcaine poise, though he knew that Gibiser was a bit challenged when it came to grasping other senses of humour than his own— Gabriel's especially, peculiar as it was, often proved a tough nut to crack.

"Oh, I know that very well," Gibiser said darkly. "Listen, Professor d'Allier, I am going to do for you something I should not do, which is to disclose private correspondence from a third party. If I do so, it is only because I hope it will do more good than ill for the community."

He handed Gabriel a letter, which Gabriel read with growing disgust, while barely suppressing his sniffles and hoping those that escaped could pass as sniffs of contempt.

"Dear Colleague and Dean,

I wish to speak to you about a Masters student called Phoebe O'Farrell.

This student has taken my class "The Pen and the Plough: The Peasant as Poet, the Poet as Peasant" this semester, and her paper on "John Clare's Use of the Word 'Croodle'" was of a very high level and by far the best I have read for this course. I have nothing more to add on this matter.

She had chosen at the beginning of the term to write a dissertation under the guidance of our colleague Mr. Allier titled "Stoned Landscapes: Laudanhomes & Hashishtecture in Coleridge's 'Kubla Khan' and Baudelaire's 'Rêve Parisien'"(sic). For reasons that she may or may not wish to explain to you (it is her own decision), she would like to ask you if it would be possible that this dissertation now be supervised by myself.

I fully support this request and I think it would be better for all if you and Allier would agree on this point, as she is currently undergoing certain difficulties in her work where I could be of great help.

She is one of my best students, and I hope you will give her your most benevolent attention.

Cordially Yours,

Prof. Albert Corkring
Full-Fledged Fellow
House of Humanities
Doges College

"What am I supposed to do with this rag," asked Gabriel, his voice as icy as the tip of his nose. "Propose it as a commentary in a poetry class?"

He could see that Gibiser was embarrassed. But he could also see, his own brain a dazzling crystal ball, that it was more over being involved in such an imbroglio than for Gabriel's sake.

"Do not get carried away, Mr. d'Allier. I'm saying this in your best interest. And please, rather, tell me if you have any idea what these... allusions might refer to?"

Gabriel could see very clearly indeed what the fuss was all about, and it was not very glorious. In the world of dark muted passions that is Academia, the witches' brew that blends scholarly susceptibility with delusions of seduction is rather everyday fare, but here Corkring had obviously been scraping the bottom of the cauldron.

"It is simple enough. Sometime around the Flood, my col-league Corkring wrote a rather derivative booklet on Coleridge and so considers that author as a private property I am intrud-ing upon. I suppose that the abduction of this student is for him a form of revenge."

Gibiser seemed to find the explanation plausible but did not want let Gabriel see that, and adopted instead a diffident, dis-approving, whatever-it-is-I'm-against-it expression that came as part of the package along with the panoply of Dean.

"If I read correctly between the lines, his allegations are, however, of another nature."

"I don't like to wallow in another's man mud," muttered Gabriel, barely unclenching his jaws to say it.

Gibiser nodded pensively.

"We are coming to a situation where it is his word against yours, then."

"It's my word against his oink, you mean."

The Dean pretended he had not heard.

"And I regret to say that in such a situation, his word is mightier than yours. First, he is a full-fledged fellow and you are not. Then, Mr. d'Allier, you are, if I may say so, a man with a past. I am speaking, of course, of previous involvements with students."

Gabriel wanted to protest, in the name of the largely mythi-cal nature of the said involvements, but he was silenced by a gesture from Gibiser, who did not want to discuss further such an unsavoury matter.

"And at last, and this may be even more crucial, Professor Corkring is, as you may know, Special Councillor of Studies for the Council of Seven. And—I am speaking honestly to you here—his defeat for the office of Vice-Regent of the College has made him, shall we say, a bit nervous and dangerous to contradict. I would not want him to carry these matters higher than they should go, which he is wont to do, if he is not given satisfaction."

"Which, if *I* may read between the lines, means I cannot count on your support?" asked Gabriel, who, as soon as he had heard the words *Council of Seven* knew not only that his case was hopeless but also that the noose would only get tighter if he struggled.

"Since when do you need support from anyone, Mr. d'Allier? You are a *loner,*" said Gibiser, as if that settled the matter. The French half of Gabriel's brain heard *l'honneur* and almost felt flattered, while the other half remained a cold blank. He got up and walked out without a word.

He went back to his office, holding his anger in himself as in a cup about to spill. Rage in Gabriel never burst out in fits but got ice-cold and crystallized into unforgettable, unforgiving grudges. Fuelled up by the snowcaine, he paced up and down, from door to desk and from sofa to bookshelves, sometimes whispering atrocities to a phantom Corkring, sometimes devising various plans for public humiliations, sometimes refusing to stoop so low as to acknowledge both the miserable scheme and the pitiful existence of his colleague. He almost did not hear the soft knock on the door, but eventually he opened it with an aggressive swiftness, only to find himself face to face with none other than Phoebe O'Farrell.

"Yes?" he asked, dark-eyed and frowning.

"Can I have a word with you, sir?" asked the girl, who looked ill at ease.

"It depends on what you have to say."

"I feel I must explain something to you."

"I feel that, too," he said, leaving the door ajar and seating himself behind his desk.

Phoebe O'Farrell closed the door and sat down. She was a

petite pale girl, with light brown eyes and long, flowing, curly hair of a subdued red, always dressed in a slightly quaint, Pre-Raphaelite way, and even to the objective eye she was cute as a red-alert button. But she was a wee tad affected, and from the little that Gabriel had read or heard from her, she had an Ophelian streak of potential craziness that he had, since day one, deemed wiser to steer clear of, so Corkring's allegations, the reader will be pleased to know, had no truth to them whatsoever.

They both remained silent for a while.

"I have a problem with Professor Corkring," said the girl.

"That makes two of us," said Gabriel while dusting off, as casually as he could, some traces of a white volatile powder he had noticed on his desk.

"I have shown him my work, the work I had started with you."

"You should not have."

"I know that, sir. He asked me what I was doing and wanted to see it. He gave me some suggestions about it, and..."

She glanced up at Gabriel in embarrassment, and suddenly he realized that he was putting her through the same kind of ordeal that he had endured this morning when facing the Gentlemen of the Night. He encouraged her with a smile that may have looked like a grin, because a little more time elapsed in silence.

"And...?"

"He told me that you wanted to steal my ideas."

"Which ones, my dear?"

The girl lowered her head. Once again, he felt cruel and remembered he should try to encourage her, if he wanted to know anything.

"So you know that is not true, I hope."

"Yes," whispered the girl.

"Very well. Did he *suggest* something else?"

"He said that what you were interested in was... you know..."

"I do not."

"... going beyond professional relationships."

"I don't think I have ever given you any cause of alarm on this point."

"Oh, no," she said quickly, and, Gabriel felt, or liked to think, almost regretfully.

"So you know better."

"And then, he said he could help me, because he knew the subject very well and also knew a lot of people who could be very useful to me, if I were to keep on working with him."

"On this, he did not lie. He knows a lot of people. And so I take it that you were interested."

"I did not want to work with him. But I did not know how to refuse."

"*Et tu, Phoebe...* " said Gabriel, pointing an accusing finger at his student. But that did not make her smile, as it was vaguely intended to do.

"I was evasive as long as I could be, but last week he..." She stopped, stumbling on something that immediately attracted Gabriel's attention.

"I'm all ears," he said softly, now beginning to enjoy himself.

"I came across him in the college swimming pool and he asked me what... I should not tell you that."

"It is only fair that you do. I need to hear it," Gabriel said, as benevolently as he could.

Phoebe blushed a light pink.

"What would I do if I saw him naked."

Ha ha. That was it. He'd known it all the time. One more of those *old* lecherous teachers, Gabriel judged, with all the unforgiving harshness of a *middle-aged* lecherous teacher. A snowcaine angel was prompting him to say "I hope you answered that you would vomit," but the effect was starting to wear off, and the angel had now a feeble voice that he could overrule if he chose.

"I don't know what to do," said Phoebe, as if to herself.

But Gabriel knew what *he* had to do.

"It's very simple. You go and work with him."

"But I wanted to work with you," said Phoebe, turning a lily-white shade of pale.

"I don't want you to get into trouble. And I don't want to get into trouble because of you."

"I'm sorry," she said, and looked as if she were about to weep.

Seeing this, the snowcaine angel found another entrance to Gabriel's brain.

"Please, don't," he said, getting up and walking toward Phoebe. He took her by the arm and sat her next to him on the red plush sofa, whose springs let out a scandalized squeak. "Let us see if we can solve this."

"I beg your pardon," she said, holding back her little selfish tears.

"I don't want you to beg. I want you to earn it," he said, his voice slightly trembling. She looked at him inquisitively.

"First, it deserves a good spanking," explained Gabriel, laying her firmly on his lap without feeling much resistance, only some surprise and a slight hesitation.

Now maybe, dear reader, it would be more becoming in you to leave the room, and I would advise you not to look back on the scene if you can help it: were you to linger and witness, for instance, that Phoebe has now her grey dress and petticoats over her head, you would be, and not me, responsible for it, and you could not count either on yours truly or on Gabriel to confirm that this vision was not a child of your unbridled imagination.

But we certainly can, if you please, come back a little later, and find Gabriel calmly sitting beside Phoebe on the sofa, and even hear him asking:

"Now, Phoebe, would you mind doing me a favour?"

CHAPTER V

Phantasus & Phobetor

●

Yes, for three francs' worth of opium he furnishes our
empty arsenal, he watches convoys of merchandise coming in,
going to the four quarters of the world. The forces of modern
industry no longer reign in London, but in his own Venice,
where the hanging gardens of Semiramis, the Temple of
Jerusalem, the marvels of Rome, live once more.
Honoré de Balzac, *Massimila Doni*, 1837

It was a brooding Brentford who was driven back to New Venice by the Subtle Army aerosled. The day, a short, dubious affair of a few hours, had started its retreat, pretexting that the grass was greener elsewhere, which, to be honest, was certainly the case. The frosted snow, which cracked and crunched as they passed, had turned a greyish blue, and above the city, where dim golden garlands of lights had started to gleam, blurred as through a tearful eye, the black airship had begun to assume a certain melancholy air. April may be the cruellest month, but in North Wasteland, February was a tough bitch in her own right.

The airship's shadow was not the only one being cast over Brentford's brain. The meeting had left a bitter aftertaste, as was often the case when Inuit were involved. As much as he wanted to be useful to them, his duties to the city could not but get in the way.

Since the natives had come into contact with the Whites, and though it was very clear that without them all Westerners who ventured there would have ended up as a dirty bunch of half-frozen cannibal wrecks, they had been exploited, misunderstood, and underestimated in every possible way. Brentford remembered that the profit margin of the usual barter, furs for needles and nails, had been around 1,000 percent for the Whites, and still the Inuit—unconscious dandies prowling the icepack with fortunes on their backs—felt they were striking a bargain, because for them, exchange value was use value, and use value was survival.

When the first trading posts had been established, with a slightly more realistic price policy (but with false weights, bottomless bushels for blubber, and exchange wares of wretched quality), the Inuit had been almost disappointed with how much less expensive everything turned out to be, as this had seemed to take away the real worth of what they had gotten so far. It also made them realize how cheated they had been, and how miserable they actually were. What the Inuit failed to see was that, at that point, they were also being robbed of natural resources, with little or no redistribution of this wealth to compensate them. Maybe Brentford had been wrong: they would not know a fair deal if it came and bit them, because they had hardly seen one before. What sort of trade could it be, anyway, that involved two economies that were, literally, different as day and night?

The Whites' contemptuous treatment of the Inuit was all the more maddening in that, given the city's new circumstances, Eskimo economics (and therefore—and there was the rub—Eskimo politics) could be one of the keys to the city's salvation. Until recently, and especially since its reconstruction, New Venice had been lavished with sumptuous gifts, colossal food supplies and enormous quantities of raw materials and luxuries. From what Brentford understood, the Forty Friends Foundation, which funded and maintained New Venice afloat, did not do so out of the goodness of their hearts (though they certainly had some kind of fascination with the place), but because they desperately wanted to ward off an overproduction crisis and to redistribute world scarcity along more advantageous lines. New Venice was a kind of bottomless pit or raging fire in which they would sacrifice the accursed share of their enterprises before it turned against them.

But since the Great Crash had not been avoided that way, the tide, of both means and conviction, was turning, and even if the citizens did not quite realize it, the city was now skating on very thin ice, drawing figures that were increasingly less figure eights than plain zeros. That was how Brentford had come, in spite of his own tendency to despise hoarding and to value sacrificial spending as the most sacred human activity, to fight on the side of autarky, and that was how, consequently, he had begun to regard the Inuit and the way they negotiated with their surroundings with more than the usual amused or amazed curiosity.

It wasn't that they were thrifty or miserly—far from it—or that they were "one with nature" in any namby-pamby way: they were in a good position to know what a bloody mess it is, breathing in and out through endless sacrifices, in the frenzy of self-laceration that lies at the bottom of all things. No, they were well aware that nature had not been made to please them, and that it would only make things worse if they added to its, and their, necessary cruelty the luxury puerilities of greed and domination. It was not simply accumulation, sweet as it was, that would get them through the night, but the exacting duty of sticking together no matter what, and the wealth of memories, dreams, stories, rituals, and visions that are the true fortune of our unfortunate species.

To Brentford, the idea was not to turn New Venetians into Inuit but to develop a system, or at least a mentality, loosely adapted from theirs ("as nearly as possible socialism carried into practice," as Nansen had written) that could get the city going forward, instead of selling everything piece by piece, including the future, as the Council of Seven was doing. But convincing the authorities to think along the lines of Eskimo economics was certainly no easy task: the Councillors were, after all, descendants of the men who had had their sleighs drawn by other men instead of by dogs, who had suffered from scurvy and died of cold in wet woollen uniforms because they were not going to eat seal or wear fur like those "savages." The True Community that Brentford had described in the Hotspur pamphlet was still, seductive as it was, one of those *fata morgana* mirages, a projection that seemed within reach but was still a long, dangerous, frustrating way down the road...

His metaphor crystallized in a memory not quite his own, but rather that of his Italian ancestor Felice Rossini, a faithful servant of the Duke dei Abruzzi and a member of his Mount St-Elias and *Stella Polare* expeditions. While they had been in Icy Bay, their party had suddenly seen rising from the mist the famous Silent City of Alaska, which appears on a certain glacier, all streets and spires, every year between June and July. It was there and then that Felice had fallen in love at first sight with the idea of a New Venice, and had striven, with thousands of others, to make it a dream come true.

It was a love that Brentford felt as well, and felt indeed to be older than himself. But what Felice could not have known, and Brentford did, was that even as you came closer to it, as he was doing now, reaching the Lotus Eaters suburbs under a lazy fall of snowflakes and soot specks, the city lost nothing of its illusory nature—a dream come true that remained a dream, as if you woke up each morning a prisoner in Slumberland. These musings, idle as they were, still gave him an idea, or even an urge, and bending toward the chauffeur, he asked to be dropped not at the Botanical Building, where he now resided, but almost a mile away from it, on the Beaufort Embankment.

They were now entering the centre of the city, an off-white grid of frozen canals and deserted avenues, lined with impressive Neoclassical and Art Nouveau buildings. In the twilight, their incongruous stuccoed, statue-haunted silhouettes, rising darker against the darkening horizon, gave the eerie impression that they had been cast down from the sky like palaces from another planet. You could not, by any stretch of the mind, imagine an architecture less adapted to its surroundings. An Ideal City punished and banished to the Far North for its marble hubris, it loomed titanic and mad, its boulevards, arches, and palaces a playground for the caterwauling draughts that sharpened their claws on its flaking façades. And as it did almost every day in late winter, that typical moist fog known to the locals as *cake* was now seeping everywhere, slowly dimming the scene in a way that gave Brentford the impression that, too tired to will themselves further into existence, the very buildings evaporated, fading like the ghosts of their own unlikely splendour.

Once on the Beaufort Embankment, Brentford saluted the driver and waited for the aerosled to be soaked into the distance. Though the Air Architecture here was supposed to be at its most protective, the *cake* felt like a block of cold static drizzle, and except for a few hurried, muffled, somnambulic shapes, the gaslit streets were deserted.

Once he was sure not to be seen, Brentford crossed the embankment, took Barrington Street, and headed toward the

Dunne Institute for Dream Incubation. Flanked by two twisted spires that made it look a little like a church, and guarded by the marble effigies of the brothers of Morpheus, Phantasus and Phobetor, the Institute was a sort of mental swimming pool for the tired or depressed citizen who could do with a good nap and some sweet dreams, but also for those who were seeking advice or answers to urgent but undecidable matters.

The hall, under its night-blue and starry dome, offered two different gates, one called Ivory, for recreative dreams (including erotic ones, and even nightmares, which happened to be a surprisingly sought-after commodity) and the other one Horn, for the more serious kind of incubation, in which it was indeed hard to predict what the outcome would be (after all, as Brentford had heard Gabriel say countless times, all dreams made you horny). Anonymous behind his woollen scarf, Brentford asked at the desk for the expensive Horn fare. "Single or round-trip?" asked the clerk, with a smile, though the joke was rather worn out.

Past the gates, the Institute consisted of long, swerving, stifling corridors, ill-lit with gas torches held by black marble forearms that jutted out from scarlet walls. Brentford pushed the heavy ebony door corresponding to his ticket. He found himself in a small, black-walled changing room, where he undressed completely, hanging his clothes on another protruding hand, before taking a shower that served both hygienic and symbolical purposes. He drew a curtain aside, and in the dim, glimmering light of perfumed oil-lamps, found himself facing the incubator, a huge brass cylinder with a small padded door. There was actually little this machine did except isolate the dreamer, bathing him in warm saltwater on which he could float, while playing some low-volume, low-frequency drones that were meant to soothe the brain.

Most of the incubation work was left to the dreamer, who had to choose from a distributor the right Complimentary

Chemical Complements, as they were called. Brentford opted for the Shower Of Stars, which had always worked wonders for him, and had to phrase by himself, on a piece of paper he placed under his pillow, the question he wanted the dream to answer, writing it in sigils, which facilitated, it seemed, unconscious remembrance.

Brentford eased himself into the incubator, set the sound waves to a classical 2-3 Hz pulse with cyclical forays into the theta spectrum, clicked off the electric lamp at his side, and closed his eyes, concentrating on the answers he wanted about what he should do with the Inuit. As a mathematician, he had always successfully practiced this lazy brand of shamanism known as creative naps, and for some time he had kept a book of dreams that had given him a good training in recall, so incubation was only natural for him. And indeed, though he preferred to be discreet about it, he did often resort to it to solve certain thorny problems at work. Or when he wanted advice from Helen.

A low whirling buzz sounded in his ears and he quickly fell asleep, vivid and ludicrous pictures circling around him at full speed. He disappeared for a while, but soon, as he recalled afterward, he emerged in a snowy landscape, a wilderness that extended as far the eye could blink. He was clad only in blue boxer shorts that he instantly knew were not his but had been borrowed, though he did not know from whom. He was cold, but tolerably so, much less than he would have expected in such surroundings. There were, not surprisingly, two moons in the sky that he thought were both made of green cheese. At this thought, he felt like retching. His stomach contracted, painfully, and he started spewing and spooling off a white, light, cheesecloth-like stuff that probably was some sort of ectoplasm. As it fell on the icy snow, its whiteness made it at first indiscernible, but as it started to pile up, it grew increasingly visible, appearing as a human shape trying to grow. After a long, nauseous while, it reached Brentford's height and became the figure of a former acquaintance, Hector Liubin V, a musician of the pre– Blue Wild era, whose face he could see delineated almost clearly under the ectoplasm but whose words he could not make out, as if the stuff were smothering them. He tried to guess: "Sandy Lake?" Brentford heard himself asking. The shape shifted and a young woman was now facing Brentford, wearing a crinoline and with her hands in a fur muff. "No, I'm Isabella Alexander," she said, "but my friends call me the Ghost Lady. The woman was now hovering slightly in front of Brentford and did not seem made of ectoplasm anymore but rather sculpted in some volatile, thin, cloudlike stuff like the blur on those ridiculously fake spirit photographs. Her eyes were made of sky and one could see through her mouth as she spoke. "Tell me, Mr. Osiris," she said, "did you ever fly?" but as Brentford tried to answer that... yes... he did... once... the woman vanished. As if a rug were being swept out from under his feet, Brentford felt he was going to wake up. He tried to call the Ghost Lady back, but all he managed to say was a row of letters and numbers that he found carved in his mind.

Brentford opened his eyes and fumbled for the lamp, then, as quickly as he could, noted the numbers on the bedside note pad, though they did not make the slightest sense to him. He realized how frustrated he was that Helen had not come to his rescue, in one way or another, as he had secretly wished. It had been instead a short, disappointing dream that bore no clear relationship to his question or his desire—a string of reminiscences and associations that had seemed, as the figures themselves, flimsy and superficial. Only the numbers he was re-reading had, in their opacity, the slightly heavier weight of an *apport*, but for all he knew, they could just as well be nonsense.

There were, of course, Dream Interpreters in the Institute, but his sense of privacy, as well as his suspicion that the interpreters could well be linked to the Gentlemen of the Night, made it impossible for him to ask for an appointment. Naked, dripping on the floor, he felt cold and heavy-headed, a bit hung over from the dream, trying to remember what he meant when he said he had flown. But most of all, he just wanted to go home.

CHAPTER VI

Boreal Bohemia

●

... an unpretending-looking fungus or toadstool
to stimulate the dormant energies of the dwellers in this
region of ice and snow.
Mordecai Cubbit Cooke, *The Seven Sisters of Sleep*, 1860

During the Wintering Weeks, those months of rock-solid night that enshroud the city in an impenetrable gloom, the Toadstool had become one of the favourite haunts of the self-styled Boreal Bohemians. Located right near the Yukiguni Gate and announced by human-sized mushrooms at its door, it offered in otherwise quiet surroundings the comforts of warmth, hot drinks, buffet snacks, live, amplified popular music, and a high-quality Sand System, that is, a wide choice of the finest and most potent psylicate products around.

There was even, on the upper floor, a large, warehouse-like, brick-walled exhibition space for local artists, called The Musheum. Gabriel d'Allier was up there, leaning on a steel pillar, quite dandy in his black double-breasted frock coat, floppy cravat, and Regency collar, which reached to his sideburns. He was talking to a gigantic man with a metallic hand, his friend and occasional band mate, Bob "Cape" Dorset, who also happened to be an artist in an avant-garde group exquisitely called Explorers' Skeletons. It was the launch night of the last E.S. event housed by Musheum, "Chasing the Chimera: Circumpolar Cryptozoology," a sculptural display of spirits, strange mammals, and other mythical creatures from the local lore. Bob was showing Gabriel the piece he had just built for the exhibition, a seven-foot effigy of the locally famous Polar Kangaroo, or *Kiggertarpok,* as this mysterious being is sometimes known to the Inuit. Gabriel and Brentford had collaborated on the work by offering Bob a little tune that was presently cranked out by a miniature phonograph hidden inside the innards of the beast and amplified by speakers located in its paws.

To Gabriel the impression this made was uncanny. Even if it had been an indirect, purely mental encounter, he was one of the rare persons to have come in contact with that creature, which redefined reality in spectacular ways, even by extensive local standards. He could almost feel, looking at Bob's expressionist, muscular, dynamic rendition of his subject, that the Polar Kangaroo was an inch away from coming alive, were it only in the telepathic, dream-inducing way that was its usual mode of self-manifestation. It was as if its wolf head was about to start breathing and as if this breath would translate in Gabriel's brain to mysterious whispers and eerie pictures.

"This would look fine in the Inuit People's Ice Palace," said another artist, Kelvin Budd-Jones, who had presented a Burning Inuksuk to the show.

"How are things going there, by the way?" asked Bob.

"The usual trouble," admitted Budd-Jones. "Lots of pressure in every shape and direction. We are quite behind schedule. I should even go back and work there tonight," he added, looking at his fob watch in sorry, White Rabbity disbelief. It was already late in the evening.

"I hear the Inuit are none too happy with the idea," Gabriel said. "It looks like a human zoo to them, and not quite cryptically."

Budd-Jones shrugged his shoulders, signifying that he had not come up with the idea in the first place. It was the North Wasteland Administration for Native Affairs that had commissioned that "permanent exhibition" of the Eskimo lifestyle, as a way to "bridge cultures" and "promote a better understanding between them." Another frozen-over hell paved with slippery good intentions, thought Gabriel.

"We are doing our best to present their culture in the most satisfactory way. But it's the living in there part that doesn't agree with them." He paused awhile, then said, "You should come over sometime and judge for yourself."

"That would give me pleasure," Gabriel answered.

"We will be busy every night until the opening. Don't hesitate to call and ask for me," said Budd-Jones.

"Hey! It seems the Fox Fires are on," said Bob, as some noise crept upstairs on long grating nails.

They all descended to the main room by a metal spiral staircase to meet an already considerable crowd, dressed with the calculated neglect and sense of detail of those "in the know," wearing mostly Victorian clothes completed with Inuit accessories made of narwhal bones and fur. These scenesters, whose metabolisms had borne the continuous impact of both the harsh polar winter and various compensating substances such as boilers, stokers, sand packets, snowcaine, zeroïne, nemoïne, phantastica, and opiates of all kinds, had started to assume a somewhat ghastly appearance, with waxen complexions and stares instead of looks.

Distance drinkers, as they had been known since a recent Arctic Administration edict, could be seen here and there at the luminous fly agaric–shaped tables, sitting on smaller-fungi stools. Acoustic respirographs round their necks, they were trying to hypnotize themselves with the sound of their own breath, in order to reach a hypnagogic trance, through which they hoped to suggest to themselves that the open bottle in front of them was enough to make them drunk.

Shisha pipes were available on nearby shelves, on the back wall beside the bar, and to the right, in front of a fresco depicting a toad swallowing the sun under the eyes of an old black-clad king, stood the "Bufetonine Buffet" and the automated distributor of sand packets.

Bob, Kelvin, and Gabriel huddled around a table that was almost free, while from the diminutive stage the Fox Fires spun around the place a web of barbed, electrified sounds, part crackling static, part ripped silk, that somehow ended, with the welcome help of a flute, by forming melancholy melodical patterns, or as they called them, "inscapes." They were pretty much all student types, this lot, all in woollen sweaters, velvety breeches, and mountain shoes, putting much effort into ripping interesting noises apart from those Electro String Frying Pan guitars that had been introduced years before by Ekto Liouven V and other bands in his wake.

Once again fashion had completed its meaningless but pleasant cycle and come back to its starting point. Well, not quite: the new vacuum-tube amplifiers were now much more powerful, and the new Nipi bands, as this batch were called, liked to slash and rip their cabinets to obtain sounds that would have been simply not tolerated by outmoded models of ears. This tolerance might well be due, Gabriel reflected, to the new drugs that were circulating, and that were themselves more violent and demanding than earlier ones, as if new thresholds had to be crossed every year, and as if music were both the seismograph and training ground of these sensory displacements. For him, who had spent the winter recording low-frequency drones on his electromagnetic keyboards under his Air-Loom Gang moniker (and had even managed to sell some of them to the Dunne Institute, where they had proved a good aid to all sorts of sticky, stifling nightmares), this new twist of local trendiness would mean that he would have to adapt, think of another idea, of another name, not only to follow but also to anticipate, and, with luck, to launch the next movement, if only to help the winter months pass away more quickly.

While the Fox Fires were explaining that their last song was about the sensations and reflections that occur at night between bedroom and bathroom, Gabriel slithered toward the toilets himself: circular cabinets decorated with exhilarated Santas in flayed-deerskin clothes dangling from the ceiling. On his way back to the table, he decided that the snowcaine had worn off and that it was time to sand up. He inserted some boreal crowns in the slot to get packets of his personal favourite, the black Flying Fantasia Flint, which gave one a sensation, typical of dreams, of levitating and walking a few inches above the ground, with a sweet feeling of muscular effort and of resistance from the air. It would, Gabriel thought, enlighten his return home, and maybe even make him actually *want* to go home, provided he would not go alone. He hoped that Phoebe, who was already late to the rendezvous he had given her, would not be too long. He was curious to know how her mission had turned out, and perhaps, though he was not ready to admit it, he was also eager to see her again and bring her back to his nest, both of them on the winged shoes that he had just purchased.

But as the Fox Fires finished their set, no Phoebe was to be seen, and the only well-known face at the bar was that of the owner, Nicholas Sandmann. As one of the models for the "Goodnight Kids" cartoon, he had enchanted Gabriel's rather dreary Newfoundland childhood, but these days, he was more famous as the man who had brought the sand craze to the city

and as the perennial leader of the Sandpackets Peddlers Syndi-
cate. Gabriel felt that some homage was due.

"How are you, Nicky?" he asked the thin, round-headed
man who never seemed to grow old.

"Hey, Mr. d'Allier, you're asking? You've heard about that
last decree?"

"Which one? Decrees come in droves, these days."

"The one that forbids us to sell sand in the City Centre."

"Oh, that one. It's a tough one, isn't it?"

"It's a rabid sled bitch, that's what it is. Doctors passing
decrees and police acting in the name of Health, what bell does
it ring?"

"Same as for you, I'd say. The Silver Age of the Silver Surgeons."

"Exactly," Nicholas said, wincing. "You've been there,
haven't you? You know what I'm talking about. Except the
Silver Surgeons, they were against the Council then, and now,
those *phoque-in-iceholes* work hand in hand."

Gabriel nodded, thinking of the innuendos the Gentlemen of
the Night had been making about his own consumption. When
Transpherence—a trick that made it possible to charge a dead
arcticocrat's memory into that of his heir, thereby ensuring the
continuity of the ruling elite—was one of the pillars on which
the City was founded, the drug that allowed it, Pineapples and
Plums, had proved so useful in asserting the Council's power
that the whole city had become a testing ground for it, the
federal capital of Altered States. Accordingly, all sorts of other
substances had been tolerated, with the view that they helped
keep suicide rates during the Wintering Weeks down to a reasonable level (only a paltry eleven times the Canadian rate), or
on the premise that a drugged people is a happy or at least a
quiet people. Gabriel had been subjected to Transpherence, and
remembered it, literally, with mixed feelings, but the drug part

had been the best, no doubt about that. But now those days were over, and even if the Council still managed to seem publicly tolerant on the matter, it obviously wanted to curb drug use one way or another, for some reason that eluded him.

"And you know why?" said Nicholas, whose train of thought had obviously closely followed Gabriel's. "Because they want to destroy the local production."

"What would be the point? The damned demand would still be huge."

"Yes, but prohibition of the local product means real drug lords from the outside coming into the game and taking over from us. Which means money, and on quite another scale. And for everyone, if you get my meaning. Because no drug lord would ever work without giving a modicum of, you know, sweetener to the authorities to ensure his own safety."

"Bribery? Is that what you mean?" Gabriel said doubtfully. He knew from Brentford how much the city needed money, but for the Council there certainly was some distance between going through hard times and organizing drug traffic for a profit. Despite his appreciation of Nicholas's work, Gabriel could trace in him the paranoid, obsessive streak that characterized drug dealers and users across the whole known pluriverse. On the other hand, he knew equally well that those who feel persecuted are right half the time and that is much too often. Twice too often, actually, concluded Gabriel, whose maths were rather idiosyncratic.

"Me? I've said nothing," answered Nicholas, with a wink.

Gabriel said good-bye and went back to the table, through a crowd that was thicker and rougher and mostly indifferent to his Mosaic attempts at parting its crashing waves. There was still no Phoebe to be seen, but he noticed a girl who he thought was watching him, and he tried to get closer to her, but in the middle of that thick, lazy crowd, it was like trying to reach the stars through the trees of a forest. He renounced the struggle and went back to the table, where John Linko, the métis music critic, had joined Bob. Judging by his gestures, the journalist was visibly excited about something that Gabriel could not quite grasp, except maybe the name Sandy Lake, but he could have misheard that completely, as the Sun Dogs were now storming the stage.

This band, thanks partly to Linko's relentless propaganda, was supposed to be the new luminary of the Neovenetian Nipi, or Northern Noise scene. They had just been signed by Perpalutok Records, which certainly enhanced their "canal cred," and their gigs so far had generated a buzz that had only grown louder and louder, and was rumoured to linger after their deafening shows.

The Sun Dogs were two well-built Brits or Scands in torn cashmere, and their gear consisted only of an electric cello, plugged into a compressed-air auxetophone amplifier that looked like a threatening tuba, and a Frying Pan amplified to the point of distortion. As soon as the room started to vibrate, and as a dark, ominous drone started to coil around the walls, it became palpably clear that this music directly linked one's eardrum to one's intestines and that it was, beyond good or bad, to be digested rather than listened to. It also had at times, under the murk, the repetitive, trance-like quality of Eskimo chant. This indeed was not without its effect upon intoxicated listeners, who swayed back and forth with the ebb and flow of the gravelly sound waves. The Sun Dogs' best song was called Hyperborean, and if Gabriel understood it correctly, it was a cryptic paean to snowcaine. It went something like this:

She blinks and she thinks she knows what's on my mind
There she goes through my nose and she is gonna find
A lonely frozen sea that's gonna blind her eyes

But if by chance she can dance this is a paradise
Hyperboreal
Hyperboreal
Lubberland, blubberland made of ice field and floe
Ruined cities, memories moving like drifting snow
I wouldn't be surprised if you'd died from the cold
But your body, baby, it will never grow old
Hyperboreal
Hyperboreal
Oh for the kind of stuff that my dreams are made of
It's never dark enough let's turn the heavens off
Northern lights polar star
However bright they are
It's all light
pollution
imperfection
of night

This was, Gabriel had to admit, the most exact captation of the collective life—and of his own—that he had ever heard from one of those bands. He had simply, in his ravishment, forgotten Phoebe. The audience must have felt the same: they all looked enthralled, unless their immobility had more to do with a fear of being noticed by that stubborn chord that whirled closer and closer and closer as if to decapitate them. Some people were even crouched on the floor, looking bleak and frightened, as if praying for the sonic scythe to spare their worthless lives.

But then, all of a sudden, as if the plug had been torn from the socket, everything stopped and a rush was heard (through slightly buzzing ears) in the back of the room. Gabriel turned to see a pack of Gentlemen of the Night invading the premises, dressed to kill in top hats and Inverness coats, their dreaded sword-canes in hand. He was not long in spotting among the intruders a monocled Sealtiel Wynne, who was equally quick to notice him. The policeman lightly touched his hat to him with the knob of his cane, adding a sly little smile that made Gabriel want to bite his head off.

One of the Gentlemen had hopped up on the stage and, carbon microphone in hand, suavely addressed the dumbstruck crowd:

"Ladies and Gentlemen. We hope you will excuse this intrusion in the middle of a very pleasant evening. We would gladly have dispensed with the interruption if a matter of some urgency had not constrained us to act on behalf of your health. I have here"—he flourished a paper—"a recommendation from Doctor Playfair, from the Kane Clinic. He informs us, after long and painstaking research by the best experts in the field, that, unfortunately, the joint exposure to psychotropic products and droning sounds is hazardous to the well-being of the persons exposed, and is even, he regrets to say, likely to have irreversible effects on the nervous system. Not wanting to take any chances with the health of the citizens, the Council has delegated us, your humble servants, to take the measures necessary for your protection. As a consequence, and assured as we are of your understanding and cooperation, we take upon ourselves the responsibility of bringing this most entertaining event to a close, and, with our heartfelt apologies for the inconvenience, we will take you to the Kane Clinic in order to ensure that we have no damage as yet to deplore."

The crowd had started to wake up and was voicing, though in a rather muted fashion, its disapproval. But it was too late. The Poshclothes Police had started, politely but firmly, and with "if-you-pleases" that had a certain "if-you-don't-please" ring to them, to tow the reluctant boreal bohemians toward the exit where the sled ambulances were "advanced." Nicholas, Gabriel noticed, was slumped on the bar, sobbing with his head in his hands, and he truly felt sorry for him. As to himself, he was, for the third time today, full of an impotent anger for which—the impotency, not the anger—he hated himself as much as he hated this police force of foppish oafs. Sealtiel Wynne walked up to him and bowed slightly.

"How strange it is to meet you again, Mr. d'Allier! But it is always a pleasure."

"Yes, isn't it. It's quite a scream, actually," Gabriel said, with all the detachment he could muster. "What a coincidence, indeed."

"Coincidences! In New Venice!" said Wynne, sincerely amused. "Maybe our presence is a coincidence, but yours is certainly not," he added, a little more seriously, pointing a white-gloved index finger at the breast pocket where Gabriel had put the sand packet. "Now would you mind joining our little party? I am sure it will not take long. After you, Mr. d'Allier... unless you wish to fly."

CHAPTER VII

An Appointment At The Pole

●

*There's a ginral wish among the crew to no whether the north
pole is a pole or a dot. Mizzle sais it's a dot, and O'Riley swears
(no, he don't do that, for we've gin up swearin in the fog-sail);
but he sais that it's a real post, bout as thick again as the main-
mast, an nine or ten times as hy. Grim sais it's nother wun thing
nor anuther, but a hydeear that is sumhow or other a fact, but
yit don't exist at all. Tom Green wants to no if there's any con-
exshun between it an the pole that's conected with elections.*
R. M. Ballantyne, *The World of Ice*

rentford did not go back home straightaway. He had
decided to walk the mile that separated the Dunne
Institute from the Botanical Building, and while doing
so he replayed his dream in his mind, stumbling on some con-
nections he had so far neglected.

The appearance of Hector Liubin V, whose stage name was
Ekto Liouven, may have been triggered by the sheer idea of

ectoplasm. Sandy Lake had been Ekto's former sweetheart, when she fronted the Sandmovers in the heyday of "polar pop." Brentford may have inquired about her because in his dream he was searching for a female interlocutor rather than a male one, and had eventually managed to conjure one. "Isabella Alexander" was, of course—how could that have escaped his attention?— made up of the names of Ross's two famous ships— now the names of two famous capes—which had been under his command on his first encounter with the "Arctic Highlanders," or Eskimos. Ross was a Scot, as Brentford partly was, and there was a time when Orsinis had been Rossinis, so his identification with Ross was in both respects more likely than otherwise. Then too, the whole thing may indeed have been a reference to Brentford's own meeting with the Inuit earlier in the day, which had provoked the need for the incubation, and his presence on the ice field may have been tied to his idle remembrances about polar explorations on his way back from that meeting.

Let us be more precise, he thought. He had wanted to speak to Helen or for Helen to speak to him—the woman (and a lot more than that) whose dead body he had left on the ice field a few years before, after her magic had saved the city. Vomiting ectoplasm on the ice field may have been merely a consequence of his desire to communicate with the dead Helen. And so must have been the Ghost Lady, for a spectre was more or less the form he would have expected Helen to take if she appeared. "Mr. Osiris" was another clue. After Helen had saved the city from Delwit Faber's coup with the Lobster Girls and the House of Hellequin, Brentford had found crumpled in her hand the formula Isis had used to stop the Chariot of the Sun in order to help the diseased Osiris. The very name Osiris could be vaguely construed as a play on his name, Orsini, which in Italian was itself a pun on *bear* (a bear even appeared on his coat of arms). It would be only logical to find a bear on the *arctic* ice field, all the more since *arctos* also meant "bear." Being on the ice, then, like the references to Ross, meant only that he was simply dreaming of himself waiting for a vision of Helen, not to mention that ice is the best backdrop for the kind of clear and sustained mental images he'd been hoping to see. The Ghost Lady calling him Mr. Osiris signified that, if she was not Helen herself, she was conscious of Brentford's history with Helen, and was perhaps some sort of messenger. "Did you fly?" was more difficult to decipher, but Brentford remembered now that when Helen had made him join her on a kind of shamanic trip, he had found himself flying over an unknown city. So, as he summed it up, the dream was just a rather simple image of his own longing for Helen, and the message he had got was, after all, pointing to her more clearly than he had first thought.

Of course, there was still the tiresome hypothesis that it was a simple circular circuit of wish fulfilment and that he had only received under a different form what he had first put into the dream. But then, there was the code, which he could not account for, and which could be in some way or another the answer he had been waiting for.

It was when he passed in front of the Prince of Whales pub that Brentford got the idea. If ever he knew someone who could solve this riddle, it was the local legend William de la Whale, the brain behind Matball, that mind-boggling blend of human chess and Basque pelota that had been both a craze and a secret laboratory behind Transpherence. The ciphers with which William encoded the moves and tactics of his team were famous for both their subtlety and their solidity. He had even taught, if Brentford remembered correctly, Cryptography as an integral part of his poetry class at Doges College. De la Whale would know instantly if Brentford's code made sense or not, and help him, or so he hoped, to solve it if it did.

He entered the pub, noted for its remarkable painting of a rather muddy and dark whale-hunting scene, asked for a Scoresby Stout and a Specksioneer Sandwich, and went to the Pneu-

matic Post Booth. There he wrote a message to Sybil to tell her
he would be home late (though she would probably be partying
somewhere), put it in a canister, sent it through the outward
tube, and set about looking for William de la Whale's address in
the Dispatch Directory, where he found it quite quickly. It was
in Yukiguni. He then ate his sandwich—the bread slices were
held together by a miniature harpoon—at the lustrous counter,
and having finished his beer with a manly gulp that recalled his
glorious days in the dreaded Doges College Ice Rugby Club, he
set forth for the Japanese quarter.

It was just a few moonlit bridges away. Added to the fact
that is always pleasant to cross bridges in New Venice, Yukiguni happened to be one of Brentford's favourite places in the
city. He entered the gate, slaloming among the smoking shadows queuing in front of the Toadstool, apparently a trendy
spot these days, and immediately felt at ease in that somewhat
labyrinthine network of narrow streets, miniature canals, and
gibbous bridges covered with a snow that seemed lighter than
anywhere else. It was deserted and dark, with a hum of its own,
distant and muted, which made the place sound calmer than the
rest of New Venice.

Onogorojima, where William was supposed to live, was a
tiny island right in the centre of the zone, circled and crossed
by convoluted paths that quickly caused orientation trouble.
The Hokkaido-style houses, with their empty bear cages and
taboo windows in front, which were for divine use only, had no
numbers whatsoever, and Brentford had to count them one by
one before he decided on which door he was going to knock.
Luckily, he could count well.

A middle-aged woman slid open the entrance door just
widely enough to poke her head through and take a look at the
visitor, who, deerstalker hat in hand, introduced himself with
the utmost politeness. The woman disappeared for a while, and
then reappeared, letting Brentford in with a bow.

He took off his rubbers, and after following the woman down a corridor was introduced into a space that was more Western than Japanese, and very disorderly. Around a solid desk, books were crammed everywhere, piled up in unstable rookeries, and the floor was littered with chessboards and go-ban, all frozen in mid or end game. The light was sparse, but though all Brentford could see of William was a flaky hand softly brushing a bald head, it was enough to make him realize that he had an aged man in front of him.

"Mr. William de la Whale?" asked Brentford.

"Plain William Whale will do," said a slow, hissing voice that Brentford could barely understand. "These arcticocratic games are past their prime, aren't they?" the voice kept on, slurring and dwindling into a crackle of slobbery static.

"I am Brentford Orsini," he answered, feeling he should skip the ducal part. There was a pause.

"Visitors are rather rare here, Mr. Orsini. I suppose I should be grateful."

The words fell slowly, as in some sort of Chinese saliva-drop torture. Brentford started to feel embarrassed by the hot, stifling atmosphere, and he remembered, but too late, the rumours that a lifetime of substance taking had taken its toll on William's brain, causing his early retirement from public life.

"I do not know whether you should be grateful. But you can certainly be helpful."

"I seem to remember you run the Greenhouse?"

"I do. Yes."

A long silence ensued, mercifully interrupted when the woman re-entered the room and put a tray with a kettle and two cups on the edge of the desk, where it just fit. A sweet-scented steam arose when the woman filled the cups.

"This is my spouse, Kujira Etsuko."

Brentford bowed as he received the burning cup. As the light fell upon her, he could see that her skin still had that yellowish-

orange hue typical of the "Greenhouse girls" who used to me-
tabolize Pineapples and Plums from their sweat while dancing
for Matball Players and Transpherees. Her love story with William was famous in New Venice. How Angry Ananias Andrew,
then the Master of the Greenhouse, had taken her away from
William so that he could secure his services as an addicted
trainer for his Matball team was part of a lore that Brentford
knew by heart. Eventually, or so the story went, William had
shot Andrew Arkansky. Brentford felt moved to meet her in the
flesh, a flesh whose secretions had produced the most powerful drug ever known to man—but then, wasn't that the case in
every love story? Etsuko retired, yet somehow lingered in the
fruity tang of the tea.

"The Greenhouse... " William kept on like a slowed-down,
scratched wax roll. "How it is these days?"

Brentford tried not to blunder.

"It is a rather uneventful place."

William nodded his head, in and out of the dark.

"In what way can I be of help?"

"I have a code that I would very much like to subject to
your perspicacity, Mr. Whale."

He felt instantly that he had pushed the right button on that
rather creaky mechanism. William turned toward Brentford and
lit a desk lamp that made his face appear more distinctly. He
had sagging cheeks, a small moustache, rings around his eyes,
and pupils with a moist glint that was not quite reassuring.

"Oh, excellent. I like codes, Mr. Orsini. Human ingenuity cannot concoct a cipher which human ingenuity cannot re-
solve," he said, baring his ravaged gums as he spoke. He had
apparently retained his abilities and simply lost his teeth.

Brentford handed him the paper on which he had scribbled
the code and watched him scrutinize it.

"It's short. Which does not mean easier, as we have less material to rely on. Maybe a bit of context would not hurt."

"It's a dream code," said Brentford uneasily. "From an incubation."

William now had both elbows on the desk, biting his thin lips as he pored over the message.

"You would be better placed than I am to crack a code your own wit devised."

"I tried, but to no avail," avowed Brentford.

"Would you tell me your dream, Mr. Orsini? And be reassured: I am not going to analyze it."

He had a conniving smile that Brentford mirrored. They were both from the Good Old Days, when the analyst was dreaded as a peculiarly perverse form of policeman who could cause endless trouble and spoil one's Transpherence plan. Brentford told the gist of his dream, without, however, mentioning Helen.

"What?" asked William, his glinting eyes suddenly sparkling. "Blue boxer shorts?"

"As I told you," said Brentford, who was not too keen on dwelling on his underwear, real or dreamed.

There was a long pause.

"Interesting," said William.

"If you say so," said Brentford modestly.

"Because it is the key we are looking for."

It was Brentford's turn to remain silent.

"I once had a good friend who wore such shorts," said William with a surprising seriousness, and even, it seemed to Brentford, a little trembling in the voice. "A great Matball player."

Igor Plastisine, thought Brentford, but did not say anything. The man had overdosed and gone crazy from metabolizing his own Pineapples and Plums. He, too, was part of the lore.

"We had a code between us. And this is written in some dream-twisted version of that code."

"But I would not know it, even subconsciously, would I?"

"Maybe you wouldn't know it, but you came to me, someone who does know it, sent by someone or... something, who knew that you would do that. So, that dispatch was in the wrong canister and the wrong canister was in the right tube, after all. Those networks can be a bit complicated, but this is Smalltown, Dreamland all the same."

William, pencil in hand, crossing out and substituting letters, was now quite animated, and seemed to decipher the text without much difficulty. It was done in two minutes flat.

"As to what the message says, I am sure that I do not have to fear your disappointment."

"And why is that so?"

"Because it is, precisely, an *appointment*. A date, an hour, and a place."

William looked at Brentford, visibly amused.

"But you may not like it."

Brentford waited, his heart beating.

"*On your own. March the 1st,*" announced William in his hoarse voice. "*90° N 65, 5 W°. H.*"

"That is the North Pole," said Brentford, happy to hear from Helen.

"450 nautical miles due north of us. Yes. That was where you must have been standing in your dream. That will be quite an interesting trip, I dare say."

"March first. It would still be polar night there," said Brentford, computing quickly. He could not even say that he was surprised. Helen, if indeed it was she, was, typically, expecting a lot from him. In a sense, it was flattering. But it put him under some rather intensive pressure.

"Oh, yes. You should bring a flashlight. And a camera to immortalize the deed. For you would be the first man ever to get there. Just imagine that."

"Why do you say that? Peary went there, didn't he?"

"Oh, no," William chuckled, "he did not."

"So you think that it was Cook."

"Oh! Him! Even less so, if that's possible."

William got up and went straight to one of the teetering piles of books. Without much fuss, he withdrew a red volume, which he handed to Brentford. It was called *Journey to the Earth's Interior* by a certain Marshall B. Gardner.

"Another of those Hollow Earth books," said Brentford with a slight disdain.

"Exactly. But this one has the peculiarity of having been written *after* Peary's and Cook's expeditions, which means the author was facing a tough challenge when, without ever leaving his library, he still claimed that the pole marked a gate to the Earth's interior. In this, you will agree that he was a brave man."

"Certainly," said Brentford, browsing through the book, thinking that Peary and Cook were, on the whole, more likely candidates for a Bravery award.

"It was vital to his theory that neither Peary nor Cook had ever reached the pole. And he spared no efforts to prove that. And if he is wrong about what he affirms, he is right about what he negates."

Brentford had found the chapter entitled "Was the North Pole discovered?" From what he read there, skimming though he was, it was evident that both explorers had stretched the truth by quite a length.

"Peary," resumed Whale, "came back much too quickly to substantiate his claim. Forty miles a day on a sled that Peary himself admitted he (or his men, since he could barely walk) had to push like a plough is simply not possible. His bearings must have been rather sloppy, to say the least, especially in a place where you quite easily get lost, and he had not taken into account the drift of the ice sheet either. So to say that he was thirty miles off the mark is really a generous estimation. As for Cook, he was certainly heroic as well, as the end of his trip more than proved, but he himself admitted that 'to touch that spot would be an accident,' and his Eskimos let him down by saying they had never lost sight of the land. Henson was probably right when he said that Cook had just 'half-hypnotized himself' over the whole matter."

"These men had certainly estimated that they had reached some North Pole inside of themselves," said Brentford, handing back the book. "It is perhaps the one that counts."

"Oh, yes, certainly. As Emerson said, 'Character may be ranked as having its natural place in the north. It shares the magnetic currents of the system. The feeble souls are drawn to the south or negative pole.' Who, really, would boast of reaching his inner South Pole? You know what Lorber said?" asked William, with a wicked little smile, while Brentford sniggered knowingly. It was usual, if not ritual, in New Venice that any mention of the solid, pedestrian Antarctic would trigger a connivance of contempt. Jakob Lorber's crackpot theory that the North Pole was "the mouth of the earth" and the South Pole the "the eliminatory canal" was, in this respect, a perennial favourite.

"Seriously," William insisted, "what you say has some truth, and we all wish we could reach that point, don't we? But there are other ways to think of this failure. The first would be the disappointment. After all, the place is nothing if not nondescript. The North Pole and four hundred miles off it are just the same endless expanse of dreary faceless desert. The very place where you would plant your flag would drift away with the pack, so you couldn't prove anything. Or to put it otherwise, the North Pole is Nothing. Just a name, an idea, that is not worth dying for, after all."

"I would think that the pole being an idea as much as a real spot explains very well the drive to go there. I have never seen that futility ever got in the way of human endeavour. Quite the contrary."

"I could very well agree with you on that. As you know, I am, first and foremost, a chess player, so I understand your argument even better than I would care to admit. Let us try something else, then. Maybe they did not *really* want to go there. Maybe they were, consciously or not, afraid or reluctant to face the fact that there was nothing there. Maybe they did not want to be the men who would disenchant the world, kill everyone's dream of Eden or Hollow Earth, dry the fountain from which so many utopias were pouring forth—the very same reveries that, in some ways, had attracted them to the pole. They wanted, deep inside, to keep it a *terra incognita*."

"I can sympathize with this idea," said Brentford. "But it does not make me want to go there, even if I considered myself able to do it, which, I must add, is not the case at all."

William looked at him with what was unmistakably benevolence.

"If I judge by the way you have been invited there, the risk of disenchantment is rather reduced. Maybe you will find the very thing that those explorers were afraid *not* to find."

CHAPTER VIII

Hypnotized!!!

●

*"I will not suffer myself to be hypnotized, or
mesmerized, nor will I place myself in such a passive state
that any uninitiated person, power, or being may cause me
to lose control of my thoughts, words or actions."*
The G. D. Neophyte Obligation

I t was not Plaster Easter yet—with its early spring
procession of clumsy, unlucky skaters—but the casu-
alty ward at the Kane Clinic was teeming with more
people that it could reasonably contain. Some had managed
to secure a seat among the rows of polished wood benches that recalled a Transaerian Station waiting room; others
were standing huddled against the wall under the paintings of
Elisha Kent Kane and his bride Margaret Fox, the medium,
and some were pacing up and down, expressing the late winter of their discontent more physically than vocally, for the

commanding presence of the Gentlemen of the Night discouraged all attempts at free speech.

You could almost, or so thought Gabriel, deduce from all these bodies and faces the drug menu of their evening. The compulsive striders were probably full of stokers, pills for blood pressure, or boilers, for metabolic enhancement, and there were even one or two that were showing the coordination disorders typical of Gibberne's Accelerator, which made everything around the user appear to be moving in slow motion. Most of the sitting bohemians, meanwhile, seemed rather sedated, by distance drinking or opiates, but you could also spot among them those who had taken psylicates or phantasticas and who were experiencing uncomfortable perceptual distortions: lids twitching from endless déjà-vu loops; cataleptic frowns disclosing a sudden fascination with minute details of the room or patterns on the floor; pupils wide open to the bright, bristling pulsation of furniture and walls; eyeballs rolling relentlessly to follow the course of Lilliputian figures, or *inugarullikkat*, having a ball on the benches. Some had started to show evident signs of distress, oscillating on their seats or talking nonsense to themselves.

Displacing drugged people from their chosen environment was cruel and made the drugs more dangerous than they already were, ruminated Gabriel, who then concluded that this may well have been the idea after all. He did his best to don the enchanted silver suit of armour that comes from keeping one's sangfroid, but he found it undersized and bursting at the joints with the pent-up anger he had accumulated.

From time to time, someone was called and taken away along a corridor. The Sun Dogs had been among the first to go (never to reappear), as well as Bob and Budd-Jones, who had both been released earlier on and had saluted him on their way out. Gabriel, thanking God (or Himself, for that matter) that he had been relatively sober, had been waiting like this for an hour or so, his shoulder leaning against the wall, legs casually crossed so they would not twitch too much, when, at last, Sealtiel Wynne appeared at the end of a corridor and summoned him to follow.

"We are truly sorry to have kept you waiting for so long, Mr. d'Allier," said Sealtiel as he stepped aside to let Gabriel precede him into the examination room. "We were ourselves waiting, for someone to come especially for you."

Two men were already sitting behind a desk. One was a thin doctor, with a long nose and a white smock, who was introduced by Wynne as Doctor Playfair. The other one, a man with a pockmarked face, dressed in a dinner jacket, top hat, and crimson-lined cape, was simply introduced as "the person I told you about." He was fidgeting, impatiently, it seemed, as the doctor indicated a chair to Gabriel.

Wynne now stood behind the pair.

"We are well aware that this has not been an easy day for you so far, Mr. d'Allier," he continued, in a tone that made Gabriel want to spool off the man's intestines with a spiked wheel at the first opportunity. "But things should go at a steadier pace from now on, especially if you would be so kind as to help us a little."

Gabriel said nothing, but looked at Wynne with a look that he hoped was unequivocal.

"We will gladly spare you the blood test. We both know what would be found in that precious blue fluid of yours. It is really unfortunate that you have dealt in drone design these last months. Not only for your own health, for which we are, as you know, genuinely worried, but also for the people you put at risk. You were probably unaware of the dangers, we know that perfectly well, but imagine that, because of the damage done, some of these people felt they should sue you. Whatever the outcome, it would be detrimental to your professional pursuits, wouldn't it?"

"I have listened to these," said Playfair, waving a wax roll he had taken up from the table, "especially 'Lobster-Cracking.' These are, Mr. d'Allier, or should I call you Mr. Air-Loom Gang, impossibly low frequencies whose resonance could cause lasting lesions in the organism. Taken with drugs, they could provoke a coma, or even cerebral death."

Gabriel felt like telling the doctor to mind his own drug business but tilted down his mental silver helmet instead. What came next, however, crushed his visor like a tin can.

"We discovered that roll," said Wynne, "in the handbag of one of your students, a certain Ms. Phoebe O'Farrell, whom we found unconscious in the street not far from the Botanical Building late in the afternoon. We are worried about her condition, since she has not regained consciousness yet."

Gabriel felt a cold sweat on his forehead and palms, and a curious buzz arose in his ears. He clutched his chair, turning his rage into images of mayhem and murder. He saw himself spoon out Wynne's eyes and spit into their orbits. Cruelty made sense to him as it never had before.

"She seems to be in a kind of cataleptic trance," said Playfair, handing the roll to Wynne. "She had some trace of snow-caine in her hair and we strongly suspect what she had taken caused a bad reaction to the music. *Your* music."

"Interesting. Could I see her later?" asked the anonymous man in an affected voice.

"Oh, certainly," said Wynne, as if he ran the clinic. "I am you sure you would be of great help to that poor girl."

"We should also keep you under observation, but this gentleman," Playfair said, indicating the top-hatted man with what Gabriel thought a slight gesture of disapproval, "has accepted Mr. Wynne's idea that he can help us by giving you a quick mental examination."

Gabriel still said nothing, slowly calming down, preparing for the next attack.

"It is nothing painful," continued Playfair.

"Just a few questions under hypnosis. To make sure everything is all right," explained Wynne.

"I refuse," said Gabriel flatly.

"Observation will take more time," said Playfair, with a sigh, "much more time. Precious time that I will not be able to devote to Ms. O'Farrell, I'm afraid."

"Not to mention that Ms. O'Farrell's parents, who have not yet been informed of the accident, may take it badly that you refuse to cooperate with the authorities. Especially given some of your colleagues' testimony about your personal involvement in their daughter's education," Wynne threatened.

"I do no doubt your own parents would be proud of you, Mr. Wynne," Gabriel said, so icily his words congealed in front of him and fell on the floor like little hailstones.

Wynne flinched, almost imperceptibly, and Gabriel knew he had turned his Guardian Angel into a personal enemy. There was a moment of awkward silence.

"I am tired of all this and have nothing to hide, after all," said Gabriel, like someone who feels he has gone far enough. "Just promise me I'll go free afterward, and I accept."

"This could be considered, I suppose," said Wynne, moodily.

"Do I have your word of honour, Mr. Wynne?"

The other two turned toward the Gentleman of the Night.

"You have it," he said, straightening up. "And I accept your apologies."

"I do not demand that much," answered Gabriel.

"Now, if you please, Mr. d'Allier..." said the man in the top hat, who seemed in a hurry to be done with the circus of it all.

He rose and stood in front of Gabriel, two fingers forking as if to poke out his eyes, and searched to "catch" his gaze with his own green intrusive irises. Gabriel felt the violence of the impact. The eyes, after all, are a tender part of the brain. A sentence crossed his mind: *The soul is a castle where even God can't look.* He was not sure what its author meant, but for him it now made perfect sense. He would lock himself inside and that beggar in a top hat could bang at the door as long and loud as he pleased. Pretending to struggle a little against the vicious little drills, Gabriel simply thought of what he had learned in the Subtle Army: if you are tortured, hold your breath and try to faint as quickly as possible. He would do it his way, trusting that he could use a little dissociation trick he had mastered during Transpherence training and years of afternoon naps. Instead of looking *at* the hypnotizer's eyes, he focused himself on his own reflection in the intruder's pupils, short-circuiting him with this narcissistic ménage-à-trois. Working on his breath and silently repeating his own name in a chant to parry the orders he was supposed to obey, he hypnotized himself into a half-dreaming state, until everything that happened was purely between *himselves*, his mind a stubborn block of solid fog that would relinquish nothing of any importance or interest to them, just the usual off-the-cuff hieroglyphics of sleep, so involuted as to be senseless. At the surface, though, he remained aware enough to hear the man say:

"Now, Mr. d'Allier, now... You will answer any questions Mr. Wynne will ask you. Will you please do that for me?"

Gabriel vaguely nodded his head. He could hear a drawer being opened and some machine being installed on the desk. He knew that sound: someone was fitting a tin horn onto a phonograph and cranking the mechanism to record every word Gabriel would pronounce under the influence.

"Mr. d'Allier," said Wynne, "how are you?"

"Fiiiiiiiinnnnnnnne" moaned Gabriel, hoping he was not overdoing it. He could feel his mind unfocused and foggy, but knew that if it was drifting, it was drifting away from them.

"Do you swear you will tell me truth, and nothing but the truth? Raise your hand and swear, Mr. d'Allier, if you please..."

Gabriel felt himself slowly raising an arm that was heavier than he expected.

"I swear," he murmured.

"Say that again, if you do not mind, louder."

"I swear."

"Mr. d'Allier, there is one thing we would like to know above all others. Would you please tell us what or whom *A Blast on the Barren Land* evokes for you?"

A flurry of images gushed forth in his brain. Whatever they were, they would have to do.

"Flap," said Gabriel, after a pause, not without surprise.

"Who?"

"Flap."

"Who is Flap, Mr. d'Allier?"

"Flap is... a friend."

"Where did you meet him?"

"*Her.* I met her in the Greenhouse in Grönland Gardens. I took a path that I thought would take me out of the hothouse but did not. It kept on, it seemed forever. At some point, I fell asleep under a tree. And after a while, I woke up, feeling a fresh sensation below the waist, and Flap was over me."

"Over you?" said Wynne, in a faltering voice.

"Over me. Yes. I opened my eyes, and I saw her. She was rather cute but a bit on the chubby side, with little dragonfly wings on her back. I asked her who she was and what she thought she was doing. 'I'm Flap the Fat Fairy,' she said, 'and human semen is like honey to me.' Then she spat something on my belly and flew away. I reached to see what she had spat and it was a little heart-shaped ice crystal she had kept in her mouth all the time. It immediately attracted two little elves or fairies on my belly, who were commenting on my withering 'snowdrop':

'Oh, you naughty Pocket!
Look, she drops her head.
She deserved it, Rocket,
And she was nearly dead.'

"Then they fought for the crystal, tugging at it till it burst in a cold blast and Rocket and Pocket both ran away, leaving the land quite barren. That's all I remember."

"Rocket and Pocket, hmmm," said Wynne, who sounded tired. "Please, kind sir, wake him up," he asked the man, hastily hiding the phonograph back in the drawer.

"Wake up, Mr. d'Allier," said the hypnotist in a low but firm voice, putting his gloved palm lightly on Gabriel's forehead. "You will forget everything that has happened since Mr. Wynne called you into the examination room."

Gabriel opened his eyes, and saw the three men looking at him with a blend of puzzlement, disbelief, and distaste. Some personal shades of disapproval, however, had been added to their looks. Wynne seemed particularly disgusted, while Playfair's eyes reflected a very light streak of irony. As to the nameless man in the cape, he seemed somewhat furious, and maybe slightly vexed.

Gabriel was careful to wake up slowly and pretended not to remember anything. He was himself a bit ashamed by what he had come up with.

"What happened?" he asked after a moment, while Playfair pretended with not much conviction to feel his pulse and check his pupils.

"It happened that you had a fainting spell in the waiting room and were brought here," he explained.

"We have probably detained you too long, so we will let you go now, Mr. d'Allier, hoping that it has not caused you too much discomfort," Wynne added with a chilly courtesy. "Do you want us to call you a taxsleigh?"

"Oh no. I'm fine," said Gabriel. "I will walk a little. The air will do me good."

He rose to his feet, uncertain as a young foal.

"You seem to need exactly that. I suppose you know the way back," said Playfair.

"I certainly do," said Gabriel.

But he did not head toward the exit.

CHAPTER IX

The Arctic Eden

●

Unnipped by daintiest frosts, in every field
Flowers crowded thick; and trees, not tall nor rude
With slender stems upholding feathery shade,
Nodded their heads and hung their pliant limbs
In natural bowers, sweet with delicious gloom.
Anon., *The Arctic Queen*

The first thing Brentford saw when he walked out of Yukiguni was the chaos around the Toadstool: dozens of reluctant bohemians being pushed into ambulance aerosleds by neat but inexorable Gentlemen of the Night cutting sturdy black silhouettes against the headlights and casting shadows long enough to reach him. Protests were muffled, reduced by the distance and the cold to disapproving cartoon balloons of vapour. Brentford restrained his impulse to intervene, deeming it wiser to stay clear of the mayhem and go home. Still, he worried about the increasing number of troubles caused by the Council itself.

Up to now it had been a tenet of New Venice that there should be no uniformed police force and that the plainclothes force must be almost invisible. For reasons he strove to understand, this sound utopian principle had recently started to tilt a little, then a little more, to the point where there was now a distinct trend toward the harassment of certain categories of citizens, such as the bohemians, who were usually too busy or too lazy to create trouble outside their own bodies and brains. Not to mention that the already subtle borderline separating a plainclothes policeman from a provocateur had on more than one occasion become rather blurred.

It seemed as if this unfortunate turn of events was what had summoned forth the black airship that Brentford now saw as he crossed Bears Bridge, floating overhead in a miniature elliptical eclipse that gave the moon a certain disquieting wink. Perhaps it was some foreign threat, or some panopticon watch keeping the Gentlemen of the Night incredibly well informed of what happened below; either way, it was anything but reassuring. When you added to the equation the Inuit Independentists and the recent *tupilaat* invasion, you had an overall atmosphere akin to what the Alaskan Inuit called, if Brentford remembered correctly, the *Qarrtsiluni*—the moment spent waiting in the dark for something to explode.

Brentford, leaving the bridge and its sculpted bears, reached the Arctic Administration Building and headed toward the Botanical Building, further on the right. Its lights were turned down, and the glass-and-metal structure loomed large and mysterious. One could sense the life inside, the silent but stubborn relentless growth that had a strength of its own that Brentford had come to appreciate. He was walking to the back door, his own keys in hand, when out of some dark nook a darker shape emerged, wearing the black outfit and white beaked mask of a City Scavenger. Secret words were exchanged.

"Blankbate?" said Brentford. "Do you want to come in?"

Blankbate did not answer, but he followed Brentford inside. They passed rows of thick curtains and glass doors and eventually found themselves under the glass dome, surrounded by palms and enormous leaves and feeling smothered by their warm, damp breath. The heat could be felt rising from the floor, along with the faint rumble of the buried resonance coils. A few light bulbs, planted directly in the soil, gave off a sparse light that made the paths visible. This might not have been what a long and noble tradition had in mind when it affirmed that Eden was to be found at the North Pole, but to Brentford it was a delightfully close approximation, and the fact that it was manmade did not spoil it for him—quite the contrary.

He sat with Blankbate on a stone bench in a bower.

"How can I help you?" Brentford asked, although—or because—he had more often been helped by the Scavengers than been useful to them.

"You have heard the news? About the Done-Gone system?"

The Done-Gone system was the principle that allowed the Scavengers to go home or drift freely in their barges as soon as the trash was picked up, instead of having regular shifts. Brentford had indeed heard that the Council, who had little hold over the Scavengers and wished to gain more, had put some pressure on the Arctic Administration to put an end to this "abuse." Working on a tight schedule did not agree with the Scavengers, who prized their freedom all the more because they had paid for it by being a caste of anonymous, invisible pariahs. The Administration, which could not refuse *everything* to the Council, had relented on this point, and now, as was only predictable, the Scavengers were angry.

"Yes. I have heard. There was nothing I could do." Brentford indicated the greenhouse to account for the fact he had no power over such matters anymore. Blankbate could not doubt, he thought, that he had done his lobbying best, but to no avail.

"There may be a strike, then," said Blankbate, who was a man of few words.

Brentford understood. This would add spice to the troubles that were presently brewing and disorganize the city even more than the usual tug-of-war between the Council and the Administration, in a way that cast both institutions in roles that were rather against type. Whereas the Council was supposed to keep intact the utopian ideals of the Seven Sleepers who had founded the city, it was now more than ever involved in all matters of business with the "Friends" who funded it, and these Friends had themselves increasingly turned from philanthropists into shareholders who wanted a return on their investments. The Administration, which had originally been devoted to the practicalities of running a city at a latitude that was anything but reasonable, had meanwhile—and Brentford was one of the main actors in this conversion—evolved toward a faithfulness to the first principles that was at times somewhat fanatical. For once, they had agreed on something, and that was going to cause more harm than good.

"Do what you should," said Brentford, though he could not say he relished the idea of a Scavengers strike and the trouble it would bring, mostly in the prowling shapes of Bipolar Bears high on fresh human garbage. But some loyalties, and debts, had to come first. During the Faber affair, the Scavengers had proved to be reliable and essential allies. Maybe it was in his power to convince them not to go on strike, but he respected them and their autonomy.

"I'm behind you whatever happens. You'll have to be aware that they'll probably ask you to resign your weapons."

Blankbate nodded his beak. "But there still will be bears."

"Yes, and even more of them. But I suppose the Council will decide that you only need the guns when you pick up the Garbage."

"Who will defend the city against the bears, then?"

"The Subtle Army, I suppose."

Blankbate thought about it for a while.

"They're not allowed to carry guns in the city."

"Not yet. But they will be. I even think the Council is only waiting for such an occasion, with that airship over us, and all the Inuit agitation. One might even wonder if the attack against the Done-Gone system is not being made for the precise purpose of having you play into their hands."

"So, no strike would be better? This is what you're saying?"

"I'm saying it's not up to me. I suppose there will be a vote. Just do not forget to mention those consequences when you address the voters."

Blankbate remained silent for while, lost in thought.

"Chipp sends his regards," he finally said.

"How is he?"

"Like a man who has made some big discovery. He brought back something strange yesterday that he thought I should tell you about, before we warn the authorities."

"Why me? Am I implicated?"

"Not as far as I know. But he knows you deal with strange things sometimes. Like that woman who talked to the Polar Kangaroo and stopped time or something."

"Hmm," said Brentford, who suddenly remembered he had an appointment with Helen at the North Pole. Maybe Chipp was right after all: he *did* deal with strange things.

"Chipp found a sled in Niflheim with no driver and a dead woman in it. It had arrived straight from the North."

"You mean the dogs took it here on their own?" said Brentford, hiding how the words *dead woman* had affected him. Could this be Helen coming back?

"That's what Chipp said. Yes. The woman was holding this."

Blankbate unbuttoned his coat and took out a small oval mirror that he handed to Brentford, who examined it as well as the lights allowed. Its slightly convex surface seemed tainted by some faint greenish hue. He held it up to his face, and the blur of his breath made something appear on the glass, a letter or a drawing, as if traced with a finger. He brought it closer to his lips and exhaled on it, so as to blur the entire surface.

"*Lancelot*" he read.

"What?"

"The word 'Lancelot' is written on the mirror."

Blankbate shrugged his shoulders, signifying it meant nothing to him. To Brentford it meant little more, except that it was his friend Gabriel's middle name (a name which, Gabriel would remind him, was not even Lancelot's real one).

"How long can you keep this secret?" he asked Blankbate.

"As long as we want. We have hidden the lady in our cold storage room."

"Can I keep the mirror?"

"As long as you need it," said Blankbate. "I have to go now anyway. Good-bye."

"Good luck," said Brentford as Blankbate's black, bulky shape receded toward the exit. The white mask turned toward Brentford and nodded, and then was seen no more.

Brentford's apartment was located in another wing of the Botanical Building, accessible through an exquisitely crafted wrought-iron spiral staircase. This led to a flat decorated in the finest Art

Nouveau style, as if the iron girders had melded with the hot-house plants and given birth to a profusion of hybrid forms, in an unseemly and probably hypocritical reconciliation of nature with industry. Brentford *knew* it was kitschy, but that did not prevent him from finding it beautiful and comfortable (though he would not have advised someone to take phantastica in there).

Sybil was waiting for him in the bedroom, and jumped out of bed in her rather transparent nightgown as soon as he walked through the door, looking very much like the *White Sybil of Polarion,* a painting of questionable taste that she had modelled for and which now was hanging in the room. In spite of the late hour, she was her dazzling, sparkling, kaleidoscopic self, a radi-ant sprite made out of glinting eyes, frothy silk, and luminous skin, who even in her negligee looked as if she were wearing jewels. Even her curls, which were exactly of the famous Vene-tian blond hue, had something fizzy about them. But, when you came a bit closer, her lightness and luminosity had nothing airy about them, but were rather the polished, gleaming surface of a lean muscular frame that executed nothing but high-precision movements: she was, above all, a dancer. As to her capacity as a singer, Brentford was, well, in love and would rather not com-ment on that (though it is safe to say he was not too fond of her band, the Clicquot Cub-Clubbers, nor of their bland, innocuous brand of jazz), but he reckoned that her main talent, maybe, was different: that of commanding undivided visual attention wherever she happened to be, as lit fountains and fireworks are usually wont to do. She was, in a word, *moving.*

"Sweetie," she moaned, hanging her arms around him like a necklace of white gold, "I thought you had left me for good."

"You did get my pneu, didn't you?"

"Oh! Very late! Oh my, that's for me?" she asked, pinching the mirror from Brentford's hands. Before he could react, she had wiped it clean with a swift brush of her gown. "It's so nice. Thank you, honey. Smack, smack."

Brentford sighed, then scowled, but what could he do now?

"You were nice with the Eskimos? You didn't offer your future wife to them, did you?" she asked, while looking for a spot to hang the mirror.

"Oh, darn, I knew I had forgotten something," smirked Brentford, sitting on the bed. "Hope you're not mad at me."

"I am *so* mad at you, my dear. I wished you had been here with me this afternoon. I was at the Ringnes Skating Rink with the band, didn't I tell you that, for the Clicquot Club Caucus."

Brentford was trying to undo his tie, easier said than done with fingers numb from the cold. He was in Sybil-listening mode, letting himself be pleasantly lulled. Even when she was close to him, she had that kind of from-the-bathing-room voice: it flew from her body, and fluttered all around, so that she and her words never seemed to be in the same place at the same time.

"I had to do a demonstration for the new Ice-cycle," she said, as she unhooked a small drawing from the wall to put the mirror in its place. "You know what they are, don't you? The front wheel is replaced by a little skate. I wished you had seen me. It was so much fun."

"What a shame," said Brentford, who regarded all these social and promotional events with what could pass as condescension. The recent occasion on which she and the Cub-Clubbers had entertained Bipolar Bears in garbage-rehab cages to celebrate the release of their cover of "You should a-hear Olaf laugh," he had found, to say the truth, a tad ridiculous.

"Here. It looks fine, doesn't it? And oh, I saw the strangest thing today when I came back. A girl just fainted in front of the Greenhouse. She must have been waiting for God knows what. A man passed in front of her, maybe he brushed against her, and whoosh, down she went. They had to call an ambulance to fetch her."

Brentford almost told Sybil of the ambulances he had seen in front of the Toadstool, but Sybil was now looking at him with a movie actress's expression of deep concern. He was used to these mood swings, and braced himself for what was to come.

"And then, there's some bad news" she said, with the pout of a spoiled child, which was, Brentford had to admit against his better judgement, more irresistible than exasperating. "Did you read the newspaper?"

"I did not have time," sighed Brentford.

Sybil took a folded copy of the *New Venice News,* John Blank's paper ("Ice-breaking the news since 1927 AB") from the bedside table and handed it to Brentford.

"Look who's back," she said.

Brentford took the paper and read:

MS. LAKE, BACK, PROMISES UPHEAVAL
BY JOHN LINKO

The Nethergate Psychomotive Transaerian Terminal, under yesternight skies.

Where has she been, what has she done? It was supposed to be a homecoming. It turned into a theophany. Psychomotive coloured steam had not finished hissing when the shrill of the crowd took over. Cutting her way through the panting pink and green puffs, Ms. Sandy Lake appeared to us simple mortals as an omen.

Do we have to recall to the neo-New who she is? Listen to the venerable stairs of Grönland Gardens, prick up your ears in the glasshouses in Glass Town, keep silent in New Boree Crescent, and you will know. New Venice is still humming with everlasting echoes of her heady "Yesterday's Skies."

The highbrow or hurried reader will be content with knowing that her "As White As..." was said to have caught the very marrow of the icy city. But that is of little use to really measure the remanence of her name to the olde-New. For the eye- and ear-witnesses are still in awe of her charismatic performance during the Blue Wild Thing.

Her lifestyle was indeed typical of the New Venetian golden age scene. Substances, unending live music parties—those were the days of roses, wine, and polar pop, of overbrimming dance cards... But in many more ways than one, reminiscences of Ms. Lake actually embody reminiscences of New Venice 'in illo tempore': open and fleeting, frail and fearless, the vanishing point of love and life.

Where has she been, what has she done: I shook myself from my reverie as Ms. Lake passed me by on the terminal berth. Cheerful applause lasted long enough to stir a hunting Inuk from his hideout. But there was more to the group than a goodwill reunion. The clatter sounded organized, as if all were chanting slogans. The little crowd was exclusively feminine, and dressed as suffragettes, which somehow did not fit with Ms Lake's tumultuous past.

I was thinking of how information slipped unto me, when Ms Lake shouted out:

— You must be the journalist.

— Journalists are not supposed to get involved.

— You are not asked to.

— Where have you been, Ms. Lake?

— My name is now Lenton, Lillian Lenton.

— When did you cease to be Ms. Lake?

— I've been to wondrous places down the Austral parallels. So many places, so different from one another. On the one hand, you are shattered by despair: no thing ever resembles the next, and the world looks like a roller coaster. On the other hand, you end up finding your way, and when you get to that point, it's like you get to another level of consciousness.

— What have you been doing?

— Wah—baking doughnuts, of course, what kind of journalist are you? I'm talking of another level of consciousness.

— There are a lot of people here tonight. Most of them are ex-fans of the Sandmovers?

— I have been away for such a long time, I don't think anyone here could sing a Sandmovers' tune. Including me.

— Did you give up music?

— Precisely, no. It's just that music has grown up in me. In my opinion, it hasn't much to do with entertainment or partying anymore. There's a kind of responsibility for those who are listened to by the people.

— Do you have a new group?

— Yes. The Lodestones. We release our new single in five

days, in North Venustown. Look, it's written on this bill.

— Are you planning to stay a long time in New Venice?

— Listen. This city… this city is a gift. But it's a gift wasted on spoiled children. I did not come back to act as if nothing happened. The Blue Wild happened, the city was more or less destroyed, I've traveled a lot since then. The city is back in place, as far as I can see. But during my long southern journey, there are a few things that sprouted in my New Venetian heart, and it can no longer be silent.

— Concerning the city?

— Concerning *our* lives in *our* city.

Two vigourous women came up to Ms. Lake, now Ms. Lenton, and helped her away from our conversation. I was left, alone on the steamer berth, with most of my questions. Where has she been, what has she done… And, above all, why is she coming back now?

"Who does she thinks she is?" asked Sybil, sitting down next to Brentford. "She's been away for years and she imagines she has just to snap her fingers to have all the audience at her feet? People have been working hard while she was away."

For it was indeed one of Sybil's pet ideas that she was a hardworking girl. But what Brentford retained of the article, apart from the eerie reminiscences it triggered of his own youth as a scenester, was its strange "poletical" undercurrent, as if Ms. Lenton promised or hoped for more than simply a musical revolution. One more agitator, then. Great. This was just what the city needed right now. He sighed, and lay down, suddenly feeling against his spine the frame of the picture Sybil had discarded. He discreetly looked at it, noting that it was a drawing in which the North Pole rose up a like ghost under a sheet, its head shaped like a grinning skull. In a flash, he thought of Helen.

"… and anyway," Sybil was saying, as she leaned over him, trapping two copies of him inside her gold-speckled eyes. "One more thing I want to ask you before I rape the living daylights out of you. Are you free on Friday night?"

He watched himself floating in the double bubble and found that he looked happy to be there.

"Free as a floe," he answered.

"Because," she explained while undoing his shirt with her slender fingers, "I have received two invitations from the magician we'll have at our wedding party. He does a show at Trilby's Temple. I would like it *so much* if you could come along."

"Why not," said Brentford, looking at Sybil through half-closed eyes, until she was golden and filmy, like the flame of a candle. "I could do with some magic, I guess."

CHAPTER X

A *Starmap* Tattoo

•

"Skate together! Can that be possible?"
Tolstoy, *Anna Karenina*

hat Gabriel did in the Kane Clinic was try to find Phoebe. He went up the first flight of stairs that he found and set about looking for someone who could inform him. In spite of all the agitation in the outpatient ward, the rest of the clinic had gone dim and silent into night watch. It was not long before he heard coming down the darkened corridor the typical clap-clap and clatter of a nurse pushing a cart.

"Hello, there," he said, with a bow.

"What are you doing here?" said the nurse, in a whispered vociferation that was not quite as impressive as she intended. As she turned toward him, she revealed, pinned on her white apron, a badge on which the name Vera could be made out. Gabriel believed in names. He felt he could trust her to be sincere.

"Listen," he murmured, "nothing that deserves much publicity. I am looking for a girl who has been brought here this afternoon, probably by the Gentlemen of the Night."

"Are you one of them?" asked the nurse.

"God forbid," said Gabriel.

Vera leaned toward him, conspiratorially.

"She has not regained consciousness, poor thing. I wonder what they have done to her."

"Can I see her?"

"There is nothing much to see. But I suppose that holding her hand and kissing her forehead won't do her any harm. To the left, to the right, seventh door on the right. Do not be long. And if you're caught, you have never seen me."

"Thank you very much," said Gabriel, as Vera swerved to the left and clap-clattered away. Once out of her field of vision, Gabriel opened his fist and looked at the small phial of Letheon he had just stolen from the cart. This was a poor way to thank Vera but he deserved some comfort after a day that had mostly consisted of persecutions and humiliations.

He uncorked it and, blocking one nostril, inhaled deeply till the fumes hit the back of his skull, and then repeated the operation on the other side. He knew he should stop there. His brain was already buzzing with white noise and more of that sharp stuff would impair his motor skills, turning him into one of those colourful clowns whose limbs are made of little felt rings. Not to mention the fits of erotomania he was bound to suffer from, which would assume the form of an exacerbated but rather illusory sense of possibility that more often than not resulted in pitiful enterprises, such as pornographic pneus to past loves and vaguely known women. So, he told himself, just a little one for the road and that'll be all. Then he took two more whiffs, for he was not a man to be dictated to, not even by himself, and he found himself moving in a world that was, already, made of a lighter more billowy fabric but still thought it funny to play at being a clinic.

If Gabriel's calculations were right, he should have been close to Phoebe's room when something stopped him in his tracks: through an open door, a girl on all fours on the floor and wearing only a hitched up hospital gown was displaying, in a ray of light coming from the corridor, the most heart-wrenching bottom he had ever seen in his entire life. Phoebe was instantly spirited away from his mind. It was love at first sight.

"Nice little icecap you got there," he said in a hoarse voice, unable to believe that he had just said this: but there's nothing like Letheon to turn a decent fellow into a hopelessly depraved cad. "Gives some perspective on the Hollow Earth theory," he added, wishing he were dead.

The girl turned toward him, and he could make out a small pale face and two eyes like black holes that sucked out his spinning planet of a heart.

"If you want to plant your flagpole," said the brunette with a lighthearted, musical vulgarity that was the sweetest melody Gabriel had ever heard, "you'd better help me first."

She plunged back under the bed and soon dragged out a pair of high-cut, thick-soled boots that made Gabriel's heart leap even higher. He approached and knelt down beside her.

"Those bastards took my clothes away. They must be under the bed," she whispered.

Thrilling from this intimacy, he groped around and quickly felt a soft bundle under his fingers. The girl was rather small and her arms were not long enough to reach it.

"I think I got them," he said, triumphally.

"Okay, just be on the lookout and we leave as soon as I'm ready."

Gabriel did as he was told, very happy to do so, almost not noticing that he was pulling at the cork again and pushing the phial back up his nose.

"You know a way out?" asked the girl as she stepped into the hallway, slipping on a kind of black hooded cloak.

"You're the little black riding hood, aren't you?"

"You're an old satyr, aren't you?" she answered playfully.

She was, he was almost sure of it, the girl he had glimpsed earlier at the Toadstool. He could now see her features. They had nothing frail or delicate about them, but even the baby fat was alive with currents of sparking astuteness that put the *cute* back in *electrocute*.

"You care for some?" asked Gabriel, handing her his phial. "It's on the house."

"I'm going to know your thoughts," she said.

She took it and sniffed quickly.

"You should be ashamed," she smiled, her eyes boring straight into his as she gave him back the phial. "So, how do we scram?"

"Hmm..." said Gabriel, his head whirling slightly. "The doors are rather busy. We should try the window. It's only the first floor, after all."

The girl went straight back into the room, and Gabriel heard her opening the double window. Before he could react she had jumped through it, and he followed her, as he would have anywhere. There was a little cornice that made the whole affair easier, and with bones made out of Letheon draughts, he felt there was little chance that he would sprain or break anything. He landed on the stone ledge and took another spring that sent him onto a welcome and welcoming layer of powdery snow. From there, there were a few yards to cross and iron railings that were not much of a challenge. She laughed as she saw Gabriel overplay his ease in climbing them and then somehow get tangled in their unexpected reality.

"I'm Stella, by the way."

"I'm Gabriel. I hope I'm not seeing you shining from a too distant past," Gabriel said, panting a little.

"You're funnier when you talk dirty," she said with a flattered smile.

"Ah. Dimple," he noticed, pointing accusingly at her right cheek. "And just on one side. You have decided to kill me, haven't you?"

"Not yet," she said. "Would you care for a drink of something strong before I do?"

Compared to the Toadstool, the John Dee was a notch lower in the underground. Owned by the now retired members of the amplified Elizabethan cult band Lord Strange's Men, it was a rather dark place, lit with a few braziers around which huddled a more sombre and possibly more dangerous species of Boreal Bohemian. Under this wavering, uncertain light, the cabalistic figures that decorated the walls were glimpsed more than really seen, which only made them more evocative. The Sun Dogs had started their career here and the band now on the stage was the Mock Moons, who obviously followed their traces, though their music was more upbeat and grating. The song that they played could not have been better attuned to Gabriel's feelings:

Did you look at the stars last night
because I was up there
and was looking at you
I kept blinking with all my might
But you had a lover
By the time I got to you.

Music knows more about you than any humbug hypnotizer, thought Gabriel.

He had gone to the toilets for that "very last" sniff of Letheon, and as he came back he could see that some sort of huge black-coated, Viking-looking hunk was pestering Miss Stella Black. He walked up, his uncertain legs pedalling over the evasive ground toward the cask that served as a table, and as soon as he sat down, Stella sprang to her feet and glued her mouth to his. It was as fresh a draught as if someone had opened a door in the back of his skull. The Viking, who seemed more than a bit inebriated, frowned and tried to accommodate the scene to his disobedient eyeballs, and finally retired with slurred apologies.

Stella stepped back.

"Whoa," she said. "One could get high on your breath."

"That's the best definition of love I have ever heard," Gabriel said to the girl, who receded, wavering like Northern lights. He thought he might have preferred a different first kiss, but then he decided that no, everything was good, and would be from now on. Just because it had happened, it was good. That was his second-best definition of love.

They had ordered two Wormwood Star absinthes, and had just a few sips to go. Absinthe and Letheon were a daring blend that reduced everything to bi-dimensional pictures, which floated here and there to the point where it became uncomfortable.

"I think I'd like to get some fresh air," Gabriel said.

"We could go skyskating," Stella suggested casually.

The part of Gabriel that could discuss the pertinence of this idea had long been dead, buried, and forgotten. He did not miss it at all.

"And then we'll test your Hollow Earth theory," she added, dimpling like the devil.

"I promise we'll use that little pot of butter," said Gabriel, always a gentleman.

They walked for a long time along a deeply embanked small canal that often disappeared under smelly bridges, and during these eclipses, they kissed slobberingly and caressed each other, as far as their thick clothes allowed. And after another clumsy stunt from Gabriel climbing over a fence, they eventually looked down on the Ringnes Speed Skating Rink.

The moon that hung overhead looked strange, as if a quarter of it had been neatly cut and thrown away. The ice spread below, dark grey and scratched with entangled traces no angel could unravel. It was like life itself, thought Gabriel, a born allegorician: bodies had come and gone, met or avoided each other, retraced their steps or someone else's, been found by and lost one another.

Stella took a pillbox from her pocket and gave him some purple heart-shaped "boilers," before taking some herself. The glycine-and-ephedrine blend made one feel warm, caused one's heart to beat faster, and pumped blood to the body's extremities, three things Gabriel did not feel he needed more of. His good education, however, forbade him to refuse a drug.

Then Stella went down the slope and started to take her clothes off over her head, quickly, keeping on only her boots, whose skates she liberated with a little gesture that was a bit of a ballet, or bullet, to Gabriel's heart. Coming closer, he watched her ecstatically, as if he had never seen a young woman before. He had more or less the same reaction every time (he believed that nude girls came from the same realm or region as dreams, from the same eternal inexhaustible fountain at the spring of time and yet out of time), but a girl like this one—no, he had never seen and never would see again. It was not only, as some bad poem put it, the "dimpled fullness of her form," nor "the midnight blackness of her plentiful hair," and neither was it— he could be as bad a poet as anyone else—the opal teardrops of her breasts. What held him mesmerized was the circular star-map tattoo that ran all around her shoulders and which, as she started gliding on the moonlit ice, was the music of the spheres made visible to his eye. He stared at the dark inky stars and figures on her pale skin and how they reflected, as a negative print, the sparkles that sprinkled the Heavens. Rapture and Terror seized his heart and tears welled up in his eyes.

"Hey!" she cried, "move or you'll freeze."

Once he was stark naked but for gloves, boots, and Elsinore cap, he switched on his skates and, shod with steel, launched himself on the tinkling ice, dizzy and weak as he was, happy not to have taken the Fly Fantasia Flint he had bought earlier at the Toadstool. He scraped his warm body against the coldness of the night and it felt like a rash all over his skin.

He tried—his legs barely responsive—to skid toward her but tripped and fell forward, hearing her laughter and feeling the burn of the ice through his gloves as he caught himself just in time. He stood up and looked around in panic, as if afraid he had lost her. But there she was, whirling round him, a comely comet whose hand he tried to grasp: she always took it back at the last moment, her laughter echoing in his head like crumbling crystal stalactites.

He launched himself again. With the hiss of a giant hand, the wind slapped him about, forcing a crown of cold steel around his burning head. He strove to move toward her, the *lodestar of desire*, going faster and faster, cutting across her ellipses, but as soon as he came closer, she would take a sharp turn and speed up again, gleaming on the glassy plain, tattooed stars tangled in her hair, her bubbly buttocks a Milky Way in the moonlight. He realized that to hold her naked brilliance, he would be willing to give all.

After a dreamlike while, as he was still pursuing her in vain, she suddenly turned toward him and waited for him to bump against her, which he tried to do as softly as he could. They clasped each other and almost fell over, but eventually stood firmly on the ground, his head spinning still as the world wheeled by them. He kissed her, his hands full of constellations, for a long time, or so it seemed, until the universe came to a standstill around them. Slowly, he took her back to the slope, where their clothes were waiting, and he laid upon them her heavenly body. She laughed and overthrew him, went on top, a cascade of steamy black hair erasing the night; then the stars fell down on him and covered him, so close now, as if he had died and been turned into one.

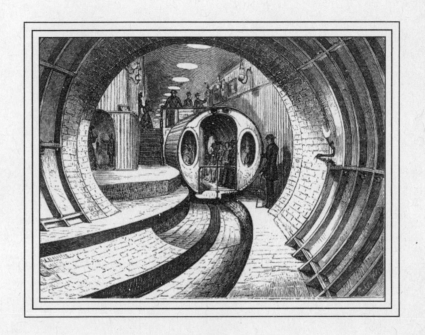

*Much to Gabriel's surprise, this led to a ghost station
of the disused Pneumatic subway line.*

Book Two

•

Magic & Mayhem

The combined effect upon the spectator of the spoken word and the eyes together is generally irresistible.

David P. Abbott, *Fraudulent Spiritualism Unveiled*, 1907

CHAPTER XI

Nordlicht

●

"Das Fest im Geist! Des Urlichts Ausbruch aus der Natur kann uns, auf der nordwärts gerichteten Heimreise, zum Ruhepol in uns, zu einer überraschenden Feiertag werden. Pfingsten erfüllt und erwartet den Nordwärts-schreitenden. Den Nordwärts-denkenden. Den, der den Norden erleidet."
Theodor Daübler, *Das Nordlicht*, 1910

oly Cod!" thought Gabriel, as he saw Brentford waving to him through the large window of the Nordlicht Kaffee. Their eyes had met and it was too late to pretend that he had not noticed him. There was no other choice but to go into the Kaffee and pray that no Gentleman of the Night or affiliated spy was witnessing the scene. However, the past few days had convinced Gabriel that this was a rather idle hope.

The Nordlicht Kaffee was an über-chic spot located off Koldewey Canal in an area of gabled, finely sculpted Gothic houses

known as Neu-Vineta. This quarter, which specialized in luxuries, drew its name from a Baltic harbour that according to
some German legend had been doomed and drowned because
of its riches. It emerged, said the tale, for a single day once in
a century, and plunged back into the depths if the merchants
failed to sell their splendid goods to some unsuspecting stranger.
Needless to say, prices tended to drop dramatically as the day
advanced. But though the mythical source of the Sales Period
could be traced back to this Anti-Venice, it had become in the
New Venetian Neu-Vineta but a distant, irony-tinged memory,
and Gabriel hoped no one was counting on him to break a similar curse these days, for the prices here were now well beyond
his grasp.

The Kaffee itself was supposed to be reminiscent of the
barocco ice city that the wintering crew of the *Tegethoff* had
built out of boredom on the floe that had imprisoned them. But
the result was nothing if not slightly pretentious. The walls and
ceiling seemed to be made out of whipped cream, the furniture
to be glazed with dark chocolate. The room was decorated, on
the rare moulded panels that were not hung with engravings of
the *Hansa* or the Payer-Weyprecht expedition, with extracts of
the famous *Nordlicht* poetic cycle by Theodor Daübler, most of
them about Venice. Gabriel's command of German was rather
shaky, and all he knew was this: It had been at a masked ball in
Venice that the adolescent Daübler had experienced his revelation, his "aurora of the soul." For him, the Northern Lights were
the proof that the Earth "longed to be a shining star again," and
would one day become "the spark of freedom in the universe."
The Seven Sleepers may have thought about this when—well,
according to the local pronunciation—they put the *ice* back in
Venice and Venice back on the ice. Or maybe they were *pillortoq*, simply stark raving mad.

Brentford was sitting on a curved plush sofa just against
the window, basking in a slanting sunray in front of a light

breakfast of coffee and croissants, a mooring post of sanity to Gabriel's loose gondola. It was a strange place and time to see him, but then it was also a strange place and time for Gabriel to be there. His own excuse, however, was this: on "sick leave" from Doges College, he had spent the night, as he had every night since he had met her five days earlier, roaming through the city with Stella, pausing in their ramblings only for strong drinks and endless kisses, and he was now heading home to sleep through the few hours of remaining daylight. To speak frankly, it showed a bit. Brentford was not long in noticing, as he shook his friend's hand, that he had sagging, ashen cheeks and haloes around his eyes that looked like pools of oil. But what he could not perceive was that Gabriel used this exhaustion to cover up his anxiety about a meeting whose outcome he feared for both their sakes.

"What are you doing here?" asked Gabriel, falling into more than sitting on the sofa in front of Brentford, and huffing a breath that carried the bitter whiff of absinthe.

"I quarrelled with Sybil," admitted Brentford, with a wry smile to show it was nothing too worrying. "About the guest list. I discovered she had added Surville at the last moment. I certainly do not want to see him."

It took Gabriel a migrainous while to understand the fuss was about Brentford's former sweetheart.

"Seraphine's husband?"

"Ex-husband, yes. But nevertheless. And the spokesman of the Council. Go figure."

"Why would Sybil invite him?"

"I do not know, really. Sybil has an address book the size of *Moby Dick*. I think he is a kind of sponsor to the Cub-Clubbers, or something."

Gabriel refrained from wincing at the name of the band, which was everything he detested. Though he had to admit that Sybil was, well, attractive.

"It infuriated me all the more," continued Brentford, after Gabriel had ordered a double coffee with the vague, but visible, hope that he would not have to pay for it himself, "because I have an appointment with the Council this afternoon. I'll spare you the details. Having to cope with them twice a day is beyond my patience, these days."

Gabriel started at the mention of the appointment. He hoped that it had nothing to do with the book Brentford was, not without reason, suspected of having written. But he also realized that if they were seen together now, on display in the window, it would only mean to *them* that Gabriel was warning Brentford of the danger, which would point to his friend as the culprit and himself as his accomplice. The noose tightened around his throat. Since his failed attempt to send poor Phoebe with a message, he had decided to stay away from Brentford, hoping it would benefit both of them. What a brilliant success, he thought, not withholding the wince this time.

"Nothing serious, I hope," he managed to grumble. He had decided not to add to Brentford's trouble and said nothing of his own interview with the Gentlemen of the Night.

"Well, they do not exactly invite you over every day, so I guess they want to convey the idea that it *is* serious. The reason is rather technical, a little litigation over hunting quotas between the army and the Inuit. But I expect they will take advantage of it to embarrass me some way or other."

Gabriel nodded, but he was not in a state in which technicalities were of any interest to him. It would give too much credit to his mind to say that it was *racing* to find an excuse to get out, but, at last, it tried to.

"You seem a bit tired," said Brentford, not wishing to dwell on his own problems.

"I met a girl."

"You look like you met two or three."

"Sort of, yes. She's very energetic. She's called Stella, but she should be called Tesla, really. High-voltage girl."

"The Earl of Real versus Stella Tesla. It sounds good," said Brentford, who wondered how long this latest fling, or his friend's nerves, would last. "What does she do?"

"Pretty much everything."

"For a living, I mean."

Gabriel smiled at the motherly tone of the question.

"Oh. She's a vaudeville artist, I guess. Relatively new to the city. She is now working for a magician."

"Handyside?"

"What?"

"The name of the magician is Handyside?"

"I don't know. She works at the Trilby Temple."

"That's the one. Sybil wanted a magician for our wedding and I'm supposed to see him perform there tonight. I guess I will see your Stella."

"You won't see anything but her," said Gabriel, with a streak of pride that did not linger too long. The coffee had arrived and he lost himself in the smoke, eyes half closed, not exactly liking what he saw reflected through a cup, darkly.

"Speaking of coincidences," said Brentford, "the Scavengers have found a dead woman in a sled in Niflheim. She held a mirror with *Lancelot* written on it."

"Cracked from side to side?"

"Not yet. Maybe next time I quarrel with Sybil, who now owns the thing. Why do you ask?"

"For no reason. It reminded me of a poem. But then everything does."

"I wondered if you might have a clue or simply feel concerned."

"I do not date dead women as a rule."

Oops, thought Gabriel, hoping he had not offended Brentford, whose longing for Helen, concealed as it was, nonetheless was well known to him. However, this time Brentford easily read his friend's mind, as if in a comic book: the arched eyebrows, the pursed lips. He decided not to take offence, but discovered that, indeed, he wanted to speak about Helen. Gabriel was perhaps among the few persons who would not consider such talk as pertaining to alienism—and the only one among them whom Brentford himself would not regard as a lunatic.

"I think I have news from Helen, by the way."

"Dream incubation?"

"Yes. She has given me an appointment on the North Pole for March the first. Geographical, that is."

Gabriel nodded appreciatively.

"You're going there?" he asked, a bit jealous.

"Well, I'm of two minds. I do not think I will risk it, but still I am getting the *Kinngait* ready."

"Nice honeymoon trip."

"Yes, you're right. I do not think Sybil would be too happy with me going there right after the wedding."

"By the way, this North Pole thing reminds me of something," said Gabriel, who felt a sudden relief at having found a reason not to stay that was nobler than simply going to bed. "I have to go visit the Inuit People's Ice Palace. I met a friend of Bob's who is helping with the staging of it all. He invited me to visit it before the opening."

"I do not think this palace is the best idea," said Brentford with a frown.

"I recited the lesson you taught me about it. But you know how it is: curiosity got the better of me. I am actually late," he added, standing up, searching for a wallet which he knew was empty. Brentford waved his hand appeasingly, to signify that he would gladly pay the bill.

"Don't forget you're supposed to be my best man on Saturday," he added, as he shook hands with Gabriel.
"Don't forget to make up with the bride, then."

Through the window, Brentford watched Gabriel go away, and felt vaguely worried. Since he had first met him twenty years before, watching in disbelief as "the hurling earl " crawled uninvited on all fours into his Doges' College dorm room to vomit in the washbasin, Brentford had acquired a rather large spectrum of expectations about what could be regarded as right or normal for his friend. Now Gabriel was undoubtedly tired and could have his moody spells, but knowing him as he did, Brentford sensed there was something else. Gabriel had seemed nervous, elusive, pulling relentlessly on his sideburns while casting quick glances at the street. This "Lancelot" story would normally have goaded him into inventing thousand hypotheses and he would have given more thought to the North Pole trip than he had, as it was a longtime fascination of his. Was this Stella to blame? Or something else? He reverted to his own already numerous problems and found with a sigh that Gabriel's eerie behaviour had been added to them.

CHAPTER XII

Eskimo Thieves!!!

●

His filthy habits unsubdu'd
His manners gross, his gestures rude
No friendly hand assists to teach
Instruction comes not in his reach;
And scarcely knowing good from ill
Being untaught, he's blameless still.
"A Peep at The Esquimaux," By A Lady, 1825

Hiding the truth from Brentford was something Gabriel could consider doing, but, as a gentleman as well as a friend, lying to him was beyond the pale of the possible. Once he had told him that he was going to the Inuit People's Ice Palace, he had little choice but to actually go there, however exhausted he was. Wondering why he had not simply admitted that he needed some sleep, he staggered toward the Marco Polo Midway.

Though it was early in the day, and not exactly warm, the Midway was already busy, people taking advantage of the few hours of decent daylight to stroll about and linger in front of the shops, cafés, and attractions that lined the long avenue. A refuge against the most dreaded Hyperboredom of the Wintering Weeks, the Midway was a poetic hodgepodge of architectural styles, but with an overall cheapness that made it more Fairground than Fairyland. Through dreary days or dazzling nights, it catered almost nonstop to all kinds of questionable tastes in mass entertainment. Panoramas, dioramas, oloramas, cycloramas, mareoramas, myrioramas, and panopticons took the spectators through all kinds of famous monuments and places, exotic lands, ferocious battles, and natural catastrophes, unless they preferred a "Trip to the Moon" or a good update on the "War of the Worlds," or even, if one believed the bold letters above the gigantic archways guarded by angels and devils, a replay of the "Creation of the World" or a peek through the formidable "Hellgate." Gabriel had patronized, in more senses than one, each of these many times and though he professionally professed to see their naïve vulgarity, he had always tremendously enjoyed them, precisely because the imperfection and mechanical frailty of these industrial visions reminded him, more than anything else, of his own stuttering fantasies, the do-it-yourself of his dreams.

Nevertheless, the very idea of building the Ice Palace right there, a few steps from the pyramid-shaped Palace of Palmistry or the Trilby Temple, said a lot about the seriousness of its planners' alleged anthropological concerns. The building itself, whose outside was now completed, was shaped, rather ridiculously to Gabriel's mind, as a rough mountain or an iceberg of huge proportions, as if the Eskimos were some kind of troglodytes living in caves of ice. He walked up to a man in a sort of zookeeper's uniform whom he supposed was a guard, and having explained his case had only a few minutes to wait— his heavy lids closing by themselves—before Kelvin Budd-Jones came to meet him at the door.

"Nice to see you. I do not have much time, however. We're under considerable pressure, here."

"I hope I won't detain you too long," said Gabriel, who was sincerely in a hurry to get between sheets that would not be made of ice. "It's really kind of you, anyway."

The entrance hall and the darkened corridor that curved toward the main rotunda were a dusty mess indeed, carpeted with crumpled blankets and tarpaulins, littered with dismantled iron scaffolding and boxes of greasy nuts and bolts.

"You've heard about Bob?" asked Kelvin, to strike up a little conversation, as they made their way through the obstacles.

"No," Gabriel answered, realizing that since he had met Stelia, he'd felt no interest or curiosity about anything or anyone else.

"His Polar Kangaroo has been stolen. Well, it has disappeared, while we were at the Kane Clinic. He's not the happiest boy in New Venice, as you can imagine."

"Oh," said Gabriel, trying to look surprised. But when you started fiddling about with the Polar Kangaroo, no surprise would be the real surprise. He could well imagine the statue hopping away on its powerful hind legs. Generally, any manifestation of that wonder or freak of Nature, fictitious, real, or anything in between or beyond, was an omen of trouble threatening the city. Gabriel had a hunch he would hear about it again.

"Here, you see," said Kelvin, indicating a blue glow running along the base of the curved corridor walls, "these are Geissler tubes full of argon. We were trying to imitate the light just as it appears over the horizon, so it's a bit like being outside."

"A bit, yes. Great idea," said Gabriel, who appreciated the effort to simulate those sensations but who could not help thinking that a −30°F temperature would have been a more efficient way to produce a real Arctic feel, if that was truly the point. Then you might get some notion of what being an Inuk was all about.

But when the corridor ended and they entered the Hall, he was struck dumb. It was towering and vast and looked bigger than a normal panorama, perhaps because one entered it at floor level and not upon a mid-level platform. A painted roll, maybe forty-five feet in height, circled the entire rotunda, showing snowy peaks and icebergs adrift in the sea. A fjord, part paint, part real water, extended right to the middle and blended into a shore scene in the hall, where about twenty igloos were scattered on the blinding white floor. A few stuffed seals lounging on floes or peeping out of ice holes completed the picture, and Gabriel wondered if the Polar Kangaroo would not have felt indeed more at home here than in the Musheum.

This cardboard sublimity, as it tricked his senses into accepting that inside was outside, left him rocking uneasily between belief and disbelief. The light was dim, with a Sunday afternoon heaviness to it that felt barely comfortable. A frayed film of mist, probably made from dry ice, hovered above the ground, curiously at odds with the rather warm temperature around them. The scene in its entirety produced a strange sensation of frozen movement and epileptic clarity that was, Gabriel felt, slightly oppressive.

"It's a panorama but also a diorama," explained Kelvin, pointing at the painted scenery. "The canvas is actually transparent linen, with a few other layers behind. There are light rigs and filters behind the paintings and in the ceiling, over those fake clouds, so we can make the whole scene look like it's day or night, and imitate sun dogs or mock moons. We can even do northern lights. I can't show you now, but it's quite something. I'm devising a trick that can synchronize them with electromagnetic sound waves. Right now, you can hear the wind, I suppose, as we're testing the loudspeakers."

There was an ominous hiss, in fact, but since nothing moved, not even the mist, except a few stray workers here and there installing props in the igloos, it just worsened the feeling of uncanny stillness. It reminded Gabriel of that night when Helen died after having stopped Time for a few minutes, and how scary it all had been.

"I'm impressed, really," he said, becoming almost dizzy when he lifted his eyes toward the vault.

A titanic amount of work and skill had gone into this scheme, and he really wondered what was the point, beyond sheer performance. It did not look like the kind of cheap entertainment that the surroundings promised, but neither was it credible as a scientific or cultural endeavour. The idea of having real Eskimos going through the motions of hunting stuffed animals seemed especially ludicrous when everything around seemed designed for wax figures. It was enough to look at those four real Inuit in furs who came out of an igloo and blinked around, hands over their eyes, seeming as lost as Gabriel, to understand the absurdity of it all.

The four Eskimos regrouped and walked toward the exit, coming closer to Gabriel, who could hear them laughing behind their sleeves, when a fifth one, in an employee's uniform, darted out of the igloo and ran after them, apparently furious. He caught by the arm the last of the group, a long-haired, bowlegged, smelly fellow who seemed to be hiding something under his parka, and whispered to him something in Inuktitut that Gabriel had not enough vocabulary to grasp but that was, by the sound of it, an unequivocal reproach. The other fellow strove to free his arm, pulling faces at his aggressor, while the remaining three seemed rather amused at the scene. Suddenly, another of the uniformed guards, a white man, strode from the entrance toward the group.

"Hey, Oosik," he said, "what's going on here?"

"Nothing, nothing, sir," said the Eskimo guard, who looked rather embarrassed, while the others now laughed openly, elbowing each other in the ribs.

"Oosik, cousins or not, I told you to be discreet when you took them in," said the white guard. "People are working here and have no time to fool around."

"They gave me good advice for the igloos," pleaded Oosik.

"And I'm giving you some as well," said the guard. "Get them out of here, before I tell Mr. Peterswarden. Hey, but what are you hiding here?" he exclaimed, pointing at the long-haired Inuk Oosik was holding by the sleeve.

"Nothing," said Oosik, blushing. "It's a little joke between us."

The oldest of the four befurred Inuit—a small, stocky man with a wrinkled face—said something to the long-haired man, who laughed and pulled out his hand from under his parka, showing a little carved knife he had stolen from the igloo. He handed it to the white guard with a smile that lacked some teeth. But the smile waned as the guard briskly grasped the knife and returned him an angry look. There was an instant of awkward silence. Gabriel could see the other Inuit get tense. The old one extended his hand toward the white guard, as, Gabriel supposed, a gesture of appeasement, but the guard violently pushed it aside, and taking a whistle from his breast pocket, blew it, the shrill sounds causing a commotion that rippled across the still-life scenery. Guards suddenly appeared from all the corners of the hall, running toward the Inuit. Kelvin stepped in, trying to calm the guard, but the man would hear nothing, and tried instead to seize the thief, who, in his turn, pushed the guard back so violently that he fell to the floor. The other Inuit looked at each other, and then, without a word, all four started to run toward the exit, though other guards were now blocking the way. The Inuit tried to dodge them, but were tackled, and a wrestling match ensued that the fur clothes of the Eskimos seemed to muffle and make more playful to the casual observer (who, tired as he was, found it a good excuse not to intervene). Screams and swearing echoed through the hall, until more guards, streaming from the rear in Keystone Kops quantities, managed to catch and control the Eskimos. Other Inuit employees of the palace, along with Oosik and Kelvin, were trying to placate the guards. The fur-clad Inuit were now being put back on their feet and dragged away through the corridors, with complaints and protestations from the other workers.

Gabriel decided it was time to leave, before the Gentlemen of the Night arrived. The incident, as far as he was concerned, had not been serious and was drawing to a close. He approached Kelvin, who was about to follow them all.

"It's more lively than it seems, here," said Gabriel.

"Sorry about this," said Kelvin. "Everybody's nervous with the oncoming inauguration. I hope it won't be too bad for them. Or for Oosik. Or the other employees."

"The Eskimos who work here?"

"Yes, the idea is that it's the resident Inuit themselves who explain things to visitors. Some of them have their doubts about the project. We've even had a little sabotage lately. This is going to make things worse."

"You should go and make sure it cools off," said Gabriel, who felt as if his head was about to burst with exhaustion. "I don't want to detain you. Thanks a lot for the visit, anyway. It's truly amazing."

"Thank you," said Kelvin, shaking Gabriel's hands before following the Eskimo cortege.

Gabriel yawned and headed toward the exit. He hadn't gone two steps when he felt a small object under his boots. It looked like a dancing bear or something, one of those miniature carvings that Inuit make when they are bored and forget about afterward. It must have been part of the whole staging. He knelt down and picked it up.

It was only in the street that, opening his gloved hand, he realized that the tiny figure he held was that of the Polar Kangaroo.

CHAPTER XIII

The Recording Riot

●

That ragtime suffragette
She is no household pet
H. Williams & N. D. Thayer,
That Ragtime Suffragette, 1913

Brentford still had plenty of time before his appointment at the Blazing Building with the Council of Seven, and he felt he could afford to make a detour to Venustown, where, according to the flyer he had just been handed by a girl in a suffragette outfit, he could attend the launch party of THIS YEAR'S MUSICAL EVENT: LILIAN LENTON & THE LODESTONES' NEW ELECTRICALLY RECORDED 10-INCH!!!

He had to admit that the newspaper article Sybil had handed him with such a charming fury had triggered his curiosity. When he was a youngster, caught in the agitation of the city's

137 * Jean-Christophe Valtat

golden age, Sandy Lake had more than once enchanted him with her good looks and crisp little tunes that would turn his brain wiring into blinking fairy lights. Her band, the fine-tuned but foul-mouthed Sandmovers, had been the epitome of what the city was about in those days, as it stood upon the two pillars of attitude and addiction. But he would not have gone for such cheap flashes of nostalgia—for he knew ultimately how useless and heart-wrenching they were—if he had not dreamed of Sandy Lake at the Dunne Institute. He had to check the connection, if only to make sure it was nothing but a coincidence, though he knew very well that a coincidence, by the simple fact of being noticed, was always *something*.

Venustown, just on the other side of Yukiguni, was not at its best in the daylight, being as it was something of a decayed tooth in the pearly-white smile of the city centre. The houses were rather greyish and their facades had little or none of the ornamental flourishes that characterized most of the local architecture. It certainly had an atmosphere of its own—especially at night, as its narrow, gaslit, cobbled streets, all mazes and byways, were haunted by the gold-plated ghosts of low life. But in the morning hours, it had a sort of sleepy, moody, unwashed ambience, so characteristic of red-light districts everywhere. The faint music that guided Brentford's steps from Boötes Bridge up to Selene Street seemed out of place, a fading memory more than a reality, like a song hummed by a drunkard slumped in a gutter, such as the dark-faced Eskimo whom Brentford was trying hard not to look at.

The "Year's Musical Event," probably thanks to Linko's enthusiastic article, had drawn a substantial crowd on Great Pan Place, mostly hipsters but also quite a few rubberneckers, and Brentford wondered, not without melancholy, in which one of these categories he should be counted these days. Hoping that Sybil would not be spying incognito—but this was a rather early hour for her—he gently excused his way to the front of the crowd to see what was going on.

In the middle of Great Pan Place, surrounded by a gang of white-clad suffragettes dressed like the young woman who had handed him the flyer, a van was parked, mounted with blaring compressed-air amplifiers from which the four songs of Lilian Lenton's last recording were being played in a loop.

It was fairly distinct from what a toe-tapping Brentford re-membered from the Sandmovers. The electrified guitar still had that tense, clear-cut rhythmic urgency that was Lilian's hall-mark, but there was a darker, droning undercurrent to it that carried the song beyond the caffeined nervousness of the past. Her voice, also, was different. Lilian had replaced her former girlish nursery-rhyme mannerisms with a talk-over that seemed at first neutral but that became, as you listened to the lyrics, laden with a certain venomous tongue-in-cheek. However, it was the content that had undergone the most drastic change. If it remained allusive, a string of seemingly unrelated, enumerated words, the accumulation drew a picture that was, once deci-phered, unequivocal: "Destroy," said the song coldly, destroy everything.

But the subsequent tune seemed to explore a quite different ground. It was as urgent, but heavier, more dramatic, with wide sweeps of noisy guitar and spine-tingling accelerations. The lyr-ics, too, came as a shock: they were a translation of a famous Eskimo chant in which a dead hunter speaks through the voice of a shaman, telling of how he died in graphic, moving images that Lilian's less distant delivery underlined so powerfully that Brentford could almost feel the vermin in the hollow of his own collarbone. This was a daring addition to the genre, tak-ing a rather innocuous form toward a whole new dimension. But most of all, it was when you added or contrasted the two songs he'd heard so far that something happened: there was a message in them that was both as encrypted and as clear as the one in *A Blast on the Barren Land*, warning that the city would go nowhere fast if it forgot exactly where it was and whom it had been stolen from.

The two remaining songs were in a lighter vein but right on the pulse: one was about the boredom that went with the city's current undirected lifestyle—or that's how Brentford interpreted it; the other, playfully but painfully, riffed on the widening gap between poor and rich, breaking again with amazing ease what had been regarded as rather taboo. The whole recording, when you summed it up, reflected exactly what Brentford thought about the city: that the utopia was neither given nor granted, but, quite on the contrary, had to be defended and redefined.

The crowd, first silent and then bursting into applause and cheers as the music ended, may have had understood the same thing, or maybe not. John Linko, on the other side of the square, seemed especially rapt. Lilian, stepping forward under a wide-brimmed hat, saluted, surrounded by her band mates. Brentford was surprised to see how much she had changed: her eyes, which used to be slightly unfocused and teary from excessive sand consumption, were now piercing and determined; she had thinner lips and sunken cheeks and generally looked as if she had been sharpened on a grindstone. She was pretty, he thought, a blade to Sybil's flame.

Brentford could not resist buying a copy of the record from a cute suffragette whom, as she lifted her head under her slouch hat, he recognized and saluted as Jay, or Guinevere de Nudd, one of his friends from the now defunct School of Night. She was a mean little troublemaker, and seeing that she was involved in this was for Brentford further proof that there was some kind of false bottom to the "musical event of the year." But the crowd was pushing behind him and this was neither the time nor the place to discuss the matter with her. Thinking a bit too late that Sybil would not be too happy with a record by her rival, he decided to find a City Courier and have it brought to Gabriel as a gift.

The scene suddenly shifted, taking him by surprise. The suffragettes had suddenly pulled placards from the van and were brandishing them. Some were carrying drums, others brass instruments, forming a kind of marching band that set about crossing Great Pan Place, pushing great blasts of brazen sound into the sullen damp skies. Brentford, caught in the maelstrom of the moving crowd, could not at first make out the signs that were bobbing over the band. Or, more exactly, it took him some time to simply believe what he saw: THE POLE TO THE PEOPLE said one, WHITE & INUIT UNITE said another, FREE-DOM FOR FREEZELAND proclaimed a third. The crowd around him became hesitant, unsure of how to react: was this part of the promotional stunt? Was it a real revolt? Which one was the pretext for the other? The borderline was blurry, to be sure, but Brentford, having paid as much attention to the lyrics as he had, felt little doubt that he was witnessing an event with little or no antecedent, a feast of all firsts, as the Eskimos said, a piece of history in a city that had always strived to keep out of history, nay, a city whose very aim, as proved by the Seven Sleepers' decision to reverse Time and impose an "After Backward" calendar, was to avoid it at all costs.

Brentford followed the parade down the street as it opened for itself a way among the perplexed, disbelieving onlookers. He was now more or less elbowing his way through them, hoping to see more of the march as it went down toward the Chione Canal and the Boreas Bridge. As long as the cortege stayed in Venustown, with its long tradition of deviant carnival events, this would come off as nothing more than a curious little incident to be added to the local lore, but if it crossed the bridge and entered the city centre at Frislandia, it would become wholly different: a poletical event with unpredictable results.

Brentford stopped at a little booth where a red-hatted Courier, stomping his feet to avoid freezing, was waiting for deliveries to make or messages to carry, and gave him the record with Gabriel's address. Seeing people in these kinds of menial, low-wage jobs never failed to make Brentford bitter about the way things were heading (down, obviously), and finding them useful did not mitigate his feelings, either.

He tipped the man generously and hurried to rejoin the crowd, but as he reached the tail of the cortege, the march stopped, and even seemed to retreat, the brass instruments tilting back like wheat stalks under the wind. False notes were heard, and slogans turned to screams. Brentford made his way toward the front, more muscularly perhaps than his good upbringing authorized, and almost stumbled into the ongoing chaos.

A host of gentlemen in black frock coats and silk hats had interrupted the procession a few yards short of the bridge. Wedging dark, angular moves into the wavering whiteness of the march, they were trampling the drums, confiscating the horns, which they'd bent beyond repair, breaking over their thighs the signs that cracked like bones. Through their spats and shiny shoes, Brentford could make out, collapsed on the slimy cobblestones, the crumpled cape and kicking legs of Lilian Lenton, her feathered hat knocked across the pavement near his own feet.

He wanted to step in, without bothering about the cost of a fight with the Gentlemen of the Night, when a group of Navy Cadets, probably just out of a nearby brothel, but chivalrous by tradition if not by trade, came to the rescue, shoving and pushing the Gentlemen of the Night away from the women they were brutalizing. It was most unexpected, but the crowd welcomed it with cheers that only infuriated the dapper coppers all the more.

Brentford, as a former cadet, felt quite elated by this turna-round and could not resist doing his bit: he took a step toward Lilian, who had managed to get up, and seized her by her firm lean arms, not without a little thrill of tactile pleasure. Unfortu-nately, however, she immediately mistook his black Macfarlane for a Gentleman's uniform, her look shifting quickly from see-ing stars to cold-steel contempt. As he opened his mouth to say "nothing to fear," a cadet, who had made the same mistake as Lilian, hit Brentford with a neat punch on the chin that sent him reeling toward the spectators. The world took some time to oscillate back into place, and all that Brentford could see as soon as he was able to regain some control over his eyes was some Gentlemen of the Night carrying Lilian Lenton toward an ambulance aerosled that had just arrived from the other side of the Bridge.

He watched the ambulance go, stroking his chin with his gloved hand and checking on the tips of his fingers that he was not losing blood. A Gentleman of the Night flew by in front of him, crashing into the cheering crowd. As he had feared, the historic revolt that had enthused him so much a few minutes ago had reverted back to the trivial slapstick of a Venustown carnival brawl. He shook his head, his brain a painful tuning fork vibrating back to the right pitch.

CHAPTER XIV

Unwelcome Guests

●

O! Sleep it is a gentle thing
Beloved from pole to pole
Coleridge, *The Rime of the Ancient Mariner*

If there was a place that Gabriel liked as much as New Venice itself, it was his apartment on New Boree Street. Not that it was especially vast or comfortable. The lower level was occupied by a kitchen at one end and a greenhouse at the other, and both were equally neglected. The space between, with bare walls but floorboards copiously covered in a quilt of thick carpets, was sparsely furnished, just an enormous stove, a round table, and four upholstered chairs, a buffet, a pianorad, a phonograph, and, usually facing the hothouse, a worn-out, puffy burgundy velvet sofa that had seen some action and still more inaction.

At each side of the flat, two corkscrew staircases led to his favourite place, a horseshoe-shaped mezzanine whose walls were covered with bookshelves almost up to the ceiling.

Behind the fine wrought-iron railing that surrounded the mezzanine, a mammoth writing desk sat in the middle of the central platform, commanding a panoramic view of the whole flat; the rear part was occupied by a bathroom boasting a round tub, and a small but cosy bedroom whose ceiling displayed a crude map of the heavens: the stars were, in curious accordance with ancient Eskimo beliefs, little holes, but the only super- natural presence beyond them was the Electricity Fairy. Large windows framed with thick velvet curtains offered a vista of St- Brendan Bridge and the leaden Crozier Canal, and beyond that the small whitewashed houses of Ballymaclinton Harbour.

To the obsessively obsidional Gabriel, this was his Troy, where he would defend himself to the last. His books, lined up with a compact precision, were the battlement from which he would shoot the poisoned arrows of his wit. Needless to say, then, that he was disgusted when he came home to find the door ajar and his place occupied by the Nemesis Brothers, Sealtiel Wynne and Robert DeBrutus.

The plundering had begun. Books were strewn all over the floor, some open and some not. Wynne was plucking them off shelves, flipping through them and tossing them aside at full steam under the benevolent, if not affectionate, look of the Angel of the Law, who was sprawled across the displaced sofa. Discipline was slackening, noted Gabriel. That was what hap- pened when you were indulging your basest instincts. He knew something about that.

"Ah, Mr. d'Allier," said DeBrutus. "We were expecting you. I hope you do not mind our having preceded you. The concierge was so kind as not to let us wait in the cold. She has been very helpful. It really is a pearl that you have."

Gabriel said nothing, slowly assimilating the scene. He felt surprised, and a bit saddened, by his own detachment from it. Maybe it was the exhaustion. Maybe he was through judging them. They were dead men, as far as he was concerned. He just hoped that when they came to realize it, it would be slowly and painfully.

"Oh, and there was a City Courier who brought you a record," continued DeBrutus, displaying some pieces of broken shellac. "Unfortunately, there has been an accident. Mr. Wynne inadvertently sat on it. These things are so frail."

"My apologies. By a stroke of chance, it was only the new Lilian Lenton record," commented Wynne, lifting his eyes from a book. "Did you know she started a pro-Eskimo riot this morning? I am really surprised that a man of your standing would have such democratic tastes."

"It's not as if I had listened to it," said Gabriel gloomily.

Wynne threw the book aside and plucked off another one.

"We are really impressed by your library," he said.

"I am sorry it has given you so much work."

"Not at all. We were eager to explore it. You can't curb a man's appetite for knowledge, can you?"

"And your phantascopic collection is *rare*," added de Brutus, tugging at a spooled-off reel of celluloid that might have been Gabriel's collection of Bourne-Cantwell pornoperatic works. "Although as a lawyer, I would have difficulty defending it."

Gabriel suddenly understood what they were looking for, and tried to hide his concern. They were not exactly hot at the moment, but God forbid—or the Devil—or anyone—that they find it.

"Ahh!" said Wynne, slapping a page of what Gabriel recognized as the copy of *Phantastes* offered to him by his former lover Christine Cranberry, "'Rocket' and 'Pocket'! This is not exactly unknown to me, is it?"

"I read books, you read my mind, so you read my books too," said Gabriel, wearily, thinking Wynne was lucky not to be reading his mind right now.

"And I suppose this is... Flap?" added Wynne, showing Gabriel a dedicated sepia photograph of Christine in a fairy outfit that served as bookmark.

Gabriel said nothing. On his Old Testament scales, the retaliation level went up from sevenfold to tenfold for this single familiarity. Unaware of or indifferent to this, Wynne plunged back into the book, or feigned to do so.

"Since we're talking about your acquaintances, how is Mr. Orsini, these days?"

"He's well enough, I guess."

"Did your conversation over breakfast interest him?"

"I'd hate to think it did not," Gabriel said, though he had to admit that he hadn't been exactly dazzling this morning.

"Should we suppose that you talked about our little private chat at the Hotel de Police?"

"We usually don't stoop that low."

Wynne threw the book aside and took one step toward Gabriel, towering above him in a threatening attitude.

"Do I detect a certain lack of respect, Mr. d'Allier?"

"Do I detect a certain lack of self-control?" said Gabriel, quavering at his own insolence.

"Tsk, tsk, gentlemen, please..." said DeBrutus. "This is no way to behave. Remember you are here on a mission, Mr. Wynne, and not to tease my dear client."

"Excuse us, Mr. DeBrutus. Now that you mention it, there is something I would like *very much* to show to Mr. d'Allier."

He rummaged through the scattered books and seized one, brandishing it in front of Gabriel as if it were the Tables of the Law. It was a copy of *A Blast on the Barren Land*. Gabriel knew instantly that it wasn't his, which had a different binding. He was not, however, going to explain that to Wynne.

"Oh! You brought me a book. How generous and thoughtful of you."

"You do not recognize it?" said Wynne venomously.

Gabriel had a flash, one of those reflexes that one's body
and brain work out automatically in times of utter exhaustion.
He saw himself browsing that very book in the Hôtel de Police,
spotting something on the first page.

"I do indeed. It looks a lot like the same copy you showed
me last week."

"How can you be so sure?"

"Just check the ex-libris. It is different from mine, as you
must know by now."

He was sure, or took the chance, that Wynne had not
thought of counterfeiting the ex-libris before planting the book.
It would have been the final "proof," in *their* rather generous
definition of what could pass as evidence. But Wynne was angry, in a hurry, under pressure from the Council, or simply not
bookish enough to care for such details. Gabriel could read it in
his eyes and in DeBrutus's, as they glanced at each other. And
more importantly, it meant they had not found *his* copy yet.
Gabriel was not exactly disappointed in Wynne, but this was a
botched job if he ever saw one.

Wynne sighed.

Gabriel tried to keep his victory modest, but it warmed his
plexus with a pleasant glow. They had failed first to unlock his
mind and now in tampering with his library. It reinforced some
irrational belief in the value of his lifestyle, even if that was
presently going to the dogs like a rotten piece of ring seal.

"Do not worry about the mess. I'll clean it up myself. See
you later," he said simply, stepping back to free the passage to
the front door, which had remained open.

Wynne fetched his greatcoat and hat without a word, while
DeBrutus pandiculated on the sofa, trying to look unconcerned.
Gabriel did not even feel hateful any more; he was merely in

that state where a man would trade Heaven for a darkened room and pair of clean sheets.

His visitors eventually shuffled moodily toward the door. Wynne, just before going out, pointed his cane at Gabriel, almost touching his breast. Gabriel thought of the sword that was sheathed inside.

"There will be no third time, Mr. d'Allier."

"I should hope not," said Gabriel.

As soon as he had heard them leave the building, he hurried toward the book's hiding place, inside the pianorad. It had been found, unlocked and rummaged through. The book had disappeared and, unless something was escaping him completely, had already been missing when the Gentlemen had searched there. Gabriel could not figure out why and was too tired even to try. Stella? But he had not told Stella about the book, having had other fish to fry, or as the French side of his mind put it, other cats to whip. He went toward the bed, his mind a foggy blank, and fell on his face, his boots still on his feet.

That was when he heard a knock on the door.

He tried to ignore it but it stabbed on, murdering his sleep. He finally stumbled to the door, barely awake, his brain sideways in his skull, promising himself to strangle the concierge if it was she. But it wasn't. Instead Gabriel saw in front of him a tall, thin man dressed in a dirty black coat, with a pointy beard, *very* bad skin, and a parcel tucked under his arm.

"Hello," the man said in a conspiratorial whisper that revealed a thick Russian accent. "I am Mikhail Mikhailovitch Mugrabin. I have come to bring back your book."

"Book?" asked Gabriel in a thick voice.

Mugrabin looked all around suspiciously.

"The one you so kindly lent me," he eventually murmured with a wink.

Gabriel, without giving it much thought, moved away from the door to let the man inside. The mysterious visitor strode into the room and pivoted on his heels, tearing the parcel to shreds and pulling out Gabriel's own copy of *A Blast on the Barren Land*.

"Excellent book. A bit reformist for my tastes. But you have to start somewhere," he said, with a grimace that would have been comical if his skin had not been so awfully wrinkled and red.

Gabriel could not believe what he saw. He was astonished—not just by the return of his book, but also by this character who looked as if someone had crudely glued half of Dostoyevsky to half of Rasputin. He was like a policeman's dream of a Russian anarchist, or perhaps more like a policeman's impersonation of one. They had not been long to send a replacement for Wynne, he surmised. But the provocation was a bit gross.

"I did not lend you this book, did I?" said Gabriel, who was not going to admit anything.

"Your girlfriend did," said Mugrabin. He leaned forward, his ugly mouth close to Gabriel's ear. "Charming girl, by the way. You're a very lucky man. What are your opinions about free love? I hope they are as liberal as hers."

Gabriel must have made a face. Mugrabin burst out in a forced laugh, as if trying to sound insane, or so it seemed to Gabriel.

"Hahahaha!!! I was joking!!! Of course!!!"

He pirouetted and launched himself onto the sofa with a sigh of ease.

"Thanks for the coffee!" he howled as if Gabriel were already in the kitchen.

Some automated part of Gabriel actually went there and prepared two cups of coffee. When he came back to the living room, Mugrabin had found the liquor bar and was drinking vodka directly from the bottle.

"Nothing like a drop of it in the coffee!" he hollered, wiping his mouth with his sleeve.

Gabriel handed a cup to Mugrabin, noticing he was missing the last two fingers on his gloved right hand.

"Little accident," Mugrabin explained, knocking his right eye with the spoon, so that Gabriel could hear the little dull glassy thud it made. "I also have metal pins all along my right leg. And a brass plate in my skull." He took off his hat and bowed. His sparse fair hair was combed across his head but Gabriel could see more of the plate that he wanted to. Mugrabin knocked on that with the spoon as well. "Very uncomfortable here. Because of the frost. But these things can happen when you're a chemist."

Then, suddenly, he shifted to a more serious mood:

"Suffering, Mr. d'Allier, is part of the cause. We suffer in our flesh to pay for the pain we inflict on the enemies of mankind."

"Who sends you?" Gabriel managed to ask between two yawns.

"My story is a rather long one," said Mugrabin, as if that answered the question. "You care for a cigarette?"

Gabriel craned his neck, trying to decipher the Cyrillic lettering on the packet.

"Lacto," said Mugrabin, squeezing the cardboard tip before putting it in his mouth. "Hard to find here, believe me," he added as he helped himself with one-handed dexterity from a matchbox that bore a drawing of a revolver.

Gabriel declined (his code of honour forbade him to deprive a man of cigarettes that were "hard to find"), but Mugrabin went on to savour his silently for a long time, his good eye lazily following the smoke as it drifted across the room, while his host sat through what he had decided was a nightmare.

"We have to kill to put an end to all killing," Mugrabin said dreamily, as if talking to himself. He nodded his head, lost in thought, as if it were a particularly worthy piece of wisdom that he had just proffered.

"I lost my faith before I lost my virginity," he kept on, for reasons that eluded Gabriel. "I suppose it's the same thing anyway."

He rambled on. Between narcoleptic fits, Gabriel vaguely heard, as a hum, Mugrabin's story as it unrolled its slimy meanderings. As was to be expected from a man with a supposedly long habit of clandestinity and false identity, his outpouring soon took on the proportions of a flood.

From what Gabriel could piece together, he understood that Mugrabin had been born among *Doukhobors* ("spirit-wrestlers," as Mugrabin translated it), a community of egalitarian peasants who rejected any secular or spiritual authority except for the Bible. Mugrabin's people lived in the Ganja protectorate, somewhere in Transcaucasia. Such radical Christians are always especially abhorrent to their lukewarm, mainstream co-religionists, and the *Doukhobors* were duly persecuted, but they refused to use violence even to defend themselves, and as a way of resisting the temptation to do so had destroyed all their weapons. "When I saw my parents take a beating from a *sotnia* of Cossacks," explained Mugrabin, "I totally lost any respect I had for them. From that day onward I was finished with family and any kind of authority."

He had fled to Baku, the nearest capital, a desolate, dusty, dreary jumble of derricks and minarets, of European streets, Persian bazaars, Tartar slums and wastelands—one of the most god-forsaken and violent cities in the world. "There's a place there, not far from the city, Ateshgyakh, it's called. It looks like a fort, but is a Zoroastrian temple. An eternal flame burns from the ground right in the middle of it. This is where I pledged myself to destruction by fire," Mugrabin said, with intensity. "A sword of flame may defend Eden. A sword of flame will regain it," he added, not without grandeur, and something in Gabriel—but he was tired—refused to find that as ridiculous as it was.

Mugrabin had then found work in the sulphuric acid factories and had trained himself as a chemist, quickly joining the thriving anarcho-communist movement. He had been part, he said proudly, of the most radical group of them all, the *Chernoye Znamya*—the Black Banner. They were the ones who put the *Baku* in Bakunin, he said with a roar of laughter, though Gabriel supposed it was hardly the first time he had cracked that joke. The Black Banner had started by murdering some strike-breaking capitalists but had soon diversified their activities to include holds-up and "ex's" (expropriations, Gabriel understood), attacking armouries and police stations, dynamiting restaurants and factories, shooting on sight or fighting in pitched battle the pharaohs—as they called the police—and detectives. They were, Mugrabin explained, *bezmotivny*, motiveless terrorists, exercising violence for violence's sake, just to purify the old world in the flames. "It was a great life. You would need a considerable amount of alcohol to imitate the intoxication of walking around with dynamite in your pockets, the detonator clicking as you walk."

Which was how, as it turned out, Mugrabin had exploded in his room one day, while heating mercury fulminate to make a blasting cap. A good portion of him had gone to Heaven or Hell; he would never know. What was left was cared for in a hospital he then managed to escape from. Death could well be the sister of Liberty, but for all his courting of the first, Mugrabin had eloped with the second, younger one. But for the honeymoon he'd had to flee Russia. Baku was done with, anyway. Anarchy was not on the front page anymore. The suppression of the 1905 revolution had taken its toll, and now all the rage was about Tartars massacring Armenians in racial riots. The vandalized Bibi Eybat oil wells burned non-stop in the night, in true Zoroastrian fashion. He regretted that he had not done it.

It was his luck that *Doukhobors* were at the time leaving the country for Canada in massive numbers, on a trip that was partly funded by Tolstoy's royalties. Relatives of Mugrabin and men from the Anarchist Red Cross smuggled him aboard one of the ships. He eventually found himself in the Good Spirit Lake colony (its real name was Devil's Lake, but this clearly would not do) located in Canada's Northwest Territories, in a village that bore the same name as his childhood home and looked uncannily like it.

He eventually emigrated with others to a place called Brilliant in British Columbia, where *Doukhobor*s soon started to disagree over their degree of assimilation and their faithfulness to the old cause. Of course, Mugrabin joined the most radical branch, the Svobodniki, or Freedomites, though the sight of his scarred, sewn-up body during the naked protests they favoured did not always uplift the demonstrators. He came in handier when, at his own incenting, the Svobodniki turned to arson and bombing, destroying schools and transportation systems but also their own properties and money, all of this done in the nude. "Burning Money is truly exhilarating. And burning it naked is quite Edenic," explained Mugrabin happily. "If you really want to drive people crazy, you should try it. Guaranteed or the ashes of your money back." Mugrabin was in a good humour now. Obviously, his mood swings worked on a ten-second cycle.

The Canadian authorities got tired of his antics and he soon had to seek other, even less benevolent, climes. How he arrived in New Venice he would not exactly reveal, but he maintained he had found a home here, though not in the Novo-Arkhangelsk district, which was swarming with Bolshevik flies. It was a moral home, rather.

"The Eskimos. They remind me of us. The equality, how they share everything. This is how human beings should live, don't you think? The *True Community*. I should really like to meet the author of this book."

If Gabriel had been not unpleasantly lulled so far, this slapped him awake. His suspicion that Mugrabin was another policemen in (black) sheep's clothing returned forcefully. The story was too good to be true, and calculated to fit some of Gabriel's pet interests, even if those interests were purely theoretical. For people like Gabriel, whose social status was going down the drain, radical politics was the cheapest commodity there was and a good thumb to suck on during daydreams. He knew that well, and kept it to the level of *motiveless* fascination.

"I do not know him," lied Gabriel.

"That's not what the dedication suggests," said Mugrabin, patting the book.

"Are you a professional policeman or just an informer?"

Mugrabin went mad at this. Jumping to his feet and advancing threateningly, he flourished a Nagant gun that made Gabriel shiver as it was agitated under his nose. "If there is one thing that would give me as much pleasure as killing a cop," howled Mugrabin, his face even more noticeably red, "it is killing someone who calls me a cop. I may not look like it but I have some self-respect, you see."

"I'm sorry if I was mistaken," said Gabriel grimly, as he was more than fed up with people menacing him. "I see more policemen than I would like to these days."

"Ah, who doesn't?" said Mugrabin, who now settled down quickly. "It makes my heart bleed that you do not trust me. What can I do to prove my friendship to you? Oh! I know. What if those two pigs I have seen going out of your building had an accident? You know, some little explosion of their Bollée sled car?"

"I do not know much about Russian terrorism, but enough to know that some infiltrated agents do no hesitate to kill policemen or even state ministers."

Mugrabin laughed at this.

"Those SR clowns, really! They were too naïve with that Azev thing. I am an anarchist, Mr. d'Allier. I live on highly different moral grounds."

"I'm sure of that."

Mugrabin nodded his head.

"I admire your loyalty, to speak frankly. I would even have been disappointed in you if you had told me who wrote that book. Imagine it as a test. We will contact you, and in the meantime, if you're in need, you will find us."

"Us?"

"It's more impressive when put that way, isn't it?" said Mugrabin with a smile that revealed his ceramic teeth.

And with that he suddenly dashed toward the door, with, Gabriel noticed, the vodka bottle bulging in his coat pocket.

"Drink to my health, Mr. Mugrabin."

"I certainly will do that. I hope it will be more beneficial to yours that it is to mine," he chuckled while putting on his rubbers. "I'm not like this character in one of our greatest novels, who thinks he should have gone to the North Pole because he had the *vin mauvais* and wanted to get rid of the habit."

Gabriel nodded, though the reference eluded him. However, he would have plenty of time to look through his books while tidying up the mess.

"Who sent you?" he asked again, his head whirling with fatigue.

"You'll know. Or you won't. *Da svidania*."

Gabriel could sleep a little at last, and soon found himself in a strange dream. It was about a polar expedition that was abandoning ships (though the ships seemed to be inside a gigantic cavern or underground cave). The sailors and officers were filling up trunks and crates, not with food or any kind of gear, but with the icicles dangling from the masts and ropes, as if they thought these were precious diamonds and did not realize they would melt inside their crates.

When he woke up, night had fallen again, and his oozing brain seemed stuck to the pillow. What had awakened him was not the dream but a pulsating void he could feel in himself and identified as the absence of Stella. It had been nagging him all day, and as soon as he had allowed himself to unwind, it had come back to the surface and it was now punching holes in his guts with its clenched little fists. His brain lit up like a Stellarama, repeating endlessly the same recorded loops of memories and fantasies. What he was doing here, away from her, he could no longer understand. The stars above his head were a cruel mockery compared to her celestial tattoo.

He got up, and turning on the lights descended drowsily into the maelstrom of his scattered books. The apartment had been desecrated and seemed to have lost all its power to attract or retain him. He did not feel like sorting things out or cleaning up. It simply disgusted him, like finding a stranger's hair in one's ice cream. The only thing that did not revolt him was the idea of spooning naked against Stella and holding her in his arms, his face buried in whatever horoscope her back would trace for him.

He returned upstairs to fill a Poirier packsack with clothes and toiletries, a bit haphazardly, and gathered all the money he could find. Just before leaving, in a last flash of lucidity, he realized that at this very moment Stella would still be at the Trilby Temple for tonight's show with that magician of hers. While reflecting that he thus still had some time on his desperately empty hands before meeting her, he tripped on a book and recognized the Sommer edition of the Arthurian romances. Getting down on one knee, he turned over the book to look at it. It was about Lancelot. *Le chevalier a la charrette* who had preferred his love to his honour. Of course. Gabriel relished the coincidence but was not that surprised; more astonishing things had happened. Books knew more than you did, as a rule. But who had told him about Lancelot today? He remembered Brentford's story. The dead woman in a coffin on a sled. Now that he was the Knight of the Cart for good, he might as well spend the remaining hours on that quest. With a little luck it would distract his mind and belly from Stella, while he waited to see her again.

He left the flat, and in New Borée Street jumped into the first eastward jitney taxsleigh that happened to cross his path, not knowing when he would come back, wondering if he ever would.

CHAPTER XV

The Blazing Building

•

"You are in a spot," said a friend, who chanced to
be near at hand, "which occupies, in the world of fancy,
the same position which the Bourse, the Rialto, and the
Exchange, do in the commercial world."
Nathaniel Hawthorne, *The Hall of Fantasy*, 1843

The Blazing Building, home to the Council of Seven,
was located at the end of the Cavendish Canal. Its
golden dome, which always seemed freshly polished,
had a peculiarly blinding, almost white sheen that seemed to
radiate from itself rather than from the reflected daylight. It
was especially spectacular when it contrasted—as was now the
case— with a dark cloudy backdrop of afternoon skies that
looked like an emanation from the black airship above.

"Snow clouds," thought Brentford, as his gondola, crunching pancakes of thin ice, approached the mooring post. He was

paying no small amount of attention to meteorology these days, as if some part of his mind were always computing, in a more or less idle way, the chances of his making it to the pole by way of ice yacht. It also diverted his thoughts, doubtlessly, from the gnawing concerns of city poletics. But as he jumped onto the embankment and headed toward the colonnade that marked the entrance, he readied himself to face them again.

Though it was not his first visit to the Blazing Building, such occasions were sufficiently rare to keep him in awe, even if he did not like to admit it. Behind the rather sober, classically designed exterior, which paled a little in comparison with, for instance, the Arctic Administration Building, the place displayed a grandeur and a certain craziness that was as pure an expression of New Venetian spirit as one could hope to meet.

The entrance archway opened onto the vast rotunda of Hyperboree Hall. Its floor was a circular map of the polar regions, where the Arctic seas were made of white marble and the islands were cut-out slabs of polished granite decorated with little figures in minute mosaics, drawn, if Brentford remembered correctly, from the Olaus Magnus and Nicolo Zeno depictions of the North. It mixed almost accurate cartography with phantom islands, mythological monsters, and imaginary people, among whom New Venetians were prone and proud to count themselves.

In the very center of the Hall, the North Pole was represented by a fountain rising from a basin of snowflake obsidian; its dangling stalactites, kept constantly frozen, were sculpted in the shapes of Northern divinities from different traditions. Through the stained-glass openings in the base of the lofty dome overhead, various shades of light fell on the translucent fountain to simulate, even by day, the colours of the Northern Lights.

The dome itself, supported by white pillars, was of jet-black jasper encrusted with diamond stars and silver filigree work that

drew a map of the night skies centred on Polaris and the Great
Bear. A motto ran around its rim in both Greek and English
versions: OVER THE WHOLE SEA TO THE ENDS OF THE EARTH
AND TO THE SOURCES OF NIGHT AND TO THE UNFOLDINGS OF
HEAVEN AND TO THE ANCIENT GARDEN OF PHOEBUS.

Between the pillars, toward the rear, stood twelve tall marble statues of polar explorers, their eyes fixed firmly on the
fountain, their stone fingers pointing toward it. Their pedestals
were ornate with episodes that somewhat belied the noble demeanour of the heroes: Barents agonizing, surrounded by his
men; the abandoned Henry Hudson adrift in his small craft;
the discovery by Rae of the infamous Franklin's expedition life-
boat; Hall half rising from his bed in the throes of poisoning;
the starving Greely sentencing the thief Charles Buck Henry to
death; Melville finding in the snow the protruding arm of De
Long; Andrée frozen within the folds of his useless balloon; Dr.
Svensen putting a rifle to his own head while Sverdrup ran to
stop him in vain; Dr. Dedrick amputating Peary's toes; Ross
Marvin shot in the back by his Eskimo guide; Fitzhugh Green
shooting his Eskimo guide in the back—these were among the
many incidents recalling the sacrifices and villainies that had
always accompanied the conquest as faithfully as a shadow,
and all were depicted in a ghastly realism that did not exactly
encourage Brentford to go to Helen's rendezvous.

Behind those statues were mirrored doors that led to the
various parts of the building. The Council Cabinet's was opposite the entrance archway, and this was where Brentford was introduced by one of the gigantic Varangian guards of the Council of Seven's Security Company, who wore the usual uniform
of figure-eight ruff, black doublet and black and white striped
pluderhosen and held a halberd in his enormous hand.

A flight of stairs led to a corridor down which an icy
draught, strong as an upwind gale, was blowing, probably,

thought Brentford, as a reminder of the hardships of going *there*. And yet, cold as he suddenly felt, he nonetheless did not hate the idea. He was, after all, as much a New Venetian as the Councillors were, and could relate rather easily to some of their notions and actions—as long, at least, as they concerned interior decoration.

As he hurried, head to wind, through the corridor, he could perceive rooms whose open doors revealed the strangest scenes, all intended to evoke memories of past events and important symbols in the dreamlike manner of a Memory palace. To the untrained eye, these scenes appeared more like a jumble of absurd props and kitschy figures. On his right, for instance, a huge stuffed seal with wings was leaving the imprint of his greasy muzzle against a snow-white sheet held by a scantily clad marble woman (oh yes, Brentford thought, this must be the *Seal* of the City), while on his left an automated gentleman in medieval garb repeatedly plunged a pointed flag into the heart of a supine Viking (this one left Brentford totally clueless).

The corridor ended at a huge black double door, which an usher pushed open, with an effort that was painful to behold, just enough to let Brentford wriggle himself in. This was the waiting room, if one was to judge by the mosaic clock that decorated the floor, with its black stone hands pointed toward a perpetual midnight.

Mason was already there, sitting on a sofa, impatiently tapping his fingers on a satchel. Brentford came up to him, offering a hand whose fingers the captain-general observed suspiciously. He finally got up and accepted the offer.

"I have to congratulate you," said Brentford, whose first impulse with Mason was always to tease him mildly, as if that were the only way he could express a sympathy he did not quite want to surrender to, while, nevertheless, he tried to create some complicity between them.

"What for?" asked Mason, warily.

"You may not know it, but the Navy Cadets have proved as chivalrous this morning as one could expect them to be."

"I'd say *more* than *some* could expect them to be," said Mason with a frown. "I just got the news myself. I'm surprised you're in the know."

"I was there. Some mysterious Gentlemen were brutalizing a girl."

"I doubt a Gentleman would do such a thing."

"Some Gentlemen have a dark, if not nocturnal, side, obviously. Your men performed honourably."

"I will be asked to punish them, though," Mason said, indicating the Council's Cabinet door.

"They did not cause the trouble. They didn't start it, at least."

"I heard there was a riot."

"There was a demonstration, which I think is different. It was peaceful until it was interrupted."

Mason seemed to be thinking hard about it.

"What sort of demonstration?"

"Hmm... A new kind. It looked poetical at first but then became rather poletical."

"And my men defended it?"

"I have been a cadet myself. Unless things have changed considerably, I think defending the fair sex was their only concern."

Mason stared at Brentford, hesitating to speak, but finally let go.

"Would you say so in front of the Council?"

"I have no reason to lie to them."

"And of course, I could take a more moderate view on that hunting matter."

Brentford raised his hand.

"I have no doubt about your honesty."

Mason nodded, which Brentford interpreted as a reluctant "Thank you."

The Council of Seven could certainly be criticized, or so thought Brentford, on many levels. But they understood that governing was not so much about words, nor even about actions, as about images, and that made them powerful.

The Meeting Room was well designed to put those called before them in awe. The room was as beautiful as could be, with its black marble floor, mother-of-pearl ceiling, and ancient geographical and astronomical maps circling the walls. It was at the long table around which discussion took place that the nightmare began.

At their end of the table, the members of the Council sat alternately with the wax figures of the Seven Sleepers who had founded the city. This was meant first as a way to mark their allegiance to the founders, but also as a sign of their own uncontested legitimacy, as if they were finishing the sentences or completing the moves started by the frozen effigies, who all directed their fixed, transfixing looks toward the guests.

The seven members of the Council were almost as motionless, croaking among themselves like a murder of crows and letting their spokesman pronounce the conclusions they reached. From where he sat, Brentford could barely distinguish these black-clad, balding men from one another, all the less so since he had seldom seen them together: ritual required that they take turns when it came to public appearances, each one always on the day of the week for which he had been nicknamed.

Bailiff-Baron Brainveil was the one Brentford had seen the most often, the longest-standing member and already an un-

pleasant old man when Brentford was a youngster. The tall
one, on his left, must be the severe Bornhagen. Froideville was
next, a thin moustachioed scientist Brentford's father was always complaining about. Then came the eggheaded De Witt,
who was also the head of the Gentlemen of the Night, followed
by the bearded Imruzudov, who was all the more dreaded because nobody knew what his business was. The remaining two,
then, must be Houndsfield, the stout so-called economist, and
the wiry Auchincloss, who was in charge of military affairs.
The Spokesman for the Seven was Philip Surville, who had
married—and recently divorced—Seraphine Le Serf, Brentford's
adolescent sweetheart.

Sitting alongside Brentford and Mason at their uncomfortable end of the table was another man who was already in
discussion with the council when they arrived. He turned out to
be Peterswarden, the anthropologist and director of the Northwestern Administration for Native Affairs, and the man behind
the Inuit People's Ice Palace, a lanky, knotty, white-haired man
whose love of the Inuit was so strong it apparently entailed
leaving them to their own devices, as if they would rather die
than be corrupted by the white men. Peterswarden was, for instance, adamant that they should not be granted citizenship.

"We will not, unfortunately, have the pleasure of hearing
the Eskimo delegation from Flagler Fjord," announced Surville,
with a certain streak of satisfaction that irked Brentford immediately—though whatever Surville might say was likely to irk
Brentford.

"Mr. Peterswarden has informed us," he continued, "that
they were caught red-handed stealing some precious objects at
the Inuit People's Ice Palace and are presently being detained by
the authorities."

Brainveil whispered something in Surville's ear.

"Needless to say," added Surville, fixing his gaze on Brentford, "this does not incline the Council to consider their request

about the hunting quotas with all the equanimity it was previously very willing to show."

Brentford and Mason exchanged glances, while Peterswarden raised his hand to speak.

"It has certainly caused turmoil," said Peterswarden after Surville, with a mechanical nod, had granted him permission to speak. "Not so much because of the act itself, which is likely to happen with people as curious and spontaneous as our Inuit friends are, but because our aboriginal employees have naturally but thoughtlessly taken sides with their own kind, and this a few days away from the opening, at a time when we need them to fully participate in presenting their own rich and fascinating culture to the public."

It was Imruzudov, this time, who spoke through Surville.

"The Council suggests that, in the first place, these persons should not have been allowed on the premises. It is your duty, not to mention very much in your interest, to make sure that the dissenting employees will no longer cause delay in the realization of a project which is, as you know, dear to the Council."

"I understand," said Peterswarden, in a voice that trembled slightly, "and I thank the Council for its concern."

"You are still invited to repeat to Mr. Brentford Orsini and Captain-General Frank Mason what you have just told us about the hunting quotas," said Surville, on his own initiative this time.

"Oh..." said Peterswarden, with visible relief, as if he were, now, treading on thicker ice. Brentford could guess that whatever he said, or recited, given the present circumstances, would be a good indication of where the Council stood on that matter.

"I was humbly advising the Council to stick to the current policy. The wilderness Inughuit should be as separated from us as possible, in order to ensure their autonomy, especially as to what regards their subsistence. They have different needs and different ways of satisfying them. Thanks to their abilities, they can hunt in the remotest areas where we are not fit to thrive, if you will allow me to say so. Getting them to hunt for us, even for a payment in kind, will make them our servants instead of the free people they are and deserve to be. I also wish to recall to the Council that they receive, thanks to its own wisdom, a limited number of munitions sufficient for their own survival and that, in their own interest, it was deemed unsound to give them more. This way, we hope to save these peace-loving people from the misuse of firearms so often demonstrated, I regret to say, in our so-called advanced culture."

The Council nodded their heads in unison like a bunch of string puppets held by a single fist. Given the recent photographs of mysterious Inuit carrying rifles, it was an argument that could not but go straight to their old dried hearts.

"Mr. Orsini?" said Surville.

Brentford chose his words carefully, in order not to sound like an excerpt from *A Blast on the Barren Land.*

"I can only agree with Mr. Peterswarden's solicitude toward the Eskimos. I am not an expert on the question, as he is, but I think that if we regard our island as the Subtle Army's hunting grounds, our use of rifles will deplete the game beyond our actual needs and force the Eskimos to go hunting farther away and for a longer time, which will in part render meaningless the Council's own efforts to sedentarize them. I also thought that they could benefit from the Greenhouse products in return for their hunt, which also would improve their diet."

"They have always had a diet adequate to their existence. They are hunters, not farmers!" protested Peterswarden, without asking permission to speak. This rebuttal ulcerated Brentford all the more in that he had on occasion said the very same things himself. It is strange how one's ideas can sometimes sound loathsome in someone else's mouth.

"Captain-General?" said Surville, dismissing Peterswarden's remark with a little gesture of the hand.

Mason seemed embarrassed in a way that Brentford had never seen before. The Lenton "riot" was no doubt on his mind and he was probably looking for a way to ingratiate his men with the Council without opposing Brentford, whose help he thought he needed right now.

"Hunting has always been part and parcel of military activities in the Arctic regions, though often, to be honest, it has been done in cooperation with the Eskimos. I consider that beyond the question of food supply in time of peace, my men should be prepared and trained to live off the land when they are in operation, which could be well the case sooner or later, given the present circumstances. I nevertheless understand that it should be limited so as not to endanger the Native way of life."

De Witt poured some words into Surville's ears, which were not long in coming forth from the spokesperson's mouth.

"The Council suggests that your men, beyond all technical considerations, should indeed get more exercise. They have been found to be rather idle and nervous lately. Maybe the city air does not suit them. The Navy Cadets especially *should* hunt other game than peaceful citizens."

Mason cleared his throat.

"I present all due apologies to the Council. There has been a misunderstanding. From my information, my men were only trying to defend a lady who had by accident fallen on the ground."

Once more De Witt ventriloquized his dummy.

"The Council reminds you that its own collaborators are perfectly entitled and able to help citizens when they are estimated to be in danger. It is the local rule that the military should not in any case intervene in civic affairs. The Council would hate to have to take the occasion of a public trial to remind the military authority of this."

Mason's face had become perfectly inscrutable. Brentford knew enough about soldiers to be sure that it was a mistake to humble one in front of civilians. They might force Mason into some sort of submission, but they would lose his respect for good. Brentford cued in, hoping his intervention would throw the Council a bit off balance and bring Mason a little further onto his side. He raised his hand, and Surville, although frowning, nodded his approbation.

"According to firsthand accounts I happened to hear," said Brentford, "it was very much a mistake, indeed. The Cadets actually did not recognize persons they thought were aggressors as defenders of the law."

Brainveil leaned toward his human microphone.

"Mistakes and accidents can happen. But these tend to have a pattern or a common origin that the Council, in spite of its leniency, can no longer ignore. Certain ideas are currently being circulated through the city, criticizing the current state of affairs and advocating a community with the Natives, in a way that is most contemptuous of their differences from us, as Mr. Peterswarden would be glad to confirm for you. A certain book, in particular, is said to exert a bad influence over the weakest minds, such as that of Ms. Lenton, as she now calls herself, and her gang of suffragettes."

It was now Brentford who sat unmoving on his chair, under Mason's scrutiny.

Surville kept on, while his eyes, the Councillors', and the wax Sleepers' all fixed themselves on Brentford, "The Council would like very much to exonerate the Subtle Army, as well as, it may add, the Administration, of any suspected support for the said theories. The Council would therefore appreciate total and open collaboration from all parties. Regarding the hunting quotas, it is, alas, not possible, in the current situation, to give satisfaction to the Flagler Fjord Eskimos. Since you care so much, and rightly so, for our food autonomy, Mr. Orsini, you will find it agreeable that the Subtle Army contributes to it in the form of a planned, reasonable hunting campaign. And you will find it convenient, Captain-General, that the hunting be trusted to the Navy Cadets as a permanent mission, so that they can show their utility and dedication to the City. The Council has spoken."

Mason had stayed with the Seven to review the details of the "campaign." Brentford had carefully avoided Peterswarden on the way out and, the boreal draught on his back chilling him to the bone, hurried back toward the hall, from which he could see that the night had already fallen. He was angry at the way things had turned out. His intervention had been useless to Mason and done nothing but strengthen the Council's suspicion of himself. As to the final decision, it had been, as usual, nothing but a sadistic show of strength, and if it ever hid some darker agenda, that would probably be more of the same.

It wasn't until he was in the hall that he managed to calm down. He walked to the fountain across the marble floor. This was at least one place where he could go to the pole. He watched the fountain as the coloured lights played pleasantly through it, but it was only when he spotted Helen's profile among the stalactites that he finally felt better.

CHAPTER XVI

The Hollow Earth

●

*Why, poor man, have you left the light of day
and come down to visit the dead in this sad place?*
Homer, *The Odyssey*

I t was dark, and cold. A blizzard had started to blow from the north, forcing its way through the Air Architecture, and though this had blunted it a bit, it was now bellowing and whirling around Gabriel as he hurried toward the low, circular Fisheries Building that housed the Septentrional Scavenging and Sewerage Service. Bowed over, he looked like a hounded man, which he was, after all: he felt that were he to look back at his own shadow, he would discover it had turned into Wynne's. He could still feel his yearning for Stella burrowing relentlessly in his stomach, but it was now blended with apprehension over having to meet the Scavengers, whom New Venetians avoided almost superstitiously. Nothing, of course, was forcing him to do so, but his growing curiosity about the

171 * Jean-Christophe Valtat

mysterious dead woman, and the possibility that she could have something to do with him, made this visit seem the best way to waste the time he could not pass with Stella, as well as his last chance to feel that he was not entirely reduced to a flayed, writhing mass of longing and love.

Two Scavengers were loitering in front of the Fisheries, seemingly waiting for their shift to start (there had been no further rumours about a strike), but more likely guarding the place from prying eyes. Since their masks hindered them from smoking, they passed back and forth a small bottle of something they sniffed at through their long white beaks. They stiffened as Gabriel approached, and he felt grateful to Brentford for having confided to him, for use if he ever "got into trouble," the secret word that would gain him a modicum of attention from them and, hopefully, entrance to the Fisheries. He advanced toward the guards, a little too close for his comfort, his hands visible and well apart.

"Ring around the rosies," he whispered, feeling ridiculous, faintly afraid of becoming the butt of some tasteless joke.

The Scavengers looked at each other, then back at him. Observing no further reaction, Gabriel felt he had to explain himself.

"I've been sent by Brentford Orsini," he said, stretching the truth a little to fit the situation. "About a dead woman."

The Scavengers did not answer, but one of them turned and went back into the Fisheries, while the other stood by, looking indifferent. They were working hard at their own myth, Gabriel could tell, but then, as much could be said about everyone in New Venice.

A third "plague doctor" came out and examined Gabriel for a long time through the glass beads that hid his eyes.

"Pocketful of posies," the Scavenger eventually grumbled in a cavernous voice, while he gestured for Gabriel to come inside. The place was known to be harder to get into than the trendiest club in town, and it was almost with an insider's pride that the not quite clubbable Gabriel followed the square, faintly smelly black oilcloth silhouette.

"Mr. Orsini's friends are our friends," said the man in a strong, hoarse accent, leading Gabriel through the entrance. "My people call me Blankbate."

The name was well known to Gabriel. Brentford had described the man, whose face he had never seen, as the "ganger" of the Scavengers: not quite the chief, as they professed to have none of that, but an elected, especially trusted member, who solved whatever problems came up regarding the outer world. If this was the same man that Gabriel had once seen crushing Delwit Faber in a trash compactor, he not only solved problems, he dissolved them.

"I'm Gabriel *Lancelot* d'Allier," Gabriel answered.

The mask nodded under its wide-brimmed black hat.

"We've met before. You may be the man we are, or the dead lady was, looking for."

He stopped in front of a door and faced Gabriel.

"But before we go there, I have something to tell you. When you arrived, we were helping someone who needs a hiding place. You are now going to meet that person, but it would be better if you kept it secret."

"You have my word of honour," said Gabriel, who was rather happy to give it sincerely for once.

Blankbate led Gabriel into a wide circular room that was decorated with a disgusting trash-made mosaic of the Fisher-King on a raft, fishing garbage with his mouth. But the most astonishing sight was that of a blonde, bony woman in a fur coat drinking coffee from a crude mug, accompanied by another Scavenger. Gabriel recognized her instantly, in spite of the thousands of days and nights that had passed "like zebras in a haze," as one of her songs put it, since he had last seen her.

"Sandy Lake?"

"I'm known as Lilian Lenton now."

He could see she was straining to put a name to his face. He helped her.

"Of course," she said pleasantly and almost convincingly. "I'm sorry. I have had a rather hard day."

"I've heard that, yes. You are... escaping the law?" he asked, recalling what Wynne had told him about the riot.

"I was rescued from the hospital before I had to. Thanks to these men."

She turned toward the other Scavenger.

"You are sure Vera will not have any problems because of me?" she asked him.

"I tied her up. She won't be suspected," answered the other Scavenger, who spoke even more laconically than Blankbate. As for Nurse Vera, thought Gabriel, she was, decidedly, quite a useful character.

It was now Blankbate who spoke to the rescuer.

"You haven't been seen?"

"We did this while collecting the Garbage. This lady here just slid down the chute into a bag. All anyone would have seen was just us picking up the trash."

"I'm flattered," said Lilian, with a bow.

"This man comes to see your finding," said Blankbate to the other Scavenger, casually switching subjects, as if this kind of rescue operation against the Council were just part of their normal job and demanded no further comment. "Which means we are all going in the same direction. This is Chipp, by the way," he added for Gabriel's benefit, "the man who found the dead lady."

"Enchanted," Gabriel said. He knew the name as well. Chipp had been part of Brentford's own gang during the duke's brief *sub rosa* stint as a Scavenger. He felt like saying he had heard about him, but given the Scavengers' obsession with secrecy, this might not have come across as the most endearing approach. Just knowing the password seemed *a lot,* Gabriel felt.

With a tired smile, Lilian handed him a cup filled with a coffee that was horrible, but still good in the way even horrible coffee can be when you badly need it.

"I almost listened to your last record," Gabriel said to Lilian. "Unfortunately a Gentleman of the Night sat on it."

"A Gentleman of the Night sat on *me,*" she answered, her smile now almost sad. Even if the brilliance of youth had gone from her face, she was still cute, in a harder, leaner, more angular way. "They're such arses, aren't they?"

Gabriel gulped the coffee quickly, sensing the impatience of the Scavengers, and slammed the mug back on the table in a display of pure Round Table attitude.

"If you want to follow us..." said Blankbate.

The Scavengers took them first through an armoury, where they armed themselves with sawn-off lever shotguns and cartridges, and then through a back door. The blizzard had worsened, and whirled madly like a trapped wolf. Gabriel offered his comforter and his leather Elsinore hat to Lilian, who took only the hat, with a smile, and tied the leather flaps under her chin. They walked through the mounting snow until they came to a kind of tube, four feet in diameter, that slithered along the Embankment. An open car on rubber wheels, almost cylindrical, was waiting at the entrance with the pensive loneliness of all things snowed upon.

It was, or so Gabriel assumed, the prototype for the Parcel Pneumatic Post that had never quite gone beyond the first experiments. A larger version of the telegram tubes network, this was, if Gabriel correctly remembered Brentford's explanations, supposed to carry packages and crates, especially from the Fisheries, right through the heart of the city, six hundred yards away. Compressed-air engines at the end of the tube pushed and pulled the cars at an astounding 70 mph. How the Scavengers had come to inherit the use of this network Gabriel did not know, but he surmised that Brentford had lent a hand, while he still ran the Office of Striated Space. Whether it had been done without the consent of the Council or by flattering their fetish about the invisibility of trash, he had not the slightest idea.

Lilian, Gabriel, and Chipp crammed themselves as best they could into the cart, while Blankbate, before adding his considerable bulk, asked a sentinel to close the valve and operate the pump. The tube was dark, uncomfortable, cold, and smelled of rust, and once the pump started, Gabriel felt like a bullet shot through the barrel of a gun. But, thank God, it did not take long before they hit the other end of the tube, where the valve opened automatically.

They now found themselves in a large closed space, part workshop, part warehouse, which might have been the former Receiving and Delivering Station. It was icy cold, but judging by the howling wind above, any shelter was a blessing at the moment. Blankbate lit a hurricane lamp, and Gabriel could see, on the one side of the room unoccupied by either tunnel entrances or sorting tables, an almost invisible door.

Much to Gabriel's surprise, this led to a ghost station of the disused Pneumatic Subway line. Of course, he had heard about this line but had almost forgotten its existence. Another half-baked idea, it had been part of a short-lived policy to double the size of the city via an underground network, which would have been another welcome refuge during the Wintering Weeks. It soon proved a failure, because boring through permafrost is, indeed, quite a bore and because lighting the whole underground would have definitely exceeded the capacity of the city's somewhat testy wattage. The idea of a Pneumatic Train had eventually been exploited on the surface, both in the suspended tube that shot people all the way through the Pleasance Arcades and in the Elevated line, with its elegant cast-iron pillars, that ran along Barents Boulevard, but the subway itself had been a short-lived fad.

However, as Blankbate turned on a gas lamp on the wall, Gabriel could see that the boarding platform (or, as it had been known, the Reception Room) apparently not only remained in good condition but also was still as luxurious as it ever had been, dust and cold notwithstanding. Pictures and gas brackets alternated on the striped tapestry above the easy chairs of the former waiting room. A frozen fountain with a fish basin, now empty, was laid out in the middle, a stopped clock stood at one end, and there was even a piano, smothered in dust, disconsolately untuned. A cylinder-shaped silver car was waiting below a staircase, its door open, and in front of it, framed by two torch-holding bronze Inuit, the perfectly circular tunnel opened toward nonexistent destinations. There was something Pompeii-like to it, though the catastrophe here had only been low rentability. But that was apparently enough to freeze worlds in time and turn them into literal Neverlands.

On the platform, Blankbate opened a door revealing a room furnished as a first-class businessman's office.

"This will be your home, Ms. Lenton," announced Blankbate. "There's a folding bed there. Bathroom's off the waiting room. You will be safe here, and once it is heated, it should be fairly comfortable."

Chipp was already fumbling with an Eclipse gas stove, which soon started to purr.

"The Gentlemen of the Night know of this place?" asked Gabriel.

"They know enough to never come around and not enough to see why they should."

"This will be perfect. Thank you very much," said Lilian, passing her gloved finger over the dusty desk.

"You have a pneumatic tube, if you need anything. We've connected it directly to the Fisheries."

As Gabriel's first glimpse of the Scavengers' secret operations, this was certainly impressive. He wondered about the nature of their underground activities. If they were not a criminal organization (though they were notoriously trafficking in some sort of black flea market economy: the Scavengers were reputed to be able to find and deliver almost anything), they certainly could turn into one at the very first occasion. It reassured Gabriel to think of them as Brentford's confederates, although Brentford had made 'clear that he needed them more than they needed him and that dealing with them was a rather delicate business that could get out of hand at the slightest mistake. But at least this was a world free of the influence of the Gentlemen of the Night, and Gabriel took a deep breath to celebrate this.

Blankbate turned toward him.

"Now, the dead lady."

Lamp in hand, he took them down the stairs and led them through the Tunnel, not minding that Lilian was blending her echoing steps and curved shadow with theirs. Gabriel tried to strike up a conversation.

"Sorry to have mistaken you for Sandy Lake," he said, with, he hoped, more complicity than indiscretion.

"Oh. No offence. I am even a little flattered that you recognized *her*. Miss Lake has been a long time gone. Who'd have thought anyone would remember her?"

"Musical memories are not easily forgotten. Nor is someone who wore luminous garlands in her hair. And so, if I may ask, what happened to Sandy Lake that she became Lilian Lenton?"

There was a little pause before Lilian answered, which she did with a gravity Gabriel had not expected.

"Sandy was a bit of a shallow, superficial girl, wasn't she? She needed to grow up and to grow old. In a foreign country, she met someone very courageous, and she wanted to become

like her, or if not, to pay homage to her. And then she had the
inspiration that this admiration would be better directed if she
could put it to use in her own hometown. She just took her
friend's name so that her spirit might accompany her on her
way back. Or I should rather say, might accompany *us*."

"Us? Your new band?"

"The band is just an advertisement for another us. The U.S.
of Us, if you like. Your best enemies and your best friends," she
added, lightening a little.

"It seems a bit cryptic to me," admitted Gabriel.

"I'm afraid it has to remain so for a little while," she said,
her slightly husky voice now striking an amused note, as they
reached the other end of the tunnel. There, they stepped onto a
wider side platform, whose cast-iron pillars and Gothic arches
reminded Gabriel of a deserted church. Ignoring a staircase that
must have led to street level, they crossed the platform toward
another door.

"It's rather cold in there," warned Blankbate as he opened
the lock with a jangling of keys.

It looked like a fabric shop, with long tables and shelves up
to the ceiling, but it had been used, Blankbate explained, as a
storeroom and workshop for maintenance purposes. It was now
something else entirely: a cave of wonders or, rather, the den
of the Forty Thieves. This was where, Gabriel understood, the
Scavengers piled up their "loot" of outmoded, discarded objects.
Strange machines with forgotten or absurd functions, baby
cribs, sleighs, skis and snowshoes, stuffed animals, worn-out
hides and moth-eaten furs, ships in bottles, sextants and other
Navy paraphernalia, Eskimo objects and weapons, and faded
paintings and mutilated statues from all places and periods rose
up from the floor, flooded the tables, and scaled the shelves, appearing and disappearing with the passing of the lamplight like
the exhibits of a spectral World's Fair.

"We call this place the Arcaves," said Blankbate, just as Gabriel wondered if there really was a profit to be made from these second-hand or last-chance objects. It was, then, in its own, dusty, stifling, desperate way, a Memory palace, a crumbling and frail monument to all the anonymous lives that the city had forgotten about. It was preserved there, smelling of shipwreck and ruin, patient and melancholy, crouching in the dark, biding its time, perhaps.

"Of course, if someone ever wants something we'll retrieve it."

"For a profit?" asked Lilian, who was much less shy than Gabriel.

Blankbate turned his beak toward her.

"Depends on who asks for what. The less you need it, the more it's going to cost you."

Somehow, that seemed logical to Gabriel.

The door at the other end led to a cold-storage room. It chilled Gabriel to the bone as he entered it, and the lamp that Blankbate held, trembling as it did, did not make the place any cosier. The mysterious sled Brentford had told Gabriel about was in the middle of the room under an oiled tarp that Blankbate lifted up with one swift, powerful gesture of his black-gloved hand, revealing the glass top of the copper cylinder. The lady's face, that of an almost old woman, was not unknown to Gabriel, but he could not quite pin it down.

"So?" asked Blankbate, who seemed now to be in a hurry to be done with it all.

"No means of identification whatsoever?"

"There is one thing," said Chipp. "There. At the back."

Blankbate moved the lamp down, revealing a coat of arms. Very simple. Gabriel had never been much of a heraldry fiend, but he knew he knew this one, and then recognized it for good. Sable three snowflakes argent. He remembered the motto by heart. *Nix super Nox*. This was incredible.

"Nixon-Knox," he said. "Isabella Nixon-Knox."

"Like the former Councillor?" asked Lilian.

"His wife. Her maiden name was Isabelle d'Ussonville."

"Like... the Sleeper?" Lilian whispered.

"His *daughter*."

"But the Sleepers weren't supposed to have children," she said.

Gabriel knew the story from his father, from the time when he had been Portcullis Pursuivant of the City's Civil Registry Records at the House of Honours and Heraldry. It was a story that his father liked to tell a little bit too often and it was he who had started spreading the rumour around various bars and she-beens until he had been deemed a nuisance and "put on ice."

"They were not supposed to. It was part of their oath. So that there would not be any dynastic complications to their promised collective 'return' from cryogenic sleep. But, even if d'Ussonville learned it too late, his wife was pregnant before the oath and could not be persuaded to go away from the city. She was to be the only exception to the rule. The daughter would be married to a councillor and that councillor would make sure that she did not bear children, so that the family line would stop there. At some point, Nixon-Knox got tired of watching her, and when he was sure she could no longer become a mother, he sent her into exile, nobody ever knew where."

"Why did she come back?" asked Lilian.

Gabriel shrugged.

"It's her city, after all."

"And why was *Lancelot* written on the mirror?" asked Blankbate, who now seemed less impatient and even interested in the matter, as far, that is, as his mask allowed Gabriel to guess.

Gabriel spread his hands, clueless. Flummoxed, that was his middle name, not Lancelot, he thought.

"How would I know?"

The idea that it might have something to do with the fact that he happened to be one of the few people to know her story crossed his mind. But if it pointed toward some responsibility, well, thank you, he certainly wasn't going to pursue the matter further.

"Can I show you something?" asked Blankbate. "It's not too pretty, though."

"If you wish," said Gabriel, checking his fob watch so as to be sure he would not miss Stella when she came out of her damn show at the Trilby Temple.

"It's fine with me," said Lilian.

"You have been warned," said Blankbate, walking toward a large tarpaulin that covered and outlined some bulky vertical shapes lined up against the wall.

"Help me with this, Chipp."

Each took an end of the tarpaulin and pulled it down firmly.

Lilian let out a little cry.

Gabriel fought not to vomit.

Seven silvery cylinders appeared in the trembling light, revealing, under their crystal lids, the mortal remains of seven old men dressed in black frocks and starched white shirts, wearing sashes and livery collars around their necks. Their swollen, blackened faces were grinning from unfinished putrefaction.

Gabriel had never believed the Seven Sleepers would ever come back from their sleep as the legend promised, and it was well known that their Claude Cryogenic Coffins had been damaged during the Blue Wild, but facing the bare truth still tore away for him some piece of persistent childhood.

Blankbate and Chipp quickly put back the tarpaulin.

"Where did you find *these?*" Gabriel managed to ask, while a pale Lilian held her gloved hands to her mouth.

"In a canal in Lotus Eaters. With cast-iron weights tied to the coffins. All of them swaying straight up. They must have been dumped before the winter, but the ice has limited the damage."

"The Council did it?" asked Lilian.

"It's cold in here," said Blankbate. "Maybe we should go back."

CHAPTER XVII

The Ghost Walks

●

*"That which makes conjuring an art of deception is
not its technical appliances, but its psychological kernel.
The working out in the realm of the senses of certain
capacities of the soul is something incomparably more
difficult than any finger-skill machinery."*
Max Dessoir, *The Psychology of Legerdemain*, 1893

Brentford turned off the faucet and took a towel from
the tray. As he bowed down to throw it in the basket,
he checked in it to see if the answer he was waiting
for had already arrived. Yes. It was there. This "waste" network
really worked. He picked up the folded paper and deciphered
the code. Lilian had been exfiltrated out of the Kane Clinic and
was safe somewhere. He tore up the paper and threw the towel
away on top of it.

Was it a good idea to have started this? He could not really
tell. Barely out of the Blazing Building, he had felt an urge to

take his revenge on the Council in one way or another. He had scribbled a hasty note and thrown it, not far from the Blazing Building, into one of the special garbage cans that the Scavengers used as post boxes and where he knew it would be collected quickly. They had acted swiftly and, as usual, efficiently. Now he owed them another debt, but he felt there would be plenty of occasions to repay them. Or to beg them for help again.

He went back to the theatre, if the Trilby Temple could be called that. It was more like a music hall, actually, and typical of the Midway. Behind its neoclassical facade it hid what was allegedly a replica of the Place St-Anatole-des-Arts in a fantasy of Bohemian Paris. The mock-leprous walls were decorated with false windows and panes and some hanging laundry, and stylized slate roofs with crooked chimneys reached up to the crudely painted starry ceiling. The floor was painted to simulate cobblestones, and rusty light-green metal chairs surrounded small, round, overcrowded tables. Brentford, however, had a table on a mezzanine disguised as a balcony. As he walked up the corkscrew staircase, Sybil waved, her face lighting up as if she had not seen him for years.

"Spencer the Clumsy Conjuror" was, thank God, finishing his routine to polite applause. Brentford had seen the act before, maybe done by the same man (the name Spencer *conjured* something in his mind that he could not exactly place), and felt rather impatient with it all. He knew it was now a standard feature in magic shows to let a supposedly incompetent assistant drop things and show the ropes, the better to amaze the spectators with the performance to come, but nevertheless the sight of an old man bungling his tricks on purpose saddened Brentford more than it amused him.

Perhaps he was simply unhappy about being there; perhaps he did not like the idea of having a magician at his wedding, as if the ceremony were just another vaudeville act; perhaps he had other things on his mind right now that no amount of magic dust could dispel. Tonight, what he appreciated the most, by far, was being with Sybil and warming to her fire. She was as usual a show in herself, as if a spotlight were perpetually pursuing her moves whatever she did. Like a silent film star just lifted from the screen, she glittered on her own plane of existence. He could not imagine anything else flowing through her veins than the champagne she was drinking.

Below them, the curtain had fallen and expectation was rising among the spectators. Many of them, judging by their animation and commentaries, had come before to see the show, but still hadn't grasped what they had been gasping at. Handyside's performances, since the beginning of his residence at the Trilby Temple Theatre, had been, according to rumours and reviews, nothing less than astounding, even to jaded tastes and stage-magic connoisseurs.

Brentford belonged to neither category, but looking at the programme propped on their table he saw nothing unexpected in the titles of the tricks. He knew that Handyside would not do—as if it were beneath him—any card or coin tricks, but just enough legerdemain to prove that he was not a mere button-pusher, and also knew that he would not work with animals. What remained, however, seemed to consist of the usual fare of disappearance, restoration, transportation and so on. If Magic was about pushing the limits, it was obviously about doing so inside a very definite frame, almost a folklore unto itself and mostly made, or so it seemed to Brentford, of references and repetitions: they, were literally, doing it with mirrors.

The curtain opened and Handyside appeared, walking slowly to and fro on the stage, probably selecting in his mind some "volunteers" for the tricks to come. He looked up, rather intently, toward Sybil and Brentford. Toward Sybil, more likely. Brentford had expected more charisma from a man who dubbed himself magnetic. But the magician, clad in a black cutaway and white waistcoat, was of an uncommanding appearance, with a pock-marked face that his stage makeup did not quite smooth and a quiff that was sprouting from the top of his head in a rather clownish way. Brentford watched him pulling his right glove with his teeth, and could not help smiling when the hand came off, neatly cut at the sleeve.

"Oh, no!" said Handyside, as if sincerely dismayed. "Not again."

The crowd laughed.

Handyside screwed the hand back in place with a frown and, after having shown his palms with his fingers splayed apart, put his hands in front of his eyes, twisted them quickly and now held between index and thumb two little spheres the size of eyeballs, while his orbits looked empty. Then, apparently blind, he juggled the eyeballs, multiplying them as they went up and down. A third gloved hand joined them, and another, alternating with the balls as they passed through Handyside's hands. The crowd was motionless, mouths open, breath taken away. Then, as he kept on juggling, the hands and eyes vanished one by one, until all that remained was two eyeballs. Handyside clapped his hand and the eyeballs stood frozen in midair. He walked up to them, picked one, and swallowed it, apparently gulping. Then the other. He put his hands over his eye sockets and when he took them away, of course, his eyes were back in their orbits. The crowd applauded, delirious, as Handyside bowed.

This was, considered Brentford, what magic was about. When the fact that is a trick is even more astonishing than the same thing *really* happening. When human ingenuity is as admirable as any supernatural power. When it is in itself a supernatural power.

A movie screen was then rolled onto the stage. This, too, was standard nowadays. Objects disappeared from the screen and reappeared in Handyside's hands, or the other way around. But Handyside had given this an extra twist. The movie showed a table with a vase on it. The magician, his back to the audience, picked out the flowers from the vase, while the editing made them disappear from the screen. He then turned toward the crowd holding the flowers that were—Brentford liked the detail—still a gauzy black-and-white. Once he had finished his bouquet, he asked a lady to come up on the stage. As he offered her the flowers, she realized, as her hands passed through them, that the bouquet was as insubstantial as it was transparent. Then Handyside went back behind the screen and appeared in the movie, black-and-white himself, bouquet in hand. Simultaneously the real Handyside emerged from behind the screen. Exchanging looks with his own greyish image, who was putting the flowers back in the vase, the magician turned the corner of the screen one more time, entering the movie as a colourized version of himself, pushing out of the screen his black-and-white doppelgänger, who carried away the vase. The image now floated on the stage, ghostlike and grey, and, though this version of Handyside looked rather too immaterial to hold them, the vase in his hands was *full of red roses*. It was so eerie Brentford found that his spine was tingling. The two images, the one on the screen and the one on the stage, bowed down and saluted as the curtain fell down under raging applause and cheers.

Sybil turned toward Brentford with enthusiasm.

"Isn't he wonderful?"

"Hmm..." said Brentford, who was as jealous as he was impressed.

Then an assistant appeared, with paste moon and sun adorning her jet-black hair. Stars painted or tattooed around her shoulders were visible through the flimsy gauze dress she wore, as the night sky would be through a thin veil of clouds. This must be Stella, thought Brentford, as he took a kind of cylinder

from his breast pocket and with a twist turned it into opera
glasses. He wasn't surprised. She was very much what he had
expected from Gabriel's description. Less beauty than charm,
not the finest features but irresistible animation, a bit of the
girl next door, a bit of a diamond in the rough. Compared with
her, Sybil was pretty much the polished and perfect product, the
gilded work of art. But then, it is hard to find glamorous a girl
who is riding a monocycle, isn't it?

Stella de Sable, as she was advertised, also held a cornucopia, identifying her as an allegory of Fortune. While she cycled
around Handyside, he took the cornucopia from her hands as
she passed and showed the audience that it was empty before
giving it back to her. He then took a banknote from his vest
and, lighting a lucifer match, started to burn the banknote,
which he put in the cornucopia as Stella passed in front of him
again. Still cycling, she overturned the horn, and an avalanche
of banknotes and little tinkling golden coins poured forth, continuing to do so as she circled Handyman another three or four
times. The sight of so much money seemed to elate the audience
beyond words, and Brentford felt it as a pleasant relief from his
constant public money–saving schemes. Handyside soon had
money piled up almost to his ankles. Untying his cape, he slowly placed it over the scattered fortune, performed some passes
over it, and then swept the cape away, to reveal that everything
had of course disappeared. From the audience came *ooh*s and
*ahh*s of wonder and disappointment. Handyside tied his cape
back across his shoulders and saluted the crowd.

The next trick, however, "A Poll at the Pole, or the Enchanted Election" entertained Brentford a little less. A gang of
scene-shifters had positioned a voting booth and a ballot-box,
two pieces of furniture that were virtually unknown in those
latitudes, except between the pages, if not between the lines, of
A Blast on the Barren Land. Using the curtain and the box as

props for a magic trick struck Brentford as both a clever but also a somewhat malignant idea.

After volunteers from the audience had checked that the ballot was as empty as the booth, Stella, dressed in the same suffragette costume that Brentford had noticed during the Lenton recording riot, entered the booth, her legs showing below the drawn curtain. She exited a few seconds later holding a large card on which she had drawn a cross under a circle and, booed by some boors in the audience, she voted by casting that Venus symbol into the ballot box. Handyside called her back as she walked away to warn her that cheating was forbidden. Stella pleaded not guilty. But Handyside opened the ballot box and, tipping it to make it spill its contents, revealed hundreds of cascading Venus-sign votes. The audience roared with a kind of laughter Brentford did not like. He found he took it too seriously. Too personally.

A new ballot box was brought out and examined by a spectator, while a sulky Stella was sent back into the booth. Brentford was fairly certain that when Handyside clapped his hands, she would disappear from the booth and find herself in the box, which indeed eventually happened, with Handyside opening the lock and releasing the pirouetting girl to maximum applause.

But this was just the beginning of the trick. Next he requested that members of the audience write down their names and slip them into sealed envelopes being distributed by his assistants. Spectators then proceeded to line up across the stage and place the envelopes in a new ballot box that had been rolled out. A new character, introduced as Little Tommy Twaddle, had made his appearance on the other side of the stage: one of those typical ventriloquist's dummies, with a big square wooden smile and bulging apple-red cheeks. Handyside sat on a chair, taking the dummy onto his lap. Every time an envelope was put inside the box, and a lever pulled down by Mr. Spencer to "make sure" it was hermetically closed, the dummy spoke the name aloud, to the amazement of the voter. This went on for a while without a single mistake being made by the dummy.

Eventually, Handyside left Little Tommy Twaddle on the chair and walked to the box, which he opened, releasing the money that had been escamoted from the previous trick. He showed that the box was now empty and put it back on the table. As he walked away, knocks were heard from inside the box. Handyside walked back to it, opened it and produced Little Tommy Twaddle, who jumped out of it like a jack-in-the-box. Even Brentford applauded that one.

The next trick, however, once again left Brentford with a bitter aftertaste, especially after what he had seen and heard that afternoon at the Blazing Building. It was called the "Greenland Wizard" and simulated or mocked an Eskimo shamanic séance. Spenser the Clumsy Conjuror tied Handyside on a sofa after having helped him out of his cutaway, vest, and tie, now folded on a nearby chair. As the lights went dim and Handyside concentrated, a tambourine at the head of the sofa started playing by itself, while the magician's clothes slowly hovered and moved about like ghosts across the stage, as they were sometimes supposed to do in igloos during shamanic rituals. Brentford recalled that the first explorers had always tried to impress Eskimos with magical tricks (which usually made them disgusted and angry) and, at the same time, mocked their shamans as ventriloquists and conjurors. This trick was quite in the same vein, and Brentford found it rather despicable.

It was then time for a little levitation. The "Fairy Funambulist," was a rather simple idea. A tightrope was installed on the stage, upon which Stella started to walk with her arms stretched apart, pretending to feel dizzy. Handyside opened a white umbrella whose pattern consisted of a black spiral. He made it spin in his hand in front of Stella's eyes, and the girl, now supposedly mesmerized, resumed her walk without any hesitation, the umbrella in her hand. Then, taking a pair of scissors, Handyside cut the rope in front of her. As both ends fell to the floor, Stella stopped, but then took another step and continued the rest of the way suspended in mid-air, closing the umbrella and waking up only as she reached the platform. This was another roaring success.

Stella came down and bowed to the audience, but as she stood up, her head remained stuck in midair, while the rest of her body faded out. Handyside, who sometimes had a bit of the mime about him, looked at the head, scratching his quiff in disbelief, and requested a lit candle to pass under the severed head, while Stella provided lively faces and winks that made Brentford understand what Gabriel would find so attractive in her.

Feigning a sudden inspiration, Handyside blindfolded Stella's head. Spencer brought him objects collected from the audience, which Handyside then held in front of himself with his back toward the bodiless girl. This routine of guessing things was rather worn out in itself, but mixing it with the Stella illusion made it really uncanny, and all the more so because Handyside, who remained silent, could not be using any word code.

Loud applause ensued, and Brentford was starting to feel dizzy and exhausted from the various humiliations and violations of natural laws he was supposed to have witnessed. Handyside's relentless inventiveness and the stifling atmosphere below the mezzanine were turning his mind into some white-noisy blank, and if it hadn't been for the atrocious blizzard outside, he would have been happy to breathe some fresh air.

But there was still the *pièce de résistance*, "Summoning the Spirits." This time, it wasn't Stella who joined the magician, but a certain Phoebe, the Phantom Princess, a lithe red-haired girl in a white gown, whom Sybil, taking Brentford's opera glasses from his hands, recognized instantly.

"This is the girl I saw in front of the Greenhouse."

"Who?"

"The one who fainted. I told you," she said, with a pout of mock reproach. It was one of their most common routines, Sybil complaining that Brentford never listened to her.

The poor Phantom Princess, explained Handyside, had been accidently mesmerized and could not be awakened without risking her life in the process. She had wandered far in the land of the spirits, and could materialize amazing ectoplasms of the deceased. This was not a spectacle for everyone, he added, and children and sensitive women should be spared the sight of it.

The medium *malgré elle* was sitting on a chair, her hands in her lap. Silence and darkness prevailed on the stage and in the audience. Handyside was massaging his left temple, the veins of his forehead bulging from concentration. As he did so, a wisp of smoke started to slither out of the girl's mouth, slowly morphing into vague, transparent, empty-eyed human faces, with lips seemingly moving. Then one of the shapes developed a full human body and, still attached to Phoebe's mouth by the train of her gown, made a few spectral steps across the stage. "The ghost walks" whispered someone in the audience, eliciting subdued laughter from the crowd, for in magical slang, that meant that the magician was being paid his due at the end of the show—the rarest and most difficult of all tricks.

But Brentford was not laughing or smiling at any of this. At all. With a shiver, he had recognized the Ghost Lady of his dream. It was Isabella Alexander, her hands in a muff of smoke, and a cold thrill ran through his spine as she turned toward him and shook her head, a gesture Handyside did not seem to notice, as his own gaze had remained fixed on the floor. This was no doubt part of the trick, and once again Brentford could not help feeling this was all addressed to him. But why the

Ghost Lady indicated "No," as if refusing him something or warning him against some action, he could not tell. Maybe he was just misconstruing this. The Ghost Lady was now bowing, saluting the entranced spectators. Handyside acknowledged her presence and, walking toward her, passed his hands through her smoky silhouette without meeting any resistance. The spectre now dwindled again and disappeared back into Phoebe's mouth. Cheers erupted as the curtain fell, only to open again on the last number of the show, "The Volunteer Vanishes."

Handyside, in a sweat, was scanning the crowd for some "brave man or braver woman" when his eyes fell on Sybil, who did nothing to hide herself and looked, quite the contrary, rather eager to go. Brentford knew there was precious little he could do about it. It was Sybil's nature to fly toward the limelight. She went down the stairs like a queen and climbed up to the stage, with the help of Handyside's courteous yet, it seemed to Brentford, slightly quivering hand. Many people, recognizing her, applauded, and Brentford with them, though with less enthusiasm.

This was a most classical trick, and Brentford really wondered how Handyside would renovate it, beyond the fact, surprising in itself, that it was done with a volunteer instead of an accomplice. Two chairs were brought on stage and Sybil was asked to lay her head and shoulders on one and her legs on the other. "Magnetic" passes were made over her sequined dress, and the chairs of course were pulled away by stage hands while Sybil, in her mesmeric trance, levitated motionless above the stage. More passes raised her a little higher. This required some magic dust, announced Handyside, taking some from his pocket and sprinkling it over Sybil, while Brentford felt a nagging anguish building up in his stomach.

Now, Handyside removed his cape and covered Sybil with it. There were some more passes, a pregnant pause, and the cape was swiftly swept away. Sybil of course had disappeared as promised, leaving just a few specks of golden magic dust where her body had been.

Handyside bowed, the audience roared, and the curtain fell. Wasn't it part of the trick that Sybil should be restored? But no. The curtain opened again, the whole troupe saluted under a thundering volley of applause, but no Sybil was to be seen. Perhaps she would just pop back into her seat at the table. Nothing would astonish Brentford anymore this evening. But another salute had not brought her back, and Handyside's nod to Brentford, just before the curtain closed one last time, was anything but reassuring. It suddenly clicked in his head. Brentford got up and ran down the stairs.

However, going backstage, as he intended, was impossible, for a thick crowd of spectators blocked the way, held enraptured, and offering a standing ovation that seemed to go on forever. Brentford forced his way through, as calmly as he could, which was less and less at each step, and under what seemed to him the ironic smiles and sniggers of the crowd, who recognized him as the tricked husband. His face flushed with anger and shame, he pushed and rushed through a scene that, in a nightmare, would have awakened him in a cold sweat.

He finally reached a door on the side of the stage, but there a large, fair Gentleman of the Night politely but firmly refused to admit him. Brentford, howling in his ear, declaimed his identity but as an answer the Gentleman merely took off his hat and bowed to him. Brentford had to explain, while the cheers continued all around, that his fiancée had just disappeared and should now be in the wings where he was supposed to meet her. He formulated this in a way that rendered difficult another refusal from the Gentleman of Night, who, visibly annoyed, shuffled aside to let Brentford in. Now he could hurry down the ill-lit corridor, crossing the dark shadows of stagehands and firemen, trying to read the names on the doors of the artists' dressing rooms.

Such was Brentford's good education that when he found a door marked A. H., he knocked on it instead of storming inside. Much to his surprise, he eventually heard someone say, "Come in." But the room, full of trunks and props, was otherwise empty. Little Tommy Twaddle, though, was sitting on a sofa, upright and grinning, with a letter in his hand that Brentford supposed was addressed to him.

He approached, noticing that the dummy's eyes were rolling, following him as he came closer. A five-year-old child would have fled in panic at the uncanniness of it; Brentford tried hard to convince himself that he had got beyond that stage. It was with a slightly trembling hand, though, that he picked up a corner of the letter and pulled. The dummy's own hand resisted, and even, Brentford felt, pulled the letter back a little, while the creature kept on flashing this stupid grin that he would gladly have bashed in. Brentford pulled harder, but this time the damned thing lunged and bit his hand through his glove. Brentford tore the letter away and slapped the dummy on his articulated jaw. He jerked to one side, but quickly sprang back to its position on the sofa.

"It doesn't even hurt," he said, in a creaking, exasperating voice.

Brentford had torn open the envelope and was reading the letter, which simply said: "Two o'clock at your Botanical Building apartment. Sybil."

Brentford crumpled the letter and threw it at the dummy, hitting his wooden head.

"You missed! You missed!" he croaked, as Brentford, massaging his hand, left the room in a hurry.

CHAPTER XVIII

Lessons Of Darkness

•

Let their eyes be darkened, that they see not;
and make their loins continually to shake.
Psalm 69

abriel thought he would never make it to the Midway and the Trilby Temple. The snowstorm was raging, pushing and shoving the few and stray pedestrians, blinding them, freezing them to the bone. More than once he almost renounced the effort, sheltering under archways or carriage doors, but he needed Stella more than anything else and did not want to miss her at any cost. As soon as he had left the Scavengers, he had forgotten the Seven Sleepers and had returned, as to a home and hearth, to his obsession with his star-studded sweetheart.

When he arrived on the deserted Midway, the Trilby Temple had already closed its door. His face rashing from the cold wind, Gabriel went straight to the Artist's entrance at the rear of the building, where he had waited for Stella two or three times before. But no sooner had he got there than he beheld, almost miragenous through the whirling snowflakes, four hooded shapes hurrying away down the back alley. One of them, judging by her rather small size, could well have been Stella. He had no fixed rendezvous with her and was therefore not surprised that she had not waited for him, but he still found it painful and somewhat suspect to see her leaving with other people. He instantly felt the green-eyed tapeworm moving in his bowels, and decided to follow the receding shapes before they disappeared from sight.

Unafraid of being heard, thanks to the howling wind and the thickening layer of snow that muffled his steps to a faint leathery crunch he himself barely perceived, he took to the alley, hugging the walls, crouching behind the garbage bins.

He must have overdone it, for when he emerged from the alley, the group had disappeared without a trace. There must have been a taxsleigh waiting for them, but it would be ridiculous to try and follow its tracks, with all this snow falling down. Gabriel sighed, desperate. The driven snow stung his cheeks and eyelids, ephemeral pins leaving a minute burn behind, but missing Stella hurt him more than the surrounding cold. He had no idea what to do, and trudged back toward the Artists' entrance, not knowing exactly why.

But someone, indeed, was there: a girl, huddled against the door in her hooded mantle, an orphan of the snowstorm. As he approached, he saw she was shaking with cold, but she stood still, her eyes fixed and glassy, not even acknowledging his presence. He recognized her.

"Phoebe?"

He took her arm. She did not react, as if lost in some kind of trance.

"What are you doing here?"

She turned toward him but still did not seem to see him.

"Can you hear me?"

She tilted her head to one side, frowning slightly, as if concentrating on some remote call or memory. What had happened to her? What had *they* done to her? What the hell was going on in this place? But though he pitied her, first and foremost he wanted to hear about Stella. Maybe she could help.

"Did you see some people leaving? A few minutes ago?"

Phoebe opened her mouth, but nothing came out except a cloud of breath.

Gabriel sighed, but tried again.

"A girl called Stella. With men?"

Another cloud answered him. But this cloud, he noticed, behaved curiously, expanding and changing shape. He thought—that was how tired he was—that a face was forming in that blur. It had something like lips, which parted as if to speak. If he squinted, he could now see hovering in front of him a girl who looked a little bit like a younger Isabelle d'Ussonville, but made out of Phoebe's breath and answering his question. He focused on the lips, and though he heard nothing he somehow knew what they'd said.

"The Ingersarvik," he repeated to himself.

It was precisely the name that Gabriel had been afraid of hearing. Maybe that was why he had heard it. A chasm opened in his stomach and his heart sank into it. But suddenly the door rattled behind Phoebe and Gabriel had just time to squat behind a garbage bin.

An old man in a fur coat and bowler hat emerged from the Artists' entrance, carrying over his shoulder a shape that looked like a child. The man took Phoebe by the arm and spoke with a husky voice.

"There, I found him. Trying to strip a string puppet in a tutu. You have been patient, my pretty. Sorry to have kept you waiting in the cold."

"The bastard struck me," complained a voice, probably the child's, though it sounded unpleasant, like some creaky clock-work.

"So what?" said the man. "He probably hurt himself more than he hurt you, blockhead."

He had taken Phoebe by the arm and was taking her with them.

"Now, we're all going home, aren't we?" said the man almost tenderly, and as Gabriel flattened himself against the wall, the little family walked away down the alley, fading into the snow as if they had never existed.

After long minutes of both moral and physical loneliness, Gabriel eventually found an electric taxsleigh going his way. It was an opportunity not to be missed, and, taking no chances, he let his money do most of the talking. The driver promised nothing, because visibility was poor and the streets were blocked by the snow, but he would do what he could to take him as close as possible to Venustown. The taxsleigh advanced slowly, but for Gabriel, tucked under the blanket on the seat, it was a welcome pause in spite of the icy wind, and an occasion to pack down his own whirling, drifting thoughts into a grid of solid banks and blocks.

What he had just seen did not retain his attention for long. They, whoever *they* were, had turned poor Phoebe into some sort of visionary vegetable, and were now, he supposed, exhibiting her at the Trilby Temple. He knew it was partly his fault, for having sent her as a messenger to Brentford, but he also knew that his responsibility was nothing compared to theirs, and that they would have to pay for it sooner or later. Later would be fine, because he had other things on his mind right now.

The presence that had been "talking" to him he dismissed as an hallucination, born from his tiredness and the extreme conditions surrounding him. Still under the influence of his subterranean trip, he had just allowed some dim memory of Isabelle d'Ussonville, or of some photograph of her seen in his youth, to shape an intuition about Stella that was maybe just another illusion. This he would be checking soon.

But why he had had that intuition was still unclear to him. If he tried to reconstruct it, he had to admit it amounted to some inborn distrust of Stella's faithfulness, though she had given him no particular cause for alarm in that respect. It was true that she disappeared all day long to rehearse and perform at the Trilby Temple. But she had explained to him that it was high-precision work, with no mistakes allowed, and so required painstaking practice, and he had no reason not to believe her.

He had not gone to see the show, though she had invited him, because he simply did not want to. From what he imagined, a magician's assistant was a half-clad doll, offered to foreign, inquisitive looks and subjected to all kinds of sadistic outrages. She would be paraded, manipulated, locked up in tight boxes, sawed in half, decapitated, and the Devil knew what else. He simply did not wish to see his love treated that way in public.

However, something nagged at him: the fact that he had met her in the hospital the day of the Drug'n'Drone Dragnet, as it was now called in the local lore, and precisely when he'd been on his way to find Phoebe, so that, in a sense, Stella had prevented him from seeing and possibly rescuing the damsel in distress. The way she had presented herself could have been spontaneous, but could also have been calculated. After all, as a trap, it would have been a rather simple and infallible one.

The fact that she was employed precisely where Phoebe was now exploited and under the command of a magician who was also a hypnotist—like the one, if not the same one, whom he had faced in the hospital (and who had voiced, if he remembered correctly, his interest in Phoebe)—did little to dispel his doubts. He hated himself for suspecting her, but as a man whose past week had been nothing but set-ups and persecutions, he could be excused for a tendency to see patterns and plots in mere coincidences. As to why the Ingersarvik had sprung to his mind, he could not really tell. Maybe it was his way of bracing himself for the worst.

The taxsleigh had given up shortly before Boreas Bridge, as weather conditions permitted no further advance. Gabriel regretfully paid the sumptuous fare he had himself promised and trudged for the rest of the way, sometimes sinking up to his calves in the fresh powder snow.

The blizzard seemed to be dying down, and it was now possible to enjoy the sight of the buildings and embankments and bridges smothered in the diamond-dusted whiteness. There's always something soothing in the snow, thought Gabriel, a promise of happiness and absolution, of a new start on a clean sheet. Snow redesigned the streets with hints of another architecture, even more magnificent, more fanciful than it already was, all spires and pinnacles on pale palaces of pearl and opal. All that New Venice should have been reappeared through its partial disappearance. It was as if the city were dreaming about itself and crystallizing both that dream and the ethereal unreality of it. He wallowed in the impression, badly needing it right now, knowing it would not last as he hobbled nearer to his destination.

Only second to the Bower of Bliss, that miragenous bordello on the Ladies' Mile, the Ingersarvik (the word meant something like "Humping Spot") was one of the most famous places in Venustown, where "famous" mostly meant "infamous." For the layman, however, it was impossible to find, as no signs indicated it. But Gabriel knew where it was and even knew it too well: down an almost invisible steep flight of stairs, in a chink between two buildings. A heavy door with a ringing bell opened, after too long a while, on a ticket booth staffed by a rather sulky Inuk girl. For singles, the entrance fee was expensive. Gabriel's money was melting faster than the snow promised to do, and what was worse, he expected little pleasure in exchange as he entered, ducking his head to pass down the low, narrow tunnel to the main "igloo."

If there ever was something about Eskimo culture that had left a strong impression on the Whites, it must have been the wife-swapping, orgiastic part. New Venice's most notorious swingers' haunt had drawn its inspiration, or its excuse, from that obsessive fantasy. In a sense, Gabriel thought, as he entered the first room dressed only in a complimentary *natik*, it was a kind of blueprint for the Inuit People's Ice Palace, a monument of perverse, projective anthropology. On one hand, if the truth be told, it was one of the rare places in the city where there was a modicum of mixity between Inuit and *qallunaat*, but on the other hand, it had a rather limited take on racial relationships and, as an unspoken rule, you saw more white men with Inuit girls than Eskimos with white women. Gabriel, who had sometimes been there in the days when he'd had an Igloolik maid, was, however, not in the best position to pass judgement on this.

Modelled on igloo architecture, the Ingersarvik was actually a labyrinth of little dome-shaped rooms of different sizes connected by small tunnels. It was hot, probably around 100°F, and some steam that smelled of laundry made the place rather smoky. The walls were made of glazed ice, and the rooms were lit by a sparsity of wick lamps, so that most people one came across were little more than faceless silhouettes. The light grew less and less intense as the maze went on, and the last lamps could even be blown out to simulate the Eskimo ritual, more a game, actually, known as "snuffing the candles," that preceded the Inuits' too-famous orgies. (Gabriel recalled from his studies that these were less a permanent feature of Eskimo life than a diversion in times of hardship and food shortages.) Niches were carved inside some of the walls, allowing people to have a drink or to lounge on fur blankets. A block of ice, or *iglerk*, covered with furs and skins, was placed in the middle or inserted in the wall of each igloo. This was where people got busy, "laughing under the skins," as the Inuit said, though as a matter of fact you hardly ever heard anyone laughing.

Gabriel scoured the rooms, in a curious predicament, afraid of finding what he could not help looking for. A woman with a stick and a masked man with a penis made of stuffed intestines fooled around the rooms chanting in a hypnotic tone, adding a touch of *couleur locale* that seemed rather tiresome to Gabriel, while meatbergs of indistinct people could be seen in a distant room, piling up like walruses on top of one another. He was rather indifferent to the spectacle—once he had made sure, as well as he could, that the participants were not known to him.

He had been there and done that, and not been impressed. Had he been inclined—God forbid—toward metaphysics, what he would have concluded from these experiments is that Sex is in Man an ancient, different, parasitic soul that can operate on its own and for motives obscure even to itself. What he had lived through here had been, in a way, happening to Sex more than it had been happening to him. Gabriel had watched himself doing things, or things being done to him, with a kind of detached curiosity that had perplexed more than enlightened him. He had been hoping for a trip to the *terrae incognitae* of life, for revelations that would flay the world alive, but instead had found scary savages huddling together in a cave around the feeble fire of a female body.

Tonight, as he passed among those silhouettes in the smoke, little locker keys dangling and jangling from their wrists or ankles as if they were lost sheep in the fog, he even felt he had descended to Hades, among fading shadows who loitered at loose ends between two stages of Death, barely realizing they were not alive anymore. But then, he had to admit he had seen better days himself.

Still, something was making him feel alive. It was less his beating heart—even though that was pounding fast and loud enough—than his constantly nagging, tugging, gnawing stomach, which, since the day he had met Stella, seemed to be the very location of his soul. It now acted as a compass, pointing him toward a drawn skin curtain and warning him he should not go over there and open it.

But there he went, and there they were.

What he saw at first was not her but a large, muscular back that in the flickering light of the flame above displayed on its entire surface a tattoo inspired by a Dürer Apocalypse, *The Seven Trumpets are Given to the Angels*. It was only as the back moved a little aside, its muscles rippling like those of some reptile, that Gabriel could perceive—and how could he be wrong—Stella's own star sign, the Scorpio on her left shoulder. The back, he suddenly realized, was Sealtiel Wynne's. He had recognized his bulk back there in the alley but had blocked the fact out as long as he had been able to, and this was exactly the kind of tattoo that the Gentlemen of the Night were rumoured to have. If he'd wanted a Revelation, now he had one. A shudder took hold of him, which was both hot and cold, the burn of cold water falling on colder skin. He fainted and woke up in simultaneous waves, as if passing through ascending hoops made of darkness and light, of ice and fire.

It was when he summoned the strength to turn away that he saw, or thought he saw, something else, on the next block of ice: the hospital hypnotist was here, the little wick flame prickling shadows on his pock-marked face, a curious sprouting quiff on his head as if he were himself turning to smoke. The goldilocks girl on her hands and knees before him, her empty eyes turned toward Gabriel but looking right through him, as if he weren't there, was Sybil Springfield.

Gabriel suddenly felt a cold, flaky hand crawling under his *natik*. He jumped and saw a thin, eye-masked old man he had not noticed before, who had also been watching the couples. Recoiling in disgust, he slapped the hand away. The man jolted back, his bald head lit for an instant, his eyes angry. Gabriel knew this face, in spite of the eye mask, knew the thin lips and the pointy teeth. He could not believe what he saw.

How he found himself outside, standing in the middle of the Boreas Bridge, he did not know. What woke him up was the wind, freezing his own cold sweat through his unbuttoned great-coat. He did not care to button it up. He shrugged it off instead, opened his jacket, put it down, stripped off his wool sweater, his shirt, his undershirt, to feel the cold better, as if it would cleanse him from what he had seen. He stood there for a while, waiting for his heart to stop or his mind to go blank.

Neither had happened, he realized after a while.

It was barely one o'clock. The only thing that resembled an idea in his head was how much he missed and needed Stella. No matter what she was up to with the Gentlemen of the Night, he would win her back. He would wait for her, but not here. He would wait in front of her place, for hours if need be, ask her for explanations, and he would listen to them, eager to grant forgiveness. Or maybe he would say nothing at all about what had happened tonight, and just hold her tight in his arms.

He dressed quickly, before he could catch his death.

CHAPTER XIX

The Magician's Menace

●

*"I wish it to be distinctly understood that I shall do
my best to deceive you, and upon the extent to which I
am able to do so will depend my success."*
Stanyon Ellis, *Conjuring for Amateurs*, 1901

rentford stood at the large picture window of his
apartment, a bandage around his hand, less admiring
the sight of the frostwork on the sleeping city than
sombrely meditating on past events and those about to come.
He could still feel the burn of the red-hot-iron-letter-day. He
had been punched by a cadet and bitten by a puppet. He had
been implicated in the kidnappings of two local celebrities—
Lilian's, successfully enough, and Sybil's, which was maybe a
payback for the first. A snowstorm had swallowed a good half
of the city and the Council was ruining the rest. And as two
o'clock struck on the Art Nouveau mantel clock, Sybil had not

reverted back from a few specks of pixie dust to a woman he could marry in two days.

A cough behind him made him jump. He turned back, his heart racing, to find Handyside sitting with his legs crossed in the Majorelle armchair behind him. "Where's Sybil?" and "How did you get in?" elbowed each other in Brentford's brain to gain access to his tongue.

"How did you get in?" won.

"Rather easily," answered the magician with a little gesture, dismissing the question as having very little interest.

"Where's Sybil?" said Brentford, advancing toward him.

"Ms. Springfield, you mean? Not here, apparently. But I do not think the message you read ever said she would be."

Brentford had to admit that, literally speaking, this was true.

"Were we here to talk about magic, I'd say that's lesson number one," said Handyside. "Most of the trick is founded on what the spectator infers."

"Thanks for the lesson. When will I get to see her?"

"You missed a good chance in my dressing room, actually."

"You were still there?"

"Of course. In the trunks. Rather cramped, if I may say so. And I had to stifle my laughter when Tommy bit you." Handyside smiled, pointing at Brentford's bandaged hand.

"That damned puppet."

Handyside chuckled.

"This is what happens when you assume things are what they seem to be. Tommy is indeed a *very* mischievous contraption," he added, almost tenderly.

Brentford had once again been misdirected, and tried to retrace his tracks.

"We were talking about Sybil."

"Do not worry. She'll be restored in time. That will be my little wedding gift. Provided, of course, this conversation leaves us both satisfied."

Brentford sat down with a sigh in the armchair in front of Handyside.

"You're not one to be trusted, I would say," he replied.

"You'd offend me if you thought otherwise," answered Handyside, with a bow. "Deception is my trade, as you know. But then, if I deceive people, I do not disappoint them, I hope. Look in your right pocket."

Brentford reached into the pocket of his smoking jacket. Much to his surprise he pulled out a crumpled scaly brown leather thing he instantly recognized: it was the pineapple-shaped mask worn by Angry Andrew, the former master of the Greenhouse, in the heyday of Pineapples and Plums. And suddenly Brentford also recognized in Spencer Molson, the Clumsy Conjuror he had seen tonight, Angry Andrew's personal assistant and master of ceremonies.

"My real name, you will be interested, if not pleased, to know, is Adam Arkansky. I am the son of Ananias Andrew Arkansky and I have come to claim my inheritance," he said, putting in his own pocket the mask Brentford handed him back.

"Your inheritance?"

"The greenhouses my father ran."

"I do not own this place, Mr. Arkansky, and neither do you. A lot of things have changed since your father ran it. For one thing, it is now a branch of the Arctic Administration. Even if I were inclined to give it back, it would not be in my power to do so."

"I know that, of course. But were you to resign, I have reasons to think the Council of Seven would consider my application with benevolence."

"I do not doubt they would," Brentford said, darkly remembering the presence of that cumbersome Gentleman of the Night in front of the backstage door. "But I am not sure you would like the job. I spend most of my time calculating ratios of sand, ashes, local soil, compost, and nitrogen, making sure steam pipes or Tesla coils warm the soil sufficiently, finding ways to fan out or recycle the heat when it's too hot because of the long periods of daylight. It bores me as an engineer, and I doubt it would have for you the glamour of stage magic."

Actually, Brentford delegated most of those tasks, but he wanted to know what Handyside, well, Arkansky, was aiming at.

"Stage magic is more math than glamour. But anyway, there's one word you said that sums it all up for me: sand, Mr. Orsini."

"Sand is not that fascinating, I assure you."

"But imagine we replace it with local psylicates. Would not that give a certain flavour to our local production?"

That was it, then. A return to Ananias Andrew Arkansky's old way of using the Greenhouse as a drug factory. When affordable *food* was so damn hard to find for everyone. Brentford frowned.

"I can see you are your father's son. But the days of Pineapples and Plums are long dead and gone. Welcome to Scarcity City, Mr. Arkansky."

"My father was a great man, a visionary, but he had not the time to fully develop his plans. The Council, as becomes the living memory of New Venice, has not forgotten them, and that is why they have searched and found me. Pineapples and Plums, for all its virtues, was mainly a local resource. And psylicates are too precious to be simply wasted on those useless Boreal Bohemians. The Council seems to think that *exporting* is very much the future. Imagine the fortune *we* could make out of it. Importing more down-to-earth food would be then quite easy, I suppose."

"You have no notion of the costs of importing food here."

"I'm rather well informed on the current situation. I have for instance read an interesting book, lately, *A Blast* or something... You probably do not know it," Arkansky Jr. added, with a wink that Brentford pretended not to notice. "I'm quoting from memory and I don't imagine you would have a copy here to check the exact wording, but I seem to remember that it said that in New Venice, the real wealth was the imaginal wealth, the generosity of dreams, the ever springing fountain of the inner eye, coming from sensory deprivation in the night and in the snow, a culture of *fata morgana* and *aurora borealis*. Well, that is exactly what I am aiming for, Mr. Orsini."

"I never said it was for sale," Brentford answered too quickly.

"Oh? You did not write the book, by any chance?"

Damn, thought Brentford, placing mental hands over his mouth.

"That's lesson two. Always watch what the other hand is doing." Arkansky was smiling wickedly, very happy with himself. "You see, if the Council were to learn your passion for *les belles-lettres*, you might have to resign for good."

Brentford tried to look relaxed.

"As little as I know them, I still think they would need more proof than a magician's word."

"Let us make this a footnote to lesson one. A proof is what people will believe. Every night, I see people whose will to be deceived is matched only by my will to deceive them. This is precisely why they come and see magicians. And this is why my ballot box trick makes special sense, even if you did not like it, as I noticed."

"But I thought the blackmail was about Ms. Springfield," said Brentford, who did not feel like discussing poletics.

"We are coming to that," Arkansky kept on. "The Greenhouse is one thing. Much to my surprise, and to my displeasure, I must add, I have other matters to discuss with you."

Arkansky sat back in the armchair, lost in thought for a while, seeming even a bit nervous, though Brentford could not see why, for he had all the cards in his hands. The magician finally spoke.

"How did you like the show, Mr. Orsini?"

"Would you be fishing for compliments, by any chance?"

"Ha! As an artist, I make a living out of compliments. So they are always welcome, I suppose. But let me rephrase my question. Did you think there was anything special in the show tonight?"

"I found everything rather impressive, I admit."

"Correct me if I'm wrong, but you seemed to have been especially, shall we say... troubled by the walking ghost."

"I was not the only one, I suppose. It is a powerful illusion," Brentford said diffidently. He still failed to see how any of this could involve Sybil.

"But you are the only one she made a sign to."

"Because you made it so, I suppose."

Arkansky leaned toward Brentford.

"Mr. Orsini. Have I, since this conversation began, given you the impression that I deserve to be spoken to as if I were some sort of dimwit? "

"Not really," admitted Brentford, regretfully.

"Well, then. Let us behave accordingly, if you don't mind." He took a deep breath and went on.

"Who is this girl?"

"Which one? The Princess? The Ghost?"

"The Ghost or God knows what it is."

"I do not have the slightest idea."

"You are sure you have never seen her before? Because *she* had seen you before."

"How can you be so sure?"

Arkansky got up, took a few steps to and fro, biting his lips, visibly wrestling with some inner dilemma Brentford had no inkling about. Then, he suddenly turned toward Brentford, seemingly pacified, or at least, with his mind made up.

"As much as I regret it, it seems that the best way to deal with this is to be relatively sincere with you. Needless to say, were you to abuse my trust, and inform a third party of what follows, you will place yourself in a rather unenviable predicament."

"Your secret is as safe with me as my authorship of the book is with you."

Arkansky pondered this for a moment, and then said, "Let us both believe it. Belief can work wonders. Are you a connoisseur of magic?"

"Not in the least," admitted Brentford, still at a loss as to what Arkansky had in mind.

"That is a good thing. We magicians have a rather equivocal relationship with connoisseurs. It is the paradoxical nature of magic as an entertainment that it dreads the capacity of its public to understand the tricks, while, to be appreciated as an art, it requires exactly such understanding. However, and frustrating as it can be, I may be one of the rare magicians to be wary of connoisseurs on both accounts. Not because I am a bad magician, but precisely because I am, as you have noticed, and I say this with all objectivity, a little above average. The tricks I did tonight, I admit, are mostly standard, and the stage was as rigged as a three-masted ship, but some of these tricks, frankly, I could not have done in Paris, London, or New York, possibly in front of other magicians."

Brentford felt it was time for his cue. He sighed and delivered, so as to get more quickly to the point.

"And why is that?"

"Because, Mr. Orsini, a fellow magician would certainly see that such tricks are not *really* possible."

"This is, I presume, what every magician would like his audience to suppose."

"It's more complicated than that, I'm afraid. There is nothing that is more despised among magicians than a fellow conjuror trying to pass himself off as some sort of sorcerer or magus with supernatural powers. As you know, some of us also make a living by trying to prove such people are frauds. On the other hand..."

"On the other hand?" Brentford forced himself to ask, remembering that he should watch that other hand closely.

"Magic as a trade would be the best cover for someone with such abilities, don't you think? Pretending his supernatural feats were but vulgar magical tricks."

"What would be the point?"

Brentford noticed that Handyside was now levitating about a foot or so above the ground while staring him right in the eyes.

"That could be one of your tricks," said Brentford.

Arkansky rose another foot, just as if he were full of hydrogen, his quiff almost touching the frosted-glass globes of the ceiling light.

"Yes. But the point would be that... you would not know."

The magician returned to the ground. Brentford noticed how flushed he was. But it meant nothing. Arkansky was, after all, in the grip of the famous paradox: who would believe a man who calls himself a liar? The magician had paid for his talent to deceive by losing any credibility, whatever he might say or do. That seemed to Brentford like some infernal punishment, the true meaning of selling your soul to the devil.

"You see, Mr. Orsini. There are two sides to what I do. Some of it I admit is trickery, and that's where some of the beauty lies. Some other things cannot be explained so simply, even by myself. And tonight, something happened that not only can I not explain, but that I could not control at all, even though I pretended to. *I swear I do not know who this Ghost Lady was.*"

He leaned toward Brentford almost threateningly.

"But she knew you and... you... know... her."

Brentford saw the light at the end of the tunnel.

"I'll tell you when I see Sybil back at home and safe."

Arkansky sat back.

"Which home? You forget I have only to tell the Council that you wrote the book for you to lose the Greenhouse."

"You are bluffing. The Council already suspects I wrote the book. What they need is some tangible proof which you do not have. Besides, I remember we have already made a deal about our mutual discretion. Forget about the resignation. Sybil comes back intact and I'll tell you who the Ghost Lady is."

"I could still trade Sybil against your resignation."

"You could," Brentford bluffed, offering his position as a gambit to protect the information he didn't have. "But then you won't learn anything about the lady who comes and goes through your performances as she pleases."

Arkansky was thinking hard. But it was too late. He had forgotten he wasn't the only one to have two hands. As Brentford would have bet, the magician's curiosity, or fear, eventually got the better of his ambition. Well, for the moment, that is, before he plotted a new way to uproot Brentford from the Greenhouse.

"The name, then. But you'd better not *trick* me, Mr. Orsini."

"Would I make such a mistake? And I won't make the mistake of telling you the name before I get Sybil."

"You will have your Sybil back. But not tomorrow, I'm afraid."

"Why is that?"

"I doubt you're interested in this, but another singer disappeared today. Apparently the Council seemed to think that it would be a good idea that not all the headlines speak of this incident. Ms. Springfield's disappearance could not be more welcome in that respect, if you'll allow me to say so. You will see her *a lot* on the front page, I suppose."

"I'm used to it," said Brentford. He still found it hard to believe that the Council of Seven had had a hand in kidnapping his bride.

"Take advantage of the Greenhouse as long as it lasts, which will not be long. For the rest, let's clinch the deal," said Arkansky, offering his hand to Brentford.

"I suppose that if I take it, it will come off and stay in my hand."

"Do not be mean. Do you think I'm some cheap conjuror for children?"

Brentford took the hand, which stayed in his.

Arkansky chuckled and turned his back to leave.

But then the magician saw something through the open door of the bedroom that made him start. Before Brentford could react, Arkansky strode into the bedroom. Brentford followed quickly and found him standing still in front of the mirror Blankbate had given him and Sybil had stolen from him.

The magician turned toward Brentford and, indicating the mirror, spoke with a hissing voice.

"What is this *thing*, Mr. Orsini?"

"It's called a mirror. I thought that as a magician you would be familiar with the notion."

Arkansky cast a dark look at Brentford and advanced toward the mirror, as if to reach for it. Brentford quickly opened a bedside table and pulled out Sybil's Browning, which he pointed at Arkansky.

"Do not touch it, unless you're ready for some bullet catch."

The gun was uncomfortable to hold with a bandaged hand, but Brentford felt confident that his opponent would get the drift. Arkansky turned toward him, frowning as if to hypnotize him. Brentford staggered under the malevolence of the look, the sheer will power that oozed from the green eyes. But when it comes to mesmerizing, few things rival the barrel of a gun.

"Oh, yes," Brentford said, "my finger feels *really* heavy."

"You wouldn't do that," said Arkansky, still trying to force his crowbar stare into Brentford's brain.

"Perhaps I'll just shoot your fingers off."

For a conjuror, this was worse than a death threat. He could see Arkansky take in the blow of the image: the torn, bleeding fingers dangling from the palm, simply held by bits of charred skin and broken bone shards. The magnetic stare went off like a light bulb.

"I'm on my way," said Arkansky, with a tone that sounded more like "I'll have my way."

Brentford took a step back, following Arkansky's retreat with his gun. He heard his steps cascading down the stairs, like an avalanche of poisoned apples, and the door slammed shut. He bent over the stairwell to make sure the magician was gone for good. At least he would know how Arkansky got out.

He pressed his eyes, suddenly exhausted, and went back to the bedroom. He wondered what the magician had seen in the mirror, and moved closer to it.

As he looked inside, he saw the Ghost Lady behind him, wearing an elegant black dress. Smiling. He started and turned around. Of course no one was there. And no one was in the mirror either as he looked into it again, except a tired Brentford in a burgundy smoking jacket holding a gun that had not been loaded, just a waxed pencil moustache short of looking like a second-rate actor in a bad crime phantascopy.

I must be really tired, he thought, an unpleasant shudder tickling and chilling his spine.

But tired as he was, he did not sleep that night.

CHAPTER XX

The Failure of the Feast

●

"Why," said he, laughing, "the barbed arrow of
Master Cupid, my dear Gabriel, has penetrated quite
through all the plates of your philosophy."
Ignatius Donnelly, *Caesar's Column*, 1890

Sybil was finally restored the day before the wedding. A party of ice-cutters working off Symmes Spit found her lying unconscious on a small drifting floe, wearing only a fur coat over her party dress. Dropping jaws and saws, they raced her on their sled to their cabin, from whence they sent a flashing balloon message to their headquarters, which immediately called a propelled sled ambulance.

Alerted by pneumatic post a few hours later, Brentford jumped on his Albany cutter sleigh and met her at the Kane Clinic. According to Doctor Playfair she was perfectly safe and healthy. She had obviously been given boiler pills and stokers when she had been abandoned, and this barely a few minutes before her discovery. She showed no signs of frostbite or even hypothermia and could resume a normal life after a simple check-up. Much of Sybil's disappearence and rescue, then, had been staged, and Brentford had not been surprised to hear that journalists from the *Illustrated Arctic News*, notorious propagandists for the Council of Seven, had been on the spot under the pretext of taking notes and pictures for a coming series on the ice-cutting industry, "the cutting edge of our economy." Meanwhile, of course, Lilian Lenton had dropped out of the headlines.

Sybil did not seem to remember anything from the previous days, and, though a bit absent-minded at times, tried to get interested in the wedding plans as if nothing had happened. However, there was actually nothing much left to do in terms of preparation, as Brentford's mother had taken charge of things in the no-nonsense way that ran in the family. Curiously, the complications this was bound to create did not spin out of control, and except for a little nitpicking, Sybil took in the situation with a surprising coolness that bordered on indifference, and she did not even react when she heard that Handyside's performance would have to be cancelled.

She had, it soon appeared, other things on her mind. When the Cub-Clubbers came by to discuss the musical program for the wedding, most of the talk revolved instead around their next recording, and the sessions, it appeared, were already booked at the Smith Sound Studio for the day after the ceremony ("I'm soooo sorry, honey"). If Brentford had overheard correctly, the idea was simply to record a copycat of a Lenton song, talk-over and all, with the subversive edges blunted and a few typical Cub-Clubbers jazzy gimmicks thrown in. If this were some sort of commission from above, he would of course never know, but he suspected it strongly. The Council's way of doing poletics was as inventive as it was pervasive.

Brentford had to admit to himself that the Handyside episode had somewhat marred their relationship. If she seemed oddly detached, maybe as an aftereffect of the hypnosis that she had gone through, Brentford, on his part, found himself feeling a bit estranged as well, as if unsure of tHe part she had actually played in the whole affair: the eagerness with which she had run toward the magician at the Trilby Temple had left Brentford with a bitter aftertaste. There was no doubt he would still marry her, but he found that a certain sense of duty was now buttressing his desire to do so. He also found himself equally, if not more, worried by the fits of Arctic Hysteria that were seizing the city. If he had ever in his youth dreamed of being that New Venetian Doge who would throw a golden ring into the Lincoln Sea and pronounce "We wed thee, O Sea, in token of our true and eternal dominion over thee," he was now aware that the ring would only rebound on the ice with a ridiculous *cling* of rejection. No ocean in its sound mind would marry a city so totally *pillortoq* as New Venice now seemed to be.

The very morning when he had been driving Sybil back to the Greenhouse, the streets—already barely passable after the snowstorm—had been blocked because of an incident involving the native employees of the Inuit People's Ice Palace. Dressed in furs and installed on a platform decorated with mock-igloos in front of the Nothwestern Administration for Native Affairs, in order to give speeches promoting the official opening in two days' time, they had done quite the contrary, slandering the Palace and distributing leaflets that had a distinct autonomist flavour to them. "Gentlemen" from the crowd had of course "volunteered" to "protect" the Inuit from the angry crowd and "sheltered" them until things cooled off. All of which could of course have been predicted, given the recent events, and in Brentford's opinion *had been predicted* by the Council, who had not only let it happen but had *wanted it to happen*, because it served their obscure plan to stoke up racial tensions.

The last straw had been the astounding accusation that the snowstorm had taken such proportions in so little time because the Air Architecture had been sabotaged. Though in normal times the Council would have been only too happy to blame the Arctic Administration for such supposed shortcomings in their protection of the city, they had this time designated as culprits *four* Inuit from Flagler Fjord, who had been jailed and released for petty theft the very same day and had, allegedly, wanted revenge upon New Venice.

This injustice made Brentford want to spew vomit like a fulmar under attack. He knew the Air Architecture very well, as his father, who had designed and run it, had taken him many times for walks along the impressive rows of Astor vibratory disintegrators that heated and relentlessly pumped the methane-gas hydrates out of the permafrost. There was no way whatso-ever that four Inuit with knives made of "starshit" meteor stone could ever damage that shiny, greasy underground beast. Now the February Freeze Four, as the press was calling them, were on the run, and that was the only news Brentford could mildly rejoice about.

Even the fact that Arkansky had kept his promise to restore Sybil and had left him alone so far was not especially reassur-ing. As Brentford had yet to reciprocate by disclosing the ghost's identity, he knew something wicked would sooner or later come his way, and he feared it was going to be during the wedding.

Speaking of which, his best man, Gabriel, seemed to have disappeared. Bah. His friend was right not to care, after all. Brentford felt ashamed and stupid to be getting married when everything, public and private, seemed to be going to the dogs.

And then a pneumatic dispatch arrived, informing him that his mother had slipped on the ice and broken her leg.

Gabriel's nerves had snapped one after the other, like so many strings on a Loar guitar.

Waiting on Stella's doorstep until three o'clock in the morning in the snowstorm had not helped his health. It was not so much the common cold he'd come away with as the way he had treated it in the following days. A steady diet of opiate pills, Freezeland Fags, Wormwood Star Absinthe, bad coffee, and almost no food had turned his body into a thin, taut, anatomical *écorché,* with no muscles and all the nerves showing, the whole offering little or no protection against the outer world.

That world now consisted almost entirely of Stella's place, a collective apartment at the edge of Novo-Arkhangelsk. The Apostles', as the demure-looking building was called, was the former site of the offices and warehouses of the now defunct Mirrilies & Muir department store. There, artists, bohemians, and dropouts had installed studios and Spartan rooms, where they shared costs, bottles, beds, and just about anything else.

Not that Gabriel—his mind open like a ruin where draughts circulate through banging doors or unhinged windows—either cared for or condemned the lifestyle in itself. After all, as someone trustworthy had once said, "the whole business of man is the arts and all things common." It was even, in a way, what he had been looking for. But, a bourgeois among bohemians, he would sooner have considered sharing his girlfriend (as long as she wasn't Stella) than a bathroom with strangers. The promiscuity made him secretly unhappy and bothered him more than he admitted, for he did not want to criticize, let alone lose, Stella's hospitality.

Among the Apostles, he was surprised to come across Mugrabin, lurking in the shadow and busy plotting with an Inuk
who looked a lot like the one who had defended the Eskimos
at the Inuit People's Ice Palace. On seeing Gabriel, Mugrabin
flashed a knowing false-toothed smile and winked a glass-eyed
wink. "Ah!!! Did not I tell you that you would join us?" he
sputtered in Gabriel's face. Shaking his hands violently, he then
informed him that "great things are on their way." The idea
of Mugrabin living a few yards away from him and probably
fiddling about with homemade incendiary bombs had not quite
helped Gabriel to relax. He later interrogated Stella about the
man, but she had just tapped her forehead in an unambiguous
estimation of the man's sanity.

But what Gabriel could not forget about Mugrabin were the
insinuations he had made about Stella and Free Love during his
visit to Gabriel's apartment. Another aspect of the local com-
munism that did not sit very well with him was that every time
he met a party of people somewhere within the Apostles, one of
them turned out to be one of Stella's former lovers. His efforts
to forget everything about the Ingersarvik would be blown to
smithereens, and sharp pangs of jealousy pierced him through
and through, as if he were an unfortunate assistant in a failed
sword-box illusion. Though Stella did her meagre best to reassure and soothe him, he often felt anguished and shameful, a
laughingstock for people who probably could not care less.

He found he loved Stella too much, not in regard to what
she deserved—for he wished everyone to be loved madly—but
in regard to how much he could handle. Of course, she was
cute, curious, quick-witted, deliciously debauched, and clownish as a kitten, but his obsession went far beyond her objective
qualities. Every trifle from her was quatrefoil to him. Any word
she said or move she made provoked instant salivation, like an
electrode in a dog's severed head. The way she danced with

her fists clenched and biting her lips with her perfectly aligned little teeth, the way she put both of her small hands around a hot mug to drink the worst coffee he'd ever tasted, the way she, well... She was like the girl you fall in love with when you're three years old and never quite recover from, the little child whose features you catch by surprise in the prettiest of your girlfriends. The sight of her receding buttocks as she got up from the bed in his St-Anthony-Pateyville Polars hockey top (which had, sewn on its back, a number that was, curiously, an exact count of the girls he had known before her), or, as she sat on her heels, the vision of her toes that were like little orphans huddling together, filled his heart with a curious blend of bliss and distress. When she fell asleep at his side, either he would prowl around her nude, half-covered body like an old hungry wolf, or he would simply bend over her and cry with what could equally be the tenderness of a father or the loneliness of an abandoned child.

He was, in a word, ridiculous.

It had even got to the point where he'd acquired a new tattoo from a nearby shop, as a token of commitment and complicity. He'd got the idea from a bizarre book that said that the scions of old families from the Bourbonnais (where the Alliers allegedly originated) used to have needles stuck in their napes to indicate the initials of the fixed star under which they had been born. The book further affirmed, even less credibly, that this was how the magnetic attraction of needles toward the North Pole had been discovered. Gabriel, his lucidity in tatters, had found the tradition worthy to be revived.

Stella, who between stage contracts also earned a living as an astrologer, had studied his natal chart and found that, with Scorpio rising, a star called Agena had been in conjunction with Neptune and exerted a strong influence on his life. She taught him that it was the tenth-brightest star in the sky, which perfectly contented Gabriel's unassuming modesty (he had already accepted living, after all, on an island that was only the tenth-biggest in the world). Its rays made him "sharp," "headstrong," and "original"—which he was only too eager to admit—but Stella did not hide from him that their influence could also result in "poor executive ability, loss through law and specula-tion, obstacles to success, many false friends and enemies, and liability to accidents or death by colds or fevers." He'd snig-gered and gone for it, mostly as a dare, drawing for the tattoo artist a sigil that he thought would look fine at the base of his neck. He was marked for life, but that was exactly what he felt like feeling anyway.

Then he'd had a row with Stella, when he reproached her for having let him shake the hand of one of her former beaus. Another nerve snapped (he wondered with curiosity when he would reach the last one, but there always seemed to be some-thing more in him that could be severed, crumpled, trampled, or broken), and he remembered Brentford's wedding as, if not a good idea, a good excuse to get out of the house. Surely, pneu-matic dispatches from the worrying groom were accumulating in his apartment. He would go there and fetch a decent suit and then, instead of reading St Paul as he was supposed to, he would tell everyone from the pulpit what the bride was doing in her spare time at the Ingersarvik, or maybe not, and then the Gentlemen of the Night would do him in for having communi-cated with his friend, who wouldn't be his friend anymore. That would be a great evening. Twinkle, twinkle, little fixed star.

The Orsini family had done things on a grand scale. They had rented the Splendide-Hôtel on the Icy Heights of Circeto, the crowning achievement of the d'Ussonville chain of hotels that had been so instrumental in the city's foundation. Winding along a ravine, two majestic, immaculate avenues met in front of the monumental stairs that rose to the Casino, where guests were welcomed by the newlyweds, and to the Kursaal, where tables had been installed for the banquet. The weather conditions were both atrocious, because of a cold that made Celsius feel like Fahrenheit, and enchanted, because the frozen snowstorm had decorated the roofs, gutters, and balconies with a crystalline lavishness of icicles that money couldn't have bought—though, to speak frankly, money hadn't spared its efforts, either. Brentford doubted that the two hundred or so persons who had been invited could make it to the highest point of the city on roads that were like curling sheets, but then, he could not care less, for he knew precious few of them.

Caught between the outer darkness and the dazzling brightness of the lustre, between icy draughts from the revolving door and warm waves from the rooms behind, he stood in the lobby and smiled at perfect strangers so bejewelled that they, too, seemed to have been frosted. He did not feel quite at ease. First, because he had never been much of a socialite. Then, because these guests were, after all, the people *A Blast on the Barren Land* had been partly written against, though they had done nothing to him except, tonight, offer gifts and blessings. Brentford's true loyalty, he reckoned, was with the Scavengers, and the Inuit, maybe. But they had not been invited, and so there he was, part outlaw, part son-in-law, a gentle Judas to all the classes he wished to reconcile.

He could comfort himself with the idea that things had been relatively under control so far. The church ceremony had been, thank God, rather short. Gabriel had finally deigned to appear just in time for the ceremony, dressed in a purple velvet frock coat that matched, with a true dandy's sense of detail, the rings around his eyes, and sporting a floppy ascot that was exactly the wavelength of the northern lights. As a former Navy Cadet, Brentford knew a loose cannon when he saw one, and promised himself to keep an eye on his friend. The best man botched his assigned epistle, reading with the voice of an automaton running on low batteries and staring at Sybil in a curious, almost reproachful way, while, lost in her thoughts, she simply ignored him. As for the priest, he looked like some second-rate beau at a Circus Of Carnal Knowledge premiere, and only the ladies paid attention to his routine. Brentford could not help thinking that if he raised his eyes he would see Arkansky doing coin tricks with the hosts, interlocking the wedding rings like Chinese links, or changing the wine to water on the altar. And that as he lifted the veil of his bride to kiss her, he would see either Little Tommy Twaddle flashing his bright square teeth at him or the Ghost Lady whispering something important he would only half grasp. But in the end it had all gone smoothly enough.

Suddenly Brentford saw Mason storming toward him through the lobby of the Splendide-Hôtel. He had a satchel slung on his shoulder and under his fur coat was wearing a field uniform, on which a holster strap cut a bend sinister. Brentford sensed immediately that trouble was brewing.

"Congratulations!" Mason said, bowing to Sybil and giving her a nonchalant *baisemain*. He turned to Brentford, and taking his arm while shaking his hand, drew him a few steps away.

"Sorry about this, but can we talk for a minute?"

Brentford looked around him, then moved toward Sybil and, whispering in her ear, excused himself for a moment.

"This way," he said, leading Mason into an empty, dimly lit smoking room.

"I had no choice. I'm leaving tonight," Mason explained to Brentford, handing him a folder he took from the satchel.

"You're leaving. On a mission?"

"Yes. You remember those Eskimos with rifles? They have been seen by one of our spy balloons on Prince Patrick Island.

Near what seems to be an airship base. I am leaving immediately."

Brentford wasn't that surprised. This had been bound to
happen sooner or later. He wondered if he should say Good
Luck or something. But Good Luck to *whom*?

"And what is this?" he said instead, opening the folder.

"My wedding present. I'm not sure you'll like it, though."

Brentford spotted the letterhead, the moon-shaped C surrounded by seven stars.

"With the seal of the Council on it, it's indeed possible that
I will not."

"These are my final instructions for the so-called hunting
campaign."

"The numbers seem impressive."

"It's not only that. How do you like fox as a food, Mr.
Orsini?"

"Fox-hunting? It means either fun or furs."

"I'm afraid that in this case it means furs."

"The fur trade is reserved to the Inuit."

"The Inuit are game, now. Not hunters."

Brentford looked up at Mason, who stared straight in front
of him and nervously bit his lips.

"Have the four Inuit fugitives been found, by the way?" asked
Brentford in a voice that he hoped would sound detached.

Mason hesitated.

"I do not think so. As you know, these police matters are
not within our responsibility." He hesitated for a while, and
finally said, turning toward Brentford, "Which I'm thankful for,
as I suspect they could be innocent."

"They are, believe me."

Brentford browsed through the folder. It was a nightmare
come true. The idea was to kill two birds with one stone, and
then get the whole flock falling dead from the sky. Driving the
Inuit out of the land by depleting the game and reclaiming a fur

trade that would bring increased profits was only the first step. Then, Brentford knew, the cleaned-up land would be offered to the Forty Friends for all kinds of probes—oil, gems, gold, whatever. They would turn the greenhouses into drug facilities, and import food that only about half of the population would be able to afford. Everything that *A Blast* had tried to warn against. That would teach him to preach in the desert, especially if the desert is -30°F.

Mason hemmed.

"I'm sorry. I cannot stay longer," he said.

"You know what they are driving at, don't you?"

"I can guess, I think." He paused for a while, afraid to have said too much. He finally stumbled on a stricture that seemed to satisfy him. "I do not like the idea of my men being trappers."

What did he think of his men being killers, Brentford wondered. Shooting a few Eskimos who had never hurt anyone so far? Surely, Mason had considered the motives behind it all. What they were asking him to do. Where it would lead. Brentford handed him the folder, saying nothing, knowing the moment would come for him to speak, or hoping it would. Any move now would be awkward.

Mason hastily put the folder back in the satchel.

"Would you sign this for me before I go?" he said, pulling out his copy of *A Blast on the Barren Land* and handing it to Brentford.

Too big a trap, thought Brentford. But smart enough for a kind of pact. But what sort of treaty could that be? Peace, alliance, neutrality? He took the chance, knowing Mason would appreciate just the courage it took to do so. Brentford opened the book, and accepted Mason's pen. He simply wrote B.O. and handed it back.

"I may have more inspiration later."

"That will do fine for the moment."

Mason saluted and went back to the door. Neither of them said good-bye.

It was only when he was about to leave the smoking room that Brentford saw the painting. Even in the dim light, he could, he thought, recognize her: the dark hair in a bun, the aquiline nose, the mouth that had a crease of sadness as she smiled. The Ghost Lady. Wearing, it seemed, the same black dress he had seen her wearing in the magic mirror. She had posed in a drawing room, and through an open door behind her Brentford perceived another painting that represented two nude women in a bathtub, one pinching the second one's nipple. He walked toward the portrait and read the caption. *Isabelle d'Ussonville, by Alexander Harkness*.

And then, everything snowballed into Hell.

Gabriel arrived in the Kursaal as people were gravitating for dinner around circular tables that bore the names of planets. He noticed that he was not to sit with the bride and groom. Allegedly, the extra room needed for Brentford's mother's wheelchair had caused his own relocation to Saturn. He did not mind that much, for he had little desire to face Sybil's eyes. He was very unsure whether she remembered anything, but consciously or not, her usually dormant dislike of him had clearly become an adamant snubbing. As for Brentford's mother, pulsating waves of anxiety almost in the visibility spectrum, she would not have amused him much either, as she did not seem in the mood for her usual witticisms and erudite poetry quotations. But then, neither was he.

Even marooned on another planet, he had to admit the place had its pleasant side. Everything around him—lustre, smiles, candles, Sybil, jewels, eyes, glasses—seemed to dazzle, glitter, or glint when it did not twinkle or sparkle. But his fresh tattoo hurt, like rusty nails in his neck, and he could feel that, quite like the feeble February sun, his mood, which had not been exactly bright to begin with, was plunging into deeper darkness with every minute that passed.

He did not know the people he sat with, but he found them a bit loud and annoying in the way friendly people can be to the melancholy man. A buxom brown girl, on his left side, seemed to take a vivid interest in him, but she was not Stella (she did not exist). There was wine, a Pol Roger '89, which in a place where even bad wine is the most expensive thing around was to be honoured in the only possible way. He hit the bottle heavily, raising his glass to Brentford as he crossed his worried look, and then hit the bottle again without even touching the excellent *Petits Patés Pivotaux* prepared by the French chef of the Splendide-Hôtel.

Neither did he touch the scallion-crusted arctic char. The wine was secreting a time of its own, curiously dissociated, accelerated on the outside (courses came and went more quickly than he could react), yet suspended inside him. He registered everything around him down to the most trivial detail—cutlery tings, stains on starched shirts and napkins, whispers at nearby tables, discarded fishbone with skin attached on filigreed fine bone china—but it all slid over his black-ice indifference. This was, he thought, the way God saw the world. His brain was levitating an inch behind his head, in a curious blend of Olympian detachment and mischievous curiosity about how badly the rest of him was behaving. He had relinquished all responsibility for his conduct, as if it were someone else's unruly child whom he could not stomach but had no business chastising. The girl babbled on somewhere in the vicinity of his left ear, about what Circeto could possibly have meant. He turned toward her and gave her a big, slobbering kiss, which silenced her, and the whole planet, for a while.

By and by the evening turned into hypnagogic sequences of related and slightly absurd events he had little control over, beyond a faint, unconvinced hope that he would eventually black out. He went to Brentford's table to carry a toast that embarrassed everybody for a reason he could not quite understand, for all he'd done was salute the bride's universal appeal. A few reels later in the phantascopy, after Brentford and Sybil had opened the ball with a rather stiff waltz, Gabriel found himself in the ballroom signalling to the drummer of the Cub-Clubbers that he was going to cut his throat, which made the drummer miss a beat and complain to Brentford at the first opportunity. The next scene found Gabriel, much to his sorry surprise, pulling down rabidly the bodice of a squealing blonde girl who was seven inches or so taller than he was (she did not exist). This could have been what caused Hasan Rumi, Brentford's friend and occasional right arm, to tow Gabriel away from the crowd and toward the winter garden swimming pool, coaxing him into doing some laps while making sure that he did not drown. As a true New Venetian, Gabriel did not miss that chance to get rid of all his clothes. "Party Naked for a Sign," he kept muttering to himself, as some sort of automated motto.

Such is the power of the mind once it is freed from the body, that Gabriel's malevolent spirit, hovering over the place, seemed to have contaminated the whole wedding night. As he woke up from some short coma, with pixie dust of dried puke on his purple lapel (thus giving him an excuse to strip bare again) he could perceive Brentford's stepfather trying to strangle the official photographer. One of the Cub-Clubbers, wearing long johns, his bare, wet feet on a lit spotlight, bragged that he was about to jump into the pool. Someone in underwear carried someone else on his back and dropped him on the piano with a thundering crash. The manager of the hotel complained to everyone he encountered that he had never seen such a shocking mess, and threatened to close the place, leaving everyone out in the cold.

Gabriel himself, meanwhile, had found another occupation. Standing on the rather barbaric pavilion of the winter garden and still in the nude, he yelled unambiguous advances at Sybil's mother, who had ventured into the semi-darkness to smell the arctic flowers. His argument was that she would lose nothing by her surrender, as she did not exist. She fled, apparently shocked by some aspect of his reasoning, even if Gabriel wasn't sure which part.

This last exploit eventually attracted Brentford to the pavilion. He looked hunched and weary, very much like a man stoically watching his world crumbling in slow motion. One of the guests had just confided to him that his son had dated Sybil in the past, and two minutes later, one of Brentford's closest friends had avowed that he himself had had an affair with Seraphine after her breakup with Brentford. It all made him stagger like a man with stilettos in his back. That he was staggering toward the guillotine, he did not know yet.

"Step back," said Gabriel threateningly. "I've had enough trouble because of you."

Brentford, taken aback, stopped in his tracks.

Scorpio pretty much rising, Gabriel went on, his voice nervously venomous.

"I've been spied on, defamed, arrested, hypnotized, burglarized, cuckolded… Talk about a *blast*."

Brentford tried to speak as calmly as he could, so as to better bottle up this noble gas, which he felt was highly volatile.

"I do not know what you're talking about. Don't you think you should sleep on all this? It would help me to get things back in order."

Gabriel sneered. He narrowed his eyes nastily, as if to take better aim.

"Yes. His Highness the Duke Brentford Orsini. The man who puts things back in order, while his fiancée is being poked by some ugly quack in the Ingersarvik, while Baron Brainveil is watching."

Brentford said nothing, only turned his back and went away.

Isaiah's ludicrous threat about scoffers who discover that the bed is shorter than that a man can stretch himself on, and the covering narrower than that he can wrap himself in, had stopped amusing Brentford. For tonight, at the Splendide-Hôtel, he was that man and he was in that bed, barely breathing so as not to disturb Sybil, trying to endure in silence his bitter restlessness. He would have gladly exchanged for a nightmare the memories of that night. The failure of the feast humbled and humiliated him. Here he was, lecturing people on how to run a city when he could not even throw a decent party. The blend of boring arcticocrats and careless scenesters had made an especially disgusting cream cake, with the world's worst best man as a poisoned cherry on top of it all. Talk about the *True Community*. As to what Gabriel had said... had Gabriel said anything? Brentford must have dreamed it. He did not want to think about it. A sentence circled in his head, lulling him until he fell asleep: *There are only a few days left; if I want to go the Pole, I should go tomorrow, or it will be too late, too late, too late...*

Then he found himself *there*: he knew because "North Pole" was written on the record label that he stood upon, with some inscriptions that were either the song duration or some spatial bearings. The record spun, and he spun with it, very fast. Sleigh tracks around the pole moved as he turned and somehow formed the grooves of the record, and at every round he made, Brentford could see the needle approaching in the shape of an icebreaker stem, pointing toward him, closer each time it passed.

And then he suddenly woke up. A shadow had shifted on the wall, as if someone were crawling or kneeling alongside the bed, not breathing but making some imperceptible buzzing and clicking. Brentford did not move, but followed the shadow out of the corners of his eyes, mentally detailing the muscles he could still count upon. All of a sudden the shadow made a wider move. Brentford rolled away as the awl struck the pillow, and then back over again, catching and blocking the arm before it could pull the point back. The arm cracked like a dry branch as Brentford twisted it. He felt teeth sinking into his thigh. He howled, and let himself fall from the bed, crushing the aggressor under his weight. The teeth released their pressure and Brentford pivoted quickly, seizing the struggling feet below him and trying to get up in spite of the pain. He grasped the ankles, and now held Little Tommy Twaddle at arm's length, dodging the fist that aimed at his knees and the teeth snapping at his groin. He started turning on himself, more and more quickly, knocking the dummy's head into everything that met its trajectory, bedpost, mantel, commode. He couldn't see very well, but he could hear the head splinter and crack and burst, shards of wood and scraps of metal flying everywhere, and the croaking screams of the automaton. Brentford soon felt dizzy and had to stop before falling down, but kept on bashing the dummy down against the floor, sending cogs rolling everywhere, until the croaking stopped and the legs he held did not twitch anymore and were just two useless logs he threw across the room. Almost tripping over an eye that looked at him in a moon ray, he kicked it under the bed in anger and disgust. It rebounded against the wall, rolled a little, like a marble, or a ball in a slowing roulette wheel, and then everything went still. He turned toward Sybil, surprised that she did not wake up. As he approached the nebulous whiteness atop the bed, he saw that it was her wedding dress.

And the wedding dress was empty.

*The crew jumped out to stabilize the ship,
mooring it to the crystal pillars.*

Book Three

•

No Earthly Pole

But suddenly a perfect veil of rays showers from the zenith out over the northern skies; they are so fine and bright, like the finest of glittering silver threads. Is it the fire-giant Surt himself, striking his mighty silver harp, so that the strings tremble and sparkle in the glow of the flames of Muspelheim? Yes, it is harp music, wildly storming in the darkness; it is the riotous war-dance of Surt's sons. And again at times it is like softly playing, gently rocking, silvery waves, on which dreams travel into unknown worlds.

Farthest North: Being a Record of a Voyage of Exploration of the Ship Fram 1893-96, and of a Fifteen Months' Sleigh Journey by Dr. Nansen and Lieut. Johannsen

CHAPTER XXI

Qivigtoq

●

So swift, so pure, so cold, so bright,
They pierced my frame with icy wound;
And all that half-year's polar night,
Those dancing streamers wrapp'd me round.
George Crabbe, *Sir Eustace Grey,* 1807

That was it. Gabriel had gone *pillortoq*, now he was going *qivigtoq*.

He had seen it all and done it all. He had lost his love and forsaken his friend. Stella, he would love forever (especially now that forever was simply the next couple of hours), but his love for her had drained him of his will to live. By going crazy at Brentford's wedding, he had severed the last tie that had linked him to a city where in the past week he had seen nothing anyway but hypocrisy, violence, and injustice. His friend's efforts to ameliorate it now made him snigger at his well-meaning naivety. Gabriel would never come across a better allegory of society, he thought, than the one he had been privy to at the Ingersarvik: orgy under hypnosis for the benefit of old vicious vampires.

His mind was lucid as ice crystal, and about as brittle. But he had taken his decision, or, as with every true decision, it had taken him. Dying in the cold was the coolest thing to do. In the time-honoured Inuk tradition of the *qivigtoq*, he would lose himself in the polar wilderness, and if he ever came back as one moody, melancholy ghost, he would not be very different from what he had been, anyway.

Easier said than done, though. The Air Architecture, even in its present state, precluded almost all amateur attempts at hypothermia within the city limits. Technically, the city temperatures were such that the trick could be tried if you were determined and had time on your hands. But the numerous examples of people who had been found frostbitten by the Health Angels and brought back to life to be amputated without their consent were enough to make one consider alternative schemes.

Still, getting beyond the city limits was a boring business. Gabriel trudged directly from the hotel, on rather slippery slopes, to the top of Icy Heights and then eastward toward the Black Cliffs, where he knew he could slip beyond the pale. He had to walk atop the precipitous crag, along a narrow path where greasy black rocks emerged from under the snow.

On his right, beyond a wire fence, an immense field of indistinct, spectral wind vanes roared loudly in the darkness, while narrow light beams coming from the mills at their base caught in their pale white glare the slow flakes of a lazy snow. Gabriel had the feeling, which occurred frequently, that he was living out a scene lifted from a book, but usually that was a sensation that soothed him more than it disquieted him.

On his left the city spread and sprawled beneath him, its silver and golden lights strewn in Marco Polo Bay like ducats and doubloons from a burst treasure chest. It moved him, even if he had no tears anymore. Clusters of distant lights was the view of Mankind that he liked the best. The lights had the archaic charm of little fires on a plain, and the frailty about them, if it did not excuse anything, at least explained a lot of Man's stubborn ruthlessness. Mankind had not started the mess that was life, after all. And on the whole, it had been an interesting species to be a part of, the girls especially, as long as you remembered to watch your back.

New Venice, of course, he had loved. It was the quintessence of what Mankind was about, when he summed it up: the single-mindedness of surviving at any cost, even if it meant eating up the rotting corpses of your friends, and a certain sense of the grandiloquent gesture and gratuitous ornament. But he knew the New Venetian scene by heart, and lately he had seen too much of the wings. There were no regrets to have. The heydays, he was sure, were over. He had lived like a New Venetian, quite to the full, and he would die like one: frozen to the bone, his shape deep in the snow, like another footprint toward no earthly pole. Soon the city disappeared from his sight, preventing the seductive winks of light that could have brought him back, and now, on his left, he could divine, more than he could see, the frozen ocean, a greyish rough expanse of chaotic nothing, like an immense crumpled sheet of paper imperfectly flattened out.

The way the Air Architecture worked was beyond his comprehension. But he could clearly make out the barrier of turbulent yellow-tinted flames—the Fire Maidens, as they were called—that surrounded the city at wide intervals, and the kind of hazy airwall that they built. It made him think of the sword of flames Mugrabin had talked about. Leaving Eden of one's own accord, as he was doing now, certainly showed, he thought, some strength of character.

Maybe that was what had happened to Mankind. That original sin story was an embarrassed cover-up. Man had simply walked out, bored or angry at being ordered around. Or he'd lost any interest in God as soon as he had the girl to fool around with. He had abducted her, starting a long tradition of romantic elopement. God had first thought good riddance, but had soon missed his favourite pet. Animals were less fun to play with. Eventually God grew tired of promenading alone in the evening breeze, and for the first time, like an ill-loved, ill-loving father, He learned the pangs of regret and bitterness. He closed the Garden and let it rot like an old fairground park. An angel still kept the rusty gates, just to make it desirable again. By and by, time passed and the Ice had covered everything. When men came back to the pole, even those who remembered Eden and thought it could well have been there did not recognize it. But they still had the Adamic streak and had taken pleasure in renaming everything, beast and plant and crag. What a brilliant theology, chuckled Gabriel, reassured to see that the effects of alcohol had not quite worn off and would carry him, light-headed, a little further on.

The Air Architecture area was forbidden because the concentrated methane fumes it emanated were notoriously poisonous, but Brentford had once told him of a small opening in a fence near a power plant where someone (let us say a Navy Cadet from the Belknap Base looking for a short cut while on a more or less authorized leave) could go through with minimal fuss. Gabriel found it easy enough, indeed, to crawl through the fence that surrounded the brick building (no light coming now through the strange curlicues of its cast-iron windows) and run, holding his breath, to the other side of the site, to the gate beyond the derrick, and then onward to his death.

As soon as he had left the plant behind and drawn close to the edge of the cliff, Gabriel felt the difference. New Venice was nothing close to hot or even warm, but outside was certainly *airsome,* and the atmosphere was as solid as a hall of mirrors. Cold is an element unto itself, with a whole physics of its own, and even a metaphysics, if he remembered what Boehme had written—that the Deity, at its innermost kernel, is dark and cold, "like winter, when there is a fierce, bitter, cold frost, when water is frozen into ice," and that is what holds the Creation together. Deity or not, the universe was certainly at heart a cold and dark affair, and here was the best place to never forget it.

Still, Gabriel advanced, bent forward with his fists clenched in his pockets, the cold plastering him in great swathes, as if to mould his death mask. He would have been curious to see a wine-spirit thermometer (mercury would have frozen, no doubt), but some part of him deemed it better not to know the truth. With every breath, vapour crystallized and fell to bits on the ground. It made him feel like that fairy-tale girl whose every word is turned to diamonds, whereas at the wedding he had rather felt like her wicked sister who ends up spewing toads.

By a stroke of luck, though the air was wet, it wasn't too windy, which Gabriel found a favourable omen. If he wanted to die from the cold, he did not want to suffer from it too much before going numb. Walking headlong through thick curtains made of millions of hanging, tingling razorblades is one thing, but you don't want buckets of cold water thrown in your face while doing it.

For someone who was on his way to hypothermia, he was not so badly equipped, after all. His warm-whiskered face was bare, because a comforter or balaclava would have caused his breath to freeze right on his moist skin, and that was even more displeasing than having some ice-fiend tricksters slap you and pull your nose in the dark. A fur-lined greatcoat with pockets full of warming *qiviut*—musk ox wool—, thick-soled boots insulated

with bladder-sedge and several pairs of hareskin socks, Knudsen
of Copenhagen snow-goggles, an Elsinore hat with comfortable
earflaps, wolfskin gloves and woollen overmittens—these were
a few of his favourite things. He chuckled at the paradox, and
thought, I could always shed some of them on my way, giving
dramatic clues to a potential search party. Being found dead in
the purple frock coat was a flourish to be considered. Such were
his musings as he arrived at Black Cliffs Bay.

On his left, the Lincoln Sea shone moodily, waiting for some
better demiurge to put some order into its chaotic rubble, which
looked like ruins, or a like a building site. On his right he could
make out the mile-high peaks of the New America range, like
a starless area of the night. Gabriel tried to advance calmly. He
knew he could take a good thermal shock, as long as he was
not drenched in sweat. It wasn't pneumonia that was on his
agenda. He also knew, as he had been told countless times, that
most people who had died in similar conditions had succumbed
to exhaustion rather than from the cold itself. They were persuaded they had to move until they could not move anymore,
when a bit of rest could have saved them. So it was important
to never ever stop if he wanted to die properly. So he plodded,
and tumbled, and trudged onward.

It was rough going, but the tattoo pushed him on, holding
him by the neck as if he were some unclean, reluctant kitten.
Somewhere above him shone the star that promised death by
fever or cold. As soon as Stella had told him about it, the dis-
astrophile in him had known how it would all end. Sometimes,
he stopped for a little while and looked up at the night sky,
trying to localize the aster that was his (no: *he* belonged to *it*).
But he would not have known the Centaur even if it had kicked
him in the face with its hooves, just as the cold was doing right
now. Stars were nameless to him and constellations remained
dead letters. He would have liked Stella to be with him, both

of them sitting right on that cliff, passing a bottle to and fro, and laughing as they baptized them all again: the Tambourine, the Lobster, the Bearded Woman, the Carrion, the Skunk, the Poleaxe, the Legless Cripple, the Skull, the Fool. He remembered how the zodiac on Stella's back had made stars out of her birthmarks, and this wrung out a tear from him that stung as it froze on his cheek. He slipped on the treacherous shale and fell, inches away from the cliff edge. "The Fool, huh?" he winced with a painful face that he felt was being flayed alive. It was a good thing again that he was so muffled up in clothes that they cushioned the fall and he did not break any bones. That would not have made things easier, oh no. He got up, a small bruise on his buttocks, relieved that nobody had seen him and that he could still hobble on toward his farthest nowhere.

Well, he had to admit he wasn't nowhere yet. He thought of the explorers who had been there before, on a death wish more unconscious than his own, and had left behind them a whole archaeology of dirty, desperate picnics. He knew that if it were daylight, he'd have been able to spot some of their half-crumbled cairns and disembowelled depots, rusty cans of bully beef, empty rifle shells shot at mirages, those illegible scraps of papers with mistaken bearings that are the epic poems of the place. In the least prophetic act of all human exploration, someone had even planted not far from here the flag of a temperance society. Gabriel wished he had a glass of frozen whisky to raise to this seer. But he was turning to glass himself and the alcohol left in his blood would have to do for the toast, too little as it was. Oh God, he thought, don't let me sober up now.

What these people had done here, and what he was doing now, was a rather dark business, even to those involved, Gabriel ranted on in the wine-fuelled boiler room of his brain. He remembered that in *Venus in Furs*—a best-seller in New Venice—Severin, the main character, has a dream in which he finds himself stranded on ice. An Eskimo arrives on a sled (absurdly "harnessed with reindeer" as if he were Santa Claus) and informs him casually that he is at the North Pole. Then Wanda, Severin's love, skates toward him wearing a rather inspiring—at least to Gabriel's taste—ermine jacket and cap. They clasp and kiss, only for the foolish Severin to discover "horror-stricken" that Wanda is now a she-bear and is tearing him to shreds. This is how wet dreams freeze below 32°F, and it's about all one needs to know about North Pole psychology. And, oh yes, beware of girls on skates.

He could hear the ice shelf on his right snap, crack, gnash and growl, a perpetual slow-motion apocalypse, making him start every time. Gabriel did not buy any of the Earth-as-living-organism theory, but the Arctic, she-bear or not, had much of the beast about her. A man called Tremblay had once gone around Igloolik Island shooting at it with a gun to tame it a little and punish it for all the explorers it had rejected or killed. Gabriel realized he liked that story a lot and wondered how many people knew it—tens, hundreds, thousands?—hoping that he was not the only or the last one to remember it. It was too good for the grave.

But the grave, it seemed, was creeping up on him. A metamorphosis was overcoming him as if his blood were being drained drop by drop and replaced by an equal quantity of liquid nitrogen. Numb as he felt, the notion of a skin that separated outside from inside seemed like a good idea, but now downright unreal. In spite of his boots and skin socks, his feet almost hurt as he walked. His tingling hands, too, protested against going numb. It struck him as vaguely ludicrous that the fight taking place inside him was for the pain to be allowed to remain. As long as he suffered, he would be alive, and vice versa.

An Aurora Borealis was now breaking over him, slowly pulsing and wavering, like a reversed flame on gently tossed water.

The February Lights were the most beautiful, and it would be great to die watching them, he thought, while lightning strikes of shivering hit and dislocated the icy rod of his spine. He had always had a liking for the crackpot theory that said the Northern Lights were emanations of the Earth's rut, its sexual longing for the Sun, and that one day they would form a permanent crown that would give warmth as well as light. It made more sense than it seemed, when you lived in New Venice.

Another thing he almost regretted not believing, as the Inuit did, was that the lights were the Land of the Day and that he would go there. There, the souls of those who had died violently would play football, kicking seal skulls about and laughing like crazy. Eternal childhood and laughter of Flame. Other Eskimos, however, thought that if you whistled to the lights, they would come down and cut your head off. That, too, was tempting to try, but it wouldn't be that easy with a mouth sealed by conkerbells of snot.

At least, he could still whistle in his head: as he trod on marble feet, his teeth chattering until the enamel cracked off, he discovered that a stubborn song had now burrowed inside his mind, an old ditty from the Furry Fruits that was broadcasting from a younger part of himself. It was rumoured to have been about Sandy Lake, who had given the cold shoulder to the singer from the Sandmovers' archrivals. Personally, Gabriel had a theory that it was about self-abuse, but he was not so sure anymore.

She was all dressed up in candles and garlands
And presents in her eyes
Falling from Christmas skies
Have you ever held angels in your hands
Have you ever been blessed
She said and then undressed

But her kiss was colder than if I'd been alone
The girl below zero
Has covered me with snow
And it soon grew darker than if she had been gone
She sure can smother you
Till you're frozen and blue

The loop revolved in Gabriel's brain, in the curious way music is remembered, immaterial but as inexorably real as the grooves in a shellac record. This what was the brain was, maybe, a phonograph of some sort, which would eventually repeat one silly tune in a lock groove before the needle was lifted up for good. Damn, would he have to think halfpenny thoughts until the end? Why couldn't the brain go numb first so that it could not feel the rest being...

He took a step on a snow patch that hid a crevice and fell through. Time suddenly shifted, reduced to successive still frames. The brain took the pictures, but gave no further orders. The body, after all, did not want to die: it had taken over, a deck hand going mutinous. Pivoting as it fell, it sent its left hand darting toward a jutting edge of rock, clinging to it as tightly as it could. It stayed there for a slow-motion second, while the brain looked down in disbelief. Then, with a jerk, the body shook its shoulders and threw the right knee over the edge of the crevasse, quickly rolling over to pull itself out of the chasm. Its throat ached all of a sudden as if someone were strangling it. The cold had suddenly disappeared. The world was pumping blood, veiling the eyes with an explosion of red, an inner aurora. Then, slowly, the veil dissipated, and the cold rushed back with a shock, waking up the brain. And then the brain saw the body. It was lying at the edge of the crevice, exhausted or dead. The body was also, the brain noticed, neatly decapitated, showing the white of the spine, the neck caked with already frozen blood. The brain understood that it was still in the head, which had been projected a few yards away from the rest. Maybe the strings of the overmittens had become tangled somehow and, turned to wire by the cold, had cut through flesh and bone as the body had slammed against the edge of the crevice. Bad luck. The brain started to feel cold. Icicles stuck to its lids and lips, gluing them shut. It tried to keep its eyes open and focus on the body, but wondered how long it...

CHAPTER XXII

The Kinngait

•

I have asked for ice, but this is ridiculous.
John Jacob Astor IV, on the *Titanic*

As a little boy in Nova Scotia, and as perhaps any other child would, Brentford had first imagined the North Pole as a gigantic, 500-mile-radius skating rink, on which one could glide as in a dream. But as an older child, when he had been deemed strong enough to come to the city where his father worked, he had soon discovered that this was a far cry from the truth. Even the stubborn denial of reality that was at the heart of the New Venetian way of life could do little to alter that saddening fact.

The permanent ice shelf, starting roughly—in every sense of the term—where the city ends, is first signalled by a glacial fringe that is nothing but a tumbled-down great wall of white china. The Arctic Ocean crashes and crushes relentlessly into it, but the frozen waves it throws up form an ever-changing maze of rolls and ridges that complicate or block the way. Brentford's first position at the Arctic Administration had been Chief Administrator for City Access, which simply meant that his job was to supervise and maintain the roads people used to come and go. It had been one of his first a: ignments to make sure that the seldom-used Northern road to New Venice remained somewhat open and practical. It must have been some kind of initiation ritual, for this was a job that it was simply not possible to carry out. Brentford had been happy when he was eventually promoted to Striated Space and given work that could actually be done.

Once this chaotic expanse of tidal ice is crossed, you come to an ice field that is supposed to go all the way to the pole, but as has been often remarked, this remaining icescape is actually little more than a jigsaw puzzle with blank pieces all badly mixed up by a very mischievous child. Still, depending on weather conditions, it is more or less level and cohesive. Had the fall and winter been more windy that year, Brentford would not have even dreamed of going there by ice yacht, but it was his luck that the dark season had been rather calm before the recent snow storms. That meant, he hoped, that he would find stretches of relatively smooth and even ice for the *Kinngait* to run a steady course over the frozen ocean, right in the middle of which stood, like a movie monster, the dreaded, carnivorous North Pole.

Brentford, as a former Navy Cadet and as a regular regatta runner (he had even once won the Cape Durmont d'Urville Challenge), knew the ropes as far as ice-sailing was concerned, and knowing them as he did, he knew very well why ice yachtsmen seldom attempted to go all the way to the pole, and why those who did rarely came back whole or alive. Pressure ridges, ice boulders, and water leads just took the fun out of it (just

try hauling a two-ton ice yacht over a jagged hill in temperatures under -60°F), and should an accident happen—crushed
hull, broken mast or split runners—then, in the best of cases,
the trip back home would be very lonely. Of course, like most
New Venetians rich enough to own an ice yacht, he had a personal "farthest north," and a rather honourable one, around
85°, but that was still wide of the mark.

Going solo in wintertime did not exactly tip the scales his
way: if it meant that water leads would be rare due to constant subzero weather, it also meant there would be little or no
visibility. People had received psychiatric care for less absurd
ideas than this. His best bet was simply that Helen would not
have sent him lightly to his being crushed, frozen, drowned, or
starved. He trusted her more than he trusted himself.

An engineer by trade, and a survivor at heart, he had nevertheless prepared rigorously and, he hoped, cleverly. If he could
not allow himself to forget the *least* detail (in a zone where, if
God doesn't lie in the details, then Death certainly does), he
also did not want to overburden his ship with useless junk—
for, when all was numbered, weighed, and divided, the *Kinngait*
was his best asset. At first an amaryllis-class three-hull sailing
ice yacht, she had been upgraded in every possible way. Since
Alexander Graham Bell's recent groundbreaking trials with his
Ugly Duckling in Nova Scotia, propelled fanboats were thought
to be the future in the Arctic, as they allowed travel on water
leads as well as on ice fields, and Brentford had been one of
the first to take the costly step of making an airboat out of his
ship. Now, she was rigged with windmill fan blades coupled to
a series of Trouvé electric motors. She certainly wasn't easier to
manœuver, but she thrived against the wind, and given optimal
conditions, let us say a clear day on Lake Hazen, she could go
a steady 60 mph. In most respects, she was now state of the art,
and in her berth at the Nouvelle-Ys Marina, her solid dolphin-

grey silhouette compared not unfavourably to most other crafts, even under the gloomy, unflattering light.

Brentford, with as much agility as his fur clothes permitted, jumped aboard and slipped inside the round cabin. It was small and Spartan but convenient, well padded all around, with the helm at the front, a central gas stove in the middle that he immediately lit, a half-circular desk on one side covered with charts and instruments, and a small but well insulated bunk on the other. In the rear, a hatch in the floor led down to the hold, and flashlight in hand, Brentford checked once again that everything he needed, or hoped not to need, was there as he had ordered: pellets of Cornwallis zinc to recharge the motor fuel cells; one month's supply of "Vril-food," dried soups, pemmican cakes, cod roe, whey powder, aleuronate bread, bars of his favourite chocolate, lime juice, and coffee; a small sled and harness; a primus stove; a pharmacy; a 16-bore Paradox rifle with boxes of shotgun shells and cartridges; a caribou-fur sleeping bag; spare warm clothes; oil-cloth tarpaulins; ice-axes and guncotton powder; a toolbox with everything necessary to build and live in a snow house or an improvised cave; a captive oil-silk balloon that he could send up to project light signals on—everything that could come in useful to prolong his life or his agony. Satisfied with what he found, or thinking that *alea* was pretty much *jacta* anyway, he went out to unmoor the ship, and, with a leap that was very much of faith, went back to the helm, started the motor, and headed northward-ho.

The routine of leaving the harbour and setting the course correctly was not engrossing enough to prevent Brentford from ruminating on his current situation, which wasn't, he had to admit, exactly Polaris-bright.

His marriage, to start with, had lasted but a few hours. He had always suspected that it would be more an end than a beginning, for Sybil's light was not one that you could easily put under a bushel, however benevolent. But he would never have thought its demise would be so quick, nor so loathsome. Brentford fancied himself as a bullet-biter, but it did not mean he had to swallow everything. If he resented Gabriel as much as he could, or could not, for his behaviour and his aggressive way of breaking the news, he knew instinctively that there was more truth in all of it than he would care to admit. He had been too tired and confused to take any decision the night of the wedding, but having slept badly over it, and woken up to find a dummy trying to stab him and Sybil gone sleepwalking back to that damn magician, he had decided all of a sudden that it would be better to call it a day, even if days, in New Venice, could hardly be called that. Did he really need to accuse Sybil or anyone else? Brentford, after all, had got the *Kinngait* ready the very day after his meeting with William Whale. The call of the North was one thing he could feel, the call of Helen another, which went deeper still. He could have resisted either separately, and he had tried, hadn't he? But as soon as the hand that retained him had let go, there he was, darting like a wobbly arrow toward an invisible mark. It was as if he had been waiting for the catastrophe to happen as an excuse to flee.

He wondered if he had done anything wrong, if there might have been another way out of his predicament. Certainly, he had not respected his part of the deal with Arkansky Jr. and had never meant to. Had he *really* known who the Ghost Lady was at the time, he could have considered trading the secret against Sybil, but instead he had deliberately bluffed about it. When he realized that the ghost was Isabelle d'Ussonville's, he'd also had a hunch that neither Arkansky nor the Council of Seven should hear about it: first because everything connected with the Seven Sleepers made the Council grow even more threatening than they usually were, and then because, sooner or later, some way or other, this secret might turn out to be a trump card in the game

Brentford was playing against them. Anyway, because Arkansky had cheated him as well by not telling him at the Greenhouse what he had done with or, as Brentford preferred to phrase it, *to* Sybil, he had no tactical regrets, only sentimental ones, and those were hard enough to live with for the moment. So, goodbye to the circus. He did not know whether Sybil would miss him, or even notice his absence, and he did not want to know. He had simply taken his French leave as soon as, coming back from her sleepwalking, she had entered the studio with the Cub-Clubbers, whose name seemed now strangely prophetic in light of the recent hunting frenzy of the Council.

For there was of course another side to the matter, one that went beyond personal grudges. They were all—Sybil, Arkansky and he—part of a wider picture, whose monumental size Mason had revealed to him. It was no less than the city that was at stake, and they were all, in this, nothing much more than pawns believing themselves to be either tricky knights—like Arkansky—or dependable rooks, like Brentford. But Brentford wanted to play a different game, a game of icy-cold draughts, a game of *dames*, as the French called it: he now hoped that if he went to the edge of the checkerboard he could compensate for losing Sybil by "crowning" himself with Helen and, with her help, moving backward with a vengeance. He was aware that this was a rather fuzzy scheme, but he saw no other options. He just hoped it would not pass, even in his own eyes, as a flight from trouble.

That would have been unfair, really. Trouble was as much in front of him as it was behind. Passing under the narrow archway that cut through the ramparts of the glacial fringe and heading toward Mushroom Point, he was now entering the hard, hummocky, hillocky stretch of his trip and he could feel the *Kinngait* snort and vibrate unpleasantly on the uneven ice. The carbon-arc searchlight at the bow showed nothing but a landscape that was about as easy to skate upon as the broken lumps of a gigantic sugar bowl.

But Brentford had a secret weapon upon his nose: Second Sight goggles. They allowed him, through some cutting of their Iceland-spar lenses, to foresee obstacles before he arrived at them. It only worked, however, if a few bothersome conditions were met: continuous scanning of the surrounding area (hence the half-circular windshield of the ship and the serious risk of a stiff neck), as steady a speed as possible (no mean feat in itself), and, the most mysterious and exacting of them all, possession of at least one quarter Highland Scottish blood.

Brentford Orsini had plenty of that fluid, being related through his mother (though he had inherited from her more insight than Second Sight) to the Mackays of Anticosti Island, the very house of the Nova Scotia baronetcy. By some fold in the fabric of things, Anticosti had always been known to the native Innu as Notiskuan, "the place where bears are hunted," and this was where his mother had indeed met and made herself bearable to a polar Orsini. His mother's mother was a Matheson of Cape Breton, and Matheson meant "son of the bear," exactly what the Orsini heir apparent, then, was to the second power. There was some transcendence in such coincidences, no doubt, and Brentford liked to think about them, or would have liked to, if he had not had to steer, "by his strong arm," as the Mackay motto boasted, the ship away from the ice boulders that jumped up in the searchlight. The Matheson motto was *Fac et Spere*, "Do and Hope," and seemed good advice for the time being.

The Second Sight goggles were useful but exhausting to use. After hours of searching and finding roundabout ways through the messy maze, Brentford often had to slow down, stop, and take a few minutes of nauseated rest in total darkness, or cup his head in his hands and slowly turn it from left to right, trying to alleviate the ache in his crackling cervical discs. He could hear all around him the ice crunching like splintered bones and the assassin cold mindlessly whistling a tuneless song as it tried to get inside the cabin. But soon Brentford had to get up and shuffle back to the helm, his shoulders and his eyes still painful from the strain.

He did not go as fast as he had expected to, but it was the number one rule of any arctic trip that expectations were worthless and that everything that could go wrong would eventually do so. He had now about five days to get to the pole, which could be done, depending on the ice, and provided he lost no time. A full day of sailing, if it could be called that, had taken him only fifty miles closer to his target, but these had been, he hoped, the hardest miles.

He tried to sleep for a few hours, but he could not find the switch to turn off the lamp in his head that was called Sybil. He remained seated and shivering in the cabin, with only his breath for company, making out through the thick blurry windshield the rough unfinished shapes of angry, growling, roaring ice sculptures mutely howling at the moon. This was pure Phobetor territory, here, a nightmarish wilderness with none of Phantasus' creatures to animate it, the true kingdom of Icelus, as Phobetor was known among the Gods. If Brentford peered into the landscape long enough, he could see, like many explorers before him, something like the outlines of a city emerging from the icy pandemonium: buildings out of ice blocks, domelike hillocks, razor-sharp spires of crystal, the dark canals of water leads. It occurred to him that the icescape tried to imitate New Venice, unless New Venice, in its moonlit marble whiteness, was but one more dream mirage from the mind of Icelus. Maybe there was a message in this metamorphosis about how useless or impossible it was to go away, or about how badly he already missed the place. For a while, he was tempted to go back, but somehow that demanded even more fuss than continuing on. He knew well that he was, quite literally, pursuing a dream, but this did not make it any easier to call it quits, when everything else seemed to be lost.

He was half asleep when the dawn caught him by surprise, a drowned pale sun that rolled slowly on the horizon like a coin about to fall. Mumbling about losing precious time, he shook off sleep and went out to do the chores, defrosting the windshield, scrubbing the runners and greasing the cast-iron shoes with a mixture of tar, tallow, and stearine, checking that the hulls and the rudder-skate had not suffered any damage beyond a few scrapes and minor blows. The air was so clear that he could see for miles a landscape as precise as a painted miniature, with distant sheets of ice flashing like planted mirror shards, and breathing it turned his lungs inside out. But that felt good, somehow.

He took out the sextant and theodolite to try to take his bearings, because the constant search for a passage and the effect of the drift were likely to have made him stray off course. Under these latitudes, the compass indicated a stubborn southwestern direction, and even travelling at night, the stars could not be depended upon with Polaris too high overhead to be seen. If he was right, he had been carried away to the east, but not to an extent that rendered his trip more absurd that it already was. So he kept on.

On this second day, the going was getting somehow smoother, with less steering around and more sastruga snow. At some point, the *Kinngait* even picked up speed, and the landscape jolted past in a blur of blue. Under the whirr of the fan blades, Brentford could hear the crackling and ringing of the runners, the spraying of crushed gems they spurted in their wake. In front of him, under the bow, the faint shadow of the ship, the rows and rows of swallowed rollers, the complicated lines of cracks quickly tangling and unravelling themselves wove a moving web that lulled and mesmerized him. The *Kinngait* went on steadily enough, except for some unexpected bumps that woke Brentford up as he dozed off at the helm. This was where he saw her for the first time.

A woman hurried on the ice in front of him, either guiding or fleeing the ship. He first took her for some eddy of snow, but even without his goggles he could clearly make out her white shape against the bluish ice, the train of her misty dress a hundred yards ahead of him, going as fast as the *Kinngait*, so that it seemed impossible to reduce the distance that separated them. It was of course a hallucination. These were inevitable, but he had not thought that they would occur so early in the trip. He felt lucid enough, though, but lucidity required that, lost in the middle of the paleocrystal sea, you did not trust your own lucidity. The woman slipped behind a boulder and did not reappear.

For a few hours, that is. Twilight soon followed dawn, and his searchlight now etching deeper, ink-black shadows in the icescape as it jumped past and dodged the yacht. At some point, when the night had risen all around him, he caught a glimpse of her again, as she advanced in front of him, almost beyond the reach of the light, straight ahead through the yellowish ice and snow. She was, it seemed, running on her bare feet, but he could not be quite sure of that. He could not see her face beneath her hood, but he figured out this much: if he thought about Sybil, then she would be Sybil; if he thought about Helen, she would be Helen; if he thought of the Ghost Lady, then it would be her as well; it could even be Seraphine, his first love, if his spirits ever went that low. The choice, he felt, was pretty much his, and it was a cruel choice to have to make.

What surprised him most was that—as he lost her for a while, caught another glimpse of her, then lost her again, then found her once more, as if she had been waiting for him—he had not done anything but follow her, without asking himself any questions. She could well have been leading him to his death, toward some crevice or some rising ridge he would see just at the last moment before crashing into it. The siren of the frozen sea. But still he followed on, not even persuaded that she would lead him somewhere, but just because it was the thing to do. He had come here because a dream had told him to do so, and for all he knew, while he was at it, he might as well chase a ghost, faithful to the feeling of love and longing he felt toward her flight. He did not even want to catch up with her. That was how he understood what William Whale had told him, in his own way, about Peary or Cook not *really* wanting to go to the real pole. Because there is no real pole, or if there is one, it's only real as long as you don't get there. You destroy it, and yourself, by reaching it.

As soon as he started to muse on this and lose his focus, he felt his left runner crack against some treacherous hummock, and the ship suddenly spin out of control. He threw himself on the port side to act as a counterweight, but it was too late, the *Kinngait* was capsizing, its right runner sliding as well, the windmill blades toppling and about to crash and break themselves on the ice. His only hope was that they would not burst through the roof and kill him as the ice yacht tumbled liked a rolled die.

The last thing Brentford saw before the searchlight broke was the girl standing on a hillock, slowly turning toward him, her hand pulling her hood backward, and revealing herself as totally faceless.

CHAPTER XXIII

A Wizard in Strange Trance

●

May the wolves devour the dreamer.
Kalevala, X

hen the wolves came. *Kajjait.* A pack of a dozen famished-looking silvery beasts that sniffed Gabriel's beheaded body and started to tear it apart, growling hungrily, their jaws snapping with excitement.

Once the thick clothes had been torn to rags, they started gnawing at the balls. "He who liveth by the sword...," thought the head, shaken awake from its slumber at the first bite. The head, which dared not call itself Gabriel anymore, could still feel the teeth sinking into the distant body and the flesh tearing off, ripped apart in tattered shreds. It hurt, but in an eerie way, as phantom limbs are said to do, but also, because of the cold, maybe less excruciatingly than the brain would have expected. It was like being operated on while under anaesthesia, when the numbed body becomes an abstract map of muscles and nerves, reacting unpleasantly to the surgery, in a dull, precise way that sets one's teeth on edge, more an expectation of suffering than an actual pain. Still, this relative loss of sensation carried with it a certain anxiety, as if the head felt buried alive and was knocking itself repeatedly against a coffin lid made of its own skull bone.

The head did not know whether it should close its eyes or not. The sight was awful but fascinating, as the body was flayed and mangled, the limbs jerking from the tugging of the wolves. One of them ran a few steps away, the left arm between its teeth, the gloved hand tightly curled in a fist. Gabriel's head could see the shoulder joint protruding out of the trunk, the ribs appearing on the side, even whiter than the snow. The blood on the ground had curdled purple under the northern lights.

One of the wolves, turning toward the head, finally noticed it, half buried in the snow. Their eyes met. But, instead of coming closer for a sniff, the wolf suddenly growled, looking at some point above it. The other wolves moved nervously, casting glances in the same direction, moving in ripples of fur as if grouping to attack. A groan resounded above Gabriel's head, and a shadow covered it. The brain remembered the story of a dead explorer who'd been eaten by his own pack, except for his head, which was found being watched over by the lead dog, in some token of loyalty, or perhaps it was waiting for the head to give it an ultimate order. Now some animal was protecting Gabriel's head as well: the wolves retreated and hurried on to finish the rest of their quarry, dragging it a few inches here and there with scraping sounds on the snow, cleaning up the carrion in a messy way that left strips of bloody muscle dangling from broken bones. They looked up from time to time, baring their fangs at the shadow but not daring to move toward it, as it towered above Gabriel's head. Was it a bear? But a bear would have attacked, and why would a bear have cared about the head anyway? To reciprocate the pains the Eskimo took to groom and feed the head of a killed *nanuk*, so that the beast would not speak ill of the hunters when it reached its own afterlife? Whatever it was, its looming presence spoiled the party. Sometimes, a few of the wolves tried to get closer to the head, then retreated again, fearing to lose some fine morsel of the half-eaten carcass.

Then, all of sudden, as if they had silently plotted among themselves, they attacked together. Before they could reach it, the shadow jumped over the head, a white furry beast knocking the wolves about with its powerful hind legs or its swinging tail, sending them rolling in the snow before they had a chance to bite. One of them, though, circled and darted at Gabriel's head, catching it by the earflaps of its hat. The white shape turned around and, with a thunderous roar, scared the wolf so badly it dropped the head, sending it rolling into the nearby crevasse. The head plummeted down, having just enough time to notice that a disarticulated body was lying down in the crack.

There was a shock and, coming toward the head at full speed, a light so strong it blinded the brain, piercing and melting it as it passed through. The burn peaked and receded slowly. Gabriel opened his eyes. He was now lying on the ice at the bottom of the crevasse, his head back on his shoulders. He tried and found he could move his limbs. They hurt in a diffuse way, but nothing, unbelievable as it seemed, had been broken by the fall. There was a God for suicides, he thought. He turned over and saw, ten yards above him, a dark streak of starry night between the narrow ice walls, and, from time and time, the muzzle of a whining wolf. No traces of the white shape remained visible, but Gabriel could feel its presence somewhere close by.

He got up, wondering, with less concern than he would have expected, if he were alive or dead, or both, or neither. He noticed that he now stood totally naked and freezing, though he remained rather indifferent about it, as if his body, after what it had gone through, would not bother him over so little. Maybe he was simply agonizing somewhere, as he had planned, and hallucinating in his agony.

A bluish light seemed to emanate from within the ice walls, and he could see that the crevasse went on, in front of him and behind, in a nearly straight line whose ends were invisible. He decided to follow it northward, hoping for some exit at the base of the cliff side, or for the moment when he would wake up, or forever black out.

The path sloped downward, and at some point he noticed that the opening above had disappeared and been replaced by a glazed roof of ice. He was now, by his own reckoning, somewhere under the sea. Then he saw them: bodies inside the walls—hundreds, thousands of them, standing frozen at different depths, like dummies in thick frosted-glass shop windows. They were not lined up in a row, but seemed occupied with everyday activities or maybe, Gabriel thought, arranged to mimic their last moments. He remembered who they were: the Qimiujarmiut, if that was the correct name, the People of the Narrow Land. Those who, according to some Inuit beliefs, had died a peaceful death and were therefore not allowed in the auroras. The sight was gruesome, but after having seen himself mutilated by wolves, he found their still, blurry silhouettes almost soothing. Except that, as he kept on walking along the walls, the corpses seemed to be observing him with some curiosity, wondering why this newcomer could walk around freely. He now hurried past them, without looking back if he could help it. He had no idea what he was doing here. This was not the kind of afterlife he had wanted. His first choice would have been the good materialist Nothingness, with Heaven a close second. Even the kickball games in the northern lights would have appealed to him. But the Narrow Land had never been an option. Hell, he had certainly died violently, hadn't he? He would have to talk to the manager.

Then, it dawned on him that perhaps he wasn't dead. Not quite yet. Not to the point where he would be kept in that translucent freezer he was passing through. He wouldn't be shaking this way if he weren't made of quivering flesh and rattling bone. This was good news, after all. A body is not unlike a pet—stupid and dirty as it is, one becomes attached to it.

He walked on, until a smooth slab of snow blocked the ice corridor. Some voice inside Gabriel told him he would have to go through it, but he had no pick or shovel to clear the way. He took a few steps backward and then ran toward the snow slab, but this did nothing but print his own silhouette in the snow. His face flushed from the cold, he had to charge again, and this time he crashed all the way through, as if he'd burst through a paper hoop. On the other side, the crash woke up a dog with red insomniac eyes, which growled at Gabriel as he got up. He was now standing under a dome completely filled up with frozen bodies, which he could perceive through the thick ice and which were all looking back at him. An igloo stood beneath the middle of the dome, with a low narrow entry, but the dog prevented all his attempts to come closer.

Once again, Gabriel had an inspiration. He noticed a corpse lying near him—his own, in fact, as he had seen it devoured by the wolves. Wincing with disgust, he bent to tear off a piece of his own forearm—the flesh resisted a bit, and Gabriel even thought he heard a moan—and threw it as far away as he could. The dog ran off to fetch it, stupidly wagging its tail. Barely holding back his nausea, Gabriel ran to the entrance of the igloo and advanced on all fours through the narrow corridor, as if he had always known that this was the way to behave in such a situation.

The tunnel seemed to go on forever but eventually opened onto the inside of the igloo, which was much wider that it had seemed from the outside. Its roof, in a way Gabriel could not comprehend, was transparent, and from where he was he could see not only the starry skies but also a wide expanse of land. New Venice was on his left, not so far away, its lights visible from below, as if the ground it stood upon were made out of dark ice or glass. It made his head dizzy. Then he saw her.

A long-haired woman. Sitting near a huge circular well. *Saana*, thought Gabriel. The Inuk Goddess of the Sea.

"Oh. You can call me Helen," said the woman, turning toward him, her face half-lit by the flame that danced from a lamp in the ceiling. It was Helen Kartagener all right, but in the trembling chiaroscuro light, Gabriel thought she also looked a little like Lilian Lenton. He stood up, and noticing her amused downward glimpse, he covered with his hands his penis, which the cold had shrivelled into a shrimp.

"How are you, Mr. d'Allier?" asked Helen, the amusement now in her voice.

Gabriel tried not to look impressed.

"Very well. Thank you. I've just fallen down a crevasse and been devoured by wolves."

"Rather classical part of the initiation. How do you feel right *now*?"

He thought about it for a moment.

"To speak frankly, like I've fallen asleep during my anthropology class."

Helen chuckled gently and indicated the surroundings.

"It's not so bad, though. I'll give you an A for this project. And a diploma for the crash course in shamanism. The underground trip toward me wasn't bad either. You may have confused or conflated one or two things, but after all, it has to remain an individual experience, your own version of it."

"As an *angakoq*, I may disappoint you when it comes to ventriloquism and sleight-of-hand. I may not be very entertaining during the long winter nights."

"I know. Things have been rushed a bit. But you already have the modesty of a true Inuk and you also have a *very* powerful helping spirit."

"The Polar Kangaroo, you mean?"

"We know him as Kiggertarpok here," she said. "You could not have chosen, or been chosen by, a better ally. He protects the city much better than I could do. Now, if you will..."

She showed him a comb made of narwhal tusk at the edge of the well. "I suppose you did not sleep through that part of the class."

Gabriel advanced and took the comb. The well was so deep the eyes could not fathom it. It was full of seals and walruses gliding around in a complicated choreography, and it stank atrociously, he thought. As he drew closer to Helen, he could see that she looked tired and sick, her skin waxen and wrinkled, the hands on her lap awfully maimed, with all the upper phalanxes neatly cut away, as if devoured by some wild animal. But for someone he had seen dead a few months before, she was not so bad.

As the ritual demanded, he started unravelling and combing her long tangled hair, slowly, carefully, hoping she would not notice that his penis was slowly metamorphosing back into some bigger, harder-shelled crustacean. For a man who thought a few hours (years? centuries?) earlier that Stella would be the very last woman he would ever desire, this was nothing short of a miracle. Such was the power of the Sea Goddess.

She sighed with pleasure, her eyes half-closed.

"So what brings you here?" she eventually asked.

"I supposed it was you."

"No. *You* brought *me* here. If I can be of any use."

"I have no idea. People usually come to find you about food, don't they? But that would be Brentford's business, not mine."

"Yes. I have heard, through the grapevine, so to speak, that he's been running the Greenhouse. I'd be curious to see the kind of crooked vegetables he grows. It's not my line, however. As you know, I specialize in animals. I was quite a huntress in my youth."

"I seem to remember Brentford was having a problem about hunting quotas. But I could not tell you what the problem was, exactly."

"I know and I'm taking care of it. Just pass the message along, if you will."

"You'll have more chances to speak to him than I will. He also told me you had given him some kind of rendezvous. At the North Pole."

Helen stood silent, for a while.

"To be quite exact I sent a messenger. Brentford is on his way, I think. And, as you see, I'm not," she conceded.

Gabriel tried not to sound reproachful.

"You have sent him to his death, then."

"I sent him *away* from his death. You did not approve of his marriage any more than I did, did you? He's worth much better than that... What's her name? Sybil. She was the last girl who should have been allowed to be called by such a noble first name. Very much the girl-next-stage door, isn't she?"

Gabriel could not believe it. *Women*, he thought, nodding his head as if he had hit the mother lode of philosophical truth.

"I hope he will pull it off, though." said Helen, as if to herself, with an accent of real concern.

"It is not too late to help him."

"I'll help him by not helping him. He can do more by himself than he thinks. He only has to find out how much. You, I can help. Or, at least, I can help some people who want to meet you."

"And who would that be?" asked Gabriel.

She sighed and turned toward him.

"You talk a lot... Maybe you should quit shamanism and become a hairdresser instead," she said. "In any case, thanks for the combing. I badly needed it. I see fewer and fewer shamans these days. But you seem to have appreciated it as well," she added in a teasing tone. Goddesses, thought Gabriel, move in mischievous ways.

"Isn't there a part where my clothes come flying back to me?" he asked, her downward glance reminding him he was naked.

But the voice that answered wasn't Helen's.

CHAPTER XXIV

The Phantom Patrol

●

Wonderfully—really wonderfully—like the Tree
of Knowledge in Eden, he said, was that Pole: all the rest of
earth lying open and offered to man—but That persistently
veiled and 'forbidden.' It was as when a father lays a
hand upon his son, with: 'Not here, my child; wheresoever
else you will—but not here.'
M.P. Shiel, *The Purple Cloud*, 1901

It was the cold that woke Brentford: a sudden revolt of all his shaking flesh. His head hurt from some blow that had knocked him out, but passing his gloved hand over his cropped hair, he felt only a swollen knot at the back of his head, probably from a clomp against the stove. Thank God he'd had his hood on to protect him. Things could have been worse. They were merely catastrophic.

He was lying, he realized, on the ceiling of his ship. The *Kinngait* was almost upside down, tilting slightly to the side, sustained in that position by the stump of its broken mast. It was dark, as all the lamps had been broken, and freezing, because the stove had gone out. This was better than its having started a fire, but there was little chance, if any, that he could make it work again.

Brentford had no idea of what time it was, or of his bearings. He was lost in the middle of the closest earthly definition of nowhere. Walking back the hundred-odd miles to New Venice in the February night would be nothing short of suicidal, but waiting for help in the overturned ship this far from the city did not make much sense, either, especially as the ice, which he could hear grumbling around him like an empty stomach, could very well crush him at any moment now. Both options seemed equally bleak, but they were still options... which also meant that a mistake could be made. As the clenched-jaw survivor he was supposed to change into, he would almost have preferred to have no choice at all and instead go for broke without further soul-searching. Being dead was one thing, dead and wrong another.

There were priorities, though. Light and warmth had to be found, or the weather conditions would decide for him. He did not want to end up like the captain of the fabled ship *Octavius*, found frozen, brittle quill in hand, in front of his logbook after thirteen years of drifting and wintering around the Arctic seas.

He got up and dizzily raised his hands toward the deck hold, struggling to open the latch, his arm across his face to protect it from the tumbling contents. A manna of material crumbled down to what used to be the ceiling. His limbs quivering from the cold, Brentford groped about in the heap, hoping to locate a spare flashlight and the primus stove, which he hoped hadn't suffered from its fall. He found the time excruciatingly long before he could place his hand on the Ever Ready lamp. And then there was light, revealing the disheartening chaos of the topsy-turvy cabin, the instruments broken, the maps scattered everywhere as if a storm had blown inside the ship. By chance, the solid glass windshields had been spared. He rummaged for the extra batteries, and for the primus stove that would save his life—whatever it would be saved for. From time to time a loud crack from outside made him start, but he controlled himself, remembering that he was going to suffer more from loneliness than from intruders. The stove was there, and it seemed in working order. It would not be enough to heat the cabin, but he would have warm meals for a while, and maybe reach Heaven with a full stomach, something many dead explorers would have envied him for.

He retrieved a watch that, still ticking, informed him that it was around two o'clock, probably A.M. though maybe he had already reached a latitude where the polar night still extended throughout the entire day. From where he barely stood, the unhelpful stars were invisible, and he did not feel like going out to check them just then. His idea was to hope for the crack of dawn that would come sooner or later, then use his sextant and, according to his bearings, either abandon ship, dragging the spare light sled he had in the hold, or stay there and send some flashing balloon message.

Rubbing his limbs through the extra fur clothes he had picked up, and using his flashlight as sparingly as he could, he Robinson-Crusoed or, rather, Allan-Gordoned his way through the following hours, trying to organize his anti-cabin in the most sensible manner while waiting for daybreak. The top of his bunk, seemingly solid enough to hold his weight, had been fitted with a mattress and a caribou fur–lined bag, inside which he could enjoy relative warmth. That way, he would make, he thought, one of those comfortably tucked-in corpses that rescue parties sometimes end up finding, a grin of welcome on his blackened face.

Using a wooden spoon, he ate clam soup from a half-warmed tin can and drank a little brandy straight from the bottle, trying hard to think of a way out of his situation while trying equally hard to forget about it for a while. Outside, the ice snored uneasily, grumbling in its sleep, having nightmares, no doubt, about all the men it had killed, ready to turn violently and smother the *Kinngait*. Great, thought Brentford with a sigh. He understood he was not going to sleep, as deep down some primeval, childish fear had gotten hold of his guts. Even the faceless banshee whom he had followed so blindly now filled him with a retrospective awe. He was finally dozing off a little, though, when the voices woke him up.

He could be wrong, of course. It could have been some trick of the wind, some spillover from an interrupted dream, a classic Arctic hallucination. But as he pricked up his ears, now sure that he was awake, he could hear them again, not only the voices but also the steps that crunched closer to the ship. He could not believe it. People. Here. So soon. Grasping the flashlight, crawling out of the caribou sleeping bag, and banging his head against the lower edge of the upturned bunk, he managed to land on the ceiling and hurried toward the windshield. He had not dreamed. There were human shapes, all around the ship, all carrying hurricane lamps and cautiously approaching. He was about to flash his lamp when one of the shapes lifted its lantern to its own face.

Brentford recoiled in horror.

There was no face, nothing but a mummified grin and eyes bulging out.

Brentford's stomach knotted and he felt himself melting in a prickly cold sweat. He closed his eyes and looked again, trembling. There were seven figures, moving closer, their bearded faces all visible now, some yellowish and cracked, some swollen and black. They wore ragtag clothes, woollen greatcoats heavy with ice, sealskin jackets with fur hoods, frosted welsh-wigs or leather hats with earflaps, duffel knee boots or *kamiks,* large woollen or fur mittens—all holding rifles. Some of them wore wire snow-glasses that, thank God, hid their eyes. Their motley clothes, like their body parts, seemed to have been patched up and sewn together haphazardly.

The Phantom Patrol. This couldn't be true. Brentford, trembling, fumbled for his rifle and then tried not to move.

The undead advanced slowly, silently, their rifles cocked. One of them stood a few feet in front of the ship, waving his lantern from left to right. Brentford tried not to breathe so as not to leave a blur on the glass that separated him from them. The phantom put the lantern at his feet, casting a long shadow behind himself, and then placed his fists on his hips.

"Ahoy there!" he cried with what seemed to Brentford an American accent.

Brentford crouched a notch lower, feeling as if he were being trussed up with ropes made of shivers.

"We expected a warmer welcome, sir," the man continued after a moment, turning toward the others as if to gather their approbation. "What kind of man would have such a hardened heart as not to salute fellow travellers in such a wilderness? Especially when those travellers have walked a long way to meet him and are, shall we say, rather hungry."

Some of the other men burst into a yellow, unpleasant laughter.

"Believe me, sir," the man went on, as the others came closer to him. "We have spent long periods of wintering in cramped cabins or tents, and there is nothing that we understand and value more than a man's need for a little privacy."

The others nodded with conviction, some saying "Aye, aye."

"But, as we have also experienced, there is absolutely no place on earth where a man can feel more desperate and helpless when he is on his own."

A hum of approval greeted his words.

"Here, kind sir, here and only here, can you learn to truly appreciate the value of someone being there to lend you a hand. Or a fresh leg."

The patrol roared, a sickly, grating laughter that curdled Brentford's blood. The man silenced them with a gesture of his hand, before tipping his hat.

"We are unforgivable. We attempt to address a gentleman but we haven't introduced ourselves. Maybe we should do this now, mates."

Regrouping in front of the ship, the men all put their lanterns on the snow, in a row, a few feet from one another, and then, walking back together, formed a straight line behind the orator, who started his banter.

"As you know, there is nothing worse under these latitudes than the lack of entertainment. This is why we are happy and proud to present to you the best success of the famous Royal Arctic Theatre since *Harlequin Light*. Ladies and Gentlemen, *The Skating Rink Ting Ting* or *The Phantom Patrol's Polar Pageant*!"

The men applauded, while Brentford, now a paralyzed block of anguish, wondered if going mad would not be the easiest way out of this demented situation.

The master of ceremonies went and sat on a nearby block of ice, looking very comfortable.

"Come on, Geo," he shouted, turning toward the back row. At that command, one of the men emerged into the circle of light, striding like an automaton toward the "stage" lamps. He had a grey, sideburned, sallow face under his Eugenie hat, and his bulk was made larger by a thick brown greatcoat. He turned, showing, painted on his back, a coat of arms and a motto: "St. George and Merry England." This was, Brentford suddenly remembered, what British sailors did to have some target to look at as they man-hauled sleighs in snowstorms. Having pirouetted again, the man psalmodied in a croaky, pathetic voice:

I am Saint George that valiant knight
All feet no toes for England's right
My cross stands on a useless land
Show me the man that dare before me stand.

Another tall, bearded man, with a greyish hollow face, no lips over his square white teeth, and a U.S. Cavalry hat on his head, jumped into the lights and pretended to defy the English sailor:

Here comes I, I am the Snipe
And I am carrying Stars and Stripes
Saint George thinks he's valiant and bold,
If his blood's hot, it'll soon be cold!

The two men drew knives from sheaths inside their coats and, crouching on their creaky joints, exchanged murderous glares, ready to lunge at each other's throat, until a third sailor, wearing a tartan sash across his sealskin jacket and a helmetlike worsted cap, interrupted them to declaim with a Scots burr:

I'm MacGlashan, ma body's steeled
Nae man can make a Scotsman yield
I'd rather set ma blood to flow
And lay Snipe and George doon in the snow!

The first two valiant knights turned at the same time toward this new opponent, but then there came up from behind them an older, bulky, yellowish fellow dressed in thick furs, carrying what seemed to Brentford a huge piece of driftwood. In a stentorous Irish brogue, he declared:

> *In come I, ould Belsey Bob*
> *On me shoulthers I carry me knob,*
> *A fryin' pan and wid yer thighs*
> *I will make hot or cold mince pies!*

Four men now stared at each other, weapons in hand, rolling defiant glassy eyes, threatening each other and not daring to make the first move. This sick pantomime went on for a while, until a smaller ashen fellow, with his nose fallen off, trotted quickly between them and announced himself:

> *In comes I, Little Twing Twang,*
> *The lieutenant of the Press Gang.*
> *I craved money from my mates*
> *Now I'll sweep the food from their plates!*

As the others turned toward him, he put a black finger to his cracked lips, and winking a horrible wink, indicated to them the sixth protagonist, approaching slowly, like a ghost, into the mock limelight. This one was nothing more than a skeletal shadow, disappearing within a greatcoat much too large for his long bony limbs. One of his hands, cut at the wrist, had been replaced by a wooden spoon tightly tied to the stump. He spoke with a hissing voice, as if in agony:

> *Here comes I, I'm Hump-back Jack,*
> *Dyin' shipmates on my back,*
> *Out of mine I've got but five,*
> *All the rest be starved alive.*

The five others suddenly jumped on him and pretended to slaughter him with large stabbing gestures, as he dramatically knelt down on the icy ground. Then, instead of sharing their spoils, the killers turned against one another, fighting like knockabout clowns, until, one by one, they all fell on the snow in histrionic agonies, except the so-called Saint George, who, his foot on the heap of corpses, addressed the master of ceremonies:

> *Doctor! Doctor! I'll give five pounds*
> *To cure these men of mortal wounds*

The master of ceremonies stood up and came forward to observe the agonized sailors, with his hands behind the back of his fur coat. Brentford, starting at the word *doctor*, thought he detected a passing resemblance to a portrait of Octave Pavy, the drowned doctor of the hideous Greely failure. His fear now blended with a strange feeling of fascination as he followed the dialogue:

> *I'm the famous Doctor Phoenix*
> *And there is nothing I can't fix*
> *But I shall not come under ten,*

announced the doctor proudly.

Saint George:
> *For Doctor Phoenix, ten Pounds then!*
> *But please, what made you a doctor?*

The Doctor:
> *I've travelled far and then some more:*

From the fire spot, the cupboard head,
Up stairs and then to bed.

Saint George:
Is that all, sir?
That far and no farther?

The Doctor:
I've travelled high, I've travelled low,
Through Hail, rain, and frost and snow.
I have been to the farthest North
Where roasted pigs come trotting forth
Forks in their arses, squealing Eat me
All the way to the Open Sea.
I have cured Charles Francis Hall
Rubbed him dry with a wet snowball
While my friend Doctor Bessels
Made him drink warm ash with pills.

Saint George:
These are credentials for sure,
Prithee tell me what can you cure?

The Doctor:
The itch, the stitch, the palsy, the scurvy
The rummelgumption in a thin man's belly
And if a sailor has nineteen blue devils
Twenty of them I'll cast out of his skull
Seven men once I could even save
That had lain seven years in their grave.
I can even cure a man of the toothache

Saint George:
How's That?

The Doctor:
Cut off his head and throw it in a ditch.
Now, in my breeches, I've crutches for lame lice,
And a little bottle of hectrum spectrum Ice
Some bear's feathers, some wool from a frog
Some eighteen inches of last December's fog.
Three drops to their temples and one to their heart,
That's it, brothers, rise up and play your part.

He feigned to pour the potion from an invisible phial. One by one, the fallen men started to move, and, thus resurrected, painfully got up from the ice, their limbs stiff, but not suffering, it seemed, from the cold. Then, stringing themselves together, their arms around each other's waist and their awfully mutilated faces lit from below by the row of lanterns, they chanted hoarsely:

Once I was dead and now I'm alive,
Blessed be the doctor that made me revive.
We'll all join hands and fight no more,
And be brothers, like before.

Brentford, who did not know anymore whether he was trembling from cold, fear, or tension, thought it was over, but he was wrong. Another man he had not seen arrived in front of the improvised stage, his body entirely hidden under some hooded brown garment.

I am the Unseen Comrade
The last you'll see before you're dead

Gliding all wrapt and hooded,
One more than can be counted.

Then the Patrol bowed and saluted in the little circle of trembling lights. There was no applause save the crackles and growls of the ice all around. Brentford was still afraid, but most of all he felt invaded by a weary sadness that was beyond reason or words.

"Doctor Phoenix," however, had started speaking again.

"Excuse us, sir, if our little spectacle did not amuse you. It seems we have developed a humour of our own that some may find unpleasant, and we are well aware that our overall appearance does not speak in our favour. We do not, alas, delude ourselves with the vain hope that we can obtain your sympathy. In that respect as in many others, as one of us once said, the only illusions we have left are our optical illusions."

This provoked a subdued ripple of approval through the company, the way an old joke does.

"But maybe we can aim at a little pity. For once, sir, *we were like you*," the voice said with an accent of sincerity that moved Brentford in spite of himself.

The man indicated a direction behind himself, which Brentford thought might be north.

"Once, as you seem to be doing, we regarded a certain spot as the noblest place a man could tread upon, and we prided ourselves in being such men, or the faithful companions of such a man. We thought that there was no sacrifice we would not consent to in order to fulfil that ambition. And now, please, look at us, unpleasant as it is. Look at the way our pride has been punished."

The Patrol now faced Brentford, looking solemn and attentive. The doctor took a step forward.

"For, sooner or later, there comes that special moment, that *very* special moment, if you can imagine it, when that very man who deemed himself a hero suddenly decides that he will go out, dig up the grave of his friend, and with a rusty knife help himself to a slab of that half-rigid, half-rotten flesh and chew it raw, sir, as he is reflected in his dead mate's glassy, unbelieving eyes. At that moment, this man's will to reach his Farthest North has been fulfilled beyond his wildest dreams and fears. This is how God humbles some of us, sir. Those he loves, he reserves as flesh for others, as he did with his own Son."

A long silence ensued.

"There is nothing God hates as much as the pride of Man. This we have learned the hard way. It is a strong malediction, but also our noble mission to roam this land eternally so that we can protect it against Man, and protect Man against it."

Brentford released his grip on his gun, but it was then that the Patrol slowly began moving toward him.

CHAPTER XXV

Eskimos to the Rescue!

●

*"Should you meet any white men, treat them
kindly, and you shall be rewarded."*
"Specimen dialogue," *Eskimaux Vocabulary for
the Use of the Arctic Expedition,* 1850

The voice, Gabriel thought, came with a rather bad breath. Bad enough to bring him back to life. Half opening his eyes, he could make out, in the dim light, the face of an Inuk bending over him. The Inuk said something Gabriel did not understand, and then started rubbing Gabriel's nose with a fistful of ice. This woke him up completely, protesting and sputtering, while someone laughed not far from him.

His eyes were now wide open. He was lying in a dark igloo, surrounded by four Inuit who threw huge shadows on the curved glazed walls. It took a while to recognize them as the men he had seen in the Inuit People's Ice Palace. One of them, the tallest, spoke a little English.

"How are you?" he asked, his brow knitted in a way Gabriel did not find especially benevolent.

"How am I?" Gabriel repeated, returning the question. He could not feel his hands or feet and felt in his stomach the sudden fear that they had been frozen.

"It happened that the poor Inuit found you at the foot of a big rock. Lying in the snow. But the *qallunaq* is safe," said the tall Inuk.

Gabriel struggled to sit up. He was on an *iglerk*, wrapped in furs, his clothes drying on a rack over the oil lamp that also lit a scene that he found rather dismal. The igloo had been put up rather quickly, and was not very warm, with draughts swirling around. A pile of foul-smelling food lay in a corner, and the moss wick from the lamp spluttered a little, so that the surrounding Inuit flickered like the pictures of a finishing dream.

"I can't feel my hands," said Gabriel, with some anguish in his voice.

The tall man, turning toward the others, translated, eliciting a chuckle from one of them—the uncouth thief Gabriel had seen eloping with a knife. The one who had rubbed Gabriel's nose, and who wore the paraphernalia of a shaman, now looked at him moodily, then spoke to the tall one, who in turn translated to Gabriel.

"They're frozen. But it will come back."

He then took Gabriel's red, slightly swollen hand and shook it in the exaggerated Inuk fashion, the smelly man's chuckle turning to laughter this time. Gabriel had the strange, scary sensation of having a wooden limb attached to his wrist, as if he'd slept on his arm.

"My name is Tuluk," said the tall one.

"I'm Gabriel."

They repeated the name, passing it around amongst one another as if it were some sort of strange absurd object they did

not know what to do with. The oldest of the four eventually
came to Gabriel and bowed, introducing himself in a broken
English that had been fixed the Eskimo way: improbably but
dependably.

"My name Uitayok. I am very sad this poor igloo offer."

"I thank you for saving my life," said Gabriel, bowing
back.

"This one Ajuakangilak. Very powerful *angakoq*," Uitayok
kept on, pointing toward the brooding shaman, who barely
nodded to Gabriel.

"This one here my son Tiblit," Uitayok continued, in a tone
that was almost more sincerely apologetic than when he had
excused himself about the igloo.

Tiblit came closer to Gabriel and gave him another of those
Five-on-the-Rossi-Forel-scale handshakes that seemed to amuse
him no end. Gabriel wondered if Tiblit were not playing the
classic part of the Eskimo Clown, knowing it would always
work with the *qallunaat* and meet their expectations. There was
always a bit of *commedia dell'arctic* to such occasions.

However, thanks to the violent handshake, the blood was
starting to flow back into Gabriel's right hand, and rather painfully so, like a spring river break-up carrying cutting slabs of ice
down along his veins. His left fist, however, was still clenched
and remained insensitive. But as he slowly pried open his fingers, he saw in his palm the Polar Kangaroo amulet that he had
found at the I.P.I.P. He did not know how long he had been
holding that.

The *angakoq* froze, while the others looked at each other.

"Kiggertarpok!" the shaman exclaimed, before casting a
look at Gabriel that he interpreted as rather malevolent.

They had a confabulation between them that seemed to
last forever. They spoke too quickly for Gabriel to make
sense of the very few words that he happened to grasp. He

overheard *qavaq*, though, the word Inuit used to refer to southerners and idiots.

"Where you get it?" eventually asked Tuluk.

"I found it at the Inuit People's Ice Palace."

They observed him attentively and, he thought, cautiously. Maybe they recognized him, although he doubted that they had paid much attention to him in the heat of that moment. He did not know if it was a good idea to tell them that he had seen them being caught red-handed and then harassed by the guards, as he had no idea of what they would think that made him: a kind of accomplice sharing a secret or a cumbersome witness to their embarrassment. He decided he needed their complicity and he went for it.

"The same day that you were there."

This triggered another animated discussion. Uitayok said something that quieted everyone, although the *angakoq* kept casting side glances at Gabriel that did not reassure him. Tuluk eventually explained what troubled them.

"It happens that this little Inuit group is just out of *qallunaq* prison. For this little knife. But the *qallunaat* have the little knife back and the Inuit have nothing and they go to prison," he said, darkly.

Gabriel remembered how difficult it had been for the Inuit to get used to the *qallunaq* idea of justice. The Eskimos were not the teddy bears some well-meaning Whites thought they were. They were about as good savages as any other human beings, that is, they were good as long as they weren't savage. They knew about violence and retribution, of course, mostly in the ancient, time-honoured way. They had vendetta stories that would shame a nineteenth-century Corsican mountaineer's, and under the conditions in which they lived, even Jesus Christ would have been liable to jump at some apostle's throat, knife in hand, sooner or later. But why strangers had to meddle with such personal business as justice remained a mystery to them. They submitted to it in most cases, surrendering either to strength or to symbolical showmanship, but they seldom seemed to really get the point, or they reacted to it strangely. The first two Inuit murderers who had been sentenced to death in Canada, Gabriel had read somewhere, had carved little figures out of walrus tusk as presents for the executioner's wife. Gabriel had never understood if this was meant to excuse themselves for the trouble the hangman was taking on their behalf—as the Whites would have liked to think—or as some subtle way to pass on the guilt to others. He was not sure if the four Inuit that surrounded him now had learned any lesson from their prison stay except that the less you deal with those dangerous *qallunaat* bastards the better it is for your fur-wrapped behind. But as Tuluk plodded through their story, it was clear that there was more to it than a simple misunderstanding about the Philosophy of Right. In fact, it smelled even fishier than the igloo did.

"They let these Inuit go yesterday. 'You're free,' they said. 'Go away.' Then these Inuit buy a sled and they buy dogs and they buy food. It's to go home. But they go home and the *qallunaat* follow us. Like hunters. So these Inuit turn and turn, and the *qallunaat* are always behind and in front of these Inuit. So Uitayok says that these Inuit go through the sea to Kalaallit Nunaat. ("Greenland," Gabriel translated as he listened.) And it happened that these Inuit find you lying in the snow."

"I am very thankful that you stopped on your way."

Tuluk hesitated before he went on.

"It happened that they did not find you on their own...," he said, obviously struggling with some notion he could not convey to Gabriel, because he either could not or did not really want to.

"Kiggertarpok. He brings these Inuit for you," Uitayok cut him off.

Tuluk looked uncertain, then continued. "It is like Uitayok says. It is the dogs. These dogs they do not obey well to bad sled drivers like these Inuit. These dogs do not fear the whip and they have eyes not like the dogs and they listen to another voice in the wind."

Tuluk was speaking low, now, and the others nodded slowly. Gabriel could feel they were genuinely worried and maybe a little apprehensive as well.

"These dogs see Kiggertarpok in front. These Inuit see Kiggertarpok, too. They are afraid. But the dogs, they want to follow Him. And so these Inuit have to follow, too. And they follow and they follow and they find you. And around you in the snow, we can see the... shapes... of Kiggertarpok. Not from a long time ago. There to warm and save you. But, then, Kiggertarpok is not there anymore."

Gabriel nodded. He dimly understood why the *angakoq* was looking at him that way. These fugitives had been diverted from their route, which they deemed the way to salvation, by a Spirit who had led them to no better finding than a half-frozen *qallunaq* with nothing to share and unable to help them in any way. And, on top of it, this white wreck had about him the reek of the uncanny, carrying an amulet that had been apparently enough to enrol Kiggertarpok as his *tornaq*, his helping spirit. Gabriel wondered if he should tell them of his little chat with Saana, or Helen, or whoever she was, but somehow he thought that would not sit well with Whatsisname the Sombre Sorcerer, who looked either wary of a possible rival or jealous of a favour bestowed on one more useless *qavaq*. Bringing your own God to the exploration party is one thing, but stealing other people's helping spirits was certainly as criminal as stealing a knife. Gabriel tried for what he thought was Eskimo politeness.

"I am sorry you had to go out of your way for a person as useless as I am."

"You *angakoq*?" asked Uitayok bluntly.

Gabriel decided not to make any extravagant claim about his momentary supernatural powers, which he suspected had everything to do with a typical local cocktail of alcohol, exhaustion, and numbness from the cold. He also knew that Inuit were, generally speaking, more or less uneasy with their own shamans, and still more cautious about those of others. And then there was the matter of the notoriously tense relationships between shamans themselves. He certainly did not want to get into some sort of contest with one well-seasoned, ill-meaning *angakoq*. They would not believe his denial, of course, as *angakut* as a rule always play it cagey with strangers. But at least he would have tried his best to make himself understood.

"It's only the amulet," he reassured them. "You want it?" he then asked the *angakoq* as a gesture of goodwill. But the shaman took a step backward, spitting on the floor. This did not necessitate any translation. Judging by the way he had glanced at it, he was obviously interested, but probably did not want to accept anything from the *qallunaq* in front of the others.

"Do you hungry?" asked Uitayok, who was looking for some way to dispel the tension that was condensing in the igloo. He was the host and considered his guest, however unwanted, to be under his protection. Gabriel, who remembered he had not eaten anything either at or since Brentford's wedding, was hungry indeed, but the smell that rose from the food reserve Uitayok was indicating was not exactly appetizing. He said yes, though, thinking it would at least help in creating some sort of bond between them all.

But this proved even harder than he thought. Tuluk announced some *kivioq*, and dragging a dead seal from the reserve, he ripped it open with a knife. Gabriel's heart darted up into his throat. The seal was actually a kind of larder, and had been filled with rotting sea birds looking a bit like miniature penguins (guillemots or auks, maybe, but Gabriel, the typical city dweller, knew little ornithology). These were now passed around. The Inuit took the heads of the birds inside their mouths, and having gnawed at their necks with their renowned all-purpose teeth, peeled the birds like fruits, with a quick downward gesture, before eating their bodies. Then they took the fat from under the discarded skins and smeared their faces with it, as it was, Tuluk explained, good for the cold. Gabriel was instructed to put some on his half-frostbitten nose, which he did, wondering if they were not playing a trick on him. They were watching him intently, looking at each other and talking, he supposed, about the rather clumsy way he was doing things, with hands that were stinging and burning, and little better than two wood planks. Sometimes they chuckled, but he was not sure about what. He felt a bit like a child in the midst of teasing, slightly contemptuous adults.

But this was still better than having to eat raw half-rotten birds. Gabriel, hopelessly trying to hide his disgust, would have rather chewed the flesh of his own forearm than this sweet, reeking, melting flesh. His hosts' systematic spitting and thunderous belches did not really stimulate his appetite either, not to mention the miniature bird carcasses strewn all over the floor.

Once again he wondered if this was the Eskimos' normal way of doing things, or if they were putting on a show or some sort of hazing whose aim was obscure to him. Was it a kind of initiation ritual that would help him to be a part of them, if only for the short time they had to spend together? Or an attempt at self-assertion, to put him ill at ease, to make him feel how inept and useless he was? Maybe it was just his own delusion of the persecution he had come to associate with most forms of social life: two is company, three is a lynch mob, as he was fond of saying.

He thought of Brentford's book and its dream of a True Community, but he couldn't help thinking how opaque the communities would remain to one another, always misunderstanding each others' motives. Well. Society is what you have to swallow, whether you like it or not, thought Gabriel, gulping down his carrion snack with a lopsided smile that he hoped would pass muster.

"Good, huh?" asked Tuluk, with an inscrutable expression.

It was so good that after four or five rounds, Gabriel was on the verge of walking on all fours through the narrow entrance of the igloo to go out and deposit a full northern Lights yawn, as the delicate local wit called this rather frequent phenomenon. But he remained stoical, comforting himself with the idea that the next course could not possibly be worse.

"Seal's eyes. Very Good," said Tuluk, who looked sincere as he smiled, offering him a few small slices of some gelatinous matter, almost happy, it seemed, to share such a treat with their guest.

Gabriel did not sleep, but the night had been a nightmare on its own. He had been crammed, with almost no clothes on, into a *krepik* between Tuluk and the repulsive Tiblit, whose sexual jokes (if he understood correctly the general notion) amused Gabriel much less than they did the others— they even forced a mild smile onto the shaman's face. Tiblit even had sex with dogs, a straight-faced Tuluk informed him. For a descendant of dogs, as all *qallunaat* were according to the generous Inuk mythology, this was hardly reassuring, and Gabriel turned his back toward Tuluk instead, much to the others' delight.

The body heat brought back the blood to his extremities, but it was more like a long burn than a real relief. His neighbours snored so loudly that Gabriel almost expected the igloo to tumble down on them. He secretly abjured his faith in primitive anarcho-communism, or at least embraced the version which had private rooms and an à la carte menu.

He had the strange, unpleasant feeling than he was being subjected to some sort of life lesson, that he was supposed to enjoy the sensation of breathing under any circumstances or to realize with gratitude that some people had harder lives than himself. But right now he did not enjoy it that much, to speak frankly. And what he mostly realized was that however the Eskimos lived, they were no wiser or better than he was. They knew how to do things that would be hard for him to learn, of course, but they would have a hard time learning some things he knew or could do. And in the end, anyway, the lesson the surrounding conditions were supposed to teach you so brutally was only this: when all human life is boiled down to the core, it's not your race or class that counts but who you are as an individual. That is what matters when it comes time to decide if you are going to sacrifice yourself or sacrifice someone else. If you are just going to get down on your knees and offer your throat to the knife, or if you are going to turn around, knife in your hand, waiting for *them*. It is what having a soul is all about, not much more. Whether Inuk or *qallunaq,* the real mystery is what you are going to do when the end is here. And if you are lucky enough, you may never have to discover that at all. Whatever brought the best or the worst out in him, Gabriel, frankly, did not want to know more about than he already did. Great, he sighed, that's it, now I'm going to think about Stella. It was one of those typical two o'clock sequences of ideas.

The three o'clock idea was that he was somehow paying for having toyed with the Inuit's beliefs. His brain had wanted to play at being a shaman, and now he would see what being an Eskimo really meant. At some point he even had the feeling that the *angakoq* was not asleep but was staring at him in the dark, but that must have been his own sleeplessness going to his head.

Then, four o'clockish, he started worrying about Brentford. Helen, he remembered (sometimes taking for the truth what at other moments he considered a fit of delirium), was not going to help him. Gabriel had ruined his friend's wedding, denounced his bride, and now had let him go to the North Pole on what was nothing but a suicide trip. He reassured himself by thinking that he would ask the Inuit to help him find Brentford, if it was not too late.

When, lulled by the wind softly scraping against the igloo, he eventually fell into a rumble of unfettered pictures, the whole icehouse woke up.

He knew the reputation that some Inuit people had for throat singing, but their throat clearing was not to be underestimated either. For what seemed a half hour they grunted, snorted, coughed, hawked, and spat on the walls and on the floor, scratching themselves all the time, while Gabriel pretended to sleep a little longer, just as an excuse to keep his eyes shut. As he opened them tentatively, he perceived Tiblit passing through his hair the hand he had just dipped in the piss-pot, but he must have hallucinated that. At some point, though, they seemed to remember that they were fugitives, and hastened a little, leaving their *iglerk* regretfully in order to prepare some tea that had been left on the lamp to be heated. As Gabriel had done nothing to help—this was, at least, his interpretation—he was the last to be served.

He was as hopelessly useless when it came to packing for their departure. Contrasting with the Inuit's rather sloppy domestic manners, strict rules and maniacal attention to detail prevailed when they loaded the sled. Gabriel, not knowing what to do with his hands, which were still unusable and burning, trampled on the ice a few feet away, trying to ignore what he felt were reproachful looks.

He was cold as well, with his best-man clothes still a little damp, and so ridiculously smart that they made him look like some lost miniature groom standing on an endless white wedding dress. It was a foggish, greyish day, and it froze him down to the marrow of his bones, even though the igloo had been built between hummocks a few yards off the coastline to protect it from the winds as well as from being seen. The dogs were still around the igloo and Gabriel could see they had collars with little medallions hanging from them that tinkled as they moved, but although such ornaments were rather unusual for Eskimo dogs, he did not dare to come closer and check. He contented himself with exchanging looks with the lead dog, and it was a sort of relief for him to face eyes with no human intent or expectations he could not rise to. Maybe it was because the dogs were family.

The Inuit had forgotten something and were unpacking and then repacking. They were unhurried and cautious in a way that meant that they had enough problems of their own without adding extra troubles from either sled or dogs. Eventually, as the dogs were harnessed, Tuluk came walking toward Gabriel, who noticed for the first time the bear claws at the tip of his *kamik*.

"You come with us to Kalaallit Nunaat?"

Gabriel had not dared broach the topic during breakfast, when the talk had first revolved about their dreams and about how the amiable Uitayok admired the trash deposits of the Whites that he had seen while travelling to New Venice, and how, really, he dreamed of having such heaps of rubbish in front of his own house. All this, Gabriel understood, with his tongue rather hummocky in his cheek. Then they had decided to give their guest an Eskimo name. Gabriel, interpreting this as an honour, had prepared himself to receive it with dignity. It was Tuluk who proposed the name.

"*Innatuumajuujaaraaluttuujanirartauqattalaurunnainiralaurtuugaluaq,*" he had declared solemnly, setting the whole igloo, *angakoq* included, rolling on the floor laughing, slapping their thighs, and pointing their fingers at Gabriel, who nodded stupidly, a waning smile on his face.

"Sorry. I do not know translate," Tuluk said, wiping the tears from his eyes five minutes later. "It is about one who is a bit of a dreamer, who has a little dreaming seal in his head."

"Oh?" Gabriel had said, deeming it was not the right time for any serious proposal.

But now it could not be avoided any longer.

"I have a favour to ask you."

Tuluk frowned as if he wasn't sure he had understood. Hadn't they been helpful enough to the *qallunaq*?

"A friend of mine, a good friend of the Inuit, is in trouble. He is on a trip to the Big Nail. I am afraid something will happen to him."

"What friend of the Inuit?" asked Tuluk, doubtfully.

"Brentford Orsini," answered Gabriel. The name had been an open sesame with the Scavengers and he had a faint hope it might work with the Inuit as well. And actually it did seem to work a little, to the point where Tuluk called the others and explained to them what Gabriel had said.

"Orsini," confirmed Gabriel, thinking of a way to break the news that it more or less meant *bear*, as he knew that Inuit thought, just as he did himself, that *the name is as large as the man*. "He is a good friend of the Inuit. He wants them to rule with the New Venetians."

Tuluk translated, using for the New Venetians the word *arsussuq*: "Those who live in abundance." It was the same word, incidentally, by which they meant the Dead.

But the others would have little or none of it, and Ajuakangilak was most vocal about it. They had of course no reason to help, but Gabriel could feel that they still mulled over the involvement of the Polar Kangaroo and the danger of refusing anything to that white nitwit amateur of an *angakoq*, who had nevertheless secured the help of Kiggertarpok.

Waiting for the results, wondering how far Brentford could have got by now, Gabriel caught the eye of the lead dog. It was like a signal he did not know he had given. The pack suddenly darted toward the North, dragging the sled behind them. The Inuit, howling and cursing, ran after them as quickly as they could, and for a moment it seemed that they could catch up. Maybe it was only that the dogs, *looking behind from time to time*, gave the impression that they were slackening the pace, just enough to give hope to the chasing Inuit. But as soon as the Eskimos came closer, they sped up again.

Gabriel ran after them all, lagging behind, his feet full of pins and needles, slipping and tripping on rubbly ice, with the horrendous feeling that he was being abandoned on the frozen seas. He saw the sled disappear in the distance and then the Inuit, getting fainter and fainter, almost miragenous in the hazy morning.

He stopped after a while, panting, sobbing, his lungs like ice blocks about to explode, his blood throbbing in his ears, quite on his own again.

Except for the shadow that was looming over him.

Gabriel lifted his eyes. The shadow was that of a black airship that glided above his head, the very same that had been hovering above New Venice. A trapdoor opened from under the gondola, releasing a rope ladder that fell just in front of him. What choice had he but to take it and climb? He sprinted over and seized a rung, his hand burning through his glove as he did so, almost unable to grasp it firmly. But he had to go up, however painful that would be. He twisted his forearm about the rope and set his foot on the ladder. He started to climb, his clenched jaws slashed by the cold wind, jerking with pain at each new grip he took. But up he went, slowly, until the airship became the whole sky.

It took him endless minutes to reach the gondola. He did not dare look below, where the airship's shadow twisted and folded as it passed over the hummocks, but looking in front of him, he could see faintly through the fog the Eskimos running behind the sled, almost catching it, but always missing it. "Follow that sled," he said dramatically, as he reached the hatch and a powerful hand grasped his forearm to pull him inside.

CHAPTER XXVI

The Ariel

●

*That we are always against
the law—it is self-evident.*
Novalis

The Phantom Patrol had passed under the reversed runners and were now pounding on the windshield with the butts of their rifles. By chance, it was one of the new Benedictus laminated panes, and for the time being did not cave in, though it burst into cobwebs of cracked glass.

At every impact, Brentford shook himself further from the palsy that had held him in thrall. He realized that his gun was useless against the Patrol, as would be any weapon he could improvise. He jumped to reach the hatch above his head and, lifting himself with his arms and elbows, crawled into the hold, knowing there would be a way to open it up at the bottom, which now faced the stars. He closed the hatch under himself as well as he could and, lamp in hand, began looking for the trapdoor that was used to load the ship from below. Once outside, it was his plan to sprint as fast as he could: maybe he could outrun dead men. He tried to be as silent as possible, but the trapdoor was stuck and needed a good shove. Brentford worried that they would hear the thudding and climb up the sides to meet him, but it was not as if he had any choice. So he pushed, with the strength of despair.

As the trapdoor suddenly yielded, the hold was flooded with light from above. "That's it," thought Brentford. The thought flashed through his mind that he would become one of the phantoms, condemned to prowl the ice packs until kingdom come. But the light did not come from their lamps. It was the white blinding glare of a searchlight. A rope ladder fell right under his nose. Before he knew it, he was climbing it, as fast as the swaying of the rope allowed him to.

He had no idea what he was scrambling toward but it could not possibly be worse than what he was escaping from. It seemed to him that the ladder was going up straight into the sky. It was hellishly cold, and the rungs were already caked with ice, but Brentford did not care about such trifles right now. He would keep on climbing, using his teeth if he had to. Shots cracked beneath him, with rumbling echoes; bullets whistled around his head, but he was carried away too quickly to be a sitting duck for long. He looked below: the wrecked ship was now almost invisible in the night, and all he could see of the Phantom Patrol was their lamps, the shadows they threw, the sparks of their shooting rifles. He looked up and could see that the rope led to a square of light, where some silhouettes awaited him. It looked like what people describe when they are about to die, but now he knew this is what you see when you're resurrected.

He was lying on the floor of an airship, a crowd of topsy-turvy people surrounding him. He slowly soaked up the images, trying to make sense of them: Gabriel was there, dressed in mourning black, his hands in bandages. Three of the four Inughuit of the Frobisher Fortress delegation were there, commenting with animation upon his presence in front of them. But there were new faces as well. A few figures wearing black jackets and woollen hats, and a lean young man, dressed in black as well, with a large forehead, an aquiline nose, and long wavy hair tucked behind his ears.

"It is a pleasure and honour for us to welcome you aboard the *Ariel*," said the young man, in a faint German accent. "The ship, I suppose, is not unknown to you. You have probably seen her floating above New Venice lately."

Brentford rose up and shook the hand that was offered to him. He tried to express his surprise, but after the Phantom Patrol, he found it hard to be amazed.

"My name is Maximilian Hardenberg," the man added, planting the gaze of his immense eyes on Brentford's.

"Brentford Orsini. I owe you my life, sir."

"No one ever owes anyone anything," said Hardenberg, curtly but firmly. "And I pride myself on being no one's sir."

"If you say so," said Brentford, slightly taken aback.

"If you will permit me to introduce to you some of my brothers. This is Johann Treschler, from Prague," Hardenberg continued, as a clever-looking man with bushy brows and short blond hair proffered his hand.

"Herr Treschler is our engineer, and this ship is his brain-child. He will give you a tour if you are interested. This is Dr. Sven Heidenstamm, our doctor and, I dare say, philosopher," he added, indicating a stocky person who had the strangest glint in his eyes. This was not, Brentford thought, the doctor he would choose, but he was still immeasurably better than Doctor Phoenix, who still made Brentford shiver with disgust and pity.

The next up was a bright-faced, square-headed little man with cold-steel eyes.

"Saying that Herr Hans Schwarz is our chemist would be cruelly reducing the extant of his competencies," said Hardenberg. "It is thanks to him that our modest armoury is so full of

305 * Jean-Christophe Valtat

surprises. Our pilot, Hugo Trom, is of course busy, as are most of his crew, and they regret not being able to meet you at the moment. The rest of the people here, you know already, I think. We will leave you to yourselves for a while, but I would be glad if you joined us for dinner, even if you are, of course, totally free to behave as you wish."

"Nice to see you," Brentford said to Gabriel. His friend, his borrowed black clothes flapping around him, looked slightly embarrassed, probably about the wedding. Brentford decided he would not talk of it at all. It had been ages ago, anyway.

"What happened to your hands?"

"Jackfrostbitten. More ridiculous than serious. As usual." Gabriel launched a Punch and Judy show with his bandages on the edge of the table.

They were sitting in wicker armchairs in the almost cosy deck-saloon of the *Ariel*. A corridor led aft to the engine room and the cabins and berths of the crew's quarters, and forward to the wheelhouse and the magazines, where a kennel had been improvised for the sled dogs, suddenly very compliant now that their "mission" had been accomplished, it seemed, with the rescue of both Gabriel and Brentford. Gabriel was still amazed that they had darted straight in the direction of the *Kinngait*, just as he had been thinking about his friend.

The Inuit, except for Ajukangilak, who stayed sulkily in his berth, obviously trying to avoid Gabriel, were busy exploring the dirigible, pussyfooting into every nook and cranny. From time to time Gabriel and Brentford could see Tiblit passing through the lounge, usually pursued by one sturdy, black-clad, bearded member of the crew who was trying calmly but firmly to wrestle from him some object the Inuk had found especially interesting or desirable—a box of crayons, a barometer, or a brass telescope.

"So you did not make it to the Pole," said Gabriel, casually.

Brentford winced, as he had when he learned that he had been found barely fifty miles from the city. This mysterious banshee must have made him run around in circles. If he had wanted to impress Helen, it had all been quite a failure.

"No. And I'm cured of the will to go there. I would not advise anyone to try it."

He did not feel like talking about what he had seen, shivering at the idea of just thinking about it.

Gabriel remained focused on his Punch and Judy show.

"You would not have met Helen, anyway," Judy said to Punch, with a twangy voice.

"You have a gentle way of breaking the news, these days," said Brentford. "How do you know?"

"Because I met her," Judy said. "And she said you did not need her anymore."

"You *met* her?" asked Brentford, trying to catch Gabriel's fleeting eyes.

Gabriel looked up and stopped clowning.

"Well, sort of. *That* kind of dream, you know."

Brentford nodded as if he knew.

"Why would she have given me that appointment, then?"

"She did not approve of your wedding, obviously."

Brentford let it sink in and sighed, his eyes on the ceiling.

"Neither did my mother and neither did you. And neither did Sybil, and neither do I anymore, I suppose. And now even the Gods are against me."

Gabriel said nothing, promising himself not to talk about the wedding anymore. It seemed to have happened a long, long time ago anyway, and this time, he also brought good news.

"But she also said that she would take care of your hunting quota problem."

"How's that?"

"How would I know? She's the goddess, not me. Expect good seal and walrus hunts, though. In my dream, it was rather her line of work."

"Does she have anything to do with the Inughuit being here?"

"Not that I or they know of. But now that you ask, there is a kind of connection, actually. Helen referred to the Polar Kangaroo as being of great help. He was in my dream as well, and He appeared to the Inuit and took them to me just in time."

The implication of the Polar Kangaroo was big news, indeed. If the Macropus Maritimus Maximus had surfaced again, it was both the sign of a major crisis and the signpost toward some sort of solution. What Brentford had to do was follow its big footprints to wherever they led: it had already woven some threads, hadn't it, though Brentford was still striving to see a pattern. And if, moreover, the Polar Kangaroo was involved with Helen, the pattern promised to be quite spectacular.

He rose and walked to the window in the side of the gondola. There was nothing but darkness down there, with maybe something that stirred and was only their own shadow. What he saw was mostly his own worried reflection, trying to follow another thread in his head without getting further tangled.

"What do you know about magic mirrors?" he asked Gabriel. For some reason, Gabriel, sceptic though he was, always seemed to be acquainted with the strangest notions. However absurd the question, Brentford knew he might get an answer.

"You mean the mirror you told me about? From the coffin? With *Lancelot* on it?"

"The very one. I saw a woman in it," Brentford said as he slowly walked back to the table.

"It is never be too late be acquainted with that side of your personality, I suppose."

"A woman that wasn't me or in me," Brentford specified with an amused patience as he sat down.

"Hmm..." As always when he reflected, Gabriel raised his eyes slightly toward the left, as if he were reading his cue from somewhere over Brentford's shoulder. "All I know is that such visions are called phantoramas. Some seers favour mirrors over other methods, as they induce no abnormal states and show things in a more stable, less fleeting way than the usual magnetic vision. But as to the content, give or take a few specificities, it does not differ from normal clairvoyance and is entirely dependent on the disposition of the seer. Theoretically, what you saw was either a distant or dead person photographing herself onto it, so to speak—or, of course, some trick of your sick mind."

"Are you by any chance calling Isabelle d'Ussonville a trick of my sick mind?"

"A trick of your mind, very certainly, but sick I hope not, for I happen to have seen her as well. Dead in that coffin, first."

Brentford opened monocle-dropping eyes at the coincidence.

"Then," his friend went on, "I saw some younger, vaporous version of her coming from the mouth of one my students, but that, of course, is strictly between us."

"More between us than you think," Brentford answered, rubbing his chin, which was his own symptom of reflection. "I have seen her myself, besides, as a, what, phantorama. In a dream and as the same sort of vapour you describe, maybe out of the very same mouth, at the Trilby Temple. But why would this dear lady haunt us?"

Gabriel thought perhaps it was because of their shared tendency to expect wonders from women. Trying to turn someone like Sybil Springfield into a model spouse or a vaudeville girl like Stella Black into a pure romantic love was in its own way being open to supernatural phenomena, but maybe, he surmised, Brentford wanted a less speculative answer.

"Well, it seems Helen uses her spirit as a kind of homing pigeon to contact you," Gabriel proposed. He had a hunch that Helen was not too keen on appearing to Brentford in her present state, but he kept that to himself as well. "What business this d'Ussonville may have with us, however, I do not have the least inkling."

"Nevertheless, we're on to something here," said Brentford, easing himself back in his wicker armchair.

"Would you care for quick a tour of the *Ariel*?" Treschler interrupted them.

The engineer was a swift and efficient guide.

"Originally," he said, leading them through the corridors, "the *Ariel* was stolen from the French army by a group of our fellow anarchists. It was then called the *Patrie* or something. You will agree that we have improved on that, as we have on the rest of the craft. From this porthole you can see the reversible propellers, one on the rear and two on each wing, swivelling up and down for manœuverability. As you could observe for yourselves last week, the ship can remain in stationary flight for quite a long time.

"And these," he said, opening a door, "are the motors. Electric. They look rather insignificant, I admit, but they can push us to a good 60 knots, if needed. Our little secret, not patented, of course, is that we can recharge the batteries through the Aurora Borealis. It is hard enough to fly airships in the Arctic because of the ice weighing everywhere and getting encrusted in the propellers, so that when the propellers turn, they shoot little slivers of ice that tear the envelope. So it is good to have a little power in exchange for all the trouble.

"These Keely devices," he added, indicating a row of glass tubes linked to coils and batteries, "allow us, by separating air and water, to produce Vapouric Ether, much lighter and safer than hydrogen, that we use to refill the gas bags. As a matter of fact, everything in the ship is based upon a simple ether-electricity loop. We can make each from the other according to our needs, electricity for the motors or Vapouric Ether for the bag, so that we have few autonomy problems. What more can anarchists ask for?"

"Now, if you please," he said, indicating a steel ladder that led to a hatch. From there, they could access the upper gallery, at the bottom of the envelope. A very narrow walkway ran along the whole hundred yards of a V-shaped keel frame that sloped away at each end. It was very cold and they all hurried toward the nearest hatch, which was located amidships.

"The *Ariel* is, in technical parlance, a kind of Parseval semi-rigid airship. The bag holds approximately 350,000 cubic feet of gas and can lift about twenty tons. Which means there is not one useless scrap of metal or piece of wood allowed on board, except weapons, of course, which are useless until they're useful. As you can see over your heads, there are bulkheads between the seventeen gasbags, so that tears or shots through one bag do not necessarily endanger the ship. Those bags are not made of the usual Goldbeater's skin, which is nothing but calf intestines. If they were, lifting such a ship would require the slaughtering of about 200,000 calves."

As Tuluk translated this to the Inuit, Uitayok frowned, but Brentford could not tell if it was because animal intestines were exactly the kind of technology Inuit would use or because the sheer numbers involved erased any doubts Uitayok might have had about the insanity of the *qallunaat*. Impressed as he was, he was not a man to sacrifice ten generations of musk oxen, even for a flying *umiak*.

"Talk about bad karma, huh?" Treschler kept on. "Maximilian and I, as self-respecting vegetarians, would not fly in a slaughterhouse, so we had to use thin bladders of vulcanized rubber instead. Now it is, if you'll excuse me, these enormous condoms that lift us. We asked a German factory, Fromm, to make them especially for us. Now, that's the equivalent of 200,000 babies liberated from karma. Just the thought of it makes one *lighter*, doesn't it?"

"The hull itself is rather solid, or so I hope, as there are three layers of rubber-proofed fabric with five layers of dope. Unfortunately, that's just a kind of paint. The keel, on which you're walking now, is made of wolframinium, but as you can see, it's covered with rubber, so that the men do not get stuck to the metal when temperatures get really cold. The bracing and rigging of the gondola is made of Italian hemp and piano wire, just for the poetry of it. Now down again."

The visitors landed in the lounge and then headed toward the stern.

"The storerooms are a bore, I assure you, but you may like the armoury, even if Herr Schwarz does not like people to nose around. Let's just cast a quick glance. We have Maxim machine guns, mostly because Maximilian likes the name, I suppose. That's a ten-barrelled Nordenfeldt. But, as you know, we anarchists are mostly renowned for our bombs. These over there are forcite, and you would not want to introduce them to a gelatine blasting cap without a very good reason. But Hans's favourites are over there, in those quart champagne bottles. It's a compound he calls *anarchite*. The burning comes with poisonous fumes, if I understand correctly."

"You intend to use these?"asked Brentford with concern.

"You see, by tradition, the odds are usually against us and experience has proved that we have little to gain by using strength against stronger enemies. But if we have to use it, it means we have no choice but to go all the way."

While sitting at dinner opposite Hardenberg, Brentford noticed the Persian motto *In Niz Beguzared* carved on one of the plywood beams.

"*This, too, will pass*," translated Hardenberg.

"So, Anarchy, too, will pass ?" Brentford asked.

"Many things will have to pass before that, I'm afraid," Hardenberg answered with serenity.

A buffet dinner was placed on a side table so that nobody would have to serve anyone. The Inughuit had helped themselves to generous portions but rejected whatever they did not like, which appeared to be a lot. Everybody else had implicitly agreed on pretending not to notice the table manners of their anarchist role models, and but for the odd belch that caused a brief lull in the conversation, things proceeded smoothly enough.

"May I ask what brought you here?" Brentford asked Hardenberg.

"Professional obligations, mostly. We are under contract with the Council of Seven."

Brentford gagged loudly on his food, which silenced even the Inuit for a while.

"What?" he managed to say weakly, tears in his eyes.

"Some governments are very eager to have their own anarchist menace, as it allows them to pass what the French call *Lois scélérates*—scoundrelly laws. Most of them use their own secret police to infiltrate anarchist movements. But it's not always possible, so they have to resort to freelance agencies such as us."

"I thought you were real Anarchists," Brentford said, surprised at his own disappointment and suddenly worried that he might have fallen into a trap. But after all, this was exactly what he had suspected ever since the airship had appeared.

"Oh! we are very much so, as much as anarchy can be real, which is not always as much as we would like it to be."

"Reality is just one more hallucination," spat out Heidenstamm, banging on the table. "It has to be destroyed just like any other hallucination."

"Certainly, Sven, certainly," said Hardenberg soothingly. "For the moment, however, it is just that we prefer dealing with these realities ourselves, instead of seeing them in the clumsy hands of the police."

"That means you have to play into the authorities' hands," said Brentford.

"This is what we would like them to think, yes. They would not squander money on us, otherwise, I suppose. That said, the shortest jokes are the best, and since we left the city, we're now officially traitors to our employers."

"But you do not help your fellow anarchists either."

"In a way, we do. But not necessarily in the way they would like. Maybe it's because of the airship, but we have a more *elevated* point of view on what anarchist agitation should be."

"Do you know someone called Mugrabin, by the way?" interrupted Gabriel, who, when not struggling with the cutlery, was thinking that the more he looked at Hardenberg, the more the young anarchist resembled a Mugrabin without disguise or makeup.

"Ah, Mikhail Mikhailovitch! A very sympathetic fellow indeed, but once again, one of those typical anarcho-masochists. Don't misunderstand me," Hardenberg kept on, now visibly warming up to his own ideas, "I have nothing against direct action, provided it's, well, directed. I'm not one to shy away from political assassination as a principle. Some people are clearly evildoers, and you all know as well as I do that the world would be a better place without them, if only for the five minutes before others equally malevolent or even possibly worse replaced them."

"There is nothing I like as much as a good riot, and an insurrection is a thing of beauty—before it is crushed, that is.

But revolutions are another matter. For one thing, they are very complicated, frail mechanisms that demand conditions which are nearly impossible to meet. But even if they succeed, there are two major drawbacks to them.

"The first one, theoretical as it is, is that as soon as anarchism starts imposing itself on others, it is not anarchism anymore, but exactly what anarchism is fighting against. So, as the saying goes, "your work once done, to retire is the way of Heaven." The second one, sadly much more concrete, is that the outcome of *any* revolution is that the anarchists will end up being shot by both sides. Not because they will stand in anyone's way to power, but because they will stand between everyone and the *very idea* of power. It happens every time."

"So, there is no future for anarchism?"

"In a sense, that is a correct conclusion, Mr. Orsini. But it does not mean there is no anarchism. It just means that it only exists in the present, at very precise spots, for, alas, only a few people at the same time and in ways as yet undefined. It could be, for instance, happening now and here."

"What do you mean?"

"Who was it who wrote of the *True Community*? And what is the true community? Certainly not race or class, but people from all walks of life suddenly thrown together by persecution and forced to invent a new life, with whatever comes into their hands. What were the chances we'd all come together today? This is the stuff utopias are made of, as long as they last."

"It's a seductive theory," admitted Brentford, politely, still surprised at the mention of *A Blast on the Barren Land*. "But it is the city I want to save. Not throw a party for myself and a few friends."

But Hardenberg continued unabashed, his wide eyes hardened and dense with enthusiasm.

"But what else is a city, really? No, seriously. We agree with you: who needs a utopia when one already lives in one?

New Venice is a city made to fulfil all appetites. It is in itself a fulfilled appetite, or a dream come true, if you prefer. One of these pieces of paradise that are strewn all over the earth. We are well aware of that.

"You see, Mr. Orsini, after years of sailing in the *Ariel*, we have come to see things differently than we did at ground level. Seen from above, the world is a most interesting piece of hieroglyphic scripture. You can very easily decipher where the *style* gets clogged or remains fluid, where freedom recedes and where it keeps on thriving. It dawned on us that this was a way that we could help a little, you know, like an acupuncturist's needle. Smoothing out sore muscles here and there, undoing painful knots, easing the breath of the world. The Arctic is one of the last free spaces there is, be it for the men or be it for their minds—free to the point of being fearsome, actually, fearsome as only freedom can be. But now we can read as in a book that it is just being turned into one more boring knot on *their* maps. We could do a *little something* about it, couldn't we?"

Brentford said nothing, tapping his fork against the table. Had he really come to the point where he had to side with terrorists to save New Venice? He felt ill at ease about the *"Blast"* metaphor of his book and how now it was striving to get real. He had been asking for it, hadn't he? Never write anything that you won't be able to live up to someday, he thought.

"Is it true that you want to share Aqilineq with Inuit?" Uitayok suddenly asked from his end of the table.

Aqilineq. The Old Country. It was what the Inuit still called that ragged, splintered stretch of land where New Venice had been struggling to take root. Brentford met the *riumasa*'s eyes, intensely staring at him, and from the corner of his own noticed Hardenberg's little smile.

"That would only be normal, I suppose," said Brentford, as casually as he could.

Uitayok nodded slowly and returned to his meal.

There was a pregnant pause.

"Do you *really* want it?" insisted Hardenberg.

"Right," said Brentford, with all the irony he could muster. "What do we do now? Go back to New Venice and ask the Council of Seven to make room for *us*? Or do we just start throwing incendiary bombs around?"

"I thought the author of *A Blast on the Barren Land* would be more of a *dreamer*," sighed Hardenberg, putting back his hair behind his ear. "We can actually do both and a little more. *We can turn history back to a fairy tale.*"

Brentford felt a certain anger swelling up in him.

"Do you realize that at this very moment, while we're having this *interesting* little table talk, the Subtle Army is attacking and probably destroying a fistful of defenceless Nunavut independentists? *Can* you turn that into a *fairy tale*?"

"Oh yes! I almost forgot! That was our own rear base that was being attacked, and we left the city because we were supposed to defend our Inuit allies who watch over it, weren't we? You remember that?"

"*Ja!*" said Schwarz accusingly. "But we had to save all these gentlemen."

"And now *they* think we shouldn't have. What a pity!" added the doctor, shaking his head.

"I do not find this very funny," said Brentford.

Hardenberg smiled.

"But since we have changed our course and followed the direction indicated by the dogs, we've made some... I think *serendipity* is the word. Do you know where we're heading right now?"

"No," admitted Brentford darkly.

"Neither do I. But Herr Torm, our pilot, has noticed that this course seems to be taking us toward some very interesting place."

"There is no place around here," said Brentford, still a bit irritated by Hardenberg's unbreakable self-confidence, his way of thinking that he could will things into existence.

"Which is exactly what makes *this one* interesting."

CHAPTER XXVII

The Crystal Castle

•

"It is no speculation of wild improbability to picture a polar paradise, like some titan emerald in its alabaster setting."
Fitzhugh Green, *Popular Science Monthly*, December 1923

ardenberg invited his guests to follow him to the wheelhouse at the fore of the *Ariel*. The room, fitted on all sides with toughened glass windows, contained the pilot's and navigator's seats, the steering wheel, the valve cords, the control wires for rudder and elevators, the instrument panels, a map case, and voice pipes for inside communication. Lit as it was, for the moment, by a single light bulb in the ceiling, its most striking visible feature was the bearded, eye-masked reflection in the windshield of Trom, the pilot. The navigator, introduced as Petersen, was bent over the backlit map, the lead dog on his knees. From where he stood, just behind the navigator's seat, Gabriel could see that the tinkling medallion around the neck of the dog was quite familiar to him.

"Look, the Nixon-Knox coat of arms," he whispered to Brentford, who nodded in the darkness.

"Where did you get these dogs?" Brentford asked Tuluk, who stood at his side.

Tuluk hesitated, as he knew it had not been quite legal, but realizing that they were now quite literally above such considerations, he answered good-naturedly.

"The men of the Trash. The Inuit were hunted, you know."

"I know," Brentford reassured him. "You did very well." And he meant every word of it. So these were probably the same animals that had brought the coffin to New Venice and brought the airship to his rescue. He did not know if was sheer luck or something more mysterious, but after all, he corrected himself, few things are more mysterious than luck.

The animal had a paw on the map case and seemed to be scratching with excitement a particular spot that was designated as unexplored.

Bending a little, the visitors could see the portion of the ice field lit by the searchlight. Rollers and rubble slid past at full speed, rarely revealing stretches of smooth ice. But Gabriel could see something that the others did not seem to notice. Something white that was bounding along with ease at an amazing speed, like some sort of spring-heeled Jack Frost.

"You see Him?" he whispered into Brentford's ear. "He's leading us."

"Who?"

"Kiggertarpok," said Uitayok, between his teeth.

The three men looked at each other.

The dog yelped. It could see Him, too. It was the Polar Kangaroo that had led the dogs first to Gabriel and then Brentford and now to...

"*Das müßte hier sein,*" said Petersen.

"What should be here?" asked Brentford, surprised at his sudden Pentecostal fluency in German.

Hardenberg smiled, his hand clenched on the back of the pilot's seat.

The searchlight revealed a foggy area: at first simple wisps of mist, but then a billow so dense, it became a cloud of white smoke.

"Volcanic fumes. I knew it," said Hardenberg, as the ship was enveloped.

From time to time, as the clouds cleared a little, they could see that the ice on the ground was progressively giving way to ragged slopes of black stone. They were, it seemed, passing over a small mountain range. The dog whined, its tail starting to wag.

"Home," said Tuluk, nodding his head, as he watched the animal.

The smoke progressively lessened to a thinner veil, and then, all of a sudden, it cleared. Land appeared in the searchlight. A dark plateau, with stray patches of snow, and curls of vapour from numerous geysers or hot springs.

"Here it is. Welcome to Crocker Land," said Hardenberg, with a thrill in his voice.

Brentford and Gabriel looked at each other. The land that Peary had seen from afar, and that had remained part myth, part mirage, and perhaps, some suspected, something of a hoax, was now spread under their gaping eyes.

"*Da!*" Petersen exclaimed, pointing his finger at the edge of the searchlight. "*Ein Burg!*"

Trom, Hardenberg's hand now squeezing his shoulder, inclined the ship and made a wide swerve over the place to put it right in the searchlight. For those in the wheelhouse, the manœuver seemed to last forever, and the dog now stood on its hind legs, its muzzle so close to the windshield that its breath made a cloudy blur Petersen impatiently wiped off.

At last, it appeared.

It was a mountain. It was a castle. A dazzling crystal mass that sometimes took the shape of an immense palace, a jumble of spires, pinnacles, turrets, and oriels, which as the searchlight moved reverted for a while to a flashing chaos of facets.

"Greenhouses," said Brentford, as the searchlight extended to the sides of the crystal structure. Four long hothouses, made of glass or crystal, surrounded the castle at the four points of the compass. This was indeed a human settlement.

Trom adjusted the valves, filling the inner ballonets with air, so that the *Ariel* could lower itself. As it did, it became obvious that the base of the castle was inside a crater with the greenhouses located around its rim. It was as if a gigantic gemstone had been excavated and the castle cut directly into the transparent, slightly water-green crystal wherever its angles had evoked architectural shapes—columns, arches, cornices, balconies, towers, footbridges, or kiosks. All of these belonged to architectural styles seemingly piled up at random, and formed a translucent labyrinth whose depths and perspective mutated with every move of the gliding searchlight.

They couldn't wait to land and explore it.

The searchlight picked up a lantern moving to and fro at the entrance to a wide cavernous opening in one side of the crystal. It looked just large enough to accommodate the *Ariel*, and Hardenberg directed Trom toward it.

"You do not think it's dangerous?" Brentford asked Hardenberg.

"I am just too curious to care," answered Hardenberg, and that was exactly the answer Brentford wanted to hear.

Trom positioned the ship in front of the cave, following the indications of the tall man in a white tunic who held the lantern at the edge of the opening.

"They do not seem to be cold here," remarked Gabriel.

"The thermometer says 34°F" said Brentford.

"Oh." Gabriel felt frozen just at the thought of leaving the relatively warm *Ariel*.

But he forgot about it as soon the searchlight dispelled the dense shadows of the cave. Sloping down a little from the entrance, it was as deep and high as a cathedral, its vault held up by pillars of crystal. Its sides, rough as they were, exploded into myriads of dazzling ornaments as the light passed over their prisms.

Trom gently took the *Ariel* down to a few inches above the ground and stopped the motors. The crew jumped out to stabilize the ship, mooring it to the crystal pillars.

"After you," said Hardenberg, indicating the door to his guests.

The floor itself was made of crystal, so smooth one could see one's own amazed reflection in it. A light appeared at the base of one of the walls, widening to reveal an opening door. A dozen tall men in white tunics and black breeches advanced toward the visitors, carrying torches. They were very fair, with ruddy complexions, high cheekbones, and slightly slanted eyes. Besides a language that only Hardenberg seemed to grasp, they also spoke a little English. Their manner was easy enough, too, but things went even better as soon as the pack of sled dogs was released from the *Ariel*. Running toward the men, they jumped at their legs with yelps of joy. Tuluk was right. They were home. And so were Gabriel and Brentford, in a way, if they spooled back the ball of unravelled thread that had brought them here.

"So, this is where the ghost of Isabella wanted us to be, then," reflected Gabriel, looking all around him in awe, his bandaged hands crossed under his armpits. "I wonder what this place has to do with her. Or us."

"*I* was supposed to go to the North Pole, if I may remind you," said Brentford, though the memory of the mess he had made of it still stung a bit.

"Through Isabella herself, may *I* remind *you*. And it's still her dogs that brought us to you as you were, well, on your way is a big word, but you get my drift," Gabriel smirked. "And they followed the Polar Kangaroo, who apparently led us here."

"So He would be linked with Isabella as well."

"Ah, what wouldn't He be linked with? He is *the* link, after all."

Meanwhile, the landing party had been invited into the castle itself. Its topography, as might be supposed from the outside, was exceedingly complicated, full of twists and turns, but also full of wonders at every one of them. If the Inughuit expressed their awe more vocally than the others, who did their *qallunaq* best to look blasé, all shared the sense of wonder. Well, thought Brentford, when it comes to sharing, you have to start somewhere, and that was as good a place as any other.

The mauve light of mock moons shone softly through numberless openings, disclosing, with the help of the torches, adjacent halls whose furniture and decorations were entirely sculpted out of the same local crystal with all the minuteness of frostwork. Some, maybe, were less detailed than others, as if this sculpting were a work in progress that had been going on for centuries. Women in long white robes could be seen in some of these rooms, giggling among themselves and provoking in the newcomers a slight change in demeanour, an imperceptible straightening of the backbone, a refocusing of the eyes.

"Many women. Good," said Tiblit, making to Gabriel, who could not contradict him, a thunderous debut in Shakespeare's tongue.

The party arrived in a larger hall, decorated with three classical statues, all made of the same crystal. The one closest to Gabriel was dedicated to Elfinor, who, a few carved lines informed him, "*was in magick skill'd/he built by art upon the Glassy sea/A bridge of Brass, whose sound Heaven's thunder seemd to be.*" This was a rather standard New Venetian reference, and the d'Ussonville coat of arms right under the verses doubtless expressed Isabella's familial piety as the daughter of a founding father. The statue at the other side of the hall, depicting a long-bearded man, was dedicated to Elfant, "*Who was of most renowned fame/who all of chrystal did Panthea build.*" Maybe this was a direct reference to the founder of that most mysterious castle, which certainly looked like the work of a fairy king, though the statue itself surprisingly resembled Henry Hudson. Could it be that he had been rescued by these people? The third statue was a well-endowed God of the Gardens, labelled *Elfinstone*, *In Memoriam*, but whose face was not quite unfamiliar to Gabriel.

A shiver struck him as, warned by the sudden silence of the group, he turned toward the—was it one? or two? persons who had entered the hall to welcome them. The *creature* was, by all standards, a freak of nature, or even slightly beyond that. Siamese twins are one thing, if one may say so, and being joined at the side is not the rarest thing nor the worst that could happen to them; but conjoined twins of different sex were, at least by Gabriel, unheard of. These twins were also albinos, their snow-white hair and pale complexion underscored by the black velvet clothes they wore. But they were also the most beautiful, graceful, luminous adolescents Gabriel had ever beheld.

"I am Reginald Elphinstone," said the boy, who wore a little golden pendant of the sun around his neck.

"I am Geraldine Elphinstone," said the girl, whose pendant represented the moon.

"Welcome to Caer Sidhe," they said together.

It was later that night, after a sumptuous dinner of fresh food served on the finest crystal dinner service had been finished, that the twins, in a perfectly executed duet, told their tale ...

THE SURPASSING STORY
OF REGINALD & GERALDINE

The story begins in New Venice, where other stories end. Once upon a time, a woman—let us name her Isabelle, or as she was known later, Isabella—was forbidden by an unfair law to have any children. Her husband, Nixon-Knox, a respected doctor and a member of the Council of Seven, not only never touched her but also watched her very closely. But there came a time when she was required to have her official portrait painted. The painter was a young, gifted, ambitious, hotheaded artist called Alexander Harkness. Alexander fell in love with Isabella's pale face and fine features, and the benevolent sadness she carried about her like an aura. Isabella fell in love with Alexander's curly mane and bushy brows, and the way his look stripped her naked as he was painting her. Before the painting was even finished, she discovered she was pregnant.

Nixon-Knox learned about it, through, let us suppose, a treacherous maid. As a doctor, he suggested to the maid that she serve a pennyroyal infusion to her mistress. Isabella, indeed, felt so sick upon drinking it that both Nixon-Knox and the maid thought that they had succeeded in provoking a miscarriage. The maid, decidedly garrulous and malignant, informed Alexander Harkness of the success of Nixon-Knox's plan. Harkness, desperate as only a young man can be, called the husband to a secret duel on the ice field, but having counted ten steps and turned toward his opponent, it was himself he shot in the head, for having dishonoured Isabella and lost their child.

But it turned out that Isabella was still pregnant. Nixon-Knox, shocked by Alexander's suicide, or troubled by some religious scruples, eventually took pity on poor Isabella, and instead of forcing her to get rid of the child, made her swear

secrecy and sent her off to exile on distant Melville Island.
After this, he seems to have fallen under the influence of a
French religious fanatic, Father Calixte, who condemned with
the utmost virulence any attempts to reach the pole as a sin
against God and, dabbling in visions and prophecies, predicted
that New Venice would be doomed because of these attempts.
Nixon-Knox, from that point onward, is said to have busied
himself with curious medical experiments that bordered on
the unwholesome, until finally he was engaged, or so the story
went, in stealing the corpses of dead explorers from the Gallery
leading to the Boreal Grounds. He was eventually denounced
by a young doctor named Douglas Norton, who had conducted
his own strange experiments in the field of animal hybridization
so far that Nixon-Knox, though he was a longstanding friend
of the Norton family, had him expelled from the John Snow
School of Surgery. On the grounds of Norton's public accusa-
tions, the Council of Seven could no longer shield Nixon-Knox,
and he finished his life as a miserable inmate of the dreaded
Haslam Hospital.

But let us go back to Isabella Nixon-Knox, née d'Ussonville.
As you remember, she was supposed to sail to Melville Island.
But it happened that her small ship, blocked by the ice near
Cape Turnback, had instead been forced northward, until after
weeks of hardship she was rescued by chance by the inhabitants of our island, which was not yet known to explorers as
Crocker Land, or more accurately, the Crocker Land Mirage.
This island, which can mostly be seen from above, and only at
certain times of the year, is known to those who inhabit it by
a secret name that can only be pronounced when the Island is
invisible to the outer world. Its people pretend, or believe, or
pretend to believe, that they are descendants of the Irish Tuatha
Dé Dannan, mixed with ancient Arctic Tunit people and, many
many centuries later, with the remnants of the Norse colonies

of Greenland. Lost or wrecked Westerners, and whatever their cargo consists of, are traditionally welcomed, so much so in fact that the deliberate wrecking of foreign ships has been, at certain times, the tradition itself. Certain legends even mention, in that respect, a certain mysterious woman who used to mislead sailors and travellers toward the island. The inhabitants call her Oene, the fallen Queen of the Arctic.

Isabella's rescue was, accordingly, regarded less as a duty than as a gift. There, upon her arrival, and while her husband considered her lost at sea, Isabella gave birth to a little girl, whom, to honour both the father and his death, she had baptized Myrtle Isabella Alexandra Harkness. Thanks to her kindness and distinction, Isabella quickly found her place in the community, so much so that she was chosen as the Lady of the Castle, a purely honorary but much respected title granted only to foreigners by the Island dwellers.

Myrtle grew up, educated by her mother and by the library that Isabella had brought with her in a trunk. But there was among those books one that especially fascinated the young Myrtle: a little octavo entitled *Snowdrift & Reliance*, written by the uncle of Douglas Norton, Edward Hilbert-Norton. The Hilbert-Nortons were on excellent terms with Isabella, and Douglas had offered a strange pet straight out his laboratory to keep Isabella company and "remain in contact" with her, while his uncle, an eccentric bachelor and Isabella's longtime *séance* partner, had dedicated and offered this book of his to her just before her departure.

Part melodrama, part Elizabethan tragedy, *Snowdrift & Reliance* has little to recommend it to the reader's benevolence, the bewildering intricacies of its plot being further shrouded by unfathomable esoteric symbolism, not to mention an amphigoric style whose only coherent trait is its consistent lack of taste. But on Myrtle, a self-taught, imaginative young girl growing up isolated from the world on an invisible island, and not in the best position to distinguish myth from reality, its effect was devastating. She was especially struck by the fate of the heroine, Princess Ellesmere, who learns, through a prophecy imparted to her mother, the hermaphroditic Quing of Reliance, that her city will be destroyed when she loses her virginity. Somehow, Myrtle seems to have conceived the strange notion that in the same manner she could wreak her revenge on New Venice for killing her father and making a castaway of her mother.

This was probably more of a daydream than an actual scheme, until there arrived on the island, by accident, a young man named Jeremy Salmon. Jeremy, a promising steam engineer, had attempted, in what probably was a last desperate bid for funding through a publicity stunt, to drive his "pyschomotive" to the North Pole. But he lost his way and wandered through the frozen waste until he found himself, exhausted, finally reaching a mirage island he had been pursuing for hours. The islanders, of course, rescued him, and brought him to the castle. There he accepted, probably out of love, and unaware of her true intentions, the beautiful yellow-eyed Myrtle's proposal that they elope together to New Venice. Depleted as he was by the return trip, he died on arrival, leaving Myrtle to her own dark devices.

A resourceful girl in spite of her inexperience, she soon found employment in the Circus of Carnal Knowledge, a theatrical institution that specialized in pornoperas, a then fashionable genre in the dissolute Pearl of the Arctic. It happened that this cornerstone of the local entertainment scene was rehearsing its own risqué adaptation of *Snowdrift & Reliance*. Myrtle, through her thorough knowledge of the text and her eerie familiarity with the main character, had little trouble convincing the director that she *was* the part. But, in spite of the efforts of all those involved, Myrtle's virginity remained unyielding, and the play flopped miserably at the premiere. It was by a twist of fate that on the very same evening that had seen her failure to avenge herself on New Venice, her fantasy almost came true when the mad painter Edouard de Couard, as part of the "Blue Wild" event he had organized, destroyed most of the city by placing tons of toxic blue pigment in the Air Architecture ventilation shafts.

In the devastating aftermath of the "Blue Wild," strange things had happened to Myrtle. Driven mad by her unfulfilled desires, she drifted through the city in search of relief, offering herself to the hurrying shadows of strangers, who relentlessly passed her by. Amidst the general panic, however, one man did not resist her, as his state did not allow him to: Igor Plastisine, an empty-eyed muscular hunk in blue boxer shorts and a tartan plaid who under the enthralling influence of a powerful psychoactive principle known as Pineapples and Plums recited in a trance an endless series of letters and numbers. Their tryst took place, it is said, on the very soil of the Greenhouse, near which she had met him. But, whether from an explosion caused by the poisonous cobalt emanations or sparked by the uncertain consummation of their feverish act, the Greenhouse burst into flames, and crumbled in a chaos of red-hot iron girders and torch-like palm trees. One of those fell right onto the back of poor Igor, who quickly succumbed on top of Myrtle's unconscious body, saving her life by his death.

But Myrtle had another lover who had been searching for her everywhere in that pale Pompeii of the Pole. This man was known to most people as Eddie Endlessex, the larger-than-life male star of the Circus of Carnal Knowledge, but to a few he was known as Edmund Elphinstone, the heir of a family of brilliant, if slightly oddball, New Venetian artists (his grandfather Samuel had engraved a map of New Venice renowned for being exact down to the very last stone, and his father, Eben-

ezer, had completed a mammoth-sized myriorama of the Frozen
Ocean whose thirty-two panels could be arranged in any order
and create billions of combinations, though they were virtually indistinguishable from one another). Edmund's gambling
debts, diagnosed satyriasis, and well-known addiction to nitrous
oxide, vulgarly known as laughing gas, had closed to him the
doors of a respectable career in the Arts, and it was behind a
large handlebar moustache and Parseval-type pudenda that the
poor prodigal son concealed his notoriety. He had never fallen
in love with anyone before Myrtle, the pure, unsoiled, incor-
ruptible Myrtle. He had to rescue her or destroy himself. And
he was the one who found her under the blackened remains of
Igor Plastisine, and loaded her on his back.

Edmund took Myrtle to the useless blue ruins of the Heaven
and Hell Hospital, where she was recognized by one of her
servants, Olaf Jansen, who, following Isabella's intuition and
orders, as well as—allegedly—the telepathic promptings of
the strange marsupial pet offered to her by Douglas Norton,
had come to New Venice in the hope of fetching her back to
Crocker Land. But the passionate Elphinstone would not leave
her side, and in order to ensure a modicum of discretion from
him, Jansen had no option but to bring Edmund to the island
as well, before it was too late to save Myrtle. When they arrived at the crystal castle after a long, exhausting trip, Myrtle
was so deeply comatose that most doctors would probably have
declared her dead. But Elphinstone was not a doctor. He was
a man in love and he believed in the power of his feelings to
bring his sleeping beauty back to life. Isabella was too shocked
and sad, and perhaps too steeped herself in the supernatural, to
oppose Elphinstone's commitment and single-mindedness. For
days and weeks, he took care of Myrtle in a secluded tower of
the castle, read books to her and played her heart-wrenching
music on Isabella's glasharmonica, bathed and oiled her and

shocked her with an electric generator the islanders had found on a wrecked whaler. Though she was not brought back to life by such dedication, she was eventually found to be pregnant, even though her pulse was imperceptible, and her breath left no blur on a mirror.

Isabella, learning the news, cast Elphinstone out of the castle, making him so desperate that she had to resort to the physical strength and firepower of the meek Crockerlanders to keep him away. Edmund lingered outside, lying in the snow and howling through the fog during the whole seven days of his endless agony. He never lived to see his premature orphans, two little mirror images of each other, being borne out of the womb of their motionless mother. At the sight of such a wonder, the Islanders knelt down in awe, and Isabella, who had a noble heart, gave the children the name of their father; a man, after all, whose love had been stronger than death.

"That was a sad story," said Gabriel to the twins, as they walked in front of him down a narrow corridor, crystal candelabras in hand. Reginald shrugged his shoulders, forcing Geraldine to do the same. They reminded Gabriel of those little figures cut out of folded paper and then unfolded to show a string of gingerbread-man shapes.

"We have not lived it," said the boy. "It is other people's memories."

"It was losing grandmother Isabella that was the real blow," added Geraldine. "She took such wonderful care of us."

"I hear she is still around and has quite a haunting presence," said Gabriel.

Geraldine turned toward Gabriel and smiled, while Reginald explained.

"Oh, you must mean our mother, Myrtle. She is the one with that ability, not Grandmother. But she certainly resembled Grandmother Isabella when she was young."

"Isn't she very pretty? I wish we were as pretty," added Geraldine, a bit coquettishly, thought Gabriel.

He looked at the nape of her neck and discovered he felt an insistent desire to kiss it, faintly accompanied by the more obscure and unsettling urge to bite her ponytail. But with Reginald around, in his little black Lord Fauntleroy costume, that kind of privacy was, of course, impossible. From what he had heard, though, Siamese twins often got married. They were surely used to a certain amount of promiscuity. And—the thought bothered Gabriel a little—Reginald had exactly the same nape, after all. It struck him that they were fairly reminiscent of his dream about Rocket and Pocket.

"You are very pretty, I think," he said, intending to be polite, but surprised at how sincere and confident he sounded. "It is just a lot of prettiness to handle at the same time."

He heard them giggle and it pleased him.

"We rejoice that you've finally joined us as our grandmother wanted you to, Mr d'Allier," said Geraldine suddenly, turning toward Gabriel.

So that was why they had kindly proposed to take him to his room, he reflected. They had something to say to him.

"Oh, that Lancelot thing, it was really about me, then. But I fail to see where I fit in."

"She saw you in her crystal cabinet," explained Geraldine, as if that clarified anything.

"That sounds great, but I am not sure I understand."

"You can follow us there, if you're not too tired," proposed Reginald.

For a few minutes, they followed a mind-boggling series of corridors and stairways, the siblings sometimes whispering to each other in some strange language, until they reached a door that Reginald opened with a key linked by a chain to the pocket of his velvet waistcoat.

"Please, go in," he said, as the siblings stepped aside. Gabriel entered a polyhedral kiosk where the crystal all around him seemed to have a different quality than elsewhere in the palace. It was less translucent and more reflective, so that he could see infinite images of himself surrounding him, quite as if he were standing at the bottom of a kaleidoscope.

"Now, close your eyes, think of something or someone, and open them again," said Reginald, still standing in the corridor.

Gabriel, of course, could not help thinking about Stella. As he opened his eyes, he saw dim shapes coming from inside the crystal and joining each other like pools of spilled water, gaining depth, light and colour as they did. And then they were her, walking away along the Marco Polo Midway in her black hooded coat with her overbrimming satchel that always seemed about to burst. She was doing her usual tightrope routine on the edge of the sidewalk, leaving little light footprints in a thin layer of fresh snow, which always made Gabriel want to run and catch her before she fell. All around him he could see the city in the dubious daylight, as completely and clearly as if he were in the middle of the street, and could even hear, he thought, the faint sound of distant bells floating from the church of St. Anthony. He felt like extending his arms but he realized that he would only bump against the crystal. Her own arms wide apart, meanwhile, Stella dwindled into the perspective distance and the ill-starred, starry-eyed Gabriel knew that for his own sake he had to let her go for good.

"How can I stop this?"

"Close your eyes and turn away," said Geraldine.

He did as he was told and waited for a while, nauseated and disconsolate, the picture persisting, as if trapped under his eyelids. He could have spared himself that trick, he thought bitterly.

"Well, that was something," he said, peeling back his eyelids again, quickly wiping a tear with his bandaged hand before he turned back and went out.

"Did you see what I saw?" he asked, a bit embarrassed, as Reginald locked the door.

"How could we? It is your mind, not ours," Geraldine said reassuringly, but the insistent smile on Reginald's face could have been from more than politeness.

"But I still do not see why your grandmother chose me," said Gabriel, trying to shake off the memory of Stella walking out of his helpless reach.

The siblings shrugged their four shoulders.

"Maybe she liked your name," offered Reginald pensively. "But mostly she remembered that only someone called d'Allier knew of her story, someone whose knowledge of the city and commitment to its values could not be doubted."

Gabriel wondered with concern what exactly Isabelle d'Ussonville had witnessed of his antics. It also vexed him that the world and his grandmother had been spying on him, when his lifestyle demanded nothing if not the greatest discretion.

"Before she left us," Geraldine continued, "she told us that only Lancelot and the Lady of the Lake would find out who she was."

"Lady of the Lake?" said Gabriel. But just as he was about to deny any connection, he remembered that when he had identified Isabelle d'Ussonville he had indeed been with the former Sandy Lake.

"This... Lady of the Lake, what part does she play in this?"

"Grandmother didn't say," Geraldine answered.

"Not negligible, I would say," Reginald added, nodding his head.

"This is your room," they said, stopping at an open door. Gabriel peeked inside. He was relieved to see that the sheets and pillows, at least, were not made of crystal.

"It is a beautiful room."

"Oh, that's nothing, you should see ours," said Geraldine, as Reginald elbowed her in their common ribs. Geraldine blushed, which made Reginald blush as well.

Gabriel felt like laughing.

"Thank you for bringing me here."

"Thank you for staying with us," said Reginald, who was a very polite boy. He had the same voice as Geraldine, but, with his white hair carefully combed back, he looked more serious than her, or at least he tried to.

"We seldom have visitors," said Geraldine, a bit impishly. "Let alone *wicked* anarchists."

"Oh, these are just spare clothes the anarchists lent me," said Gabriel modestly.

"Wicked or not, we are in any case honoured to have met you," said Reginald, "and we wish you a very good night."

"Good night to you, and thanks for your kind hospitality."

Gabriel bowed and they stood silent in the doorway for a glowing, embarrassing while, as when people do not want a pleasant evening to end, but none of them dares to be the first to admit it. Gabriel, especially, would have done anything not to find himself on his own, mulling over Stella.

"Here, sir," said Geraldine, after a while. She handed him the candelabra she held, then noticed the bandages around his hands.

"Do you want us to call a maid to help you with your clothes?" she asked, a barely perceptible smile hovering on her face. "They are very sweet, and fond of foreigners."

"No, please, do not wake anyone on account of me." He took a deep breath. "I am sure we can work this out together," he said, his voice almost a whisper.

In the light of the candelabras, the twins looked at each other and smiled.

CHAPTER XXVIII

The Aurorarama

●

*In like manner, recollected images are attributed to the
moving lights, in the splendid exhibition of the Aurora Borealis.
The Icelandic beholds in them the spirit of his ancestors, and
the vulgar discern encountering armies, and torrents of blood,
in the lambent meteors of a winter-sky.*
John Ferriar, "An Essay Toward
a Theory of Apparitions," 1813

After having taken advantage of the pale hazy daylight
for a quick morning tour, Brentford, the Aerial Anarchists, and the Inughuit had a much better understanding of Crocker Land, that mythical place that had, under
various names, eluded and deluded so many explorers.

The Island, of which the mirage appeared much bigger
than the reality, consisted of an inner plateau about twenty
miles in diameter, rimmed all around by small basaltic moun-

tain ranges that showed unequivocal signs of volcanic activity. In that respect and some others, it resembled Iceland, particularly in the numerous geysers and hot springs scattered across it. These warmed the surface considerably, and this difference of temperature with the surrounding Arctic air produced a continual veil of vapour that made the island indistinct from its foggy, icy surroundings. Only an aerial view could, under certain weather conditions, disclose the secret of its improbable presence. Interestingly, when seen from more earthbound angles, its hollow shape could be construed as a hole leading to the centre of the earth.

As the nocturnal approach of the *Ariel* had revealed, the main feature of the Island was the mile-wide crystal located roughly at its centre. Even for a trained crystallographer, as Hardenberg had revealed himself to be, it was difficult to say whether it had come from a meteorite whose impact had caused a volcanic eruption, or had slowly emerged from the bowels of the earth. The pale emerald–like crystal resembled clinopyroxene, with some chrysolite penetration twinning, but was, Hardenberg said, unusually birefringent. The double vision it caused made orientation in the castle a little difficult, especially after a few drinks, a phenomenon the anarchists had experienced the night before while trying to find the way back to their rooms after supper.

The social life of the Islanders was organized around the Crystal Castle, though it held no power but a symbolic one. The four settlements that surrounded it were themselves long and wide tunnels, about forty feet in height, dug straight into the gemstone, in a way that left the crystal as thin as slightly tinted glass sheets, which were reinforced here and there by pillars of basalt, like some kind of Arcadian arcades. Dome-shaped houses lined these tunnels; a basalt pillar about six feet high mounted with an oil lamp stood in front of each house. A series of wells, directly linked to the hot springs, were placed at regular intervals along the central path and warmed the houses through a network of pipes of a type already known, if Nicolo Zeno is for once to be trusted, amongst the Norse dwellers of Greenland—a fact which tended to prove that the islanders were indeed their descendants.

But the most curious aspect of their organization, as one of their guides explained, was that the four villages, each set at one of the four compass points, corresponded to a season of the year, by particular settings of the pipes network: the Eastern village, Gorias, had a soft, springtime temperature, with some flower beds and bowers of small trees, and was peopled by children and adolescents, colourfully dressed and playful. Findias, in the South, was almost summery, filled with small wheat fields and springing fountains, inhabited by strong but graceful young adults dressed in white. Middle-aged persons, their hair already grey, and wearing brown clothes, lived in Murias, the Western village, where one found all sort of nuts and berries, apple orchards, and, most surprisingly under those latitudes, vines with enormous red grapes, from which they made a good ice wine that Isabella had baptized Château-Cristal. The North village was called Falias, and though it was colder than the others, the white-haired elders who lived there, all dressed in grey, remained idly seated in front of their houses, mostly occupied, it seemed, with chatting and playing board games.

In every case, as the guests were prompt to note with satisfaction, the plots and ponds (abounding with a curious amphibian animal that the Inuit recognized as the mysterious *tiktaalit*) were common to all. The overall atmosphere was apparently, perhaps deceptively, one of harmony and peace, though Brentford, while taking mental notes on the Greenhouse distribution, also found it a bit boring, like some kind of very sloooooow roundabout. This was not the kind of rustic Fairy Tale he wanted New Venice to become.

The Inuit, however, liked it better, to the point that they insisted on staying in Findias for the rest of the day. They were not very eager, one could tell, to return to the castle and meet the twins again, or as they called them, with a shiver of disgust, *tyakutyik*—"What kind of being are these two?" as Tuluk translated to Brentford.

It was only as they sat for lunch, the day already turned to a lavender twilight, that Gabriel made his appearance in the dinner room, without the twins, who, tenderly intertwined, were still sound asleep in his room.

"Our hosts aren't with you?" asked Brentford, knowingly.

"No, they're playing hide-and-seek together," said Gabriel as he sat down at the table, taking a red apple from a cut-crystal bowl.

"You missed something."

"Did I?" asked Gabriel between two mouthfuls.

"We saw some very interesting penetration twinning."

"Oh, really?"

"I don't know why, but I haven't been able to stop thinking of the Elphinstone Myriorama, since last night. All these possible permutations."

"So what? Isn't *Do All Be All* the motto on your coat of arms?"

The Anarchists pretended not to pay any attention to this cryptic teasing, but Heidenstamm couldn't help observing, "I have never heard of a case of xiphopagus twins being of different sex. It must be really interesting from an anatomical point of view."

Gabriel looked at him coldly and answered nothing. But after a while, he whispered into Brentford's ears, "They are more like hermaphrodites, in fact. And very playful."

Brentford recalculated the permutations. If he sometimes found Gabriel's pursuits to be less than tasteful, he had to admit they bore witness to a curiosity of metaphysical proportions. The previous evening must have been, he supposed, Gabriel's own farthest north, though doubtless from Gabriel's point of view, his true North Pole was the Ingersarvik. From there onward, he could only go south.

"You know, there's something else I keep thinking of since last night," Gabriel said to Brentford, more loudly this time. "That story about Father Calixte."

"The religious fanatic? You think he preached Nixon-Knox into creating the Phantom Patrol, do you? I have come to the same conclusion myself."

"That was rather obvious," Gabriel said nastily. "It was something else that sprang to my mind. You remember my godfather?"

"The archbishop? The one that had you spied upon by your Eskimo maid?"

"That's the one. He knew this Father Calixte from his days in the Marist Missions among the Inuit. Apparently, the man had made himself half-mad from privations and wanting to live like an Eskimo. He had more and more frequent visionary fits, which he thought were prophetic, and he was of course a kind of black sheep for the Church hierarchy."

"They have eyes and they cannot see," said, without perceptible irony, Hardenberg, who had overheard the conversation and was getting interested in it.

"Just before Calixte died," Gabriel went on, "he asked my godfather, who had always defended him as well he could, to execute his last will. But it was a rather hard task, even for an archbishop. The most delicate provision of that will was that

Calixte wanted one of his own prophecies to be carved on his tombstone, rather than some quote from the Bible. As you can imagine, the idea fared rather poorly with his superiors. Finally, a compromise was reached: it would be written in old-style French, with a lettering so ornate as to be barely legible to the average passer-by. Some years ago, I saw this tombstone, somewhere in the floor of a particularly ill-lit spot of the crypt of St. Mark's Dream, and, according to my godfather, it read thus: *"La ville sera la proie du serpent jusqu'à ce que le fils deux fois né devers le pôle arctique les en délivre."*—"The city will be prey to the Snake until a twice-born son from beyond the arctic pole delivers it."

"And?" asked Brentford, holding back a yawn.

"Well. At the time I would have understood this rubbish as purely allegorical. The Snake of course represented evil, or else the desire to reach the Pole, which Calixte was constantly raving about. The twice-born son could be a man baptized as an adult, a convert Inuk, for instance. That would have been consistent with Calixte's missionary work. But then, yesterday, I saw a twice-born son from beyond the arctic pole, and it just rang a sleigh bell in me."

"The twins? Is that who you mean?" said Brentford, his eyebrows arching Gothic-style.

"Who else? Not to mention that they are the only direct matrilineal descendants of one of the Seven Sleepers, whose return in one form or another is awaited by the New Venetians. And after having spoken a little with the twins, I can tell you that they are much more than you think."

"In what sense?" asked Hardenberg, inviting himself into the conversation.

"They have obviously undergone some sort of innate Transpherence. They are as d'Ussonville as d'Ussonville himself was. I suspected it in the way they told their story. They knew everything their grandmother or mother had seen or felt, and could *see* it as vividly as I see you."

"But d'Ussonville was never Transphered," protested Brentford, though he had already understood how it could have happened. "Unless... it was Plastisine."

"Yes, from what I can gather, Igor Plastisine's metabolism was pure Pineapples and Plums when he met Myrtle. He may have triggered something in her that she was never conscious enough to notice but that she passed straight on to the children she was carrying, whether they were Igor's or Edmund's—something sufficiently strong to keep them alive while they were borne by a dead mother. Maybe this was the message or, more exactly, the riddle Isabella wanted to convey to us by coming back to the city: these children, Brentford, are the only way the Seven Sleepers can come back and save the city. Because there's one more thing that I have forgotten to tell you and that you, of all people, should know."

"Drum roll, please..." said Brentford, who had become wary of Gabriel's own Book of Revelations.

"I saw the Seven Sleepers rotting in the Scavengers' Arcaves. The Council had tried to sink their cryogenic coffins in a canal."

Brentford was thunderstruck.

"Blankbate did not tell me of this."

"He did not want to spoil your wedding, I suppose. Or was keeping it for the right moment. Or he just didn't care."

"And why would the Council do such a thing?"

Gabriel shrugged his shoulders.

"Maybe they're more afraid of the prophecies than they want to admit. Maybe they didn't want to take any chances that the Sleepers would return."

The Anarchists were totally befuddled, and looked at each other wide-eyed. Only Hardenberg, a frown creasing his large forehead, seemed to be pondering what he had heard. He was the one who spoke first.

"That changes everything, then."

Brentford thought he knew what he meant, but wanted to make sure.

"In what respect?" he asked.

"It means, Mr. Orsini, that the Council has betrayed its own duty to the Sleepers and that their power is now devoid of any authority. You are now, if you'll allow me such unholy words, a *legitimist* and your revolution is *a restoration*."

"I have never believed a word of this prophecy about the Sleepers' return."

"Of course, you haven't. But the question is not to believe it or not, it is whether to make it *come true* or not. Do it, and believe me, it will become believable."

During the last few minutes, and though he did his best to hide it, Brentford had felt a rising tide of excitement within himself. As he had written, in a moment of elation in *A Blast on the Barren Land* "the axe was at the root of the tree." Ideally, he had just to seize it and swing it to fell the Council in a thunderous crash of dynastic branches. But he saw himself more as someone who pointed people in the right direction—he just never thought that he would have to lead the charge. Something in him still hesitated to take a step that would be both the first and the final one. He was true to New Venice, but two loyalties fought within him, that of the letter and that of the spirit. Of course, if he put it that way, it was because he had already decided. A thrill ran through him.

"Since you're tempting your neighbour, and offering kingdoms to him, Mr. Hardenberg, you will not be surprised if I ask you to give us some kind of proof of your powers."

"Our peculiar kind of magic deals only with reality. Be careful what you ask for."

"What can you do to save the Inuit independentists?"

"Oh, that!" said Hardenberg, taking his watch from his waistcoat pocket. "It has already started. Herr Treschler should be ready by now, if you want to follow us... "

✳

Treschler had not been part of the excursion but instead had been busying himself on a terrace of the castle with both a reflecting telescope and a box covered with studs and dials and topped with a swivelling antenna ending in a silvery ball. As the others rejoined him, the telescope was pointed at an aurora Borealis that had broken out just above the top of the Island's vapour veil, and was shimmering like an emerald gauze curtain lightly dancing in a draught.

"Now," Treschler explained to the assembly, "this device is just a little Tesla wireless transmitter that I use to send a signal to rotate another machine, called a Selenium Telectroscope, located on a distant island. This machine, which is itself coupled with a camera obscura, transforms the images it captures into amplified electromagnetic pulses, that are in turn beamed, thanks to powerful transmitters and a whole array of antennas, onto the aurora itself, in order to modulate its heat and composition according to the patterns of the original pictures, which it thereby replicates. I call this the Aurorarama."

"The what?" asked Gabriel, a puzzled look on his face.

"The Aurorarama, or the Hertzian Harp, if you prefer."

"And what is its purpose, exactly?" Brentford asked impatiently, wondering how this thingamajig was supposed to help the Inuit independentists.

"You'll see, and quite literally so," Treschler answered patiently. "But I must warn you that it is a bit laggy and almost out of range, so you will have to focus very hard, I'm afraid."

By and by, as all looked on, the striations of the aurora seemed indeed to form phantom, ephemeral shapes, perpetually dissolving and regrouping into vaguely purplish spectres on the green swaying backdrop. Small mountains seemed to be the general scene of the action. In the foreground, human shapes slowly came into focus, revealing a group of fur-clad Inuit, entrenched behind hillocks, their backs to the spectators, their weapons aimed at the landscape.

From time to time, explosions, seemingly from mortar shells, swelled the aurora, but caused little or no damage to the Inuit position. The Inuit remained motionless, as if waiting to see the "Whites of the eyes" of their opponents to start shooting at them. Straining his own eyes, Brentford could see, approaching the defenders, barely perceptible modifications of the landscape that gradually turned into figures carrying darker objects, which by and by appeared to be rifles. Brentford recognized the snow camouflage of the Alpine Marines of the Sea and Land Battalion, as they began attacking the trenches. Their snow glasses and their shoes, of a dark blue hue against the pale green aurora, made it easier to see them more precisely as they charged. It grew strange, then quite nerve-racking, for the helpless spectators to observe that the Inuit did not seem to react. Maybe they were out of ammunition and waiting, bayonets fixed, for a final hand-to-hand fight, which Brentford was not sure that he wished to see.

He turned toward Hardenberg, who in his Macfarlane and wide-brimmed Puritan hat retained an Olympian calm, while just beside him the four Inughuit cried encouragements and insults.

The first assault section of the Sea Lions reached the rim of the trenches, but the Inuit still did not move as they were shot at from above, the bullets tearing their clothes and jerking their bodies. Brentford was baffled. Had some poison-gas shells killed them before the land attack began?

The soldiers jumped into the trenches, so close now that the images, still striated and undulating, were as clear as those of a slightly damaged hand-colorized fantascope movie. The first Sea Lion, his fur-lined face mask as big as a moon in the sky, turned over one of the corpses at his feet, then suddenly jumped back, recoiling in horror, just as his comrades did when they checked the other bodies.

Eventually, an unmasked officer arrived, and Brentford recognized him as Mason himself, flanked by another man, the Count-Councillor and Army Commissar Auchincloss, wearing a black overcoat and a black *chapka*. The captain-general pulled one of the corpses upright and, with a disgusted face, tore off one arm. Brentford felt like throwing up, but then realized that the arm had not been human: it looked more like a musk ox bone or something of that kind. Mason then decapitated the corpse with a violent backward slap, and Auchincloss, picking up the head, became enraged and ripped off the wooden human mask that hid the muzzle of a seal.

"*Tupilaat!!!*" cried Tiblit in relief, as the other Eskimos laughed, slapping their thighs and each other's backs, and hugging the anarchists, who were laughing with them. Brentford looked quizzically at Hardenberg, who smiled back at him.

Up in the sky, meanwhile, Mason and Auchincloss were now having what was obviously a heated debate. Eventually shrugging his shoulders, Mason ordered his reluctant men to rearrange the bodies, as if they had been shot during the attack, or thrown in a mass grave, taking care that their "faces" were hidden. As soon as this grisly task was completed, a photographer arrived and shot a picture of the bodies from above the trench. Obviously, Auchincloss had decided to make this look like a victorious battle and something to brag about when he got home. Mason stood apart, his arms crossed, sombrely looking off at the snow.

The aurora was now fading, the images losing clarity.

Hardenberg walked up to Brentford and, taking him by the arm, led him toward the crystal balustrade of the terrace.

"Now. How did you like our little *tupilaat* troopers? Made in East Greenland, thanks to our Inuit allies. It's been a lot of work."

Maybe Brentford would have liked it better if he had not faced the Phantom Patrol just the night before. This pantomime, successful as it was, hit too close to his funny bone.

"A bit horrible for a fairy tale."

"*Tss, tss*. The most horrible are the best. Every child knows that. So you will take the kingdom I offered you?"

"It depends on what you want against it."

"Nothing I will ask permission to get," said Hardenberg with a certain haughtiness. "But nothing that should be of consequence to you."

Brentford thought about it for a while. He had, so far, no reason not to trust the Aerial Anarchists.

"I have one more condition, or favour, to ask."

"That would be your second wish. You'll have just one left," said Hardenberg pleasantly.

"I want no bloodshed."

Hardenberg smiled widely, as if genuinely amused.

"Ah, Mr. Orsini... Do you know what it is that I like about you? You like to cast yourself as a down-to-earth politician and a no-nonsense strategist, but at heart, you're like me, aren't you? An artist and a poet. You should have called your book a *Butterfly on the Barren Land*. But you are no fool, and neither am I," he added darkly. "And there is no way I can promise you such a thing."

The night before the departure, Brentford had a dream. It was night and he was walking the streets of New Venice. In the mock moonlight, the city was nothing but a self-repeating myriorama of ruins, smashed-in roofs, broken columns, toppled statues, scattered objects, and clothes half-smothered in the snow. His steps crunching through the silence, he walked and walked on in

349 * Jean-Christophe Valtat

the cold, along avenues and across bridges, past empty arcades and pillaged shops, and did not meet a living soul. Now it is mine, he thought with bitterness, all mine...

CHAPTER XXIX

Terrorists!!!

●

Others, because the prince my seruice tries,
Thinke that I think State errours to redress:
But harder iudges iudge ambitions rage:
Scourge of itselfe, still climbing slipperie place:
Holds my young brain captiu'd in a golden cage.
O fooles, or ouer-wise, alas, the race
Of all my thoughts hath neither stop nor start
But only Stellaes eyes and Stellaes heart.
Sir Philip Sidney, *Astrophell and Stella*, XXIII

Hardenberg's plan was that the Anarchists would not return to New Venice with the *Ariel*: now that the contract with the Council had been broken, it would have meant a field day for the Anti-Aerial Artillery. It was a much better idea, and Brentford had agreed, to let the Council think they had got rid of the traitors and the threat they posed.

They had hidden the airship in a cave inside the cliffs on the northern coast. Then, at night, using clever little electric motor sleds equipped with kites and spiked wheels at the front, they had discreetly rejoined the Fisheries, where the Scavengers, after Brentford's explanations, welcomed them with no further question. By way of the Parcel Pneumatic Post they had been propulsed and hidden in the underground lair of the Scavengers, where they had made both their quarters and headquarters.

But though there was to be no terror from above, there would still be some sort of loud destructive device involved. Brentford had protested, but Schwarz had made it clear that this was a question of honour for the anarchists, and therefore not negotiable. It was, however, Hardenberg's conviction that quality had to prevail over quantity, and that a single, precise, well-timed blast at the right spot at the right time would have as much *expressivity* on the battlefield as numerous blind outbursts of terror. He had looked upon the map, lost in thought, then all of a sudden had pointed straight at the Greenhouse.

Brentford protested again.

"Too bad," Hardenberg said with a straight face. "Hothouses are the best things to blow up. All those smithereens. But be at rest, Mr. Orsini, it was a just an idiotic joke. What we'll do is take the most wickedly useless institution in the city and blow it to freedom come. It would be best if it were both a warning and a well-deserved punishment. I vote for the Northwestern Administration for Native Affairs."

Brentford, though he hated the idea of any ruins at all in New Venice, deemed the idea a lesser evil. And, after all, ruins, too, were part of the life of a city. A kind of *Memento mori*. Of *Et in arcades ego*.

Mugrabin was to be entrusted with the whole operation, and Hardenberg had also insisted, for some reason, that it would be Gabriel, and none other, who was to serve as messenger to him. Gabriel was perfectly happy with his self-appointed office as a chaperone to the Elphinstone twins, and had little desire (or perhaps much too much) to go back to the Apostles'. Still, he did not want to be tiresome in these delicate circumstances, and with typical bad grace he finally surrendered.

Which was why, on the eve of the military parade organized to celebrate the Victory over the Inuit, he had stealthily walked out of the underground hideout and by numerous roundabout ways through ill-lit and slushy streets had reluctantly hurried toward the Apostles', Stella's featherweight ghost using his stomach as a punching bag.

And when he rapped the code on Mugrabin's door, it was none other than Stella who opened it. In a man's dressing gown.

They stood facing each other, paralyzed. Gabriel's soul fluttered in panic like a emptying balloon, as if trying to find a way out of his body.

"Ah, Gabriel, my good friend!" said Mugrabin from behind Stella, putting on his braces. "I am so happy to see you!!!"

He came to the door and hugged him, until Gabriel could not breath anymore.

"We were very worried for you! Isn't it true, Zvevdichka, that we worried a lot? Our Zvevdichka loves you a lot, you know," he added, in a whisper that reeked of onion.

The Little Star, however, had retreated to her room.

"Whatever brings you here, my good friend?" Mugrabin asked, still standing in the doorway, his eyes blinking with emotion.

Gabriel managed to remember the password.

"Do me business in the veins o' the earth
When it is baked with frost."

Mugrabin's face broke out into an ugly porcelain grin. He took Gabriel by the arm and pulled him inside the apartment, closing the door behind him and looking through the peephole for a while.

"At last! It has come!" he exclaimed as he turned back toward Gabriel. "And you have joined our feast of Freedom. By highways or hedges, I always knew you would. Have you heard, Stella?" he called out. "He is now one of us!"

But, locked in her room, Stella did not answer.

Gabriel, trembling and holding his hat like a shy peasant, followed Mugrabin into a small, shabby living room. On the table, near the samovar, from which Mugrabin poured him a cup of steaming tea, and next to a small phonograph, was a strange device he had been cleaning, showing a piston and a cylinder with cooling vanes at the top, small enough to be carried in a coat pocket.

"Do not worry!" blurted out Mugrabin. "It is not a bomb-chka. I have had my share of those," he winked with his glass eye. "No, no, this is a new invention, quite extraordinary. It is called a Resonator. But I prefer to call it a Liberator. It's a pun, you see—on the energy it liberates and the people it liberates. Hahaha. And where are we supposed to liberate this energy?"

"The Northwestern Administration for Native Affairs," said Gabriel, burning his tongue with the tea, which he noticed Mugrabin drank directly from the saucer. "Tomorrow morning during the parade. As it is a holiday, the building will not be occupied or guarded."

"It is as if it were already done! *Perform'd to point.* Pfuii!!" said Mugrabin, with a graceful gesture. "And thanks to you, my friend."

"I've done nothing," said Gabriel, thinking of how much it had actually cost him to come there. He wondered why Hardenberg had so badly wanted him to carry this message. Maybe the arch-Anarchist knew about Mugrabin and Stella, and had wanted Gabriel to face the truth. As if having seen Stella with

Wynne had not been enough of a truth to face. Now he had to accept that she was the sweetheart of this scarecrow, who looked at him with a tear in the corner of his good eye, and then put his mangled hand on his shoulder.

"No! I mean because of your *music*. The little piece you called *Lobster-Cracking*."

Gabriel did not understand. He had forgotten about the little wax roll he had recorded out of boredom during the winter. He had happened to have it in his satchel when he went to Doges College, and he had given it to Phoebe as a countersign for Brentford. The last time he had seen it, it was in Wynne's hands, at the hospital, on the night when he had met Stella...

"It is the exact frequency we need to start our little Liberator, you see. This device, Mr. Treschler has explained to the idiot I am, works with a force called *resonance frequency*. The bigger is the building, the lower the frequency should be, though I ask you not to ask me why. Linked to a small phonograph, such as this one, it plays the song inside the walls, making it echo through the building, and then, you just have to wait for the entire place to tumble down! It is *genius*. Russia would have been free long ago with such machines at our disposal! Mr. Schwarz, the chemist of the *Ariel*, who is a bomb fiend, was not very happy with Treschler bringing it along! Isn't that true, my Little Star, that your daddy was angry?" yelled Mugrabin.

"Her daddy?" repeated Gabriel.

"I'm Stella Schwarz, the daughter of Doktor Schwarz and a French *petroleuse*," said Stella, her eyes puffy from crying, as she leaned against the doorframe of the living room. "I'm sorry I have lied to you."

"And the song... You stole it from Wynne..."

Stella nodded and sobbed, her face in her hands.

Mugrabin whispered in Gabriel's ear.

"I suffered from this as much as you did, my friend. But it was the only way."

"But... how did you know that this song existed... and could do this?" Gabriel insisted.

Stella sniffed, and took a deep breath.

"One day, as we were rehearsing at the Trilby Temple, and while I was waiting in the ballot box, Wynne, who was in charge of Handyside's security, approached him for a private talk," she explained between sniffs and sobs. "Wynne said that he needed Handyside to come to the Kane Clinic and mesmerize a girl, so that she would look as if she were in a coma. Their idea was to blame it on the effect of a very-low-frequency song. Of course, I had heard my father and Treschler and Max... I mean Mikhail... talking of the new device in the *Ariel*, and I knew that such a song was just what they needed to make it work and that it could be decisive. At some point, Wynne explained that he would allow the Gentlemen of the Night to do a round-up at the Toadstool in order to catch the man who had recorded the song. I went there after the show, but they took us to the clinic and put me in a room before I could find out anything. Then I met you. And I swear to you, on the head of Voltairine de Cleyre, Gabriel, I did not know it was your song. Not before you made me listen to the other pieces."

"Then... *you*... searched my place?"

"Be glad she did," said Mugrabin. "That is how she found the book. She knew it was dangerous for you and she brought it to me."

"I did not find the song, and so understood Wynne had the only copy," Stella went on with difficulty. "So the next time I met him at the Trilby Temple, well... It was horrible, believe me, going to the Ingersarvik, with this hypnotized woman and that old..."

"Shh..." said Mugrabin, coming back to her.

He took her in his arms, and softly rocking her, stroked her lustrous wavy hair with his mutilated hand. "It is over now. Now you must go and prepare yourself."

Stella left the room, looking at Gabriel with a sorrowful expression. He nodded, so slightly that she may not have noticed. He struggled to understand why she had deemed it necessary to go through this ordeal. But that was typical of radicals, he thought, this ability to convince themselves of the necessity of anything, provided it would turn their beliefs into action, their dreams into realities. Not to mention the influence of that damned Russian freak, who now came back to Gabriel with eyes that were, this time, unmistakably tearful, including the glass one.

"It is a small love, the one that cannot be shared," said Mugrabin, squeezing his arm. "Sharing this one with you was... exceedingly painful. But it was also an honour."

He squeezed Gabriel's arm harder, and spoke in a low hissing voice.

"Freedom is not always a feast, Mr. d'Allier. It wants weeping and gnashing of teeth. It wants sacrifices. It wants blood. *I am* ready to make those sacrifices."

He released his grip and opened a drawer, pulling out the wax roll Stella had so dearly bought.

"I would be still more honoured if you would come with us on the mission," he said, now matter-of-factly. "And Stella would be happy, I am sure, for you to see what a brave and *loyal* young woman she is."

Gabriel shrugged his shoulders. He felt empty. His love had been mutilated beyond recognition, a revolting shambles of rotting body parts like those of a *tupilaaq* hastily knocked together. He watched Mugrabin easing his maimed body into a vest and a jacket, and knew he could never touch Stella again. But he also realized—watching the anarchist distributing about himself small fulminate phials, poisoned pins on a pincushion, phosphoric cords, and what-not—that, after all, it was more interesting to be Mugrabin's girlfriend than his.

If Gabriel had feared that the bombers would not be ready at such short notice, he was soon reassured. Mugrabin had been briefed extensively by Schwarz senior, who had previously studied, with the help of his daughter, every official building in the city and planned the destruction of each in both the most efficient and spectacular way. Blowing things up in New Venice was easy enough, since for all its pretention it was rather crudely built, but it was Schwarz's theory that each building had its own personality and its own way to be blown up that would respect its features while producing maximum damage. He called this *Anarchitecture*.

Since it had been decided that killing or dismembering people was to be avoided, Hardenberg had insisted that the Treschler machine be preferred over bombs, as it crumbled the building in on itself, with little steel or stone flying about. This had required a slight modification of the blueprints from the anarchitects, since it was now the acoustic qualities of the building and the vibratory characteristics of its material that had to be taken into account. But on the whole that was less troublesome for everyone than fiddling around with mercury fulminate.

The N.A.N.A. was the target of choice for reasons even beyond its symbolic value. First, it was impressive enough. A long redbrick building, with a central gate topped by a dungeon, it evoked a British castle or college, and it looked so defiantly colonial that it was, in a sense, asking for trouble. Then too, as a late addition to the city, it was a bit off the beaten path, on an esplanade of its own (though it shared it in wintertime with the Jake Frost Palace, which had just been closed to the public), and except for its braggart's frown it was rather defenceless. On top of that, it appeared that an Inuk informer working for the anarchists, going by the name of Oosik, had described the place to them inside and out, so that all of its tickle spots were well known to Mugrabin.

The most difficult part was simply getting there without being noticed, but at this early hour, and with everybody on holiday for the victory parade, this problem solved itself, as long as one stood in the shadows of the surrounding buildings and did not attempt to cross the esplanade in the moonlight.

The terrorist love triangle, by crouching and running and ducking for cover, soon reached the back of the building and, from there, a rear entrance that was used for deliveries. Deftly avoiding any jingling, Mugrabin thoughtfully selected a key from a key ring, and three trials were enough to let him in with Stella. Gabriel, wondering vaguely why he had agreed to come along, but too heartbroken to really care (maybe, inglorious as it was, he just wanted to see more of Stella), remained behind on the lookout. He stood in the dark, shivering with cold and sadness, at the northeastern corner of the building, from which he could see the Jack Frost Palace faintly gleaming under the moon, thinking how it would soon begin to melt, a soft and slow ruin, and he could not help imagining that all the city would dissolve with it, imperceptibly, until it left not a single trace, as if it had never been there at all. That felt better, somehow, than thinking about Mugrabin having taken Stella down to a cold, obscure kingdom from which he, Gabriel, would never ever be able to bring her back.

Meanwhile, Mugrabin had lit a phosphoric cord and, as surely as if he were in their own house, discovered with Stella a staircase that led down to the basement. There, he quickly strapped the Resonator to one of the pillars that held the vault aloft, while, equally nimbly, Stella fitted below it the muffled pavilion of the phonograph, before cranking it to play the roll.

The sounds came out too low to be heard directly, but they were echoed by the amplifier, diffusing them through the walls like the beating of a gigantic heart, so gigantic it had the power the break the ribcage that surrounded it. Mugrabin and Stella could hear the distant thuds as if someone were digging a tunnel below them. The sound waves circuited through the whole building, gaining power as they did. A faint vibration could already be felt along the pillars. It was working. It would take some time but no stone would be left upon another. Mugrabin and Stella stood embraced for a while under that strengthening heartbeat and then, as a little dust fell from the ceiling, decided it was time to go.

The sun was beginning to rise as they emerged. Gabriel still stood against the wall, and he could feel it almost pulsating. He did not recognize his own song. It was not his anymore, but, then, that was what happened to songs.

"Everything went okay?" he asked without conviction.

"Fine," said Stella, who looked even smaller in her thick, black, fur-lined jacket. She took off her crocheted hat and shook her corkscrew curls out in a moment of pure terrorist eroticism. Gabriel closed his eyes.

Mugrabin looked at the ashen dawn. They had taken too long.

"We should get away," he said. He looked determined, and calmer than Gabriel had ever seen him.

But as they reached the corner of the building, Wynne suddenly sprang out in front them, his unsheathed cane in his hand.

"Here you are!" he said.

But he had sprung a little too soon. They were still a few yards away from him and had time to turn and run for their lives.

"The palace!" shouted Mugrabin.

They had the whole building to run alongside, and a good two hundred yards of esplanade to cross. But Wynne was an athlete and he would soon catch up.

"Let's separate!" bellowed Mugrabin, running quite quickly in spite of his slight limp.

They moved apart from one another, so as to disorient Wynne. Who would he really want to catch? Stella, the girl that he thought he had stolen from Gabriel and who had stolen the roll from him? Or that d'Allier for whom there would be, he had promised, no third chance of escape? Stella was the one he had been following tonight, but d'Allier was the closest. He would be the chosen one.

A blast threw Wynne off balance. A little phial had exploded not far from him, and a few glass splinters had peppered him. He started again, his rage increased, veering toward Mugrabin, but quickly changed his mind, as he reckoned this one was *dangerous*. D'Allier was better game, and almost in his reach. A promise is a promise. He would pay for the others.

Gabriel, meanwhile, had regained the yards he had lost but, blame it on his lifestyle, was not much of a sprinter. His body shook in exhaustion and fear. He entered the esplanade, dazzled by the dawning sun, already losing his breath, with Wynne pumping his legs like pistons just a few paces behind.

The Jack Frost Palace loomed, blindingly, in front of him, a mere hundred yards away. It was his last chance. Mugrabin and Stella had disappeared. Maybe he was saving them by sacrificing himself. Maybe he was just unlucky. He was gasping, a side stitch stabbing him, by the time he reached the security barriers that protected the public from the crumbling castle. He tried to jump over them but stumbled, then regained his balance and darted toward the gate, while Wynne now swiftly escaladed the clanging rails behind him.

The place was like a maze, full of open courts and inner gates, but hesitation was not an option, though any dead end would be fatal. He panicked as Wynne's shadow almost reached him.

"Stop! Stop right now!" cried the policeman.

Gabriel was perhaps not, as he had dreamed he was, one of those men who turn around, knife in hand, to face the enemy. Especially without a knife. But he was stubborn enough to keep on running, turning left or right as soon as he could, although his lungs were about to burst and his legs were giving in. He went through another gate, but this time there was no exit, just a circling wall, its crenels about ten feet high. He was trapped. Wynne was coming closer, with the strides of an ogre. Gabriel nervously searched his pocket, looking for some weapon, and all he found was the polar kangaroo amulet. He clutched it and closed his eyes.

"Kiggertarpok," he thought, "please..."

As Wynne entered the court, he saw Gabriel leaping over the wall.

Gabriel felt as if he had been lifted by a crane and tossed through the freezing air. He willed himself to land on a parapet, and did it almost neatly, balancing himself with whirling arms. As he turned away to look down, he saw Wynne hurl his top hat onto the snowy ground. And he saw that outside the castle, on each side of the gate, Mugrabin and Stella had regrouped and, knives in hand, were silently waiting for the policeman to come out.

In front of Gabriel, the city spread its whiteness, its frozen canals gleaming like fire under the ascending sun. By and by, little black figures streamed from all directions, gathering for the victory parade.

CHAPTER XXX

Fairy Tale Tactics

●

How should the mind, except it loved them, clasp
These idols to herself? or do they fly
Now thinner, and now thicker, like the flakes
In a fall of snow, and so press in, perforce
Of multitude, as crowds that in an hour
Of civic tumult jam the doors, and bear
The keepers down, and throng, their rags and they,
The basest, far into that council-hall
Where sit the best and stateliest of the land.
Alfred Tennyson, *Lucretius*, 1868

The lightly yellowish edition of the *Arctic Illustrated News* of March 1, 1908 AB (After Backward) has always been a prized treasure among newspaper collectors, and is the only item in Brentford Orsini's collection: not only has it been deemed extremely rare, but it is also one of the most fascinating documents of that very special moment in the history of New Venice.

In five dense columns of purplish prose, its front page rhapsodized over this particular day when the Council of Seven had decreed a military parade to celebrate the "homecoming heroes" of the "glorious victory against the Inuit Independentists" during the battle of Prince Patrick Island. Not only had the rebels been crushed by a swift assault of the Sea Lions that took no prisoners, but the hangar and mooring mast of the unknown black airship had been destroyed, as well as a strange machine with antennas, which, according to military experts, was, the reporter wrote, a "secret death ray still in a phase of experimentation, but powerful enough to have wiped the city off the map." As to the dirigible itself, now cut off from its secret rear base, it had entirely vanished from the skies.

It was the first time since the foundation of New Venice that armed troops had been allowed to march through its streets, as a way to celebrate their bravery and, also, to dispel any doubts as to "the harmonious relationship that existed between the City and its loyal defenders." This exceptional measure, perhaps not quite faithful to the principles of the Seven Sleepers, had been, the newspaper insisted, "fully justified by the equally exceptional extent of the threat the city had been under."

The Council of Seven had nevertheless demanded strengthened security measures for the parade itself, in the event that "misguided members of the native minorities" wrongly interpret this military presence as a provocation directed toward them, and, God forbid, a disguised form of martial law. It would be a shame if these local independentists "put at risk by some irresponsible behaviour during the parade the majority of their famously peace-loving community."

It was therefore ordered by the Council that, in the wee hours of the morning before the parade took place, and under the benevolent protection of the Gentlemen of the Night, all the Native inhabitants of the city were to meet at the newly completed Inuit People's Ice Palace, in order to remain safely there during the time of the celebration.

The day had not yet broken over New Venice when all the local Eskimo families—about five hundred people carrying the few pieces of luggage they had been allowed to take with them—were already lined up in front of the Ice Palace, being admitted as soon as their names were ticked off the list by the efficient guardians of the Northwestern Administration for Native Affairs. Those who had been oblivious of the order or, with typical Eskimo slackness regarding punctuality, a little too slow to comply, had been collected directly at their homes by the ever devoted Guardian Angels, with the assistance of Angels of the Law, so as to avoid any ambiguity regarding the legality of the process.

Mr. Peterswarden, the director of the new facility, reiterated to journalists his satisfaction that it was "the Inuit themselves who were the first to take advantage and, in a sense, possession, of a place that respected the values of their ancient and noble culture, and which, after all, had been built with their comfort in mind."

Meanwhile, a small group of anarchists from the Blithedale Brotherhood, who had started a protest march on the Midway against a measure that seemed to them a bit discriminatory, were being dispersed, politely but firmly, by the Gentlemen of the Night. The protestors were then collected by ambulances to make sure they had not been molested, and would not be heard of again during the following hours. The parade could now take place under the most favourable conditions.

Barely had the sun risen, its pale slanting rays emerging from behind the roofs, than a large crowd, which had been given

New Venetian flags, was flocking along Barents Boulevard, Ladies' Mile, and Bears' Bridge. The weather was rather chilly,
but, as the *Arctic Illustrated News* had remarked, "there is nothing like waving a flag to·warm up one's spirits."

A dais and viewing stands had been erected on Barents
Boulevard under the aerial tunnel of the Pneumatic Train, and
it was a measure of the event that the Seven Councillors were all
attending, lined up according to their Day Names and each one
wearing across his coat a sash of one of the rainbow colours.
Even the wax effigies of the Seven Sleepers had been carted out
to sit between them, wearing the same attire, as befitted such a
rare occasion.

Behind them, one could spot the officials of the Arctic Administration, taking with equanimity, it appeared, what was
nothing if not a triumph for the Council. Other notabilities and
celebrities of the city were also to be noticed in the stands, such
as Mr. Brentford Orsini, General-Gestionary for the Greenhouses
and Glass Gardens, and his charming spouse, Mrs. Sybil Orsini-
Springfield, as well as the much-touted magician who had recently amazed the whole city, Mr. Adam Handyside. Their presence
all contributed to the idea, the reporter remarked, that the City
"was at last marching past the turmoil of these last months, head
held high, under the proud banners of unity and reconciliation."

Announced by a thunderous rumble of drums that echoed
in the stomachs of the onlookers, the Subtle Army lived up to
the occasion, displaying the most impeccable discipline as they
started to parade. Marching ahead were the heroes of the Prince
Patrick battle, the Sea and Land Battalion, headed by Captain-
General Frank Mason, who had led the final assault himself.
Buckles and barrels scintillated against the regular ranks of the
blue and grey dress uniforms, "as does the glittering froth on
the inexorable waves of the mighty ocean." A storm of flags
eddied around them, and confetti fell from the windows like

a more peaceful snowfall, in a "warmhearted re-enactment of
their hardships of the past days." It was, on all accounts, a "parade in Paradise."

But then Hell froze over.

As the Sea and Land Battalion presented its flag to the
Council to have it decorated with the "Order of the Winged
Sea Lion" (rumour had it that Mason had declined the medal
for himself, claiming that he had done nothing but his duty),
a "man of probable Inuk origin, but treacherously dressed in
Western clothes," elbowed his way through the crowd until he
found himself a mere ten feet away from the dais. Before anyone could react—except Mr. Handyside, who, putting his own
life at risk, had almost managed to throw himself in front of
the target—the terrorist pulled out a revolver and shot Baron
Brainveil, who fell instantly. As he agonized on the floor, a pool
of blood spreading beneath him, a commotion ensued so chaotic
that the perpetrator was able to escape by slipping below the
dais. Some witnesses, however, including several Gentlemen of
the Night, were positive that the Eskimo Assassin had headed to
the perpendicular arcades that led toward the Marco Polo Midway, and, taking an unguarded backdoor, had found a refuge
among his own kind in the Inuit People's Ice Palace.

In such situations, a crowd becomes notoriously volatile.
Seconds after the deed, amidst the pushing and shoving of those
who wanted to see and those who wanted to escape, amidst
the shouts of anger and the screams of horror, the word was
already spreading that the Eskimos had done it, and should pay
for it. Stoked by vociferating men of unclear origin, several large
chunks of the crowd soon directed themselves "spontaneously"
toward the arcades and the Inuit People's Ice Palace; so large
a rabblement, actually, that the Gentlemen of the Night soon
found themselves unable to hold them back, and "preferred to

concentrate their heroic efforts on saving women and children from being crushed in the panic."

By an ironic twist of fate, the army, although in full marching order, could do little to react, as the remaining crowd and policemen, separating the parade from any access to the Marco Polo Midway, prevented a military manœuvre that would have been in any case difficult in the extreme. Mason himself could hardly have given orders, closely surrounded as he was on the dais by the other members of the Council, some of them reminding him that the constitution forbade the army from intervening in the city, while others proposed ways to circumvent that particular difficulty.

Meanwhile the mob was already at the doors of the Inuit People Ice's Palace, shouting death threats while using guardrails as rams against the door.

There is little more to be found about the event in the *Arctic Illustrated News*. Probably the journalist judged it was high time for him to file his report through the pneumatic post, if he wanted it to make the evening edition.

That particular issue (and this explains its value) was actually printed but never distributed: for the simple reason that by the time it would normally have been sold in the streets, its readers already lived in a different nation.

Brentford had seen it coming. Swallowing his pride until it ulcerated his stomach, and seething with a fury he did his best to cool down, his senses were so sharpened that he could see things before they happened, as if he still had the Second Sight goggles on his nose.

He had clearly seen that the man who pretended to elbow his way through the crowd had actually been imperceptibly allowed to slip through between two Gentlemen of the Night. Though Brentford had avoided any kind of eye contact with

Arkansky, he had registered from the corner of his eye that the magician had started to move even before the terrorist had pulled out his gun. There was no doubt, if one measured it in tenths of a second, as Brentford seemed to be able to do, that Bailiff-Baron Brainveil had fallen before the first shot was heard, like a figure in a dream reacting to a noise not yet heard in real life. Then Brentford caught Arkansky's look after his rival had palmed the bullet he had just caught in his hand. *Real* bullet catch. It was unbelievable, but still the only real thing in that grotesquely fake assassination.

The organized scapegoating that took place afterward was especially abhorrent to Brentford. This was the line they should not have crossed. If he had not already taken his decision to overturn the Council, he would have taken it now, without any further soul-searching. Things were not ripe: they were rotten.

When he had resurfaced at ground level two days before, as if nothing had happened, he had felt that his part was the hardest to play. Not that he had to resume any kind of real domestic life with Sybil, who seemed to sleepwalk with indifference between the apartment and the recording studio. But having to accept the invitation to the parade, bow to the members of the Council and sit near Arkansky (who did not appear very happy to see him either) had really taken its toll on Brentford's morale and self-esteem. Now the time had come to settle accounts, for the city and for himself.

"Sorry," he said to the empty-eyed Sybil, who stood motionless at his side in spite of the commotion. He jumped off the dais, not as quickly or discreetly as he would have liked to, for a Gentleman of the Night spotted him and took up the chase, as Brentford headed toward one of the arcades that linked Barents Boulevard to the Marco Polo Midway. Blending into the rear guard of the lynch mob, whose flow was now thinning out, Brentford was disgusted to see how the otherwise indifferent

New Venetians had suddenly attained political consciousness as an excuse to take it out on innocents. Still, he was sure that most of them were not acting out of an inbred, vengeful hatred, but were simply going along with the flow, out of boredom and an appetite for Grand Guignol: rubberneckers looking for severed heads on a pike.

He zigzagged through them, using them as moving obstacles between himself and the police officer, but as he arrived at the middle of the arcade, rifle shots erupted somewhere in front of him and he realized that the crowd was suddenly rushing back, like a tidal wave of pure panic. He jumped aside, pressing himself against the door of a watchmaker's shop, as the two flows met together, the oncoming mob back-pedalling to avoid being bashed into and trampled by the retreating stampede. The arcade quickly became such a crush that the buttons of his coat were ripped off as people shoved by all around him.

As the flow of people began to thin out, he tried once more to advance, to make sure that he would stay out of reach of the Gentleman of the Night. The ice rugby player in him struggled toward the exit, ignoring the blows, focusing on staying upright, and gaining ground yard by yard. The bulk of the cowardly crowd had already passed him as he reached the gate of the arcade, and he stumbled out into the Midway, almost losing his balance among the stragglers who dashed past him.

He found the Midway strewn with scattered hats, scarves, and gloves, and even the odd shoe. But the most striking feature was this: a line of a hundred or so Scavengers in their masks and hats stood spread out across the front of the Inuit People's Ice Palace, their lever guns pointed skyward and an atrocious stench hovering about them.

"Hello," called one of them, whose voice Brentford recognized as Blankbate's.

"Thanks. Once again," Brentford said, filled with such happiness he felt about to weep.

This was nothing but what he had himself planned, though. Well, more or less.

In the Anarchists' den, various tactics had been devised, but as soon as the news arrived that the Council had decided to turn the Inuit People's Ice Palace into a temporary ghetto for the Eskimos (and possibly, Brentford suspected, a permanent one), the armed Scavengers had used the sewage system to enter the Ice Palace from below, so that when the Inuit went in, their liberators were already there, with the four Inughuit as translators, and much to the wardens' dismay. The lynch riot had been unexpected, but Blankbate, a mysterious man with, it seemed, some experience of combat, had no doubts about how to proceed.

He knew that New Venetians, threatened since they were children with the idea that the Scavengers would come and fetch them if they did not eat their clam chowder, usually tended, more or less consciously, not to cross their path, and if they did to avert their eyes. Suddenly opening the doors the crowd was banging upon and stepping outside to confront them in their full Plague Doctors regalia, the Scavengers were bound to make a certain impression. And reeking of raw sewage and armed with guns as well, they were simply too formidable to resist. Taking in the sight and stench, the mob stepped back like a frightened child and, at the crackling sound of the upward volley ordered by Blankbate, escaped the subtle control of the provocateurs and ran for its lower form of life. And so did the troublemakers on the Council's payroll.

It was looking good. Unless it wasn't.

At the other end of the Midway now marched a company of the Sea Lions, their guns pointed toward the Scavengers. Brentford, hypnotized by the spectacle, took a while to realize he was standing right in the middle of the fire zone. He recognized Mason, walking beside the first row of the fusiliers, his sabre held high, as if he were commanding a firing squad. Brentford knew enough of military psychology to know that all the orders Mason had obeyed reluctantly over the past few days could now well turn against him. Enemies usually paid for the stinging humiliations soldiers received from above: this was what could happen when you double-binded people with both a sense of honour and absolute subjection. It was very thin ice that Brentford now trod upon, and he was more nervous, probably, than the Scavengers were. He found himself waving a white handkerchief as if he were waving good-bye to his behind.

The Sea Lions stopped forty yards away from the Scavengers. Mason ordered bayonets to be fixed, and the first line to kneel down and take aim. Behind Brentford, the lever guns of the Scavengers clicked, sputtering cartridges on the ground. Everything came to a standstill. Brentford remembered that a Japanese martial arts instructor of the Navy Cadets had once taught him that life should be conducted as if constantly charging the spears of one's enemies. This included, he supposed, *actually* charging the spears of one's enemies. He contented himself with walking toward the bayonets of Mason's troops, but the sensation, he reckoned, was uncomfortably similar.

Mason moved toward him.

"I have orders to empty out the street by any means necessary," he warned Brentford formally.

"When was that supposed to be? Before or after the crowd massacred the Eskimos?" Brentford bit his lips. Perhaps he had gone too far. It was his luck that Mason liked problems to be stated clearly. Brentford could sense the dilemma the officer was in. Mason, he supposed, was not personally overwhelmed by any desire to empty out this particular street, especially if it meant it would endanger his men uselessly, but orders are orders. And certainly—and above all—he dreaded to lose face.

"The Council have forfeited their right to govern the city. I have assumed leadership during the transition," said Brentford, embarrassed at the pomposity of it.

"It's not for me to judge the Council," said Mason, surprisingly coldly. "I'm not taking my orders from you." Though the second sentence was even harsher than the first, Brentford thought he detected a thread of regret or sympathy.

"Aren't your orders that you must not intervene in the city?" he tried.

"Is any of this part of your duties as a civil servant? Mason countered. "You ask me to obey superiors' orders when you are disobeying them yourself."

They were in a deadlock.

Suddenly, a rattling agitation came from the back of the Sea Lions. A lieutenant hurried up to Mason, almost tripping on his own sabre.

"What is it?"

"At the back, sir, women with weapons."

Mason instantly pivoted and stared off where the lieutenant indicated. He lowered his sabre, dumbstruck. Brentford followed his gaze and saw—though barely believing it—Lilian Lenton, in a kind of green drum-major uniform, standing on a sled equipped with a Maxim machine-gun. All around her stood dozens of young women in arms, some of them brandishing colourful silk banners that Brentford could not read. It was the *little band* that had accompanied Lilian during the Recording Riot, back with a vengeance.

"Please," called out Lilian through a megaphone, a charming, almost flirtatious streak in her otherwise self-assured voice. "We have weapons, but we may not use them *quite* right. Sorry for the damage we would inflict on you."

Brentford felt like laughing, a bit nervously.

Mason turned toward him, very calmly, almost relieved. He had found a way out.

"I do not shoot women," he said to Brentford.

"The contrary would have surprised me," Brentford replied with a nod.

"I do not help revolutionaries, either."

"I understand perfectly."

"I will therefore order my men to retreat and remain neutral," he added, in a lower voice, his eyes avoiding Brentford's. "However, I have some doubt that the Navy Cadets will obey me. They have been very dissatisfied with the Council's orders lately. But would they be mutinous... I would be myself very reluctant to send my other units to march against them in the present confusion."

"Would the Cadets be mutinous to the point where they could, let us say, help us against the Council?"

"I do not wish to know," sighed Mason, shrugging his shoulders. "There's no 'us' I'm aware or part of. I'm going back to Frobisher Fortress. If you're looking for the Council in order to surrender yourself, which I strongly advise, it is now heading back to the Blazing Building. There is a *good chance* Brainveil will survive, in case you were worried."

Without waiting for an answer, he turned to his men and ordered them to shoulder arms and about face.

"Forward march!" he called.

The Sea Lions complied in an almost perfectly synchronous rhythm of clicks and jangles, but as they advanced toward the Arcades, Brentford noticed that their faces were turned toward the girls. But then, so was his, as soon as the last soldier had walked past.

Brentford strode quickly toward Lilian, who was, he had to admit, very eye-catching in her braided dolman and feathered hat. The forty or fifty young women who surrounded her wore no uniforms, but a hodgepodge of the fashionable and the military, flouncy skirts with battle-dress jackets, flat-heeled shoes with wide-brimmed hats or fatigue caps, carrying rifles in kid-gloved hands and cradling Maxim guns in moiré or velvet arms. It was in the time-honoured custom of revolutionaries to dress as women, except that these *were* women, but disguised as, what… disguised women? He could now read the green, white, and purple banners they brandished: Sisterhood of the Sophra-gettes, they proclaimed in bold embroidered letters.

This, he supposed, was one of Hardenberg's surprises. It was a good one. Hardenberg obviously insisted on Brentford having a ball while taking the city by storm. *Fairy Tale Fight Tactics*, he called this. Brentford wondered if Lenton was as crazy as the Aerial Anarchist.

"Lilian Lenton. This is most unexpected," he said as Lilian handed him her hand and he helped her to step down from her brougham sled.

"We have been underground for too long. We thought it was time for a little stroll," she said urbanely, as if they were quietly discussing the opera season in a drawing room. "I suppose you are Brentford Orsini, the author of *A Blast on the Barren Land*. I can see you are working hard on the second edition."

"Be assured I will take your advice into account."

"That might lead you further than you want to go," she said, smiling. Undercurrents of her past cuteness passed through her bony, determined face, but quickly dissipated.

Among her followers, Brentford recognized his old friend Jay, as well as Boadicea Lovelace, whom he knew as Bay. Both seemed delighted to be among the Gnostic Girls, as they had nicknamed themselves, and with Lilian Lake, as they now insisted on calling Ms. Lenton. There was another girl, smaller and younger, whom he had seen before, but could not remember exactly where or when.

He had plenty of questions to ask, but Blankbate, much less assured in the midst of these rather elegant, obviously well-bred females than he had been in front of the Sea Lions, slouched toward him and interrupted.

"We have just caught some people you may like to meet."

"One of those agitators?"

"More like a magician," said Blankbate.

"I'm coming," Brentford said, inviting Lilian to follow them.

But as he turned away, he could hear a loud rumble shaking the ground, and some of the Gnostic Girls began screaming. A cloud of dark dust slowly drifted over the roofs of the Midway coming from the east, by and by darkening the pale blue sky. Brentford sighed, as if he suddenly realized that the city would never be the same again.

"What is it?" asked Lilian between two coughs, dusting off her dolman.

"The Northwestern Administration for Native Affairs, hopefully," said Brentford—hoping, mostly, that Gabriel was safe and sound.

They entered the Inuit People's Ice Palace. For Brentford, who had never been there, it was quite a shock. It was as if he had been transported on a magic cape to a frozen strait surrounded by mountains. The hundreds of Inuit, standing equally stunned in a circle around the place, completed the illusion. He shivered at the thought of the faceless banshee that wrecked the ships and of the Phantom Patrol (what a good pensioner's home for them this would be).

In the middle of the circle, guarded by Scavengers, stood Arkansky, his hands in his pockets, trying to look detached; Spencer Molson, the clumsy conjurer, in his Westerner-disguised-as-Eskimo-disguised-as-Westerner disguise; and, both lost in a mute, motionless trance, Sybil and Phœbe.

Brentford walked up to them.

"We caught these three as they were trying to reach the Trilby Temple," explained Blankbate. "The young miss was waiting inside."

Arkansky looked defiantly at Brentford, who stared back with a barely repressed anger. Now was the time to prove, thought Brentford, that he could conjure some act of justice out of a top hat of rage. The gaze of the Inuit, of the Scavengers, and of the Sophragettes weighed on him. Sybil's look was empty, but that, too, was a burden. He had not the least idea of what to say. Instead, it was Arkansky who spoke. The magician certainly had nerve.

"Mr. Orsini. I hope you have no intention of behaving stupidly."

"You're the proof that one shouldn't."

Arkansky tried to focus his basilisk stare on Brentford, who, legs apart and hands behind his back, deliberately looked up at the ceiling, ignoring the attempt.

"I suppose that a democrat like you will not refuse a little discussion," Arkansky said eventually.

"Not until after you have liberated Miss Springfi... Mrs. Orsini and that young person from your tyrannical influence," said Brentford, now facing Arkansky.

"Why would I sacrifice my best assets?"

"Because that would be better than having the bones of your hands crushed one by one by a rifle butt." said Brentford, a tremor in his voice that was not only of impatience.

"This is the kind of democracy I understand," said Arkansky, with an irony that made Brentford uncomfortable. "I will not force you to demonstrate it, however."

But he was not a man who could resist a trick when he saw the possibility of one, especially if it gave him the last laugh. Leaning successively toward Phoebe and Sybil, and making passes over their foreheads, he whispered in their ears: "You will faint in five minutes and when you wake up, you will fall madly in love with the first man you happen to see."

"Expect a few minutes before this works," he said with a grin, as he turned back toward Brentford. "It has to be progressive, you understand. But you have my word of honour they will wake up, much to their satisfaction. Now, can we discuss more serious matters?"

"Certainly. But quickly."

"I like challenges. This is what I propose. Instead of a bogus judgement, I want to fight a duel. If I win, I will leave the city forever and as a free man. If I lose, I am at your disposal. Does this satisfy your hunger for justice?"

"I have little time to play games, Mr. Arkansky. You're quite at my disposal now."

"Yes, but not without some sort of trial, I should think. That would be too unfair. What I'm proposing to you is a kind of ordeal to make up for it."

Why not, thought Brentford. This would settle the matter quickly and prevent his personal feelings from interfering with justice.

"What sort of duel would it be?"

Arkansky looked around and spoke loudly.

"Is there among these dirty savages one wizard who thinks he has greater power than I have? If so, I want this man to step forward and engage with me in a duel of wonders."

A murmur ran among the Inuit, as the offer, and the offence, were translated.

"No? Uncouth cowards! You admit that the White Man has greater powers than you have? That your gods and your helping spirits are just strong enough to animate children's matinees?"

Brentford looked around. The Inuit were shocked. They protested and spat on the ground but did not move. Could they possibly be afraid? If nobody accepted the dare, Brentford could not do anything but let Arkansky get away. Maybe that was still better than having one *angakoq* publicly humiliated, as Brentford feared would be the case. But then again, it would be shameful as well for the Inuit if they merely accepted without further discussion Arkansky's contemptuous claim of superiority. He looked for Uitayok and saw that he was speaking to Ajuakangilak. The shaman stepped forward and walked toward the centre of the Ice Palace, very calmly, Tuluk and Tiblit escorting him.

"Ajuakangilak is ready for the contest," said Tuluk.

Brentford was not sure if this was good news or bad news, but Arkansky's smug little smile was not a favourable omen.

"Very well. Could the spectators close the circle around us?" requested Arkansky.

The spectators slowly complied, tracing an arena around Arkansky and Ajuakangilak.

"Well," said Arkansky, looking past Ajuakangilak to address the crowd, "I suppose that this little wizard, used as he is to flying to the moon, will have no trouble doing this."

And, turning up the palms of his hands, Arkansky suddenly levitated a few inches above the ground, as he had done in the Greenhouse.

A whisper of awe rippled among the Inuit.

Arkansky lifted himself slightly higher, his arms apart, his belly now roughly in front of Ajuakangilak's face.

"I'm waiting for you," said Arkansky.

Ajuakangilak swiftly unsheathed a knife and violently thrust it into Arkansky's guts. Blood gushed out as he withdrew the blade. He stabbed again. Arkansky remained in mid-air for a while, arms apart, his eyes wide open in disbelief, as blood trickled from his mouth. Then his eyes closed and he fell down noisily, his real blood smearing the fake ice. Spencer Molson ran to the slumped body. Sybil and Phoebe fell in a swoon, as if suddenly unplugged.

"No bloodshed, huh?" a sarcastic voice whispered in Brentford's horrified brain. It was under his own responsibility that first blood had been drawn. He could only hope that it would be the last.

Ajuakangilak walked out of the circle, wiping his blade on his sleeve, and saying something to Brentford.

"Ajuakangilak says he does not show his powers to *qallunaat*," Tuluk translated.

Molson was leaning over Arkansky, trying to look at the wound. As he undid the blood-soaked jacket and vest, he also revealed the copper bands, the metal wires, the compressed air tubes and other curious works that rigged the magician's body. But it was insufficient body armour. The meteorite-stone blade of the shaman had pierced him all the way. Molson hung his head down and sobbed.

"Please. Let him go," Brentford said to the Scavenger who kept watch over the old man. He turned his back to the scene, sighing, trying to conjure the image away.

The women were slowly coming back to their senses, Phoebe in Blankbate's arms and Sybil faintly smiling at Tiblit, who had kneeled over her. Brentford felt relieved that they were safe and unharmed, but after some hesitation decided that he did not want to confront Sybil now, and turned away as quickly as he could.

"We have lost enough time," he said nervously to Blankbate and Lilian. "We should hurry to the Blazing Building. Please, Mr. Blankbate, let the Inuit go home, and send a few men with them to make sure nothing happens on their way back."

He turned toward the Inughuit:

"Consider this place as yours."

Uitayok looked around the dome.

"This place? he said, with a barely hidden irony.

"The city," said Brentford, almost bristling with emotion at this historical moment.

Uitayok seemed dubious, but thanked him politely.

✳

Canals were the fastest way to reach the Blazing Building. The unlikely little army of Sophragettes and Scavengers ran to the embankment, where *chasse-galleries* and gondolas waited for them at the mooring posts. Brentford found himself wishing that everything in the city were as well organized as this upheaval had been so far.

A large icebreaking scow opened the way, and the overcrowded crafts followed it, like ugly ducklings, in a ruffle of feathery rifles. The city seemed tranquil enough. The crowd, impressed by the Scavengers, had scattered and gone home. A few shots cracked out from time to time, celebratory or lethal, Brentford could not guess, lowering his head all the same. He could not control everything, could he? They glided past the distant smoking ruins of the N.A.N.A., which made quite an impression, more of melancholy than of glory, but the city could use the space, after all. Build another greenhouse, maybe. Or a two-hundred-foot snowman. Everything was possible, that much at least was true.

At one point, Brentford thought he glimpsed a man leaping from rooftop to rooftop, but he had barely turned toward Lilian to point out the phenomenon when it disappeared. Stranger still, he was persuaded that it had been Gabriel.

As they approached the corner of Nicolo Zeno Canal, they saw a group of soldiers building barricades on the embankment in front of the Naval Academy. A thrill ran through the crowded gondolas, and rifles were cocked, ready to fire. However, the sailors saluted the gondolas with cheers, throwing their berets skyward. These were Navy Cadets, Nobles of the Poop, as they liked to call themselves. All rifles were lowered. A young officer in white spats and a navy blue uniform with little silvery snow crystals on his collar ran to meet them, followed by a constable with a cumbersome Colson telephone round his neck. Brentford recognized the young man who had punched him during the recording riot. It was the first time in his life that he felt like offering the left cheek. So to speak, that is.

"I am Ensign Paynes-Grey. Are you Brentford Orsini?"

"I am," said Brentford, almost flattered by his new celebrity, though, after all, he was the only one here in civilian clothes, and could be easily singled out.

"Captain-General Mason just told me that, from now on, if I were to disobey anyone, it had to be you."

Brentford laughed.

"Then do not encircle the Hôtel de Police under any circumstances," said Brentford, indicating the building on the other side of the barricade. "This is an order."

The young ensign nodded.

"As a free man, I have no choice but to disobey you," he answered, "and, as a matter of fact, we have already started."

"How is the situation?"

"Under control. Just a few skirmishes. The Gentlemen of the Night are not soldiers, you know. Unless they're ten to one, they'd rather take it out on defenceless people. I think they'll just wait to see which side is winning before taking a stand."

The other Cadets had approached, very curious about the Sophragettes. Brentford saluted and gave the signal to shove off before the fraternization became too incestuous. There would be plenty of time for that.

The ships pushed off again, and it was hard for Brentford not to think that their procession was not becoming a ceremony. He remembered his grandiose childhood dream, and for a while actually felt like the doge who would marry the Lincoln Sea. The Council, obviously, had relied on symbols more than on sheer firepower, and now that they had sawn off the branch on which they had been sitting, their strategy showed its limits. The Subtle Army was out of the game, the Gentlemen of the Night were contained by the Navy Cadets for the time being, and there was little chance that the people of New Venice would risk their skins for the Councillors, especially now that John Blank had promised to publish photographs of the Seven Sleepers' desecrated coffins on the front page of tonight's *New Venice News*. But do not let it go to your head, Brentford admonished himself. This was not over yet: there was still the Varangian Guard to be reckoned with—a dreaded body of well-seasoned warriors—and, of course, the Council itself, from whom the worst could be feared.

They landed at the dock before the Blazing Building. Brentford's first idea was that the Sophragettes should not be endangered.

"Blankbate, stay with me! Ms. Lenton! To the rear of the building!" he ordered, hoping he sounded credible as a commanding officer. But he saw Lilian gracefully raise her hand, and instead of obeying his orders, the Sophragettes stopped in their tracks.

"Sorry. I was so thrilled by the sheer virility of your tone of voice, that I did not pay attention to what you said," explained Lilian with a smile. He could see her little canine tooth, slightly but charmingly unaligned.

Brentford hemmed and corrected himself.

"Ms. Lenton. Would you please be so kind as to make sure the rear of the building is safe from any intrusion?"

"Be sure I'll gladly see to that," she said, with some obscure irony that totally eluded Brentford. "Ladies, if you want to follow me. One half with me this way, the other half with Ms. Lovelace to the other side of the building, if you please."

Brentford watched them go, in a colourful and determined rustle, almost losing his train of thought at the spectacle.

"We should go," Blankbate said.

"Yes." said Brentford, nodding. "Yes. Of course." He had, he discovered, a slight case of stage fright.

Brentford and the Scavengers passed through the gate to find the gigantic Varangian Guards silently lined up in a row, their barbed halberds pointed at the intruders, and quite impressive in their shining armour plates and morion helms. Of course, the Scavengers fanned out around Brentford were armed with guns, but he could well sense their own hesitation. Under fire or not, the guards were close enough to charge and, should they go berserk, to make a carnage out of it. Brentford did not feel like taking the risk: besides the fact that he was on the front line again, he had seen enough blood for today.

His mind racing in search of a speech that would end up in fanfare and confetti, Brentford was suddenly startled when a door screeched from behind the guards. Though no orders had been given, their line gaped in the middle and Reginald and Geraldine appeared, dressed in burgundy velvet. Though they looked quite tiny amongst these well-built Scands and Finns, the guards simply stared at them as they walked majestically through their ranks. It was one of the twins' most salient traits that their appearance usually provoked silence.

While Geraldine held her chin high and kept her eyes planted unflinchingly on the awestruck guards, Reginald handed their commanding officer a roll of parchment. Lieutenant Lemminkaïnen, as Brentford remembered he was called, unrolled it and read it silently, first frowning, then casting bewildered looks at the twins.

"This," he announced to his men in heavily accented English, "bears the official seal of the Council. It announces that we should now pledge allegiance to the new rulers of New Venice, Geraldine and Reginald Elphinstone."

"In other words, said Reginald, haughtily, "*we* are now paying *you*."

The Varangians looked at each other and one by one took off their caps. Lemminkaïnen was the last one, but he went down on one knee with a chivalrous abandon, nonetheless remaining as tall as the twins.

Geraldine turned toward Brentford.

"Ah, Mr. Orsini," she said, with the mock-tone (or so Brentford hoped) of a princess speaking to a servant, "we almost have been waiting for you."

Shivering from that damned upward wind still blowing through the corridor, Brentford pushed open the heavy door of the Council Chamber and started in fright when he saw the Phantom Patrol standing around the table where the Councillors should have been.

"It's always a pleasure to see an old friend," said Doctor Phoenix with, Brentford was relieved to hear, a different, familiar voice, one with a slight German accent.

"Hardenberg, is that you?" Brentford asked in a cold sweat, his heart banging like a madman begging to be released from his padded cell. He wished he had been warned of that plan. You really had to wonder who was in charge, here.

"It is but me," Hardenberg reassured him. "Not dead yet and with little desire to die today or ever. Your little adventure out in the wilderness gave us this idea for a disguise. A masked ball is a fairy tale in itself, after all. How is your revolution going?"

"The restoration, you mean. Well, you tell me," said Brentford. "Did the Council escape?"

"Very much so. But not in very good shape. I am afraid that Baron Brainveil has gone through too many emotions today."

The anarchists started to peel off their false flesh and tattered rags. This was almost as horrible to behold as the real
Phantom Patrol had been. They had an atrocious smell, like
rotten seal flesh, so strong as to make the Scavengers pass for
white-robed virgins with baskets of rose petals.

"You mean you just... scared... them?"

"That was the point of our disguise. I have often noticed
that people who detain some power are prone to superstition, as
if they were afraid their little secret, which is nothing but luck,
could be easily discovered and reversed."

"You had no problems with the guards?"

"We never even saw them. The twins took us through a passage known only to the Seven Sleepers that passes beneath the
canal and then straight up into this room. Needless to say that
their knowledge of this shortcut greatly helped them to convince
the Council of their identity."

"You mean the twins were recognized as legitimate?"

"Certainly. They made quite an impression. It was as if
the Councillors knew they had it coming. They knew the Calixte prophecy very well, as a matter of fact, and interpreted
it exactly in the way that your friend Gabriel predicted. The
Seven did not question for a single moment that the twins were
d'Ussonville reincarnate, protesting against the desecration of
the Seven Sleepers' coffins, nor that the Phantom Patrol were
the instruments of Nixon-Knox's revenge for their having had
him expelled from the Council and for "prostituting the Pole."
It was a huge spoonful of a bitter medicine, but they swallowed
it in one gulp. They were, anyhow, in such a hurry to get away
that they signed their surrender without reading the small print
that establishes you as Regent-Doge of the city until the twins'
majority."

"I never asked for that," protested Brentford.

"This is our little surprise for you. We added it ourselves.
You know, the last minute inspiration, just to make it more

formal. But you can very well go back to your plough, if that is what you prefer."

Brentford looked around him, at the marble and the jasper. Hardenberg, the anarchist kingmaker, had truly offered him the keys of the city.

"Where are the Seven now?"

"Trying to save their wrinkled skins, I would say. Tiptoeing away like Old Man Winter. Gnawing at each other's skulls in some icy circle of hell. Why, you wanted them to kneel in front of you?"

Brentford sighed. He felt light-headed and burdened, happy and prostrated. Things had gotten out of hand, and yet they were in hand—in his hands.

It was only later that he would learn what had happened to the Councillors, when Lilian told him the story, or at least some of it.

Passing in a flurry of silk and steel through the curved colonnades that extended on each side of the Blazing Building, the Sophragettes had soon reached its rear. There, a narrow embankment with a semicircular landing stage led directly to a discreet canal, hidden from public view by the surrounding livestock farms on the opposite bank.

Lilian and the Sophragettes stumbled on the Councillors huddled there, hastily dressed for the great outdoors, while some servants and ushers still in livery were loading steamer trunks onto a few reindeer-drawn brougham sleighs bearing the arms of the Council members. Lilian noticed that no Gentlemen of the Night or Varangian Guards were there to protect them, nor was there anyone from her own side, it seemed, to watch over this evacuation. Were they attempting to escape unnoticed? Had they just been kicked out? Should she arrest them and tow them back to the Building? Should she make sure that they would be banished for good? She was unsure of what she should do, but knew that whatever had to be done, had to be done now or never. This was the moment she had been waiting for, true, but in panoramic way, and she found it hard to step forward and tear down the picture her own imagination had drawn so often, for fear of making a bloody mess of it.

"Do not move!" she improvised, as the Sophragettes advanced cautiously from both sides of the pier, their guns aimed at the men. With the little training they had, she hoped none of them would fire without her order, or the situation would be totally out of her velvet-gloved hand.

Thus the scene froze before her, looking like a bas-relief. The Councillors, not knowing what to do, kept their hands up or stuck in mid-motion. She approached their dazed hebdomad and their startled servants, stiffening her backbone, cocking the hammers of her eyes. She had not the slightest idea of what she was going to say.

"What is it you want from the Council?' asked a dishevelled Surville, stepping in front of her as if he were ready to get himself cut to pieces for his masters. "They have been forced into resignation by the vilest imaginable means, with no respect for their age or their service to the city."

"I am certainly glad to hear that," said Lilian icily. "I just want to make sure that this is where we say good-bye."

"We have been granted free passage and we expect you to respect at least this," said a sturdy fat bald man, who she supposed was De Witt. He tried to assert his authority, but she could sense that it was more to reassure himself after whatever had happened in the Blazing Building. The Councillors, indeed, looked rather crestfallen and ghastly, more eager to get away than dwell on recent events. She could not resist knocking one more nail into their coffin.

"You're right. There is *at least* something to respect here."

A livid and trembling Brainveil, whom some ushers were propping up as best they could, cast her a venomous look.

"Lake," he hissed, "Will nothing be spared us? First those monsters and now you, little ungrateful trollop. You should be ashamed of yourself!"

His imprecation ended in a fit of throaty coughs that shook his frame. A drop of saliva that he was too weak to wipe off slowly rolled down his chin.

Softly but firmly, Lilian pushed Surville aside and took a step closer to Brainveil, planting her eyes in his.

"Please, Mr. Brainveil, what is it that gives that you the right to tell me what I should be ashamed of? Is it the dazzling intellect that has led you to the position in which I'm seeing you right now? Is it the moral integrity that you have demonstrated these past few weeks? Shhh...!" she said, with a commanding gesture, as Surville tried to silence her.

She could feel the anger seething in her, and how helpless she was to control it.

"Is it the *fear* you have of me? You who cannot bear the sight of a woman except in bondage?" she kept on, looking straight into Brainveil's narrow, malevolent eyes. Weak as he was, he held her look with a strength that surprised and further enraged her. His body may have been a wreck, but something in his soul still refused to yield; there burned some stubborn fire that would rather set the whole world aflame than let itself die out. Suddenly, it occurred to her that she knew this gaze, had known it, in fact, for longer that she could remember. And she could see that he, too, slowly recognized something in her eyes, as his stare had got lost in hers and seemed to contemplate not her person but a distant, infinite horizon. Her fury turned into something different, something she was fearing herself: the light suddenly changed, becoming brighter all around; she could hear a buzzing in the air, as a cold sweat broke out on her palms and her neck. A thrill ran along her spine. The Councillors stared at Lilian in disbelief as if her face had undergone some metamorphosis she wasn't aware of. Then she heard herself speak with a different voice, huskier and deep, and she felt scared as words that were not hers forced their way out of her mouth.

"A trollop, you poor old fool Is that any way to talk to your mother? Have you forgot where you came from? Will I have to watch over you again, or will you put an end to your pranks for good, you and your repulsive associates, whose very name blackens the universe? Look where your arrogance and stupidity have brought you, you who think yourself a lion when you are the vilest snake, unworthy to even creep at my feet. Oh, you, shameless tyrannical child, see how this world that you deemed your plaything has been wrenched away from you in a single moment. The day will come when you will have to think of your own end. Before I think of it myself."

At her first words, the anger in Brainveil's stare had died down. He now looked at her with an awe that bordered on terror, searching around him for a proof that he had not dreamed it all, that he was not going mad. He felt his mind slide away from him. She had known him. She had seen through him. "Forgive me... mother," he babbled, grasping the arms of his servants. The Councillors ran toward him, as he slumped down to the ground.

Lilian progressively came back to her senses, still a little dizzy, trying to make sense of the scene in front of her. Embarrassment seized her, and, God knows why, some pity for the fallen old man. Helen... you old bitch... doing this to me... she muttered to herself, while a distant peal of laughter echoed somewhere in her head. She cleared her throat, and resetting her feathered hat, said to Surville, who trembled at her side, "No man calls me a trollop unless I ask him to do so."

Leaving him gaping, she took a deep breath and turned toward the Sophragettes:

"Let us not delay these gentlemen any longer."

The day had darkened, and the cold had become stinging. As if working under some invisible whip, and without so much as a word, the servants of the Seven hurried, passing luggage from hand to hand, cramming it and piling it into the carriages. The Councillors themselves stepped down to lend a hand, except Brainveil, who, reduced to some sort of puppet with tangled strings, was carried into the leading sleigh and wrapped inside a fur blanket.

"What is your destination?" Lilian asked Surville, who still avoided her eyes.

"It is a secret. The farthest away from here we can get, I hope."

"This at last is a hope we have in common."

Eventually the sleighs were loaded and the Councillors installed. They did not seem to care that their equipment or clothes were not quite fit for a ride in the wilderness, or for the cold night that was about to fall. Lilian almost felt like asking the girls to fetch some extra blankets, but renounced the idea for some reason. This ain't the time to go maudlin, she said to herself, clasping her hands behind her back. The Sophragettes weren't at their service, were they?

"Well" said Guinevere de Nudd, watching at her side, "you certainly got carried away."

"Did I? Oh yes. Very far away," she answered pensively, "or maybe a little too close."

The sleighs started to move, vanishing one by one into the dusk with a ghastly jangle of bells. However much she hated the Councillors, Lilian could not help feeling their departure was sad, lacking in dignity. She felt, with a distant pang, the cruelty of the situation. So what? She had not made this world, had she? Brainveil had. Or people like him. And she was not like them, or, well, she had been just a little today, to beat them at their own game. But not tomorrow, she promised herself, as the last sleigh disappeared into the night, not tomorrow.

"The aurora, the aurora," Gabriel muttered.

EPILOGUE

The Not So Serene Republic

•

... The old impossible Haven 'mid the Auroral Fires
Fiona McLeod, *The Dirge of the Four Cities*, 1901

I t was around midnight, and the city was quiet. The cold, the uncertainty, and the Scavengers had sent people home with little resistance, and the Navy Cadets had done the rest. Brentford could be sure that Venustown was well under their control tonight.

News had come that in the afternoon and evening the Inuit had looted some of the arcades, but Blankbate and Hardenberg had advised him to forget about it. Brentford did not mind the poetic justice. He merely worried about how he would make it up to the looted shopkeepers. Now, at any rate, only a few people prowled the streets and the canals, out of curiosity and excitement—some of them, Brentford had heard, wearing carnival outfits. This, too, seemed apt.

A kind of celebration had broken out in one of the reception rooms of the Blazing Building. Maybe Hardenberg was right: a city was just a petrified party. But this "feast of all firsts" was a portent of the difficulties to come. Brentford had never seen such a motley community, if it could even be called that. It looked like some mirage that would vanish with the dawn. Scavengers were flirting with Sophragettes in a hall-of-mirrors staging of *Beauty and the Beast*. The Inughuit were trying to joke with Varangian guards twice their size, playing around with their halberds as if they were harpoons. Anarchists clinked (many) glasses with Navy Cadets. He could even see the Ghost Lady walking among the living, who did not perceive her as she glided past them, but still they shivered and hushed, and looked about with a worried frown at some empty space in the room.

And then the kaleidoscope rotated again, showing new scenes Brentford found equally unlikely.

The sight, which had at first gutted him, of Sybil following Tiblit everywhere with amorous eyes, her slender jewelled arms around his fur-clad muscles, was now starting to make a little more sense, if only as an allegory of the days to come. It was better than poor Phoebe, who had fallen in love with a masked Scavenger, and not knowing which one, made advances to all. Here, the allegory escaped him. It couldn't be Love, could it?

One Sophragette came up to him, the one he had seemed to know from before, and, red-cheeked with glittering eyes, introduced herself as Daria Norton, Lilian Lake's protégée, and Douglas Norton's daughter. Brentford smiled at the co-incidence. He always liked it when things clicked together. As a young girl she had been in direct telepathic contact with the Polar Kangaroo, which was, if he had got it right, the very companion pet her father had offered to Isabella Nixon-Knox. Daria had fled to England after the Blue Wild and Lilian had found her there, a boarding-school rebel known as Lucy Lightning in the thriving suffragette scene, and had brought her home. He had no doubt that the Polar Kangaroo would be glad to have her back.

Daria handed him a little propaganda leaflet the girls wanted to distribute across the city. Brentford read it quickly, but his eyes stopped on one particular sentence that said: "*This community aims to be rich, not in the metallic representative of wealth, but in the wealth itself, which money should represent; namely, LEISURE TO LIVE IN ALL THE FACULTIES OF THE SOUL.*" He could not have phrased it better, he thought.

Lilian had joined them.

"Lake or Lenton?" he asked.

"People give different names to the same things, and the same name to different things. You will see plenty of that quite soon, I'm sure. I like being Lilian Lake today. It is a sort of homecoming."

"What is gnostic in all this... display of military charm?" he asked her, pointing to her uniform.

She did not feel like telling him what had really happened on the embankment. When Helen had started to appear in her dreams, calling her back to New Venice, Brentford's name had often surfaced, for reasons that were unclear, but that she now began to understand better. But she knew little of the nature of his own relationship with Helen. Men were fragile creatures, easily scared of what they could not grasp, and she did not want to scare this one, for the moment...

"Same answer as before," she said, growing more serious with every sentence. "Not much to some people, I would say. Maybe it is just a way to recall that procreation is not always the supreme good, and that some women may dispense with it, if they deem it *wiser*. Maybe it is just a way to remind men that if my belt gets loose, it does not make me the great whore of Babylon, and that I still have a soul."

Brentford was slightly in his cups from the celebration and felt a sudden masculine urge to show off in front of Lilian. "You're the Harlot and the Holy one, then," he said, quoting as casually as he could from *Thunder, Perfect Mind*, an ancient gnostic treatise Helen had often talked about.

She came closer to him and said softly, "Certainly, as any other woman, *I am the one who is honoured, and who is praised, and who is despised scornfully*. Or, if you prefer, in political terms, *I am an alien and a citizen, I am the substance and the one who has no substance*. But as to being the harlot and the holy one, I'm afraid I'm neither. Just a loyal and normally depraved girl."

Suddenly she glued a kiss on his mouth while painfully squeezing his testicles. In a flash, Brentford understood in his flesh the paradoxes of *Thunder, Perfect Mind*.

"And of course," she whispered in his ears as she released her grip, "like any suffragette, I carry a bomb in my muff."

There were, Brentford reckoned, four or five levels of interpretation to this. But before he could sum them up, she had disappeared.

He felt, God knew why, like walking around a little.

He passed a crimson cabinet, where hung portraits of the Seven Sleepers. He took a long look at the one that depicted the tall, aquiline Louis d'Ussonville, just to notice with a jump that Myrtle, the Ghost Lady, was behind him, faintly reflected in the glass sheet that protected the painting of her grandfather.

"How can I thank you?" her voice said in Brentford's head.

"By not appearing anymore," Brentford thought quickly and half in jest. But as soon as he finished the sentence, the ghost had evaporated.

"Don't worry," said another voice, behind him, this time. "She is still with us."

He turned to discover Reginald and Geraldine. They had a way of looking all around them, but not in the same time at the same direction, that reminded Brentford of a clockwork armillary sphere and that made him feel dizzy and ill at ease, just as when they talked very quickly to each other in some language no one understood. He also suspected them of changing sides and playing each other's part at times. But of this, he had no proof.

"We also wanted to thank you," they said, finally standing still.

They claimed to be over fifteen, but were rather small, in a frail elfin way. Brentford crouched in front of them, holding their hands. Well, some of them, at least.

Thank me, he thought, almost bitterly—when he had taken them away from their enchanted castle, only, maybe, to serve his own ends?

"You do not miss home?" he asked.

"This is home," said Reginald.

"Without Grandmother, we would not have been safe forever on the Island, anyway," added Geraldine thoughtfully.

Brentford got up, his hands on his knees. It was only now that he realized how vulnerable they were.

"Do you think we will go over well with the people here?" she asked.

"When you show us to all of them, that is," her brother added.

Brentford felt embarrassed.

"I am not showing anyone to anyone else." He tried to reassure them, not even reassuring himself.

"Should we remain hidden, then?" Reginald insisted.

Brentford sighed. They were right. Chances were that the people would see in these little wonders some sort of dubious entertainment. He did not want this refoundation to turn into a freak show, whatever the circusstances. The idea came to him that they could appear in public *one at a time*. This could be done, just wedging a mirror at a certain angle, with the surroundings matching properly. He would have to ask Molson, if he still was around.

"Do not worry," he said, "we'll work things out."

The twins looked at each other dubiously.

"Where is Gabriel?" asked Geraldine, with an almost imperceptible pout.

"I wish I knew," sighed Brentford.

He found himself in the central corridor (where, he observed with relief, someone had stopped that damned cold wind), but soon perceived, in one of the adjacent rooms of the Memory Palace, Bob Dorset's effigy of the Polar Kangaroo. It had been found earlier in the day in the basement of the Hôtel de Police, when the Gentlemen of the Night had finally condescended to surrender and, a waving luminous starched shirt as a flag, had come out of the building with champagne bottles and cigar boxes. As Paynes-Grey had predicted, their resistance had not been long. They had never worried Brentford much, anyhow. You could always count on the Police when it came to siding with the winner. One of the first moves of the Gentlemen of the Night had been to send an emissary to Brentford with the Kangaroo as a little present and as a token of goodwill. Probably because they knew (they knew everything) that Brentford and Gabriel had made a little tune for it as a present to Bob, as a souvenir of the time (it seemed eons away) when they had been together in a band called the Black Harlequins. Brentford, upon receiving the statue, had immediately ordered it to be installed in the Blazing Building.

He now approached the statue almost respectfully. So this was the creature to whom, unknowingly or not, Douglas Norton had entrusted the protection of the d'Ussonville dynasty and, by the bye, the continuity of what remained of the Seven Sleepers' dream. Bob's version of it was impressive, to say the least, worked down to the most minute details, such as the ice crystals tangled in the fur, just as if it had recently been out on the icefield. Maybe it was its muscular bulk, maybe its sparkling glassy eyes, maybe it was the canines showing through the bare chops of its wolf head, but this depiction radiated something eerily powerful. It was part of the myth that images of the Polar Kangaroo held the same power as He did, and contemplating this one made Brentford feel as if he had come to consult an oracle. Maybe he should have it brought down to the Hyperboree Hall to stand on the fountain, as the official tutelary spirit of the city, and people could come to it with offerings and questions. If he did not manage to rule the city, he could always found a religion. That was so much easier.

He was curious to know if the miniature phonograph inside the statue was still working. "Sorry," he said aloud, as he opened a trapdoor in the statue's posterior and cranked the mechanism. He put his head, almost resting, against the paw, hoping nobody would see him. But, for some reason, instead of the tune, what he heard was Daria Norton's voice, joking with Lilian Lake in a distant room about what had just happened to him. Obviously, Daria had lost nothing of her telepathic link with the Polar Kangaroo. The conversation vexed and disappointed him, but he also felt relieved, somehow, that at least two persons were not taking him seriously. Three, with himself included. He suddenly missed Lilian. He meant Sybil. He meant Helen. No. He meant Lilian.

"What are you doing here?" asked a familiar, German-accented voice.

Brentford lifted up his head, so quickly it bumped against the Polar Kangaroo's jaw.

Hardenberg was at the door with Schwarz.

"I was wondering where you were," said Brentford, rubbing his skull.

"You don't *doge* very well, said Hardenberg, suavely sardonic. "We have just come, Herr Schwarz and I, from giving a little present to Mr. d'Allier, who is, shall we say, *lounging* in the Hall. In case you were wondering about his whereabouts."

"Good. I'm glad he's turned up."

Brentford stood silent for a while, rubbing his temple.

"I was looking for you in order to—well, I wanted to thank you," he said awkwardly.

"My pleasure." said Hardenberg. "It is the only thing that counts."

"What are you planning to do next?"

"Frankly? I had the idea that I should go and plant a black flag at the pole. But if there is any place in the world that is better off without any kind of *standard*, even that one, it is certainly the North Pole. There are places where no state should install itself. We have heard—for we have informers everywhere—that the pope has offered a twelve-foot-high cross to an Italian airship captain, to have it dropped at the pole. I'll just take that airship down, believe me, before the Phantom Patrol does it."

"What was it you said that you'd take that would be of no consequence to me?"

"Oh! That! It is just that I clinched a deal with the good people of Crocker Land. A permanent rear base against supplies and protection. I hope you do not mind."

Brentford minded, but he was not sure why, and anyway, what could he say to Hardenberg, after what he had done for him?

"I can very much imagine you in a crystal castle," said Brentford.

"I can, too, obviously. As Nero once said of his palace, *I am now lodged as a man*. Every man should have a castle for himself, don't you think, for every man is a king. Anyway. That makes us neighbours, so to speak. Do not hesitate to come and see us," said Hardenberg as he warmly shook Brentford's hand. "And don't forget to bring the kids."

"It's a pity you did not like bombs," Schwarz muttered as he saluted Brentford.

"Sorry about that. Maybe next time," Brentford answered, trying to be polite.

He watched them recede down the corridor, their black clothes fading into the darkness. If he remembered correctly, he had one wish left.

Walking down the hall, he passed in front of the guardroom. A huge fire was roaring in the fireplace, and around a long table some Varangian guards were challenging a group of Navy Cadets to a drinking contest that the Nobles of the Poop, in spite of their good will, had not the slightest chance of winning. Lieutenant Lemminkaïnen, his eyes glinting with alcohol, perceived the Regent-Doge in the doorway and warmly saluted him, expressing how happy he was to be rid of those contemptuous, picky old men that he had had to protect. Brentford had first to accept a drink of *Akvaviitti* that fell like a stone to his stomach, then listen, not without interest or pleasure, to the sympathetic red-cheeked Lieutenant telling him of the Sampo, a mythological magic mill that made flour, salt, and money from the air. "This is what we need here," said the lieutenant, with conviction, banging on the table. Brentford agreed politely and thought he would have Treschler built him one. Lemminkaïnen, finally, could not resist quoting, in a somewhat slurred voice, a few lines from the *Kalevala* about, he explained, the truce between Pakkanen Puhurin Poika, the Frost-fiend, son of Blast, and some shamanic hero.

These the words the Frost-fiend uttered:
"Let us now agree together,
Neither one to harm the other,
Never in the course of ages,
Never while the moonlight glimmers
On the snow-capped hills of Northland.

Brentford thanked him, more moved than he allowed himself to show.

Finally, he reached Hyperboree Hall. It looked deserted in the cloudy moonlight, but atop the magnificent floor map, he could make out a dark shape, sprawled on its back all over Frislandia Island.

Brentford sat on the fountain ledge, unfastening his bow tie.

The shape made a move, and with a screech, a can of Ringnes beer slid upright toward Brentford.

"A drink. In a helmet," said Gabriel, in a somewhat slurred voice.

Why is it that people were suddenly constantly pushing beverages on him? Did they want to *poison* him? Brentford chuckled to himself. He wondered how long it would be before he took that threat seriously. He took one sip.

"How was your day, then?" he asked.

"Ups and downs, you know," answered Gabriel, who had done nothing all day but running and jumping to avoid the odd stray bullet. He had seen the revolution from above, like little figurines in a model city, and however much he approved of it, he found that was the best view of it. But mostly, he had been mourning his lost love. *Thinke now no more to heare of warme fine-odour'd snow:* such was his *serrat,* now, the magic formula that was only his own and by which he would live henceforward. His thighs ached from his repeated leaps and he had taken a pinch of Sweet Surf Silicium to cool down a little. He lay on his back, tides and ebbs of white noise in his ears, the only man to hear the motionless waves of the frozen sea as they crashed upon the shore. He looked through the dome openings and thought of the light of the stars and how it belonged to everyone, like the air or the earth. Who could be so vain and stupid as to claim that as his own? He tried to shake himself from his lethargy.

"So we're on to some Golden Age?" he managed to say.

"It seems," said Brentford, not sure himself if he was joking or not. "It is now officially the land of milk and honey. Money will flow and manna will fall. I heard you already had a gift from Hardenberg, by the way."

The answer came back with a curious lag.

"It's a farewell present from Stella, actually. It must be close to you, on your left."

"Sorry to hear that," Brentford said. Wasn't today supposed to be a celebration? A day of solace for every wrecked marriage or love? He had not noticed in the dim light the frame resting against the fountain. He lifted it and moved it about until he could faintly see something. It was some sort of Renaissance engraving.

"Looks nice. What is it? Dürer?

"The Seven Trumpets are Given to the Angels."

"It looks like it's on parchment."

"Almost. It's fresh human skin."

Brentford shivered and put down the framed tattoo with disgust, as if he feared to have bloodstains on his hands. He did not want to know more about this atrocity. He had found revolution easy, but apparently it had been harder for some.

No wonder Gabriel did not feel too happy or talkative. He could understand, he thought. When he had shown him the first draft of *A Blast*, Gabriel had said that the only true community worthy of that name that he knew was that of lovers, a society against society. Now that Brentford had got his own community, Gabriel had lost his. But Brentford's community was meant to be shared, and he would see that Gabriel got a piece of it. Or two.

"The twins miss you. They seem to appreciate you."

"They're swell kids."

"I wondered if you would be interested in being, let us say... hmm... *Prime Preceptor for the Dauphin-Doges*."

"I have nothing to teach to those miniature Elagabaluses."

"I meant in a more general way than in bed."

"*I* meant in a more general way than in bed. But precisely, yes, I want to hump them, not corrupt them."

Brentford laughed.

"Nice curriculum. It's no wonder you've been a success story in Doges College."

"I supposed charges were to be conferred through a democratic process, anyway," said Gabriel, with as much gentle tease as his weary, far-out voice allowed.

Brentford was about to answer that this could be arranged, but he corrected himself. This was how, he supposed, things had started with the Councillors. Dignified, decent, dutiful men who had suddenly let themselves believe that things could be arranged a little here and there, until everything was defaced and distorted.

"Well. I suppose there won't be many candidates, anyway," Brentford said.

"If I'm sure to win, that's different. Put me in. Just add *Plenipotentiary* to the title. The word fascinated me when I was a child."

Plenipotentiary. Indeed it was a potent and portentous word. As was Regent-Doge. Brentford felt the responsibility weighing on him again. His revolution had been, almost literally, a gala dinner. It was as if the Council had never had a chance. The Seven had reached some invisible limit, the edge of the world that they themselves had created, and had run out of their own reality. All that was needed was a little push to send them reeling over the top. Almost everybody had wished and waited for someone else to give this nudge. It was as if the dream had tunnelled from consciousness to consciousness and finally crystallized. Today they had all pushed together a little at the same time.

In the end, Brentford was amazed at how many allies he had with him: the Scavengers, the Aerial Anarchists, the Sophragettes, the Navy Cadets, the Inughuit. Even the Subtle Army and the Varangian Guard had deserted before they knew it themselves. He had carved himself a magic wand from the d'Ussonvilles' crooked family tree. He had the blessing of the Polar Kangaroo, which was a little like the soul of the city. Helen had not helped as he had expected, maybe, but was he so sure? She had given him a rendezvous at the Pole for March 1, and this was, in a way, exactly where he was sitting right now on the map, except the appointment was only with himself, or with his own North Pole. And she had promised, hadn't she, that she would feed the city. No. She was here as well. Watching over him in her usual unfathomable way.

He had so many cards in his game right now that he would have needed a Siamese twin to hold them all. More cards, even, than the Seven Sleepers had ever had, more than anyone would ever have again. But it was now that things were going to be difficult. Revolution is not only revolution. It is slowing it down. Living up to it. Learning the legerdemain that changes promises to compromises.

His mind drifted off toward blueprints for a new constitution. A Council of the Commonwealth, with members elected by all the inhabitants from each of the Seven Sectors. The Council would designate the Organizing Officers. Their charges would be held for one year only. (Even his own? Wouldn't he need more time?)

He shrugged. Whatever it was that he put on that paper, he knew that once it was built, it would work as well as a square wheel, and that the Commonwealth would always threaten to turn into a Commonwaste. Because, as it was written in *A Blast*, "some were wise, some foolish, some subtle and cunning to deceive, others plain-hearted, some strong, some weak, some rash and angry, some mild and quiet-spirited." Because it would be his dream or vision, but not their dream or their vision. They all would live together under the same flag, playing at being a nation, but the only flag that would truly represent them would have to be a Penelope's shroud woven and unwoven for someone who would never return, someone who had never been there. A banner as moving, as ever-changing, as ephemeral as the images under one's eyelids before one falls asleep.

Through the archway and stained windows, colourful lights of all hues began to play more brightly, more wildly on the icicles of the fountain. Gabriel mumbled something to himself that Brentford could not make out. He came closer.

"The aurora, the aurora," Gabriel muttered.

Yes. There could be no better flag.

Later, a thick, steady snow began to fall. Somewhere along Barents Boulevard, on the half-collapsed stands, the forgotten wax effigies of the Seven Sleepers had remained seated, slightly tilted, on the armchairs that propped them up. The surrounding street lamps gave a pale yellowish hue to their faces and a deep black sheen to their clothes, until the flakes dotted them, then covered them in patches, getting stuck in their beards and their eyelids. Their glassy eyes, faintly glinting in the gaslight, seemed to be all turned in the same direction: that of two small huddled figures sharing the same duffle coat, who stood in the snow, watching them in silence.

"And if any should like the world I have made, and be willing to be my subjects, they may imagine themselves such, and they are such—I mean in their minds, fancies or imaginations. But if they cannot endure to be subjects, they may create worlds of their own, and govern themselves as they please."

Margaret Cavendish, Duchess of Newcastle
The Description of a New World,
or The Blazing World, 1666

INTERVIEW WITH
JEAN-CHRISTOPHE VALTAT

By Corry Cropper and Robert J. Hudson

RJH: How does your research inform your writing experience,
your experience as an author?

JCV: When I write in French, I really try to separate both activities; but the book in English, *Aurorarama*, is somewhat more
related to my research, especially in that I have recently been
working on hallucinations, and hallucination plays an important
part in the novel...

CC: You mentioned that you work on hallucination and you've
done a lot of work on nineteenth-century authors. Are there
nineteenth-century authors that influence your work today that
you are particularly indebted to?

JCV: The authors who have most influenced my work are the
writers, not necessarily famous, who wrote adventure novels at
the turn of the century. The arctic theme was big then—so were
airships and anarchy, and there were often anarchists in airships.
You just have to connect the dots between such themes to get
an idea of the era.

CC: What particularly interested you, when you wrote this?

Were you trying to get a turn-of-the-century feel in *Aurorarama*? Why that period, and why snow, why white? Is there a connection between the blank slate of the white north and the idea of the dawn of a new century?

JCV: There were many things that interested me and New Venice is precisely designed to accommodate them all. The pre-World War I period is indeed one of them, as it was perhaps the last utopian period of Western culture. As a utopia, New Venice is explicitly modeled on the world's fairs at the turn of the century, with its typical architecture, which veers between neoclassical, iron-and-glass structures and art nouveau. The North Pole and the Arctic were recurring themes at the turn of the century, because it was a time when everyone felt the pole was about to be reached and there was a lot of speculation about what it would be like, because the place was not really mapped yet. So, this was a real place where you could still project your imagination. Accordingly, and this is another thing that interested me, it is really a book about visualization, about mapping the mental image. I found it interesting that, in Elaine Scarry's *Dreaming by the Book*, she explains that snow and ice allow the reader to have precise, detailed mental images, because there is no interfering background, and you can better concentrate on the characters and scenes. So, there is a certain logic between what I am trying to do in terms of visualization and the fact that the novel takes place in a snowy or icy landscape.

RJH: Staying with the nineteenth century and the idea of anarchy that you mention, in an earlier conversation you noted that Mugrabin is something of a mix between Dostoyevsky and Rasputin. I find him to be a very important character, and he reminds me of another radical Russian, Souvarine the revolutionary anarchist from Zola's *Germinal*: "*Faut qu'ça saigne*" seems to be his refrain—much like your character. Is this another source of influence? How do you explain this character?

JCV: As I was saying, the book is about themes at the turn of the century, and anarchists—and especially Russian anarchists—were omnipresent at this time, as mysterious, dangerous strangers. If you read *Paris* by Zola, you will find a similar kind of character. So, Mugrabin is less influenced by *Germinal* itself than by the clichéd figure of the Russian anarchist from this time period.

CC: You mentioned the visual, and I know you've made a film before. I was wondering if you have any plans for this book yet, or if you would like to eventually see this become a film because of the visual aspects you talk about?

JCV: Well, I'm a bit in two minds about this because you never want to see your imagination confiscated by an industry—not to mention that all readers' individual visualization would then be determined by the movie. At the same time, yes, I'd be curious to see it as a movie, of course—but, not by me.

RJH: So, by whom, then, if not yourself?

JCV: One of my favorite movies is *Archangel* by Guy Maddin, a Canadian filmmaker. I would really like to see it done in that style, you know, like a black and white, silent movie. That would be the most adequate way to do it for me.

CC: Interesting.

RJH: Returning to the characters, the main characters, you have Gabriel d'Allier and you also have Brentford Orsini. Both are very endearing characters, they're characters you're drawn to as a reader, but at the same time, they're very flawed characters. What can you tell us about these characters and even their pretensions as aristocrats?

JCV: The aristocrat—or Arcticocrat—theme is part of a joke in the book, because the Arcticocracy was invented by the people who founded the city, and who wanted to have something to pass on, a kind of inheritance to their descendants. This is what aristocracy is all about, after all: a few people giving themselves titles and the myth that goes with the title. It is a case study in the effect of language on reality. As characters, Brentford and Gabriel are a bit different from adventure novel characters— there is more soul-searching, especially with Gabriel, than there would be in an adventure novel, I think.

RJH: I can definitely see that. So, with these two characters, you establish this myth, and there's also the mythical, anarchic text that begins the novel and that Brentford is seen working with, *A Blast on the Barren Land*, signed by the infamously rash Henry Hotspur. This is incorporated as part of the novel and becomes a dangerous, subversive text for Brentford to possess. What are the creative origins of this text? And, why set up your two main characters as anarchists?

JCV: The Hotspur text is a real text and the quotations come from the seventeenth-century English pamphlet *The True Levellers Standard Advanced*. The political elements of this book exist because, of course, New Venice is a utopia, which, like every utopia, is actually a dystopia waiting to happen. At some point anarchy is regarded as an alternative, but it is anarchy in a very special sense: people from different walks of life getting together under pressure from the outside and trying to fix the situation so that they can regain some control of this utopia.

RJH: That seems to sort of be Brentford's conclusion when he meets with the "real" anarchists aboard the battleship Ariel. That seems to be his idea of a utopia, really, different people from different walks of life, different ideologies coming together and learning to work together.

JCV: Of course, it has to be improvised. It's an improvisation because planning a utopia turns it into a dystopia.

RJH: It is this excess of planning that leads to a police state with the Gentlemen of the Night, the Council of Seven, and the different organizing groups. Speaking of dystopia, the book has a feel similar to that of *Fahrenheit 451*, by Ray Bradbury. This whole idea of books, the organization of Gabriel's library and the way the books are all rifled through—leaving Gabriel feeling violated—resonates with scenes from Bradbury (or even Truffaut's film version) where they're breaking off the fronts of the television sets to find the books. (Bradbury's) conclusion is to have leftist anarchists who are trying to preserve culture at the same time, much like Brentford. There is also this "Big Brother" *1984* feel, a George Orwellian nightmarish dystopia. Were any novels from this genre of dystopian literature influences for you in addition to the turn-of-the-century adventure novels you've cited? Additionally, as the book is written in English, are there any influences from English-language literature?

JCV: Well, to answer first on the police state, I think that is more of a contemporary concern, you know, with the shrinking of private lives under the eyes of increasing technological surveillance. Regarding American influences, there are certainly a number of American authors who have influenced me over the twenty years I have been working on these New Venice books. Pynchon of course comes to mind. Another strong influence is Nabokov's *Ada or Ardor*, where Russia and North America actually converge in a sort of hybrid imaginary land, which really inspired me for this Arctic setting. Nabokov also insists, mostly through puns, on the French/English duality of Canada, and this is also something that, as a Frenchman writing in English, I relate to, of course, and which explains why the city is explictly located in the Canadian Arctic.

CC: Speaking of the French/English identity, you chose to write in English. I wonder if there was a bit of a, kind of Beckett moment, where you chose to write in English because it forced you to create differently than in French.

JCV: I think the first reason is that the book's influences are more American or English than French; so, it's logical in a way to do this in English, because it's not the kind of book that would really be possible as such in France—which is strange because all these adventure novels are more or less based on Jules Verne. But, in France, if Verne is really famous and widely read, he has had much more influence in the English-speaking world... On a more personal level, English makes my writing more concrete, more visual—perhaps because I associate the language with so many movies. And it also makes it more metaphorical, because, in my mind, the words may lag a little behind the images, and I often have a simile before I find the right expression.

RJH: I noticed in the official dedication, you dedicate the book to Serge, with whom you say you invented this world of New Venice. If it's not too indiscreet of a question, how did this— you just said twenty years ago—story take form? How did you and this Serge person invent this world of New Venice?

JCV: We became friends during a super-8 movie project I directed at High School and we have always done artistic stuff together. In the early 90s, we were looking for new ideas and brainstormed New Venice and its characters into existence in a single afternoon. At the start it was perhaps something more of a film project, but when I went to live in the States for a while it became a book, *Pineapples and Plums*, which we wrote 'four-handedly', just shuttling the chapters back and forth between France and the US. I wrote the second volume, *Lutes & Lobsters*, in 2008, as a birthday present. I had so much fun doing this that

I decided I was going to do a third one, and it was only normal that I dedicate this book to him.

CC: So, this is the third volume in the series. Was anything from the first two published?

JCV: No, no, they were not good enough to be published. They will remain secret. The esoteric tradition behind the exoteric one. But some characters will reappear in the second and third books.

CC: You have ideas, though, from those first two that have helped inform this world, right?

JCV: Yes. Even if it's not really explained, and *because* it's not really explained, when I mention things that happened before, in the other books, it seems to me that it gives a little more substance and a little more depth to the city and its inhabitants.

CC: I want to ask you a question about something that's personal to all three of us. Obviously, Gabriel is a professor. And there are several descriptions of the professor's life in this book that are pretty negative. Is that a way to distance yourself from your own profession? Or are you informed by the life of a professor at all? Is that description formed by that?

JCV: To speak frankly, it's just a personal revenge on a colleague. Among many other things, books are made to avenge wrongs. I don't want to make it too personal on that account either. I mean, it's kind of like a dream. When you dream, there are some elements that are from your life, and then there are some elements that come from books, and then there are the pure workings of the imagination. So, even if there is a strong personal, even autobiographical component in the novel, in the end, it's mostly fantasy.

CC: Hallucinations, it would seem, are a theme in this novel. You have the dream machine... the dream incubator. And then there's drugs as well. Are those, for you, different, or are they both means to a similar opening up of creativity and of imagination?

JCV: I think it's part of the Arctic as a theme, because the Arctic is always described as a place of hallucinations by the explorers. Accordingly, the title, *Aurorarama*, refers to the Inuit seeing their paradise through auroras, and to the use of the Northen Lights as a common romantic metaphor for imagination. The book is really interested in altered states of consciousness, and in everything that veers between lucidity and dreaming; drugs are naturally a part of this interest, even though most of them are imaginary.

CC: Can we ask you, if you don't mind talking about it, about the next book?

JCV: Not at all.

CC: You mentioned that it would be set in Paris. But could you tell us a little about, give us a little preview of that book?

JCV: Yes, I suppose I can talk about it even though it's not finished yet, and it might, of course, evolve. Some of the characters in the first book, including Brentford, Gabriel, and Lilian, will be sent on a mission to help the Parisians overcome a series of terrible winters. It will be a Paris smothered in snow and ice. It will be the same chilly atmosphere but with a different setting.

CC: And will it be set in the same time period, the turn of the last century?

JCV: Yes, definitely, with a little time travel involved. It will be

1895, precisely, because there are so many weird things going on in Paris at that time that you don't have to invent them...

I was especially interested in the way science and the occult were mingling. One of the objects in the book—a magnetic crown that records and transmits hypnotic suggestions—is a real invention, for instance, and was not regarded as utterly crazy. Some places also fascinated me, like a skating rink that was really called the *North Pole*. I like the fantasy to be as reality-based as possible...

CC: We'll look forward to that—and to seeing Paris covered in snow...

Adapted from an interview conducted at Brigham Young University on September 21, 2010.

An extract from the sequel to Aurorarama

LUMINOUS CHAOS

. . . ON THE ADVICE OF GABRIEL, who had lodged there previously during a stay in Paris that, technically, had not yet happened, the New Venetian diaspora had settled in the Grand Hôtel des Écoles on the rue Delambre. It was a slightly presumptuous place, its façade studded with lion heads and crescent-crowned Dianas, and Brentford wasn't surprised that it had appealed to Gabriel's unerringly New Venetian taste. Except for a few Englishmen, who relished the opportunity to see Paris going to the dogs under all this snow, tourists were rather rare at the moment, and there had been no difficulty in lodging their entire party. The rooms were tasteful and comfortable enough, some with a view onto a small courtyard. There was even running water, and therefore no need to spend three sous for the carriers to bring it hot to your room. However, the taps had to be left on at all times so they wouldn't freeze, and the pipes gurgled constantly. Not exactly the conditions an ambassador and his retinue might expect, but then . . . an ambassador of what?

While Lilian and Thomas went for a drink together at the nearby Eden-Parnasse, in the busy, flickering rue de la Gaîté, Gabriel had gone back to the hotel, staggering with exhaustion, his temple throbbing relentlessly. At the desk he found a message confirming the presence of the others, as well as their room numbers. He climbed the stairs, and noticing light spilling under the door of Brentford's suite on the fifth floor, he allowed himself to knock.

Brentford was propped on his pillow, counting money from a small chest open on the striped bedspread. At least they wouldn't want for anything. Gabriel cleared his throat and sat at the foot of the bed.

"Well, that was quite a trip," he said.

Brentford smiled a weary smile. "If you thought that was hard, wait for the journey home. Travelling backwards in time is one thing, but travelling forward to a city that doesn't exist yet ...?" He shook his head, then noticed Gabriel's bandages. "How's your head?"

"It still holds most of my brain, I suppose. Everyone all right here?"

"Given the situation, not too bad. Blankbate is already out, prowling for God knows what. He's quite the night creature, as you can imagine. And resourceful, too—for all my reluctance, his idea of scraping the real dates off our Canadian papers and replacing them with something more credible not only got us out of Iceland but has worked wonders getting us into this hotel. I suppose a little forgery on an already false passport isn't too terrible a crime, is it? As for Tuluk, he's cleaning and feeding the Colonel. He's become practically Branwell's right-hand man now. They get along famously and joke in Inuktitut all the time. How did it go at the hospital?"

"Oh, it was nothing special, really. Lilian and Thomas were pumped full of morphine and Jean-Klein Lavis is dead, except that he's alive."

Brentford turned pale.

"Take me through that last bit a tad more slowly, will you?" he asked.

Once Gabriel had finished his tale, Brentford carried on nodding for a while. Then he said, "Did you try to explain things to the young Jean-Klein?"

"Well, you know, explaining something I don't understand wouldn't normally scare me. Hell, I used to teach literature in college! But, this time, I was tired before I began, and not feeling especially willing to end up in a straitjacket."

Brentford pursed his lips. "It's troubling what you say about Jean-Klein—that is, *our* Jean-Klein—not remembering the weather being like this. It sounds as if we're in some alternate past, but the circumstances are curiously similar to the ones we were supposed to deal with in the present."

"You mean that Peterswarden knew this would happen and sent us back in time on purpose?"

"I have no proof of that—and anyway, I don't see how he could have planned it," Brentford admitted. "We don't have much choice, in any event. If we want to understand what's happening, we've got to start at the beginning and get in touch with Jean-Klein Lavis, Jr., again. At least, we should see if he can give us the lowdown on the *couronne magnétique*, since the old Jean-Klein had heard about it. I agree with the Colonel that it might play a part in this adventure of ours. Let's go first thing tomorrow."

"You sound as if you're enjoying this," Gabriel said, between two gaping yawns.

Brentford looked surprised, but realized that it was true: the more trouble he was in, the more excited he became. Getting everyone back home—well, everyone but Jean-Klein, alas—was a challenge that made governing New Venice look like a breeze, and after a brief bout of despondency, he had discovered that he was not only ready but willing to take it up.

"Let's say I find it ... interesting."

LUMINOUS CHAOS *is available now.*

TOWARDS A NEW STEAMPUNK

Jean-Christophe Valtat

First published on io9.com

In October 2010, Charles Stross published a spirited critique of steampunk, "The Hard Edge of Empire," saying "there's too much of it" and it's suffering from "second artist effect."

Talk about the wrong moment for my time machine. Just when I set up shop as a steampunk writer, I hear not only that there's too much of it around, but also, according to *Charles Stross,* that "steampunk is in danger of vanishing up its own arse," like a vulgar hadron collider. What a birching. It would have made Swinburne weep with joy.

My first line of defense, gentlemen of the jury, is that *Aurorarama* is not steampunk. For one thing, steam power isn't used much, because the novel takes place well above the Arctic Circle, where the reserves of coal are somewhat difficult to exploit. So the founders of New Venice naturally turned their sights to electricity, and were especially interested in the work of Nikola Tesla, maverick scientist and icon of pop culture. Which brings me to my second point: *Aurorarama* is not very punk either. I must admit, unless "punk" is a polite and paradoxical synonym for "geek," I never really understood what was punk about steampunk. For me it's more a collage of references from popular literature and popular science—a "pop" form. So, what I write is definitely Teslapop.

There's a hint of cowardice in that defense, isn't there? Maybe I should come forth and speak up in favour of steampunk. Stross's argument is twofold: first, that steampunk is revisionist through its undue romanticizing of the past; secondly, that the "Science in steampunk is questionable at best."

The first argument is the most interesting, because obviously there is some escapism and nostalgia involved in steampunk.

For one thing, I think that escapism is good and healthy and that there's more to man than reality, just as there is more to language than the present tense and affirmative sentences. Regarding nostalgia, though, I just feel that the argument is wrong. When Stross tries to jerk the tears from our eyes with "the fading eyesight and mangled fingers of nine-year olds forced to labour on steam-powered looms," he sounds very much like the average steampunk novelist, who is bound to overplay rather than downplay the melodramatic aspects of Victorian life: forced labour, high crime rates, violence towards women and minorities, social inequities, disease, pollution, irresponsible use of new technologies, political cynicism, etc., which are all ingredients of the genre.

What I find more curious is that Stross seems to think that those days are over in the "developed world." In many respects—I'm thinking of the ongoing onslaught of welfare policies through the western world, the renewed drive towards the cheapening of the labour force in favour of shareholders, the subsequent widening gap between social classes—the nineteenth century might be our future as well as our past. This is partly, I would suggest, what steampunk is about.

Zombies, here as anywhere else, are just another metaphor for the forgotten, the downtrodden, the disease-ridden poor out

427 * Towards a New Steampunk

to seek revenge; and airships are most likely the symbol of a technological hubris that, being hubris, is both empowering and bound to fail. Likewise, recurring figures or names such as Darwin Babbage or Galton simply reflect our current concern with genetics (and eugenics) and artificial intelligence, and where they could lead us.

It is very naïve to think that we are through with the nineteenth century: it is, in many respects, a nightmare we haven't quite woken up from. Most of what we experience today—in urban life that is—has its origins in the nineteenth century. I always find it fascinating to think of the moment when the things we are used to, and pretend to have adapted to, were experienced for the first time: huge capitalist production and commodification, enormous cities and crowds, speed, networking, mass media, the rise of a visual culture, unprecedented destruction in warfare ... And what makes it more interesting is that it all fell on dazzled, unprepared brains. The impact of this mode of life on the nervous system and the way that people tried to shield themselves from it (self-mechanization, neuroses, alcohol, drugs ...) were analyzed and debated instead of simply being regarded as normal. One of steampunk's ambitions might be to go back to the source of the life we now live and, by exploring those "first times," try to make our own times a bit clearer.

Of course, I do not deny the seduction of the era. Unlike us—citizens of the developed twenty-first century, happy simply to wallow in our hard-earned shallow vulgarity—nineteenth-century society insisted that there were such things as manners, honour and beauty, at least for those who could afford them. It's true that this insistence might have been an exercise in saving face: that the century suffered from a massive case of false consciousness, if not downright hypocrisy, is beyond doubt, and maybe we are all the more clever because we can chuckle about these things. Perhaps what steampunk writers see in the nineteenth century is the poetic appeal of that spectacular gap between appearances and reality. As the great steampunk thinker Walter Benjamin explained, the nineteenth century was a fantasy about itself, a daydream about a utopia that never was. In this sense the nineteenth century was as steampunk as "steampunk" is: always imagining itself to be different from its grim reality, and always trying to give a sense of purpose to the sufferings it bred. Alternate history, which is a huge part of steampunk, is quite at home in that context of struggling technologies, compulsive explorations, delirious social reforms, and failed revolutions. There was then a pervading sense of possibility that we, in our "finished world," may have forgotten. In the nineteenth century there was the certainty of a future, while the only thing we are sure of is that we have a past: no wonder that it is this past that so interests science-fiction writers.

Another good side of that civilized fantasy is that, to my mind, the nineteenth century was a time when extravagant beauty could be enjoyed without guilt or a second thought. It is moreover my theory that all writers belong, more or less consciously, to the nineteenth century, that time when literature was taken (too?) seriously and regarded as able to educate, elevate, delight, and even change life. Perhaps that is what we are missing, too. After all, steampunk writers may be no more nostalgic about the nineteenth century than people who like to read a novel by Balzac or Dickens, or a poem by Hopkins or Rimbaud. Perhaps it's a certain idea about literature's power that we are nostalgic about. Whether we live up to that idea, of course, is another question.

Now it is true that steampunk is riddled with every kind of self-duplicating cliché—zombies, airships, clockwork humans, anarchists ... —but isn't complaining about this a bit like saying that mathematics is riddled with clichés because it uses the same axioms over and over? Clichés (or myths, if you prefer) are technically essential to alternate-world building, because it would be too complicated and boring to present the reader with a world where everything had to be explained, down to the least detail. You can only present something new if it is delineated by familiar objects, if only for the reader to complete for himself what the book cannot explain or describe. The novelty—in all senses of the term—comes from the collage, the montage, the crisscrossing and hybridization of historical and fantastic references, the spark that comes from banging the clichés together. A steampunk novel is a laborious and volatile dosing with the pleasures of recognition and discovery. Of course, the dose can fail miserably, but it is not necessarily the genre that is to blame.

As to Stross's second argument: the science, bad as it can be, is just another aspect of that collage of clichés. Steampunk science is less interested in the facts of hard science than in the growing vulgarization and the social discourse of science in the nineteenth century, with its relentless inventiveness, its striking advances but also its ridiculous duds, its delusions of grandeur and control, its inability to set its own limits (as seen in its misdirected forays into psychic science and supernatural events), its almost total lack of restraint or ethics. It is no wonder that science fiction (and the mad scientist) were invented in the nineteenth century, ripe as the period was with all the fictions that science created about itself. It is the actual science of the nineteenth century that is, to use Stross's language, "questionable at best"—which is also what makes it so fascinating. Instead of bemoaning fiction writers' lack of seriousness in approaching science, we might say that steampunk is a study in scientists' lack of seriousness in approaching science. But that too, I suppose, is a thing of the past.

So it seems there is more to steampunk than meets the goggled eye, and if there is so much of it around, well, it could well be simply because it is symptomatic of and relevant to our times. And don't even get me started on Teslapop.

JEAN-CHRISTOPHE VALTAT is the author of *Aurorarama* and *Luminous Chaos*. Born in 1968 and educated at the École Normale Supérieure and the Sorbonne, he lives in Montpelier, where he teaches comparative literature. He has also written a book of short stories, *Album*, and two other novels, *Exes* and *03* (published in English), as well as award-winning radio plays and the screenplay for *Augustine* (2003), which he also codirected.

READ BOOK TWO IN THE STEAMPUNK TRILOGY
THE MYSTERIES OF NEW VENICE

"Packed with eccentric feats of pure imagination… If you like pure imagination, you will relish this dreamlike tour de force."
—*THE TIMES* (UK)

"A clever, exceedingly well-written adventure."
—*BOOKLIST*

$26.95 U.S./CAN.
978-1-61219-141-6
ebook: 978-1-61219-142-3